TRUTHFUL ROOTS

Victoria M. Steinsøy

Book One of The Seeds of Ascension Series

Victoria M. Steinsøy

https://www.victoriasteinsoy.com

First Edition: June 2021
ISBN: 978-82-692572-2-9

For my dear father who read to me before bed till I was eleven and who always bought me books for my birthday (even when I had specified that all I wanted was a dog). You seeded the love I have for books and fiction. Thank you.

About the Author

Born (and later raised) in Norway in 1996, Victoria Steinsøy has restlessly been exploring the world ever since. She's always had a love for writing and storytelling, and it was during her last semester at the University, that a spark of inspiration made her turn away from Academia and immerse herself in the world of fiction.

Her intention was simple; bringing what she'd learned from her travels, her history bachelor, philosophy courses and perhaps most importantly; her self studies in subjects like spirituality and psychology, and write a layered and multi-dimensional fantasy novel. Seeds of Ascension initially started as an idea for a singular book, but was then rapidly channeled into a much vaster, fictional world with plot lines that keep on evolving and expanding.

As a writer, who's been hit quite hard by the "muses", Victoria mostly spends her days word-vomiting over her keyboard, way too many notebooks, manuals and any other defenseless sheets of paper. As a human she is now stationed in Egypt and navigating through the author's journey, at least half gracefully, in a combination of gratitude and overwhelm, as an ascending universe unfolds itself from the touch of her fingertips.

Acknowledgments

Finishing this novel, a big and a great many thank yous' are in order.

First and foremost; thank you to my **family** and **friends** in **Norway** who have been motivating me and giving me the time, shelter, support and space to finish this book. Thank you to all my **teachers** through the years, who have provided me with important criticism as well as confidence in my writing. Thank you to my **flat-mates** in **Vienna** for accompanying me in my introvertedness when this journey began in 2019. Thank you to the **University of Vienna** for showing me how dreadful I find academia and for clarifying, once in for all, that my passion is on the other side of the scale. Thank you to all the **travelers** I've met these past two years (if you're reading this, as many of you said you would, you know who you are). I'm so grateful to all of you. A special thanks to all my wonderful, motivating **friends** in **Dahab**; Especially **Veronica Merlo**, for being my writer-buddy. Our conversations always brought me so much joy and energy.

A big thanks to my editors: **Federica Cavasinni** – for all your initial inputs, your excitement about this project and most importantly; your kindness and sincerity. **Yara Aly**, who's enthusiasm and positivity for the series has been of another world. I appreciate both of you so much. Finally, and most importantly, a very special thanks to **Samir Tal'at**, who showed up at the most perfect time and whose support has been boundless. Your faith in me, your editorial work, enthusiasm, motivation, brilliance and your overall dedication has been beyond compare and the publishing process (with its many intense periods) wouldn't have been the same without you, nor would the final version of Truthful roots. Both me and the book are forever grateful to you. Thank you.

* * *

PROLOGUE

"Araktéa's nature is changing. The new rivers are coming soon. Stay, and you will see it with your own eye." These had been the last words Wind had spoken as The Dark Loon had left him for the second and the last time. Though not a predictor, he mostly trusted their foresight, and now, looking down the valley between the unnamed mountains, he thought he could see their vague silhouette down there. Three decades had perhaps changed either of them, but despite of having similar visions, they continued to be creatures of different directions – different roots and slightly different truths. Though again tempted to see it all to an end, The Dark Loon had decided not to stay to watch the ground change. No, from now on, his direction was north.

There were certainly things to be done before he could retire from his many roles – things and strings that needed to be tied, executed, or weaved together. Not every game needed to be played out – this was something the land had forced him to learn. Lives were much too short in this realm and seeds grew much too slowly, but prophecies, he believed, would always come true in due time. "Perhaps even false ones," he thought. Brushing off this seductive intrigue with a squeaking roll of his stiffening neck. Whatever sinister truths were lurking under the surface, he would see it all ascend from afar. Turning towards the rising sun, he saw a crow diving playfully in the lower lands, and at last, he felt a readiness to go back home. "Now, I will be an observer," he said, stating a loose vow of a sort as he took his first descending step down the slope.

CHAPTER ONE

THE HARVEST

ENTERING the small piece of land that bore the closest resemblance to the outside forest, Isaiah saw the sun rising behind the taller pine trees, surrounding both the insides and outsides of the rusty-colored, northwest wall. He stared at the ground where he had planted his seed a year earlier. Certain it had been exactly a year, for it was day three, which happened to be his eighteenth birthday. With no major seasonal changes in central Araktéa, these were things you had to keep close track of, if of any interest to you. He'd personally done so by carving the wall underneath his bed every morning since coming to the Huxley fortress. Not because he thought the third to be any more special than the other days making up a year. It seemed every day was somebody's birthday after all, and seen away from the lords, the sirs, patrons, and other *great men* – celebrating theirs as if they'd been miraculous godly events – Isaiah thought all of them quite similar. It was rather due to his seeding he bothered keeping track. This, as well as his wall carvings, he'd kept to himself of course, for although it was nothing like the pagan rituals that'd been banned from the fortress, the line between what was permitted and not, seemed to be in an ever-changing flux.

The ritual itself was a simple one. Last year's seed had been given to him by Lady Huxley's gardener, and whether he'd been kind enough to spare or smuggle it out for him, Isaiah was not certain of. In normal circumstances, his grandfather would have gifted him one on the

1

morning of his birthday. They would go to their garden and he would ask a question as he planted it. It was a good training of his patience, as he'd then need to wait a whole year before observing its response. He'd always considered it an intelligent way of celebrating, having been taught there were few things more precious than having your questions answered. It was for this reason that the art of asking the right ones was something every person should strive for – a skill that saddened him to see, most people did not acquire in the slightest.

In his life, he'd never had any doubt about the accuracy of a plants' answer. He was of course well aware a plant could not talk – such nonsense was a thing of village lore. Instead, there were ways to interpret them, ways they could tell you things that only nature itself could know with certainty. Leaving behind his expectations while going through the process was perhaps the most challenging part. Because of his grandfather's botany book he normally knew what kind of plant the seed would grow up to be – sometimes making him overly hopeful. The Lady's gardener had no books of the sort and had only given him a strange, foreign name he'd never heard of and had forgotten soon after. And so, he had not imagined anything during last year's seeding or expected it to blossom into some lush, colorful flower. It wasn't about a plant's beauty after all, but how it grew according to its own nature. Just as his grandfather always said, "*A rose is no more precious than a corpse flower. Both have their place, and both have their says.*" Thus far their '*says*', or perhaps his interpretations of them, had never turned out to be untrue. No seed had ever failed to respond, and yet, there he was, now a grown man, standing on the very same ground he had a year before and it was no less flat.

The climate was different and more unpredictable in the Nahbí region, and so he'd suspected that quite possibly, whatever it was, wouldn't fully blossom within a year like seeds did at home. He'd thought he'd need to give it a few more weeks for a clear answer, but the fact that the seed had not left as much as the tiniest of sprouts for him, was something he had not prepared for. For a moment he considered if he'd gone to the wrong place, or that someone had perhaps seen it from afar and foolishly gifted it to some woman they fancied. After digging his fingers into the cold dirt, both hopes were soon disconfirmed. The seed was exactly where he'd left it – two inches underground, three steps away from the surrounding oaks that'd been shedding orange and yellow leaves around themselves, making the area almost look pretty for once.

"There will be no answers this year." Isaiah thought, observing it as it laid heavy in his palm. On any other birthday, this would have been a disappointment. An annoyance that might have left him muttering in the garden for half a day, before finally coming to terms with reality, and choosing a new and more relevant question to ask for their next seeding. But last year's question had been the most important one he'd ever asked and not one he'd made out of curiosity (a luxurious and juvenile emotion he could no longer afford). "I need to know!" He moaned. Giving the ground a childlike kick. Crisp leaves lazily lifted, then fell back down whilst some crow mocked him from afar. Slightly embarrassed by his tantrum, he looked around to reassure himself nobody was watching.

Studying the seed more closely, he wondered if it was dead but found no signs of damage to it. It was bigger than any other seed he'd planted, and so he'd had a hope it would perhaps grow up to be something he'd never seen before. For a moment he considered planting it elsewhere that might be slightly sunnier, but quickly concluded it pointless. The earth was perhaps not fertile enough to nurture it, and besides, he had not taken the time to think of a new question for this year's seeding. His plan had been to be gone long before. By then he would want to be home - home in Delta, where everything grew effortlessly and where you didn't need to worry about anyone stealing your plants, or for the soil not to do what soil was meant to do. And so, still hassled, he threw the seed away and marched over to the fields, where more reliable things grew.

It was as silent as ever and slightly chiller than it'd been for the past weeks. Still, he pulled off his woolen sweater, as its itch seemed particularly eager to torment him. The only wind meeting his arms was the one made by his own movement, and he noticed his temperature rising strangely. Finally, he stopped somewhere right in the middle of the fields for no particular reason. Squatting down, the smell of smoke from the clay oven placed on the courtyard right next to the main building, and the steep ladder that led to its bell tower reached his nostrils. Some two hundred yards east he could see there was still an hour left before it would ring, signaling the time for breakfast. For now, it was only him out there, and seven gray-clothed women flocking around the oven, with huge pots to serve the late risers. As usual, he'd been the first to have his breakfast. It'd been the same porridge they'd been serving for the past moon span or so. A little too sweet for his taste, but edible still, and enough to keep him fueled for a few hours of labor.

For his daily chore, he'd brought his smallest spade with him, as well as three, hessian sacks that were to be filled within the day. More than usual, he wanted it done quickly, but before even having pulled the first potato out of its obscure misery, he heard the sound of panting. Looking up, he noticed two, large dogs standing a couple of feet away and lurched backwards. One light and one dark, both gray and fiercely yellow eyed. He'd seen them many times – walking around unbound – and he'd been very relieved that they'd never paid him much attention. Now, they were glaring straight at him, and he was about to panic, although their gazes flickered with something more resembling expectation than blood thirst.

"Good morning." A man's voice said, and once again he was startled, until he noticed Archilai's slender figure approaching. His shadow laid long behind his impressive height, making him easier than most to recognize from afar. Isaiah had previously estimated that he had to be sixty or older, though his large, silver beard and bushy eyebrows did well in concealing what might either be signs of age or youth.

"Hello." He responded, his voice thin and revealing. The two of them usually didn't converse, and so, even if they were the only ones in the fields just then, it seemed strange he would greet him. Had it not been for the dogs he needed rescue from, interacting with anyone would have seemed especially troublesome just then.

"Hope these fine beasts didn't startle you, boy. Violet, Dusk, come on here!" His panic dissolving, Isaiah realized he shouldn't be surprised as the dogs often seem to be following Archilai around. He'd warned the children about them numerous times and on many occasions had to stop them from pulling their tails, ears, and whatever limbs they could grab a hold of. The children in the fortress, he'd decided, were often very foolish and their parents seemingly incompetent in changing this fact.

"They weren't." He assured him, relieved as Violet and Dusk obeyed and turned their vicious eyes towards a stick that Archilai waved around. He threw it across the field with an impressive range for someone so scrawny looking. Grinned as they ran, before looking down at him under the wide, stray hat (covering an otherwise bald head).

"I guess it's me then. You'd prefer to be alone, lad?" He was quick to say, grinning even wider as he noticed the boy's rosy cheeks flaring red. A tendency he'd observed on more than one occasion already.
"No... that's alright. There is more than enough space here." Isaiah tried, surprised by his bluntness.

"Worry not, I won't bother you for long. Tomorrow you'll have all these roots for yourself – well, at least for the early hours." Isaiah glimpsed at him, wondering if he'd sincerely come with the intention of bothering him, or if he'd attempted to make a joke.

"I am not bothered." He said and started digging again as Archilai took a step closer.

"No? Well, don't you wish to break free, lad?" He asked, glaring straight at the sun that had started rising higher behind the boy's back. Where the dogs chased each other in giant, joyous circles. There was still some beauty left in this place.

"Don't we all..." Isaiah responded absentmindedly as he placed the first potatoes in his sack.

"Oh, I doubt that. But I'm asking *you*." The young boy sighed and Archilai noticed the tension in his arms and shoulders that seemed to have grown much wider and harder this past year.

"Of course I do." He said. Escaping, he'd noticed, was a topic spoken of quite consistently and attempted quite rarely. Yet, there was a certain edge in Archilai's tone, almost suggesting he was being serious.

"It appears to me, you're a clever and strong young man. Why don't you?"

"For all you know, I might be planning to."

"Oh. So, you *do* have a plan? That's terrific!" he said, with an enthusiasm that made his accent more evident than usual.

"Quite possibly." Isaiah answered as plainly as he could, pulling another potato from the ground. Placing it in the sack. "Leave me alone." He thought, suddenly grossly aware of how his undershirt had already started clinging to his back.

"Well lad, won't you tell me about it, then?"

"For obvious reasons, I cannot, but I assume you will know soon enough – once I'm gone." It was the first time he'd even indicated that he had an escape plan, and he instantly felt himself regretting it. Not knowing Archilai very well, and still preoccupied with the unsuccessful seeding, he was in no mood to contemplate on his crumbling agenda.

"If *I* was the one assuming here..." the bearded man began, cleansing his throat and leaning towards a tall spade that looked like it would be of no good use out there, "I'd say you're waiting for the event that is to happen in ten days' time. If this were the case, I'd tell you getting through the northern gates won't be a good option unless you've come up with a very clever scheme, as they've planned on having more guards this year." Isaiah paused for a moment, his stomach twisting even tighter than it had whilst facing the dogs. He then resumed, trying his best to keep up the same, casual disengagement, as he asked, "Has anyone attempted this before?"

"Of course. Quite a few actually, which I guess is why they're being more cautious this time." Had he made a greater effort to look for a bright side that day, it would've been the fact that he'd just received the answer to his question – a loud, and terribly clear, *no*. It was after overhearing how drunk and sloppy the guards tended to be during this particular event, he'd decided to ask the seed if he'd be able to escape that night - without getting caught. Asking this, he'd almost sensed his grandfather sighing and shaking his head at him. "Limiting questions will bring you nothing but limiting answers." He knew it was true, but with the limitations of his particular circumstances it had seemed inevitable. Simply asking if it was possible for him to escape wouldn't tell him when, and he already knew some captives succeeded on occasion, just to be taken by the Kadoshi and brought back shortly after. He guessed he should feel happy for the ones who'd gotten out before him, but he wasn't. Not even in the slightest, and even less so for the ones who'd been sluggish.

* * *

There was a lot more to escaping than just getting through the gates. The woods surrounding the fortress were thick, and the path through them leading north was crooked as a sorceress' nose. He would need food and supplies for the journey, as well as a horse he at least felt somewhat comfortable with. He'd made sure all of this would be at his disposal just in time for the event – which now, for some reason – would be happening earlier than planned. All he'd been waiting for was his seeds' final approval to go through with it. That wasn't to say he hadn't prepared that it might signal him to stay put, but in any scenario, the message would come as it always did – from a plant that had the certainty of nature at its core, and not a man that was practically a stranger.

"You would've known this earlier had you consulted with someone. Nearly *anyone* in fact – there's been plenty of discussions in the Cave. You're hardly the first one to think of this." Archilai broke the silence, noticing the gloom look on the boy's face. It was a handsome, angular face, though the way he carried it gave him the impression nobody had ever told him anything of the sort. Framed and often hidden by a dark mane of hair, it was only now, in the early rays of sunlight, he saw its subtle, golden touch. His almond eyes were shy, but the few times they'd met his, he'd seen they were a rare, deep blue, reminding him all too much of similar ones he'd once known. His strong jaw seemed particularly tense as he said, *"This isn't something that should be spoken of so openly here."* His voice was low even to his own ears, though Isaiah knew well that both Lord and Lady Huxley were still asleep and would continue to be so for some hours more. He assumed Archilai knew this too, yet he felt desperate to make an end to their conversation without being ruder than necessary.

"Many things shouldn't, but you see, complete silence can just as well lead to the death of a man." Now, Isaiah stood up to look at him, discovering that the old man's expression had turned serious in a way that didn't quite suit his face or character. His oval eyes, like light, blue ponds, stared so intensely at him that he instinctively lowered his own.

"Thank you for informing me, I will not attempt to leave during the event. Worry not." Even if he didn't know exactly how Archilai had guessed his plan so accurately, he knew he should in fact feel grateful about the warning. Yet, being in an unusually sour mood, he had to force the words from his mouth, leaving an odd cling to them that sounded anything but genuine.

"You might have saved my life..." he tried, knowing it was a little overdramatized, and once again Archilai's face turned cheerful.

"Oh, don't flatter me too much, lad. They wouldn't have killed you – you are much too good of a worker for that. But they might have sent you to the chambers for a few days, and I wouldn't wish that upon you." Just the mentioning of the place, made a cold, unease spread down Isaiah's spine. Like everyone else in there, he'd heard of the chambers a few times too many – and more importantly, what happened to the troublemakers that were sent there.

The stories were usually told by the triplets, who always made the biggest riots, not to say, encouraged and engaged in foolish behaviors of many variables. Isaiah didn't quite understand *why*, for by now, they should be more than well aware of the consequences. More often than not, their rebellions sprung out of insignificant matters and minor disagreements. Nobody ever seemed bothered with asking why, and instead listened to their stories wide-eyed and petrified. Stories of the sort, nobody should want to hear but couldn't resist listening to. As for the chambers, they claimed the pain was unbearable, and much more than any common man would endure. Before the actual beating started, they would have no food, and sometimes no water, for three whole days. Then, they would meet with the torturer, which they'd explained was a terrifying, masked man from the Zura tribe. What happened next was different each time, but the captive would always receive a devilish beating until finally losing consciousness. Isaiah had seen their deep scars as proof of this, and though making their broad backs uglier each time, all three seemed to consider them symbols of their manhood, and so, soon after one had gone, another went.

These were stories that made it easy for him to get up early and to consistently make sure he was among the most hard-working people in the fields. He'd never heard of anyone being sent to the chambers for insignificant matters, but he still wanted the Patron's grace if he – accidentally – should end up in any trouble. This was also the reason he needed absolute certainty he wouldn't get caught escaping.

"Don't look so frightened, lad. The chambers are not really as bad as they make them sound." Archilai said, seeing his expression bore the same grimness he'd seen in too many young faces before, as the roughness of reality washed away their hopes of simple solutions. It was a rough time to be an Araktéan and it seemed he himself had always known this. Even back when things had appeared to be simple – and that was a very long time ago.

"I'm not *afraid*." Isaiah frowned, as Archilai pulled up the sleeve of his own gray, loose sweater. Parts of his arms (covering his hand and halfway up his wrist) had a strange purple-like color. The rest is marked by thick, blue veins shimmering through his skin like tiny rivers.

"These are just a few injuries from working." He explained, "For now, I think it's better if I don't show you the ones from the chambers."

"Oh." Isaiah said, somewhat relieved by this fact. Then he kept on digging again, making an effort not to look at him. He'd never seen scarring like that in his life, and he did not want to know exactly what had caused it.

"It might be unnecessary to say, lad, but I want to encourage you to escape soon, so that your *immaculate* skin can stay smooth for a little longer."

"I would have to wait for a new opportunity, but I will get out soon enough."

"So," Archilai leaned on his spade again, "Your solution is to wait *even* longer?"

"I'll be patient, and eventually I'm sure I will come up with something." If he had looked up on his companion at this moment, he would have seen an expression so soundlessly condescending, it'd bring about an argument between anyone with the slightest of a temper. Perhaps fortunately, Isaiah still pretended to focus on the stubborn roots.

"Boy, opportunities don't just show up out of the blue around here, you need to make them yourself – use your creativity."

"*I am* using my creativity."

"Wouldn't it perhaps be better for you to pursue your writing outside these walls?" With this, Isaiah couldn't help but stand back up again. It was no secret he had a book with him, but for someone who'd always felt skilled in blending into the background, he was unpleasantly startled to find he'd been watched. Facing Archilai, he realized he couldn't make a clear point out of the indecency – knowing quite well it was no different from what he himself did. The art of observation was one he'd found to be rather fascinating, allowing you to absorb people's mannerism and behavior, without the need of actual interaction. As far as permission was concerned, he was no better. He calmed himself as best as he could before speaking, tightening the grip around his spade.

"For the moment this is not a bad place to be. There is food, there is shelter. Both the Lord and the Lady treat me well..."

"Listen lad – *this...*" Archilai interrupted him, holding out his long, white, veiny, arms, "*This* is a prison. It might look pretty, and it might not seem an awfully *cruel* one, but it is a prison nonetheless. And I assure you, it is not as safe as the one you've made it out to be in your head." He pointed a finger towards his own, and the tense look in his eyes made Isaiah wonder if he'd perhaps lost his mind, like he'd heard many men did these days. Surely, the area within the fortress' walls was unimpressive compared to the larger, more beautiful villages in Delta, but if there was something everyone seemed to agree on, it would be that they felt safe there. As long as you finished your chores (which for most of them was nothing overly complicated) and followed the rules, you wouldn't be bothered by anything else than perhaps the snoring from your dorm companions and at times an overcooked, or over salted, supper.

"We are safe here." Isaiah affirmed.

"Safe from what? Zuras? Sorcerers and bandits? Wild animals, and furious beasts luring around in enchanted forests? Are you afraid of the war with these "barbarians", from the north *beyond* Dabár?"

"No." Isaiah responded, but his voice didn't even convince himself – and of course, he was indeed afraid of all of it. Wasn't everyone?

"Well, then you sure need to get out."

"From what I've heard, you have been here for over thirty years yourself. Why haven't *you* escaped?" He knew better than being rude to his elders. In fact, he'd been raised much better than that, but he couldn't help himself – not today. Archilai didn't seem the slightest bit insulted by the outburst. Instead, he made a long sight, as if preparing to explain something to a very young child.

"Isaiah, I am old. I've lived a full and *eventful* life as a free man, but *this* is my home now and I am planning to end my days inside this golden cage." There was a flare of a smile underneath his beard, making him seem almost content with his chosen fate. Isaiah strived to give a prompt reply, but not without a glimpse of hesitation. "Perhaps this is my home too." He said, and then, meeting with a wary expression, he added, "At least for now..."

"No, lad. This is *not* your home, and we need to get you out of here before you get too familiar with that thought." Despite his richness in facial hair, Isaiah noticed he had more expressions than almost any other man he'd ever laid eyes on. Normally, this might have been the sort of thing that would've fascinated him. If he hadn't felt so unusually unlike himself, he might have taken more note of it. Chosen to interact with him and observe them further. Now, his blood was boiling hot, rising to his cheeks, and his eyes were unable to look beyond the blunt, and rather unjustified, anger that he noticed creeping into his companion's.

"What do you care what *I* do? You don't even know me!" Archilai's lip tightened, his head turning slightly towards the main building. Now, slowly filling up with captives from all over Araktéa, or at least from a great many parts of it.

"Do you want to know why I went to the chambers?" He asked, only now sounding cautious.

"People say you stole from a guest during Lord Huxley's birthday celebration. That it was some important noble man..." Isaiah felt a slight satisfaction saying it, quite unable to think of anything more foolish than stealing from a noble and thinking to get away with it.

"That's only half the truth. But, yes – I did steal the cape of one of our *guests*. Of what actual importance he was, I couldn't even care to guess..." he smirked, "the point is, I did it to help someone escape." He waited for a continuation, but Archilai just stared at him expectantly.

"By dressing him up as a noble..." he nodded.

"That is... quite a big risk to take."

"And yet, not by far as risky as staying here and letting your spirits starve. Since the first day I arrived, I knew I would spend the rest of them within these walls." He took a breath, glaring down at scarred hands that had done things his mind till this day couldn't permit itself to remember with perfect clarity. "I've done many terrible things in my life, Isaiah. When one of them finally brought me here, I was forced to spend more time thinking than chasing my desires. I started asking myself *one* question." He held one finger up, pleased to finally have caught the boy's full attention. "If there was something – *anything* – I could still do, to be a better man. After thinking of this for longer than I'll admit, I decided to never try escaping from here. It was tempting, of course. I knew about every little hole in the wall back then. Every guard's sluggish habit and preferable distraction. Still, what I decided to do was to help others get out. People whose freedoms I felt would be worthy ones." Archilai's eyes were as blue as his veins, and Isaiah saw they were ones of sincerity. Right underneath it, they carried a sort of pain that not all the tears in the world could clean out. It was a strange sight, and though he believed whatever he'd done to end up there, must have been a just punishment, he couldn't help but feel empathy crawl its way into his chest.

"Why would you do such things for strangers? Risking going to the chambers – your life even... why not escape and help people on the outside instead?"

"I've found it to be a purpose for me in this life. Being a part of a whole that I am yet to fully understand..." The older man blinked and looked away, staring straight at the sun again, now standing higher over the horizon and illuminating the shade that till now had kept people at the second floor of the dorms, in comfortable darkness.

"Since I made this decision, not a soul entering the gates has been a stranger to me, but pieces of this whole that I've chosen to take part of. A whole that all of us have a part in – whether we like it or not." Isaiah thought about this for a moment as Archilai once again turned his gaze towards him.

"Like a family, you mean?"

"No, not like a family, lad. You are young, and even if you were very old, I don't think I could explain it to you adequately. Or even to myself..." It'd been a long time since there'd been anyone talking about such things in the Cave. They were often referred to as *loons* and the rumors had it they were exiled Khantalins. Despite being considered "not fully there" Archilai felt they had a strange, but intelligent air about them. A calmness he himself yearned for, but no loon ever stayed around for long. No loon ever told him enough.

"For now, it is not important for you to fully understand why I do the things I do. What is important, and what you should know, is that during all these years, some people have been in need of a bigger... *push* than others. The young boy for instance. Even when he was dressed up as a noble, he was shaking like a leaf as he passed through the gates. Poor lad got caught and confessed to everything."

"He betrayed you..."

"One might say that, but I never blamed him for it. I knew the risk when I decided to help. He got sick shortly after, and until his very last day he couldn't dare look me in the eyes. Poor lad thought I hated him, but I hate nobody... especially not the fragile and fearful."

"Fear doesn't excuse betrayal."

"Perhaps not, but it doesn't justify hatred either. I am not telling you this to convince you of my bravery or generosity, but so that you understand that I am willing to go *far* to get you out of here."

"So, you think I am weak too? Like that scared, *fragile* little boy?" Archilai laughed and shook his head.

"No, Isaiah, you are not *weak*. You're simply putting your focus in the wrong places."

"Perhaps I am and should resume my work." For a minute Archilai had managed to gain his attention – but once again he felt himself stepping on nerves he hadn't been aware Isaiah had.

"Boy..."

"Patience is a virtue. Once you have planted the seed you need to wait for it to grow." As these words (that he'd always considered very wise) left his mouth, he remembered the incident of the same morning. Surely, it had to have been nothing but an exception to the rule. This lesson that he'd been told innumerous times, still had to be true beyond a doubt.

"Perhaps with a plant boy, but in a place like this, action is needed and only the solid and fierce ones grow to see the light of day. Take a look ..." Archilai bent down and grabbed a handful of dry, powdery dirt.

"The soil is not what it used to be around here. I should know – as you just said, I've been here for over thirty years..."

"There is more than enough for everyone to eat, so I wouldn't worry too much if I were you." Isaiah turned his back to him, took one of his sacks and started pulling up roots from another row.

"For *now* there is, and you still look healthy and well-fed. You have handled your surroundings better than any other child I've seen coming in here by themselves. Your weak*ness* is that you get lost in thoughts, hoping they will lead you somewhere. From the little I know myself, they sometimes do. But it's been four years and it's time *to do* something, if only accepting some help from an old, mad man. Dreams don't come *alive* so easily around here you see..."

"I don't need your help. I will get out by myself, and I will rather continue working alone now – if you don't mind."

"Seems you're more like your father than I thought. Wanting to do everything by yourself..." Archilai chuckled.

"I'm *nothing* like my father." Isaiah felt his pulse rising, for if nothing else, this needed to be the final straw. It was not a surprise to him that Archilai knew who Ares was – it seemed a great many of the captives did. What he didn't understand was how he knew he was his son.

"Perhaps not. Ares would have escaped from here long ago." Archilai bent down again, then approached him with yet another hand of dirt. Even if there hadn't been any threat in his voice, Isaiah wondered if he would throw it at him – mad as he was. Instead, he grabbed him by the wrist, making a flat hand out of what had become quite a tight fist.

"A birthday gift. Now, consider if it's better than nothing, or if you'd be willing to risk losing it *if* you could make a jewel out of it." Before he could come up with a response to the absurd gesture, his recent wish came true, and Archilai walked away from the fields. Half relieved and half confused, Isaiah looked down on his hand for the second time that morning. in between soil and tiny rocks, he'd gifted him a tiny, deformed potato. "Mad man." He muttered. Threw the unripe thing away and again focused on his spade, sacks, the starches and that sticky, cooling sweat on his back.

CHAPTER TWO

A DECENT POET

ISAIAH spent the rest of his birthday trying to avoid thinking about the rude suggestions Archilai had made about him. Despite his best efforts, his mind kept recalling the incident, and so he had no option but to convince himself of what he knew to be true. Surely, if anyone took action in there it needed to be him, and he was certainly not among the many captives lost in childish fantasies and delusions. Quite on the contrary. Whenever strange occurrences arose (leading most of the captives into superstitious misconception), he would usually find a logical explanation. There were reasons why the brick walls would suddenly change to a darker shade overnight, and it had nothing to do with sorcery and everything to do with dust brought by the southern wind.

Born and raised in the Delta region, the south was completely unknown to him, but he knew a few things about nature's movements. Deltans, it seemed, were generally known for being simple-minded people – rather uninterested and even unwilling to accept the newer sciences. Even though he'd never studied at the academy in Nagár himself, he'd been fortunate enough to learn quite a lot about the world from his grandfather that once did - enough to know that a man's impulses (more often than not) were best kept contained, and that reacting to the vicious words of strangers should be below him. No, if anyone in the fortress did, *he* certainly knew where to put his focus, and if someone was delusional it would need to be Archilai himself – thinking it appropriate to speak so bluntly to a perfect stranger.

Having concluded both the man and his so-called gift, ridiculous and invalid, he still felt curious as to what a jewel was. Over the past four years, he'd heard plenty of wild stories about magic and alchemy – at times, entertaining ones, but usually far too outrageous to be credible. He was yet to hear anything about turning potatoes into jewels, and so he went to consult with Rim as soon as his sacks were full. The elderly woman (who had more common sense than most) had explained to him, it was a beautiful sort of stone of no practical functionality – the sort the patrons carried. This gave him some peace of mind, as he could at least answer Archilai's question to himself: yet another clear *no*, as he saw no reason for major risk-taking, only to turn something edible into a pretty stone.

After spending some more time further convincing himself there was no point in evaluating the matter any further, he headed to the ballroom. All the rooms needed to be spotless whenever the capitalers visited, and though it was still many days away, he wanted to make himself useful. He began scrubbing the quartzite (light yellow and brownish pink in color and more layered by dust than dirt). Its uneven tones laid the foundations of what was by far the largest room in the fortress, both in width and height. A mostly empty space meant for dancing. Other than the five white statues of unfamiliar faces (lined up against the left wall), it currently collected nothing but dust – and of course "Greatest Nagár". The large, proud painting of Araktéa's capital, framed in gold and placed between the two arched windows.

Soon enough he found his thoughts again returning to the conversation and realized he needed a different approach to it entirely. With neither solitude nor cleaning easing his mind, he saw no other option than going to the noisiest, and quite possibly, the dirtiest place within the walls – the Cave.

As the smallest of the fortress' four structures it would be easy to overlook for an outsider. Placed at the northern edge of the fields, and a healthy range away from the dorms, it was usually the first place the workers would go once they'd fulfilled their daily chores. Many would often spend their nights there drinking, playing cards and for the most part, speaking nonsense. Consequently, it was not a place Isaiah himself visited with much frequency, and yet this particular evening he went with a hope that external chatter might finally put an end to the one in his head. For once willing to waste precious paper, he even brought his book with him. Cave conversations mostly consisted of dull fortress gossip or village lore. Still, he'd written down a few tales, knowing all too well such adventures were the reason he'd left home in the first place. He'd come to terms with the idea that writing stories was much more preferable than living them. Being surrounded by big-mouthed people (with either wild imaginations or pasts), had thus turned out to have some benefit after all.   Reminding himself of this, as he paced towards the noise of the sad-looking structure, he still found himself little at ease as he entered.

"Care for a beer, boy?" one of the triplets, named Khair, asked him.

"No, thank you." He answered, not impolitely and yet wondering why he bothered asking, as he'd already made it quite clear he had no interest in their poisons. He then remembered he hadn't been there since the coldest day of last year. During what the people of Nahbí considered winter, but, that felt more like fall. Khair had asked him the same question then, as he'd told a tale about the resurrection of an Amnos King (what number in the lineage he hadn't been certain of), that everyone but Isaiah had found thrilling. Khair had had his normal conspiracies about it, which had led to arguments he luckily had left too early to witness.

"Alright, boy. You're welcome to sit with us, but I see you've brought that little book of yours." The broad-shouldered man grinned, flashing a bridge of teeth in at least four different tones of yellow. Isaiah instinctively held it tight to his chest. He'd caught him once, trying to steal it. Paper was a rare privilege in there – and nearly anywhere else for that matter. Perhaps if he had asked him nicely he would have shared some pages, but Khair had been unwilling to even give an explanation or apology, and so he'd kept it underneath his madras ever since. If nothing else, it'd been a good reminder that all of these people were true criminals.

Making his way past the triplets, sitting in a row at the bar among five other drunks, Isaiah found himself a table-less corner nobody else had claimed. The benches were of faded, brown leather, matching the ambience in every sense (color it seemed, was understandably of no concern to the Patrons, except when it came to their own garments). His seat was next to some cooks, still smelling like the dinner they'd prepared some hours earlier, and it had a lantern above it, that he knew beamed just enough light to see the pages clearly. With thick, wooden walls and heated by dozens of captives (most on the heavier side) it was almost unbearably hot in there. This first moon span was warmer than usual, and their breaths (smelling of beer and potato stew) filled the room faster than it could escape from the two tiny, half-opened windows. Despite the discomfort, he didn't think it wise to go anywhere else. Instead, he remained seated, waiting for any sort of compelling distraction to captivate his mind.

As it turned out, there were for once no wild stories being shared among the captives that evening. The triplets were once again rambling about where the Jalas had gone to - a tribe that had once lived by the river running through the valley of the unnamed mountains. Some Deltan villagers were complaining about the food, and a couple of new Dabárians were criticizing the injustice of "the system". Overall, it seemed little had changed since the last time he'd entered, and after once again trying to understand exactly what system they were referring to, and which part of it they disagreed with, Isaiah gave up. Opening his book, he looked down at the blank pages, meditating. He only wanted it to store important writings. Good stories. Of course, it had to do with integrity, but most importantly the fact that his grandfather would read it as soon as he was back home. "Well, that won't be for some time now, anyway," he thought, oddly nervous as he pulled out the charcoal pen that Lady Huxley, quite generously had gifted him, from his inner pocket. They hadn't offered him ink yet – being much too precious to gift a captive – but he felt charcoal did just as good of a job. Either way, he'd be a fool to think the issue was with the materials at his disposal. As he tried thinking of words making up a story worth telling, he couldn't help but hearing Archilai's – uninspiringly flowing around his head again. "You're putting your focus in all the wrong places."

"Are you having problems writing, lad? Maybe I can tell you a story or two." Lost in thought and surprised that Byron, the biggest of the triplets, all of a sudden was paying attention to him, Isaiah looked up.

"Oh, no, thank you... I am just working on a poem." Poetry was a concept Lord Huxley had introduced to him to some moon-spans ago. Though he hadn't gotten enough time to understand the rules of the genre very well, he found it fascinating. While most stories were expected to be thrilling and exciting, poetry seemed to have no such rules. It had given him the idea that perhaps, instead of an ordinary storyteller, he'd someday become a poet himself.

"Poems you say? Let's hear one, then!" Byron said with unsettling enthusiasm, choking Isaiah's hope that he'd lose his rare and unasked for attention, if he spoke of things he didn't understand. Apparently, Byron wasn't completely unfamiliar with the arts after all, and he knew how to get people's attention with his loud, broad voice. Within a very few, and uncomfortably rapid heartbeats, the Cave had quieted down. Most eyes were directed at Byron, but as he explained Isaiah was the self-declared poet of them, more and more were turning towards his dimmed corner. The faint fire of the lantern suddenly seemed to be burning on top of his head. In his whole life, never had he felt so many eyes on him at once, and to make matters worse, he was nowhere close to prepared to share any of his writings. He opened his mouth to protest, but as he couldn't find any sensible words, he started flickering through the fine pages. His fingers trembling awkwardly. "It's just some words on paper. Nothing to make a scene over." He told himself, finding the whole thing rather ridiculous.

"Uhm, yes, let's see..." he stuttered, and finally, he found the one he'd written a few weeks prior. It was the only poem he hadn't ripped out, penned instantly after coming out of a dream he now only remembered as a pale blur. He cleared his throat and tried soothing it, but it seemed every drop of saliva had dissipated from his mouth to further thicken whatever was left of the cave's air. The lump that lived in it, that he was growing much too familiar with, pounded aggressively, as if warning him that saying the wrong words would lead to death and misery for them both. "It is just words." He reminded it, as well as himself, and then took in a long breath, before speaking to his first audience:

"They were two

19

Two walking through
Through an invisible war
Cold, and in bliss
Looking for more

Together,
forever in a dream
Both hungry
both freezing
both yearning
One burning

For some God
Or all the stars
Shining brighter
in the north
The north beyond Dabár

A place only to reach
with little more
To learn and teach
Still not until
One is left behind
at a quiet place
left behind
in vicious flames."

Isaiah didn't dare look up from his book, having quite awkwardly ended his performance stuttering the word "flames", and feeling as if it had materialized inside his head. He realized he hadn't actually finished the piece, and that it didn't sound as good read out loud, as it once had in the dream or inside his head. Furthermore, his voice had been too quivery, and though the Cave wasn't large, he felt it hadn't reached far enough. Slow seconds went by in an unusual silence that rarely occurred in Captive's Cave, as he thought of these many shortcomings.

"That's all." He finally stated, feeling they were waiting for something more – misreading his words as a story with a clear beginning and an end. It didn't need to be so. This was poetry after all, and that much he knew.

"That's all?" Timotheus, the third triplet, asked. Isaiah nodded, confirming and closing the book as if it is the action that would make everyone turn their attention away from him and go on as usual. It didn't of course, and the throat-lump seemed to ascend to a whole new state of existential distress.

"You wrote that?" Byron asked. His ungroomed fingernails scratching through his beard.

"Yes. Just the other day." It might have been a few weeks back, or even a moon span ago now, but his voice was trembling too much for him to correct himself.

"And *how* did you come up with these things?"

"I had a dream and..." Isaiah stopped himself, feeling his cheeks flushing, "It doesn't really matter. What... what did you think?" He felt both bold and silly for asking, for it should be the least of his concern, and they probably hadn't understood. As Lord Huxley had explained, poetry was all about the unsaid. None of the captives seemed particularly familiar with silence or keeping things to themselves. Not to say, he hardly understood the piece himself anymore, and wasn't sure if he was even meant to.

"I think it was good." Timotheus smiled, his teeth just the slightest bit brighter than his larger brother's, and his tone quite a bit friendlier. "I would prefer a song, but it was alright." he added, looking over at Byron who looked inside his half empty jug of brown ale.

"I didn't find it too extraordinary, lad. Besides, *Khantal,* as you should know, is the land north of Dabár, and it's not a place a *child* should be making up stories about."

"You...didn't like it then?"

"Not very much, no. Sorry." Byron said, and the apology would've almost have sounded sincere, hadn't it been for his cunning smirk. Now, the others started mumbling, clearly uncomfortable with the lack of chatter.

"You don't know what you're talking about." Isaiah was very surprised to hear himself say. It was not the first time he'd felt an urge to speak up to one of the triplets, but he'd never thought he'd be stupid enough to actually do so. Perhaps it was because it was the first poem he'd ever written, and because he felt *almost* certain it was, at least, a decent piece of writing. The lump seemed to dig its way through flesh and veins, and if nobody had heard his heartbeats before, there wouldn't be any way of ignoring them now. At last, every thought having to do with Archiliai had successfully dissipated. His head, and every other part of his body, were occupied imagining which way Byron might grab a hold of him – just like he'd seen him do numerous times with rude, or just plainly unfortunate, men. As the large man got up from his seat and took two slow steps towards his corner, even moving an inch seemed impossible. In the dim light of the lantern, he saw that Byron's narrow, green eyes bore an unsettling seriousness to them. Like a large animal ready to assassinate its prey, or a Zura preparing to punish a captive, and yet, Isaiah's throat remained free as he placed his hand on the wall above his right shoulder and bent down towards him.

"You read your words to us, thinking we know *nothing* about literature and would be impressed with *anything* you've written. Now, I might not be an academic like that grandfather you've spoken so fondly of, but I'm a Dabárian, and I've read some poems in my days, *lad.*" Time seemed lucid, as the two of them eyed each other. Byron then lowered his voice, as if out of courtesy, as he said, "Your writing is not bad, boy, it is just... unremarkable. *Real* labor suits you better, so my advice to you would be to keep focusing on just *that*." It was so silent just then, that even if he'd made a bigger effort to whisper, the nearly sophisticated insult would've been heard by every ear in the Cave. He followed up his advice with a stiff smile, and a hard patch on Isaiah's shoulder. Before the rest of them had a chance to take in what had just been said, Byron turned and raised his jug from the bar – to everyone's relief, signalling for things to go on like usual. This was Captive's Cave after all, and not some Nagárian salon. Certainly not a place for poetry, or for innocent, young dreams to blossom.

Isaiah walked out immediately. The fact that he could do so with his breath still intact, and all his bones in the right order, was a minor comfort. It didn't just feel like the slightest hope regarding his potential talent had died. Rather, it felt like it'd been publicly executed, hung, burnt and ridiculed all at once. Though he knew he shouldn't pay attention to what uneducated men like Byron said, his words had rung too clearly for him to deny. Still, the fact that he allowed himself to be so affected by a drunken fool's words, was perhaps more unsettling than both the stuttering and his audience's confused eyes in the aftermath of it. "Why would I even ask their opinion?" he wondered, thinking he should know better than asking questions he did not want the answers to.

He'd never been fond of surprises and after a long day when nobody, not even himself, was acting as usual, he wished he could become calm enough to sleep. He walked at a rapid pace over the fields, feeling as if everything that'd been reliable, or at least predictable, was flying around like dry, meager soil – blinding him and unwilling to land anywhere. Looking up towards a nearly completed moon, with a head full of questions, he realized it was still not too late to go through with his birthday ritual. There was still enough time to ask. He did not have any seed to plant, but could at least look for the Lady's gardener and tell him that any seed would do. As he stumbled over a misplaced rock, he threw the idea away as soon as it'd come, sensing his skin crawl by the very thought of owing *anyone* in there anything at all. Besides, he had too many questions at once, all graspingly desperate and hysterical. Reaching the end of the fields, he found himself nearly unwillingly walking towards the seeding place. Looking down at the ground, he started wondering. Wondering if perhaps the earth simply had grown tired of him and his questions. Offering no objection nor confirmation, he finally laid down on the bed of leaves in mutual silence.

For some time, he looked up towards the sky, appearing like dark velvet in between the leaves that still clung to the oaks behind him. It'd been some time since he'd given the night sky his full attention, and he wished the stars would write out what he should do. They were silent of course, but less static than many other things, and so he allowed himself to hope they could at least see him. That they were somehow staring back at him in their own heavenly way. His grandfather had once explained that the stars could guide you home – yet gazing for too long could turn anyone into a lost and irrational star-chaser. He hadn't said anything about how long 'too long' was, but having felt both lost and irrational (looking down or straight ahead) the whole day, Isaiah thought looking up couldn't possibly cause any further harm. There were low whispers tingling through the trees and the faint smell of something sour he hardly ever noticed anymore. It resembled vinegar, and though always present, he'd failed to notice it for some time. He continued gazing, focusing on the moon as his lump slowly eased. Some captives claimed the moon to be magical – a distant god watching over them. He'd thought they'd been spending too much time looking upwards, for though beautiful, he thought it had more of a resemblance to a glowing potato than a god. Or perhaps, he now realized, it was more like a flying jewel. Hanging over their heads with no other use than to please their eyes. "Not the worst of fates." He realized.

Letting go of analyzing these distant mysteries, Isaiah took a deep breath, allowing the night air to fill his lungs. Eventually, as he claimed a few more, his mind calmed, and came to the acceptance that he wouldn't be planting anything on this birthday – nor any other day of this year. He then decided to make this lack of action a promise to himself – a promise that he would do whatever it took to get out of there. No questions asked. Even if his writing was unremarkable and his escape plan had been foolish – even if he was a failure, he was at least no longer inside the delusion of being anything else. It seemed clear enough now that it was time to leave, but right there and then, he didn't need a plan, a plant or the sky telling him how. He just needed some rest and silence. Some time to look upwards until his own existence seemed insignificant enough, for it not to bother him anymore. For some precious moments it seemed that a beautiful, useless, flying circle was all he needed.

CHAPTER THREE

THE RETURN OF THE DEAD KNIGHT

THOUGH having spent the night no more than half asleep, Isaiah woke up to an even darker morning than usual. Squinting towards the clock at the opposite side of the room (after all these years, still annoying him with its repetitive ticks and tacks), he saw it was only some minutes past five. Nevertheless, he slipped his feet onto the cool, wooden floor, sensing an unusual restlessness in his bones as he slipped underneath the bed to carve the wall. Pulling on his last set of clean clothes and slipping into the leather boots that were still a number too large, he made an effort to stay as silent as he could. The sound of unrhythmic snoring from his seven roommates remained, while the clock persisted its torment. Only within the last few "ticks", the door creaking as he opened it, he heard them turn and murmur in discontentment. He was usually better at opening doors discreetly.

Walking outside and down the steep, stone stairs facing the courtyard, the air was chill and the sky still dark with the faintest touch of purple from the little he could see of the horizon. There was no bird song, and he felt himself missing it, just like he did every morning. The clay oven stood cold and abandoned still, and having less patience and hunger than usual, he walked over to the fields while rethinking the promises he'd made to himself some hours earlier, fading promises he felt far less clear about now, he realized. There was an urge to forget them and start plotting another day. Perhaps after the event, which he'd been interested to witness from afar. "Men in our family *keep* our promises." his grandfather's voice rang in his head and Isaiah sighed. He would need to begin today. Maybe he could begin by searching around the walls and find a place to dig a hole. Or perhaps start talking to the guards and find out about their weaknesses like Archilai had once done. Neither of these approaches seemed efficient to him. No, he'd have to think of something better, and he was sure he would by the time his sacks were full. The field's, or the silence that was often found there, tended to bring him clarity.

To his relief, the fields were empty when he reached them, and didn't have a man, dog or even a crow in sight. Archilai had kept his word in that regard, and he considered finding him in the afternoon and apologizing for what he increasingly felt had been rather ill-mannered behavior on his own behalf. Though not very fond of conversing, feuds were an unfamiliarity he felt particularly uncomfortable with. Though his bluntness had been unasked for, he seemed to be meaning well, and perhaps he'd been sincere about helping. Regardless, Isaiah still wanted to make the escape plan himself, and so he thought he'd wait till he had an idea, before seeking him out. Eager to fill his sacks, he started pulling up the starches. A few minutes passed as he listened to the satisfying sound of them giving in to his grip, before he heard the sound of light boots.

"Isaiah, Lady Huxley is requesting you." It was the Lady's gardener – the little man with the broken seed, that seemed to come and go with odd inconsistency.

"At this hour? What has happened?"

"I know not, but we should not let her wait." He insisted, his face a map of confused lines and round corners. Shrugging, Isaiah left his sacks and walked along with the long-bearded man, who only reached him to the shoulders. Though he wanted to ask him about the useless seed, he instead worried the patrons had somehow overheard the conversation from the previous morning.

"Did she seem angry?"

"No." he answered. "A little... tense perhaps." Isaiah swallowed hard at this. They'd been alone. He was certain of it, and yet he had a strong sense he was in some sort of trouble.

Dressed in a yellow dress, patterned with golden flowers that could only be seen from up close, the Patroness stood, straight as a statue, waiting for them at the end of the fields. Her hands (the only thing Isaiah always allowed himself to admire of hers) were clasped together Infront of her. It was the first time he'd seen her out at this hour, and he needed to contain himself not to look directly at her face, as the first flares of dim morning light met with her radiant, olive tinted skin.

"Good morning, Lady Huxley." He said, bowing and then keeping his gaze lowered towards the grayish, green grass as he straightened his back. Although unreasonable, he always watched his thoughts (along with his gaze), whenever she was around. There'd been rumors suggesting she could read and even control the minds of men, and as ridiculous as this sounded, he'd long since decided to be on the safe side of certain superstitions.

"It is a very good morning indeed. Tzelem has returned to us." She said, her voice as sweet and cool as if she'd spoken of the weather. For the briefest of moments, Isaiah almost wished she could read his thoughts, and perhaps clarify exactly what it was they wished to tell him just then. He opened his mouth, as if to say something, then closed it again, feeling his cheeks flaring. Once again, the dead knight had returned to the living. After mumbling a response of vague comprehension, he walked along with her towards the main building in silence.

Minutes later, he was back in the same dining room where he'd first met the patrons four years earlier. It was half the size of the ballroom and seemed even smaller with its black floors and heavy, scarlet curtains. Next to the long, lacquered table in the center, stood the man that (though appearing older and slightly less muscular), was very much alive. His so-called master and teacher, who'd never taught him anything at all. The man that had taken him under his wing for some days, before riding off and abandoning him there. His brother's fortress had been meant as a very temporary placement. They'd told him to blend in and not speak of why he was there, and so Isaiah hadn't. Not once. It was not until everyone had started addressing the knight's absence as his *death* two years before, Isaiah had stopped actively condemning him for his circumstances. The patrons had insisted he should stay till there were any further notice of Tzelem's body being found and Isaiah had found himself guilty of hoping for such a message, until nearly forgetting about it entirely. Now, that he was standing before him, he felt the same, biting resentment returning. Had he come a few days earlier, he perhaps wouldn't have reawakened it, but just as usual, the timing couldn't have been worse for Tzelem Huxley.

"You're alive." Isaiah said.

"I am." His voice was still deep, slightly rasp and so whispery, people needed to pay close attention when he spoke. "For now," he added, his hard, gray eyes staring at him curiously.

"Where have you been?"

"I am sure you have many questions, Isaiah. Now is not the time..."

"It's been *four* years, Tzelem." He had to control his tone, reminding himself that though not a lord, it was indeed a knight he was speaking to. "One that owes me an explanation, nevertheless." He thought. Not to mention an apology, although none of it could ever make up for what he'd done – or *failed* to do.

"I know. And it seems they've done you good," the tall man said, still standing with his hands behind his back, measuring him from the head and down. "Now he looks like his father, perhaps the messenger was right, afterall." Tzelem thought, and then he said, "I believe you're ready to come with me now."

"Come *with* you? Where to?"

"South." Tzelem said motionlessly.

"When?" Isaiah stuttered. This had of course been the plan from the very beginning. Yet, the plan had felt as dead to him as his master had, and he hadn't made even minor preparations to go on any mission that wouldn't take him straight home.

"We leave tomorrow." He didn't smile with the statement, but his steely, narrow eyes seemed to lift ever so slightly, being about as much of a pleasant expression his long face was capable of making.

"Tomorrow?" Lady Huxley interrupted before Isaiah got the chance to. The sudden sharpness in her voice made him look directly at her face for a brief second – enough time to notice the anger in those large, dark brown eyes of hers. Khair claimed she'd arrived around the same time as him, nearly twenty years back now, but that could hardly be the case, seeing she looked so young still.

"There's not much time, m'Lady. The sooner, the better."

"Surely, you will need some days to rest. And you won't want to miss the event – *neither* of you." She protested.

"I sleep better outside..."

"Isaiah needs to get a chance to say goodbye to everyone. He has been here for *four years* – you need to give him some *time*." The Knight cleansed his throat.

"Four years seems a long enough time to me, m'Lady. He has all day to say goodbye to his *friends*. There shouldn't be too many of them." Despite Isaiah's disliking, he knew he was right. Except for a few of the young children, and perhaps the gardener, he had no actual friends – nobody to miss or to be missed by. Even less so now, after last night's humiliation.

"It's quite alright, Lady Huxley. This was the agreement."

"Please, if you would like to stay, Isaiah, I will talk to my husband. As you know, he is quite fond of you - as am I." He could see the edge of her mouth smiling from the side of his eyes. Lady Huxley never looked straight at him, but now she turned her head towards him ever so slightly.

"Celeste, please. This was the agreement. I *need* the boy." Isaiah had not known her birth name till just then, and thought it sounded foreign. There were different opinions as to her origins, but it seemed she'd first come to the fortress as a captive too, and that Lord Huxley had fallen in love with her – "just like in a hero tale", as Khair had described it. He'd been less convinced about this specific detail but hadn't found the story itself too unlikely. From the little he'd permitted himself to see, she was a beautiful woman. Long, raven black hair, rose-red cheeks, and full lips that spoke with the sweetest voice he'd ever heard. Hers was a forbidden face only for the eyes of the patron, and from what it now seemed, his discourteous brother.

"The agreement was also that you would come back within seven moon spans." She argued, and Tzelem took two steps towards them, favoring his left leg, Isaiah noted.

"Have you trained him, m'Lady? That *too* was a part of our agreement. Now, I see his puppy flesh has hardened, but has anyone taught him how to use a sword or a bow? How to hunt and navigate?"

"No." the Lady sighed. It was the first time Isaiah had witnessed her unable to control a situation, and he felt an overpowering urge to protect her. "This is my way out." He reminded himself, biting his tongue.

"Just like I thought. And so, since I brought him here, he will come with *me*."

"Or perhaps we shall let him choose for himself, now that he's a grown man." Lady Huxley said, placing her jeweled hands on her hips as Tzelem looked at Isaiah expectantly. He froze for a moment, finding the presence of choice a rather unfamiliar matter.

"If it wouldn't displease the Lady and the Lord too much, I would like to go with Master Tzelem - as was our original agreement." Isaiah finally managed to say, only disguising his puzzlement to some degree. It seemed unheard of that he, as a captive, would be allowed to make such a decision for himself. "But I'm not really a captive." He remembered. That had been a temporary agreement - a disguise of a sort.

"I see. Well then, my husband will be awake in a few hours and free you from your duties." She said, once again, her composed self. It seemed she'd put up all the fight she was willing to endure for him. They had a great many captives, and the numbers had been increasing for the past moon spans, as the newest plague had people fleeing across the land. How many Isaiah was uncertain of, since they often came and went, but certainly more than one hundred and less than two.

"You may go now. I'll brief you on the journey on the way." Tzelem said, suddenly impatient.

"Go where?"

"Back to your *roots*, or whatever it was you were doing before." Isaiah tightened his lips and fists, forced a nod and a discreet bow, before turning on his heel. He had a new master now, and he did not like this fact even in the slightest. Yet, there wouldn't be any need to find holes in the wall or some inventive way to distract the guards. For a moment he allowed himself to wonder if the moon had truly heard him and given him a free pass to the outside. He was quick to correct himself, knowing that getting away from Tzelem wouldn't be an easy task. There were still numerous matters and details in need for careful consideration. "One step closer." He told himself. No more and no less.

Returning to the fields, there were now four other men there. Three of them looking disengaged and still half asleep, and one of them being Archilai, appearing content and not doing much at all.

"Unlike you to break your routines, lad." He commented.

"Tzelem is back and I will be leaving with him tomorrow," he admitted, seeing no reason to hide this fact. He noticed the last bit of annoyance he'd felt towards him was gone, and that he nearly felt content to have found him there. Now he could apologize before leaving, *as well* as making a point out of the effortless development of the matter.

"Already?" he asked, raising his eyebrows.

"You should be pleased now."

"Very much so. I think I've *never* had such quick results with anyone." Isaiah shook his head, as he reached for one of his sacks.

"Cheer up, lad, I'm just messing with you. This is all your own earning." Isaiah considered this, knowing he hadn't done anything but agreeing with the only man he truly hated to assist him in some impossible mission (one that both of them should know he was nowhere close to fit for). It almost seemed a disgraceful escape attempt, but he wasn't ready to feel ashamed about it just yet. Not until something went terribly wrong. "Which it might" he thought, and he feared it most certainly would.

"I am sorry for being crude yesterday. I don't know what came over me..."

"Oh, don't apologize, lad. Anyone would be a little defensive with a strange, old man approaching them during their sacred morning hour. If you add telling them they need to get their head out of their arses, the old man would be lucky not to get a fist in his face." Isaiah snarfed.

"Truly, Isaiah, compared to most of the men I've met here, you have proven yourself a true gentleman. Those are rare these days..."

"Lord Huxley is the only gentleman I've ever known, and I don't feel our characteristics overlap much." Archilai chuckled at the comment.

"Not at all... Lord Huxley is a very special sort of gentleman. And his brother perhaps even more so." Isaiah nodded to that.

"Would you mind telling me what sort of mission you two are heading out on?"

"I know nothing yet and even if I had, I've already been sworn to silence four years ago."

"Of course. And as a gentleman, you should always keep your promise. Where I come from, keeping a secret and speaking truthfully, are equally important virtues. Probably like this stubborn *patience* seems to be in Delta." It sounded like something of a contradiction, Isaiah thought, but it did perhaps explain why Archilai was the sort of man that he was.

"Would that be north of the Deltan river? In Dabár?" he asked.

"That's a good guess, lad. We call it the Dabárian river. I was born on the western coast by the Pyrios ocean. Ever been there?" Isaiah shook his head. He'd never been anywhere but right where he was now and home.

"No, but you're very fair skinned. Even more so than the triplets, and they keep reminding everyone they're Dabárian."

"Well observed, lad. Do keep in mind, we're not all fair up north. Rim for instance, is Dabárian. Don't let her thinning accent fool you."

"I'll keep that in mind." He promised, and finally the two of them smiled at each other, realizing that perhaps if it hadn't been Isaiah's last day, they might have learned to get along rather well.

"Well, I'll leave you to it now. The potatoes will surely miss your attention more than myself." Archilai winked, then placed two fingers in between his lips and whistled. The dogs came walking rather than running this time, like little gray clouds from afar.

"Remember, lad, dreams that are too wild and grand can soon turn into beasts."

"Nothing wild about mine, I just want a peaceful life." Archilai smiled thoughtfully.

"Now that is a wise wish, Isaiah." He said, wondering whether peace could ever be obtained by someone with such a resistance to disorder. Having been wrong before, he nodded and strayed off, deciding he should not inflict the boy with the very same madness that had led him there. The world had changed in thirty years and its new saviors, it seemed, had very different paths ahead of them.

CHAPTER FOUR

NEW DIRECTIONS

"ISAIAH, we are so *very* sad to see you go. You are among *the best* workers we've ever had." Lord Huxley rewarded him with the very same compliment every time they spoke.

"Pleased to be of service, my Lord."

"Oh yes, boy. Indeed, it seems you have been immensely pleased here. Brother, are you sure you will need him? He is probably no good for those *wild* journeys of yours anyway." It seemed to be something in between a joke and a half-hearted attempt to keep him there, for they had already discussed and agreed on the matter, and both he and Tzelem were ready to ride out. Isaiah felt slightly offended by the remark – although it was true, and although he suspected it to be a strange way for the Patron to show his appreciation.

"He's coming." Tzelem replied, and Lord Huxley rolled his eyes and sighed exaggeratedly.

"Well, alright then." He said, turning towards his former worker with a throw of his cape (dyed with a similar shade as the wine Isaiah suspected he'd consumed at least half a glass of from his pacing). The Patron then mimicked an apologetic frown, twirling his blonde, finely trimmed mustache that was at least two shades lighter than his younger brother's.

"This is the price we pay for our heritage boy, and all we can do is to bear the burden with grace. If you decide not to, you will always be welcome back here, and we'll make sure there's a free bed for you." His words felt more comforting than they should have, for Isaiah had already told himself that there would be no going back. Still, it was nice knowing that if things did turn *very grim,* the fortress would be his sanctuary. Though a potentially dangerous thought, the assurance calmed his nerves.

"Now," the Patron said for everyone to hear, holding his arms out before searching the pockets of his vest. They always appeared terribly tight, and this one had delicate, golden threads drawing a plant-like pattern over the silky, black fabric. "*Here* is your salary." He pulled out a small, dark, green bag from his pocket and handed it over to him. Looking inside, Isaiah found four large, gold coins.

"My Lord?"

"Your payment – one coin for each year. If you come back, I'll give you two a year, maybe even *three!*" He winked at him, now standing so close, Isaiah could see that strange flicker in his eyes. Some had prattled about it, suggesting the patron was unwell in more than one way, and with this gesture he wondered if there might be some truth to it.

"Thank you, my Lord." He uttered, astonished, as he'd already been gifted a new, black cloak identical to Tzelem's. His impression had always been that they, under no circumstances, were getting paid for their labor – that this was the very reason that captives complained about being captives. Gold coins were not the usual form of payment in Delta, and it was the first time he'd held any in his own hand. Unlike many of his companions, he'd never really cared for them either – still he thought he'd might be able to spend them while still in the Nahbí region. Perhaps a good spade or a rake would be of use – a nice gift to bring home. He put them in his pack, taking nothing more than his knife and one change of clothes (initially, he'd brought a spade too, but Tzelem had told him it was foolish and unnecessary). Before turning to the saddle, he nodded towards Lady Huxley that was standing in the shade some feet away. She had looked straight at him earlier that morning, not even minding him lifting his gaze as they'd spoken together. To ease her worries of his departure, he'd promised that he would return safely and without a scratch. He regretted this now, realizing there was no certainty to this premise at all. The Lady's expression was still tense, puzzled almost, and in a way her silence was a better compliment than any of her husband's words could ever be.

* * *

Some of the children waved as Isaiah rode towards the gates on the largest (and only) horse he'd ever sat on by himself. Nineteen hands long, it seemed to him Indra had to be the largest animal in the world. He'd suggested taking a smaller one that he'd made himself familiar with for a year – but Tzelem insisted he needed a horse that could keep up with his own stallion. For once Lord Huxley had agreed with his brother. The mare had recently been given to them from the Zuras – seemingly being a way of paying their respects to the patrons. Due to the fact that Lord Huxley never rode, he had kindly re-gifted her to Isaiah, seeing that he was on a mission on the Patron's behalf. She was a wholly black and marvelous animal. One he did not feel worthy or competent enough to be riding in the slightest. Climbing her for the first time had been an awkward and apologetic act, and nothing like he'd once pictured it would be. Still, he rode out, hoping his gift would be fast enough to escape whatever danger they might encounter. If he was as lucky as he felt there and then, she might even be able to outrun his master, carry him back home and give him something more than just gold coins and a rake to show for.

*

It took less than an hour of riding, for Isaiah to notice that four years' time had turned his master into a slightly more cheerful man. That wasn't to say they'd brought happiness upon him necessarily (he was yet to actually catch him smiling). Nevertheless, his tone bore less irritation and was far less condescending than it once had been (the fact that he was talking at all, was something to take note of in itself). Perhaps it had to do with the more comfortable, physical distance between them – as they were riding separate horses this time. Perhaps he had truly changed and wherever, or whatever, had kept him from coming back before, had taught him some manners. Whatever the reason, Isaiah decided it was not so important, seeing he wasn't planning to stay around for very long - regardless of how bearable his company might be.

Unknowing of his protégé's lack of commitment, Tzelem had briefed him on the route he'd planned for the next few days. Though giving little detail on the mission itself, he assured him it would be a difficult journey – but that it would be worth all the troubles. "Trust me, you will thank me in the end." He'd said. This didn't encourage Isaiah, of course, having no intention of making it till this *'end'* of his, or going through any unnecessary inconveniences. What had been a pleasant surprise was that their first stop would be in a village further north where they were to get necessary supplies. This meant they were at the very least going in the right direction, and if they stayed the night, he would perhaps have a chance of escaping sooner than he'd dared hoping for.

Tzelem was not at all fond of providing answers, and so he tried his best to ask the fewest questions possible. On the occasions he found himself with a burning one, such as: "Will Indra get angry if I give her a kick to go faster?" or "Will it be very long before we eat?", his master did not ignore him or respond with his usual hostile muttering – he simply replied back. This was not to say, he'd gotten any fonder of pointless chatter or breaks. Isaiah had never been one to mind silence, and being inside this particular one, he realized this was perhaps the only thing the two of them had in common. As to the breaks, riding the whole day with no more than one stop to drink, was a much more displeasing experience. His stomach had grown used to the regular feeding hours of the fortress, and though he'd eaten an even larger breakfast than usual, it still felt unsettling. Tzelem had said they wouldn't have supper till they stopped to camp for the night, and knowing he had a much bigger appetite for movement than food, he was well aware they'd be riding till they couldn't see the path ahead of them anymore.

The Nahbí forest was dull and lifeless, and compared to the one in Delta, Isaiah thought it could hardly be called a forest at all. For hours, there was nothing to see but repetitive roads of tall, gloomy trees and a narrow path (hosting a troublesome number of edged, gray stones). Though twisting its way forward, it hardly ever split into more than two directions at once. It wasn't the lack of pleasant scenery or his empty stomach that came to be the worst of it. The most displeasing side of the matter did not appear until the night sky did. It was a grim sight, that didn't come in the shape of some scary beast or a group of bandits. No, it was as innocent as him looking up at the stars and remembering something of crucial importance – though Tzelem had *said* they would first head north, they were further south than they'd been earlier. He had followed his master quite mindlessly until then, certain he was bringing him closer to Delta every minute.

"Do you mind me asking, master – were you not saying we would first go to Duroya where they produce the best ropes?"

"I did, but we can get a hold of rope in another village and instead tie them together. It isn't so important we should let it delay us." For Tzelem it was perhaps nothing but a minor change of plans. Nothing else than some knots and a different village, so considering his tendency to spare his voice, it was not so strange he hadn't mentioned it. For Isaiah, it had quite severe consequences, and he had to contain his urge to turn around and run. Even if Indra had proved herself to be just as fast as Tzelem's stallion, he would surely be lost – if not dead – within a few hours out there by himself. The Nahbí roads were notorious for its robberies, rapes, and manslaughter.

"I was hoping we could visit my grandfather on the way." Despite the obvious unfairness in his situation, it was not a sort of request he was entitled to make. Even if Tzelem thought he needed him, he was still expected to act as his humble apprentice.

"On the way? I just told you, we're heading *south*."

"I am aware, Master Tzelem... but, could we perhaps ride back – I just want to make sure he is alright. We don't need to take any breaks tomorrow." Isaiah tried.

"There's no time for such nonsense. Maybe if you'd asked earlier, I would have considered it." He damned himself for not realizing they were moving in the wrong direction before. At the same time, he suspected such a *consideration* would have been short-lived and eventually declined, regardless of the given distance.

"Theodore is fine. Now, focus on the road ahead."

"How do you know?"

"I went to see him." He said this casually, as if it was something he did frequently.

"When?" Isaiah asked, daring to make his way next to him, although the path just barely allowed it. Tzelem's gaze didn't stray from the road, the lowered corners of his mouth and pointed nose just vaguely visible underneath his black hood.

"Just before I came back for you."

"Did he ask about me?" Though he wasn't quite sure he believed him, he felt the slightest of relief. Tzelem was yet to tell him the reason for being gone for so long, so It was possible he'd actually been in Delta.

"I told him you were at the fortress being trained. That I was on my way to get you. He seemed pleased." Training wasn't exactly how he would have described it himself, but it sounded much better than "working the fields". Still, he was skeptical, as he couldn't see any reason as to why he'd visit him.

"If you must know, I had an injury and went to get some of that salve of his. Remember that day?"

"Yes." Isaiah said. Of course he remembered. It'd been the last where he'd felt his bare feet on the green, wet grass and heard the thrushes sing in the morning. His heart ran warm by the very thought of it – their garden, their little wooden house, and the person he loved more than anything. He would never ask for anything more, if he could just have it back, and the only thing keeping it from him was riding right next to him – bringing him further away than ever. Then, out of seemingly nowhere, Tzelem stopped and looked to his left. There was not much to see there other than more trees that, though darker, looked no different from the ones they'd been passing for the previous fifty miles or so.

"I believe this is a good place to hunt. You haven't gotten any better at it, I assume?"

"They hire the Zuras to do it." Among many things, the tribal people were masterful hunters. Once he'd seen a young girl through a hole in the wall, as she arrowed down a deer from two hundred yards without blinking. Even if he'd had half her talent, the probability of dinner that evening would still have been low. There was little game left in the area and it was dark.

"Having slaves out hunting, would perhaps be foolish. But *you* wouldn't have run off... they should have given you the chance to practice."

"Yes, well...they didn't." Having no desire to kill anything, Isaiah was happy they hadn't. Tzelem jumped off the horse, signaled him to do the same and handed him his arrow.

"I thought you said we were going to camp and eat at nightfall?"

"Yes. But unless you want to eat my hairy, wounded leg, you'll need to catch our dinner first." Isaiah wanted to protest. He knew very well they'd been provided with plenty of food for the next few days.

"Listen," Tzelem said, looking at him for the first time that day. "I might have been a little rough on you before. But this is for your own good. Not only for the sake of your survival out here, but *the thrill* that makes it worth living for." It seemed well-intended, but this thrill he spoke of, simply couldn't bring him any joy. Even after eating their flesh for years, killing another creature still seemed barbaric to him.

"Off you go." Tzelem commanded, and so Isaiah went.

After perhaps an hour of searching in the falling darkness, straining sounds that seemed unfriendly, Isaiah returned to the roadside where their camp was – just as empty-handed as he'd been after his first hunt. In the end, it was not so much about his unwillingness to kill. When it came to it, he realized he still considered his own survival more important than that of an animal.

"You failed me again." Tzelem said, his tone dismissive and his face unsurprised. Isaiah bent his head, muttering an insincere apology. Fortunately, his master didn't bother wasting his breath and had enough sense to make use of their resources this time.

"No fire?" Isaiah asked, a slight hope of warmth as the hunger and chills crept back into his core.

"No prey, no wind – no fire." Tzelem said solemnly. Unheated, the potato stew tasted blander than usual, but at this point Isaiah was ready to eat almost anything – including Tzelem's leg. Despite feeling cold sitting on the bare ground, he was somewhat relieved he didn't need to fetch wood or worry about getting burned while sleeping. He knew how dangerous fire was, having burnt down large parts of the Nahbí forest. Entire villages even. In comparison with such large things, he'd be an easy prey, and exhausted as he was, even the hard ground came to be a good enough nest for him to finally rest.

CHAPTER FIVE

ALL THE WAY SOUTH

THE next day their morning conversation quickly lulled into a pensive silence (once again forcing him to reflect upon the rash decision to come along). The only thing that made him feel slightly less aggravated with himself, was the consideration whether it had truly been his decision in the first place. It seemed unlikely Tzelem would have ever bent to his will if he'd decided to stay in the fortress. Exiting the gates with everyone's blessing had appeared to be an obvious opportunity to regain his freedom, but now he was further away from where he wanted to be, with every passing heartbeat.

The only option, it seemed, was to reach Tzelem's destination as quickly as possible. This wasn't to say he had any ambition of actually *completing* the mission. Both because it was of no interest to him, and because he obviously wouldn't be fit for whatever task that lay ahead (it certainly wouldn't have anything to do with harvesting, botany or unremarkable poetry). The best solution would be continuing to prove his uselessness on the way there, and so perhaps his master (ever so slightly more reasonable than before), would let him go. If he saw his mistake for what it was, he might even pity him, having stolen four years of his young life, and then risking it out of his own bewildered delusions. Isaiah would ask for nothing more than being taken back home to Delta to make up for this grand error. He would still hate him for what he'd done – but as long as he never had to meet with Tzelem's icy gaze again, it would have to make them even.

40

* * *

Considering this, he knew there was still a chance he would instead grow angry and make him run off into the wilderness. Even so, he'd be better off keeping such an event as a potential problem for the future, than making it one he'd throw himself into voluntarily. And so, deciding to stay put and follow along, he figured it'd be worth asking some questions regarding their overall route. Even if his knowledge of geography was limited, he could at least get an idea of how far and how long they would be riding for – how long he would need to survive out there.

"I thought you understood when I said we were going south – *all the way* south." was the only itinerary his master provided, his long back crumbled forward as they'd seated themselves in an open area of fallen pines during that evening.

"I have never been very far south, Master Tzelem, and it has been some time since I've laid eyes on a map of Araktéa." With a slight shiver to his tightened lips, Tzelem did not immediately respond to this. Instead, he stared into the fire he'd decided to light up that evening, though Isaiah felt it was no colder than it'd been the night before.

"We are going to the Parda." He finally announced underneath his breath. His eyes still fixed on the flames as if it was speaking to him – telling him things of unease and despair.

"The Parda?" Surely, Isaiah thought, even if it might be for the very first time in his life, Tzelem needed to be joking. The first time he had heard any mention of the place, had been from the songs and screams of children running around the fortress's courtyard. He hadn't thought anything of it, till hearing it mentioned once again in the Captive's Cave. Neither source being particularly credible, he had asked Rim. According to her, it was indeed as real as the two of them combined, for her brother had been among the few who'd entered, and he'd come back telling the wildest of stories. Being a man of a particularly serious sort, and not having told a single tale all his life, she'd concluded the Parda had changed him forever. These dramatic implications had for the first time made Isaiah doubt her intelligence, and he'd regarded it as pure village lore.

This didn't stop people from talking about it, of course. At times the tales were so disturbing they kept him awake at night, and so finally he had found the courage to ask Lady Huxley herself – though he suspected she'd find him foolish for even entertaining the idea. "The Parda exists, but it is no different from any other forest. Do not believe everything you hear in the Captive's Cave, Isaiah." She had responded quite plainly, to which he'd said that he didn't, and then thanked her for confirming what he already knew.

With even less belief in these tales than before, he had continued listening to them more peacefully – for the sake of entertainment and inspiration. A subject that often led to heated discussions, circled around what was truly hiding in there – ranging from terrifying monsters to gold and magical treasures of all sorts. Some even believed the fountain of youth was hidden in there, but it all seemed like absolute nonsense to him. Just when he thought he'd heard all the fantastic tales that could possibly be told of the place, the most disturbing one had been presented one night in the Cave. If nothing else seemed certain about the Parda, everyone had agreed that Ares had been the last to enter, and that he had stayed inside for longer than *anyone* in modern times. Isaiah's father had been gone for nearly twenty years now. Some claimed he'd lost his mind and was still wandering about its wicked paths. Others said the Parda had devoured him alive and that he now haunted the place like another one of its many phantoms.

All Isaiah himself knew was that Ares had run off before he'd been born. His assumption had been that his grandfather simply did not know where he'd gone, but seeing that this forest *did* exist, it didn't seem a complete impossibility. The rumor did not excite him, as he had no desire to find a father that had left him and his dying mother behind – to chase danger and fantasies of hidden treasures. Nor did he have any faith that anyone could survive for that long inside any forest, without being killed by someone or something. To him, it was easier if he remained dead, and as to where and when, he'd rather not know.

"You do not believe in the tales, do you, master?" Regardless of his skepticism, Isaiah knew he needed to choose his words carefully – no man liked the implications of being gullible, men like Tzelem, even less so.

"No – I do not believe in *tales*. I only believe in what my eyes and my gut tell me."

"I see." Isaiah wondered what his gut had said about bringing him along. If it was because he knew he was Ares's son, he certainly needed to be a fool. Had a so-called *legend* like him gone there unsuccessfully, it was unlikely his untrained offspring would make it any further. It was said that before him, only twelve brave souls had successfully gotten through its thorn bushes. This didn't need to be true of course, and Isaiah hadn't believed it was either, until Byron had added one important detail to his tale – all of them had been taught by the same teacher. A man once considered the most brilliant academic alive – Master Raziel Mongoya. Growing up, his grandfather hadn't spoken more highly of anyone. He had been his teacher before the revolution, and so, he was certainly very real.

"What is it we will be looking for in there, exactly?" he asked. There was a strange tension in the air, and he didn't like the sound of the fire or the way Tzelem's eyes seemed consumed by it.

"None of your business for now." He muttered, marking an end to the conversation. Seeing they were on a mission on the Patron's behalf, Isaiah assumed Lord Huxley *thought* it to be gold or possibly these *jewels*. Other than his Patroness, fine wine and hardworking captives, these were the things that seemed to be of interest to him. It made him wonder whether the lady had been oblivious of it. If she'd intentionally lied about the Parda or that (as the intelligent woman she was), simply thought the legends to be just as ridiculous as he himself did – hopefully, this was the case. He couldn't imagine she would allow him to leave knowing there was this kind of danger involved. Unless, of course, this was why she'd seemed so distressed.

Out of the twelve, it was said seven had survived the Parda but had come out "stuttering and half-brained." He could understand how obsessing about finding a non-existent treasure might have such an effect. If this was all there was to it, he might survive. On the other hand, he knew there were smaller things than beasts and sorcery that could kill a man. It took no more than a deceptive plant or the spark of a fire blowing in an unfortunate direction - the possibilities of dying on the way alone, seemed rather endless. Yet, he couldn't do anything but follow Tzelem for now, with a slim string of fate he might save him from whatever laid ahead.

CHAPTER SIX

ROPE SCOUTING

"ARE we far from the next village?" Isaiah asked. It was their third day of riding, and the darkening sky bore a cloudy promise of an approaching storm. Though feeling slightly less clumsy in the saddle, Indra seemed more tense in her movements, despite the road having straightened as they got closer to the center of Nahbí.

"We will be in Bharoos in a few hours." Tzelem grunted. "Hopefully it won't be completely uninhabited..."

"Uninhabited?"

"People are fleeing to where the grass is greener."

"To Delta?"

"Most go to Nagár." Isaiah had never been to the capital before, but his grandfather had described it as chaotic, stinky and so noisy only deaf men could hear themselves think. Why anyone would flee there, he could hardly understand, but then again people often seemed to make awfully odd decisions for themselves.

"The town has been an important merchant center for years. My brother has contacts there and knows the Patron. Should be safe enough. We shouldn't stay too long though."

"You don't trust the village people?"

"I don't trust *people*. Everyone has an agenda these days, and we don't have time for any other than our own."

"Your own." Isaiah thought, but remained silent. The sooner they could get down south, the faster he'd be back north.

* * *

Arriving in Bharoos, it soon became clear it was nothing more than a large ghost town – similar to the many they'd ridden by, but the size somehow made the sight more daunting. They rode by rows of abandoned homes (mostly made of rusty, red bricks). The shops seemed to be placed around the center of a square, rooming a large, waterless fountain, sculpted by the same white material as the statues in the Huxley's ballroom. Flower beds circled it, and it might have made it beautiful if anyone had bothered investigating what bloomed this time of year. Instead, it just made the site look browner. Blending to the dusted, gray stone that made up the foundational flooring. Loose hens and half-filled sacks of grain spread across it. As they rode past broken store windows, and locks, hoping to find someone that might be able to assist them with supplies, an elderly man appeared in front of them. He was well-dressed, in a long, black cape reaching to his ankles, and a silver brooch holding his linen shirt together at his thick neck – equally tight as his expression.

"There is nothing left here, you need to carry on to the next town." His brown eyes were empty and his mouth carried a polite, hopeless smile that seemed to struggle against gravity, along with the rest of his face.

"When did people leave? Everything seemed fine a few weeks back."

"People have always been fleeing from here Sir. And dying..." He sighed.

"Are you the only one left? We're seeking the town Patron, Damien Orin. We're on a mission on the behalf of the Huxley fortress, and Lord Huxley..."

"The Patron has departed too, I'm afraid." The man interrupted him.

"Are you... alright, Sir?" Isaiah asked. Away from the struggling smile, he didn't look well. He was fortunate enough to never have seen anyone taken by plague, but knew the skin turned paler, then grayer, before finally spreading red and black spots across the body. Most didn't live long enough to reach the latest stages of it.

"Yes, young man. I have everything I need. In fact, I've never been better. It was always so very noisy..." he responded non-convincingly, then paused as he met the young man's eyes. Had it not been for the long, brown locks of hair, hiding the familiar, firm outlines of his chin and jaw, he might have allowed himself to believe he'd seen another ghost that day. It hardly mattered anymore, so he regained some momentum as he resumed: "If you ride north for a few hours you will find another town. From what I've heard there are still people there. Not as many as before, but their fields are still fertile, and they seem to be doing... alright at least."

"Thank you, but we're moving south." Tzelem said, turning his horse abruptly.

"You'll be riding for days, Sir. The plague has acted most cruelly in this area. Most managed to flee before it reached us, but I assure you there won't be anyone left in the next three villages..."

"We shall see what we find. Goodbye."

As usual, Tzelem seemed to have little time to spare, and the flatness in his voice revealed his annoyance all too clearly. Indra was eager to follow along, but Isaiah slowed her down, feeling they'd acted impolitely towards the poor stranger. Even if he claimed he'd chosen to stay, he pitied him, but as he turned to make some sort of apology, the man was already gone.

"We didn't pass any village a few hours back, did we?" Isaiah asked, finally catching up with Tzelem.

"No. That village *fool* doesn't know what he's talking about."

"Are you certain?"

"*Of course* I'm certain." He quickly regretted the question, reminding himself that though he didn't trust Tzelem's judgement as far as his plan went, he should with anything geography related. After years of wandering, he ought to know the area as well as a Zura.

"Will we need to ride for days with no supplies then? What about the rope you needed? They must have left some rope there..."

"Let's see what happens. These journeys are all about the unpredictable..." It was true, and other than the constant discomfort of hunger and fear (both being rather predictable), it was what Isaiah found the least appealing about it.

They'd only ridden a few miles before hearing the sound of galloping hooves behind them.

"Somebody is coming. They might know something, a town closer to here or..."

"I know these roads, *boy*. We have all the information we need, and I don't like talking with strangers. You can't trust *anyone* in this area."

"Why are we speeding up?"

"They might be bandits, angry tribal men – or worse." He hissed, and with that in mind Isaiah gave Indra a kick of encouragement. He had no desire to meet with any of it – especially not whatever might be considered worse than a bandit or a tribal man. The Zuras were fortunately far away, but he knew there were other tribes. For the most part, you could avoid them as long as you stuck to the roads, but there was no certainty to it. Whoever they were, they were getting closer, and when a man's voice demanded them to stop, it became very clear they were indeed being chased.

Tzelem took a quick left turn, leaving the road and riding into the woods on what could barely be considered a sideroad. All of a sudden, Isaiah felt he had no control over where Indra was taking him, and they followed right behind the stallion's wringing, black tail. The further away from the path, the more the forest thickened, and he had to duck down to avoid the heavy branches throwing him off the saddle.

"We need to change direction!" Tzelem ignored the suggestion and continued riding at what seemed a deathly speed, hardly noticing the thorns rasping his face. Turning back for the briefest of moments he saw the boy taking a sudden right turn. "This way you fool!" he hissed, but Isaiah was even less in control of Indra. Even if he had been, he thought he much prefered the far more open path she'd chosen for them (though he'd somehow forgotten how to breathe, he could at the very least see the path ahead). Tzelem came after them, cursing vicious insults that Isaiah could only hear half the content of, as Indra leaped over fallen trees and rocks. The chase seemed to have no direction or end, but just as his master caught up with them they reached a sharp, grassless cliff, leading straight down a long valley. For a moment Isaiah thought it looked like Tzelem wanted to take his chances and ride down the ridge, but before such a wild escape plan could be further considered, the three chasers had surrounded them.

"You both ought to be deaf men. We commanded you to stop in the name of King Amnos." The one in the middle spit, in a sharp, unrecognizable accent. He had long, rope-like braids, and a pair of thick black eyebrows under his narrow forehead. At first sight, Isaiah thought he resembled a Zura, but he wasn't dressed like one. He had boots for one, and they were all wearing the same black uniform, leather pants and cloaks open enough to reveal prominent shields, placed upon the sigils on their chests. "Guardians?" Isaiah wondered, thinking it looked like Gs. Then, as he met the vivid, dark eyes of the braided man again, he thought "Zura".

"We are just travelers passing through to get to Mudir." Tzelem's voice was fragile and out of breath. His head was bent, and he crooked his back in a way that made him look severely older.

"Mudir is no more. The only village near here is Hoshonto." Another of them said, a large, broad-shouldered beast of a man, with a fair, northern complexion.

"Then I guess we shall go back in that direction." Isaiah said, filling in for his master's absence of words. The braided man, who seemed to be the commander of the three, and the last of them (a fair, young-looking, red-headed one) turned their attention towards him.

"Why didn't you stop?" The commander asked, clearly suspicious.

"There are lots of bandits around here..." Tzelem said, his head still bent.

"Speak up, Sir, I can't hear you well."

"We worried you might be bandits." Tzelem said, a tone louder.

"We are guardians of the Kadoshi." The large one affirmed, clear pride in his voice as his tall, white horse took a step closer to them. The Kadoshi recruited men and women from the villages, and guardians ranked just over the gate guards and right under the collectors. They were the protectors of Araktéans, and their task seemed to be keeping the roads safe. Though not as beloved as they seemed to think themselves to be, collectors were the least popular, as children were often recruited at a very young age these days. After their training period, they would receive different rankings. The fiercest and most talented became soldiers and were sent to fight the barbarians in the north. It was considered an honor, but they rarely ever returned to their villages. One of the triplets, Khair, had claimed he'd spent most of his life as a guardian. The reason he'd ended up in the fortress had apparently been an unfair matter, where he'd been forced to kill a man. Isaiah had thought the situation seemed mostly unfair for the dead man, especially considering Khair seemed quite pleased with his captive-life. Fortunately, killing had been strictly forbidden in Araktéa for a long time now. The guardians wouldn't hurt them.

"We appreciate your service, gentlemen. Will you please let us go, for we have done nothing wrong, nor do we have any intentions of doing any wrongs on our way south." He tried, sensing rather than seeing Tzelem's long, vicious gaze turning towards him.

"People don't always *intend* to do harm, yet a lot of harm happens every day." The commander said seriously, and the northerner turned towards Tzelem with a rather striking pair of blue, suspicious eyes.

"You seem awfully familiar... do I know you from somewhere?" he asked, moving his horse a few steps closer. Isaiah noticed he had no hair underneath his hood, and a long, deep scar arrowed through his right eyebrow, making it look as if someone had attempted to cut him in half – unsuccessfully. Had they gone through with it, he would've still been considered a big man.

"I've ridden through these woods many times – so likely from right *here*."

"Raise your head." He demanded. Tzelem looked up slightly, revealing his piercing, silver eyes, carrying tiresome sacks of early ageing underneath them.
"Rise your head, *properly*." He repeated, and so Tzelem did. Blood running down his temple and a crude cut on top of his nose.

"Hold on now – aren't you the shoemaker from Hoshonto?"

"No."

"If you must know Sir, we are on a mission on behalf of the Huxley fortress." Isaiah said as confidently as he could, hoping it would lift their status a little. Perhaps they wouldn't be considered the finest of gentlemen, but neither were the guardians, and despite the looks of him, Tzelem was a knight. They wouldn't have the right to interfere with a noble mission, unless the realm had commanded it. The guardian ignored him, his eyes fixed on Tzelem.

"*Nonsense*, I've seen you there many times. You even fixed my boots once." He argued, showing off one of them – large, muddy and otherwise seemingly intact.

"You must be confusing me with someone else." Tzelem said between tight lips, and the commander turned his head slightly towards the redheaded one. He was yet to say a word and now only made a nod – so subtle it was hardly a nod at all. Isaiah met his gaze right after, and it almost felt as if it could have thrown him off the cliff if he'd bothered nodding again. His eyes were green, and with his background being the faint, gray-like forest and a sunless sky, they looked unnaturally bright. His cheekbones were tall, and he had a narrow, almost feminine, chin without a single facial hair to cover it.

"Both of you are coming with us back to Hoshonto." The commander affirmed.

"We're in quite a hurry, and I see no legal reason for this interruption." Tzelem's voice was steadier now, the same he'd used with Lady Huxley – but it didn't seem to have any effect on them.

"Do you have papers proving you are who you claim to be?"

"We don't…"

"Perhaps there's no punishment for making shoes or lying in this land, but no papers mean you could be *anyone*. You're coming with us." They were not just anyone and Isaiah sensed the guardians knew this. Still, it seemed to give them the right to legally bring them. The realm was not fond of undocumented drifters.

"You *will* regret this." Tzelem's voice was almost inaudible, but furious enough for everyone to hear.

"You like it the hard way, don't you?" the commander sighed. Then they tied up their hands and horses, before leading them back to the path. Once again heading north, Isaiah realized.

"At least we found some strong rope." He said, attempting to lift his master's mood. Tzelem gave him an almost murderous look, as there had probably never been a worse time to try cheering him up.

CHAPTER SEVEN

THE THRILLS OF THE CORRUPTED

AS the dark clouds fulfilled their promise and rain started pouring down on them, the guardians led the way to a hillside, made camp and concluded they should better bring them to Hoshonto the next morning.

"If you're as familiar as you claim to be in these woods, you must already be aware of the bears. They won't ask any questions before eating you." The bold one said, with a grin assuring that escaping unarmed, was not at all a good idea. He then unbound them, leaving Isaiah and Tzelem alone while the three of them prepared the campfire.

"Listen, Isaiah. Either the big, bold one is playing a trick on the commander, or *all of them* are playing us. Guardians make these schemes all the time..." Tzelem whispered as soon as they were out of ear's reach.

"A trick?" Tzelem nodded solemnly.

"Most likely it's an excuse to bring us *all the back way* to the fortress, just to get a payment from the Huxleys. They know my brother would pay a great deal to have them release us and prevent a long trial." He whispered intensely. The thought of the fortress made Isaiah feel nostalgic for a moment. Though not what he truly wanted, the comfort of a bed as opposed to the cold ground they'd been laying on for the past nights, was more of a temptation than he dared to admit to. The cloak had prevented most of the rain, but his hands had turned pink and numb from holding the reins. Tzelem didn't wear gloves himself, and so he'd decided Isaiah didn't need them either, seeing it wasn't "that cold".

"This is why I never carry my papers – too many bloodsuckers out here. But we'll get out of this." Other than his book, Isaiah didn't have any papers either. He'd never quite understood the concept, but it seemed they were meant to tell others who he was. Even so, it didn't make sense why theirs would be so important to the guardians, seeing they hadn't broken any law he knew of. As Tzelem continued explaining how the trials "really worked" and how much time they might lose, it all made more sense. He'd heard stories of people being taken hostages in the woods, and so it dawned on him that even if he was free from the fortress, he'd now turned into a double captive of a sort.

"Maybe if *we* paid them?" He suggested. They had a few valuables with them – including his four gold coins. It was certainly much less than Lord Huxley could offer, but if the guardians were as concerned about time as Tzelem seemed to be, they might be willing to trade it for their freedom – saving themselves the trouble of the journey. Tzelem shook his head, the lines on his forehead deepening as he hissed, "No. We need to *kill* them."

"*What?*" Isaiah had thought killing animals to be terrible enough. Murdering humans was out of the question. "Can't we just escape during the night?" All the horses had been closely bound together, but he was very good at being very quiet, and almost certain he could become almost invisible and unbind them once the guardians were asleep.

"Too risky. Even if we did get away, they know our faces and could put out warrants."

"We haven't done anything…"

"People are fools. They'll believe the guardians, thinking they're protecting them…"

"Even so, killing them is… *that* is wrong."

"Killing for the sake of completing the mission is a small price to pay – and our only option. It's all a trick. Even if it wasn't, they'd still be robbing us of precious time, and have caused great delay as It is." Tzelem took a long breath, his eyes fixed on their capturers approaching with dry wood about a hundred feet away. Suddenly, it occurred to Isaiah how foolish he'd been for telling them they'd been sent by the Huxleys. He'd been sworn to secrecy, and so it was at least partly his fault they'd become hostages. Though not having wanted to help in the first place, he'd certainly not planned on getting them into trouble either.

"Don't look so dazzled. This will be the first time you'll kill a man, but *not* the last. These men are *corrupt,* and corruption is the greatest sin made in this country."

Other than a brief retelling of the revolution of 44, and how a group of young academics had taken over the palace for three whole moon spans, Isaiah had only heard his grandfather speak of politics once. He'd been six years old and understood very little of what had appeared to be a serious discussion with a visitor. Other than the guest's face – mostly taken up by an intense look in his eyes – he only remembered one thing from this conversation. Against his will it'd been imprinted into a corner of his mind and every time it came to greet him, he could hear his grandfather's hand hitting their kitchen table – "Their *greed* and *corruption* will lead to the death of Araktéa and the *whole* world with it!" Isaiah had found the thought of the world dying as terrifying as any child would, and so, he'd asked him what corruption was after the visitor had left. After being scolded for eavesdropping, his grandfather had finally explained it was like a disease – spreading through people's minds instead of their bodies. As this same word left his master's lips, his heart started to pound as if they were being chased again. By something nearly invisible this time.

"How would we do it?" He asked. Although murder was something he'd avoid at almost any cost (something that had never even crossed his mind really), staying there with them – possibly catching this horrendous mind disease – was not a risk he was willing to take. It seemed to him that if there ever had been a good reason to kill a man, it would need to be to prevent the death of the world.

"We'll stay awake and wait until the silent one is keeping guard. He's the smallest. I will count to one thousand then get rid of him. In the meantime, you will take down the large one with the ugly scar. By then, the commander will be getting up, and I will take care of him before he attacks you."

"What if he attacks me before you get the chance to... *take care* of him?"

"He might. I never said this would be an easy mission." He hadn't.

Not once had he mentioned the word *easy*. He had said it would become easier as he got used to it. Isaiah had hoped he wouldn't need to. He didn't want to get used to any of this horror, but it seemed that meek hope of getting out of this sinless, was the first thing to die that night.

"They took our weapons."

"Lay down next to the big, bold one, and you'll find my best dagger on the right side of his belt. Go straight for his throat." Tzelem whispered, pointing to the side of his own, pale neck.

"But why do *I* have to... handle the biggest of them?"

"Trust me, the largest ones usually sleep deeper and move slower. You just pretend he's a large, hairless bear." He said, and with this final instruction, there was no more time to plan, discuss or refuse any further, as the guardians approached to light up a fire they thought would keep them safe and warm for the night.

*

As Isaiah waited for the signs, he felt his heart jumping with the slightest of movement from the others. The hairless bear was still sitting guard by the campfire, and to maintain his credibility as a sleeping hostage, he had to use every bit of effort to resist glaring at him. He knew he didn't need to look, for he had looked a hundred times already, and it didn't seem like he would become any smaller than he currently was. His neck was probably double the size of his own, and from the look of his scars (the less prominent ones but still severe), it seemed he'd been through many battles and won all of them. Other than the detail that he would be sleeping this time around, Isaiah couldn't see how the results would be any different this time.

After what felt like hours, he finally heard them moving posts. The hairless bear laid down next to him – so close that, even if he hadn't been planning on assassinating him, Isaiah would've still felt uncomfortable. Reminding himself it was better than having a knife through his throat, an uninvited empathy came over him, and he started counting. Each number was helpful in neutralizing the situation, and in between them, he tried reminding himself of this nasty disease they all (most likely) were hosting. All along it was nearly impossible to lay still, and only when he'd reached five hundred he dared to open his eyes. White and round like the moon itself, he stared straight at the man's naked scalp. Another inconvenience, as he couldn't be sure he was sleeping or just breathing heavily, but sudden grunts of snoring reassured him. Isaiah had heard real bears did this too. They slept for months without waking up, and he wished that had truly been the case, so that he wouldn't need to go through with what he'd promised to do.

Isaiah had always had a hard time believing in things he couldn't see, and for a moment, staring at the scalp, he thought he could actually spot the corruption swirling inside it. Like, little, black leeches sucking out and feeding on both the man and the bear-mind. A mere trick of his own mind, he figured. Still, it somehow helped. Reaching eight hundred, he started slowly moving his hand towards the dagger. Sweaty, trembling slightly and the rest of his body followed soon after. Sensing this, and unable to stop, he reconsidered his option. He could flee. Disappear into the forest, hide, and take his chances he wouldn't meet with something more terrifying than corrupted guardians before sunrise. Perhaps they wouldn't even bother looking for him. It was not *him* they'd accused of being a shoemaker from Hoshonto, after all. Even if the Huxleys were fond of him, they'd pay more to get a knight of their own blood released – at least the guardians wouldn't have any reason to think otherwise. Isaiah wished he'd been brave enough to negotiate while he'd still had a chance, and so maybe they would've just taken Tzelem as their hostage. While thinking about potential past discussions that hadn't happened, he forgot to count, and only remembered as his own trembling was matched with a gasp. He heard Tzelem's boots moving, followed by the silent guard's scream just a moment later.

Isaiah felt sure he'd never heard a more dreadful sound. Loud enough to wake up anything and anyone deep asleep. In panic, his hand fell to the bald bear's belt. It was an unplanned and clumsy movement, and just as surely, he turned around. Undoubtedly awake, and with the silent man still screaming with all his force, he trapped him with the massive weight of his body.

"What in the nine hells do you think you're doing?" he roared. He didn't seem to notice – or care – that he himself was unarmed, while the boy, somehow, had managed to get a hold of the dagger in his belt. He pulled Isaiah up by the throat in a single grip – as effortlessly and carelessly as a child would've done with a rag doll. It seemed Tzelem had already killed the silent man, and now he and the commander were battling on the other side of the fire.

"If you want the boy to live, leave him be and *lay* down!" Isaiah couldn't say anything in his own defense. He could hardly breathe, with the iron hand around his neck. With his free hand the man disarmed him of the knife he'd stolen seconds before – if possible, leaving him even more defenseless.

"So, this was what you were grabbing for? And here I was, thinking you were flirting with me." Barely standing on his toes, Isaiah felt sharp, cold steel towards his skin. In the same moment he met Tzelem's eyes through the fire – as cold and ruthless as the blade itself. Though usually stripped from emotion, he thought he could see disappointment in them. If nothing else – he'd at least proven himself unworthy and incompetent of his master's mission once and for all.

"Raise your hands so that we can bind them." It only took this brief moment of distraction for the commander to grab the knife from his belt and hold it towards his master's neck – the very same spot Tzelem had been pointing to himself some hours before. The commander kicked him in the stomach, leaving him gasping for air in the wet mud.

"You bloody snake!" he spit. Then he cursed out strange, furious words, finally confirming what Isaiah had first suspected – he had to be a Zura. Standing over his fallen friend he soon realized he was unsavable – his green eyes empty, his lips doomed to everlasting silence and blood deepening the red of his hair. The commander spent some moments with the body, whispering underneath the sound of flickering fire and the tension pumping through the air like distant thunder. Finally, he got back on his feet and turned towards Tzelem, still laying gasping for air. He bound his hands, tightened them while still cursing viciously.

"Are you *insane*? You were merely being taken back for an *informal* trial, and now you're the murderer of a brother of the Kadoshi!" The bald bear finally let go of Isaiah, pushing him forward so that he fell awfully close to the fire. He coughed, gasped and felt certain the flames would have taken a hold of his hair, if it hadn't been dripping with rain.

"You gave me no choice. Your *brother* is a liar, and as I said, We don't have time for this nonsense." Tzelem uttered.

"Is your time so precious it is worth killing innocent men for? Worth risking the life of your son?"

"He's *not* my son."

"Then he is an even bigger fool for sticking with you. Do you hear that boy? A *fool*! Do you have any idea what sort of punishment you'll face for murdering a guardian? Do you have any idea who this man was?" Isaiah shook his head, having pulled away from the fire, without getting too close to the other guardian.

"He was the commander of our entire squad – in charge of half of Nahbí. *This man* was a Birdú and when the word reaches the tribe they'll be ruthless..." Isaiah was not quite sure what all of this meant, or even exactly how big half of Nahbí was, but it was by far the largest region in Araktéa. Still, it seemed the silent man's position was more important than they'd assumed, and that the Zura hadn't been the commander after all.

"Luckily for *you*," he pointed at Isaiah. "I'm not a heavy sleeper, and Dove here, too soft-hearted to kill young boys like yourself." In between him and the fire, Isaiah did not feel lucky in the slightest. Soft-hearted was the last thing he thought this *Dove* character to be, and surely there would be great consequences for what he'd attempted. "I was a fool to trust Tzelem" he thought. Meanwhile, Dove and the Zura looked at each other, and though not uttering a single word, it seemed a lot was being said.

"We will leave it to you to decide, boy. We can kill your master – or whoever he is to you – here and now. There is no need for a trial in such an obvious case. Both of you would be imprisoned for a very long time. Most likely, forever." Isaiah glared at them, confused. From what he knew, everyone – except from himself apparently – had a trial before any sort of imprisonment or punishment. The fortresses were usually where the most fortunate were sent and some captives had come from much worse places. For obvious reasons, he was yet to meet someone who'd gotten a death sentence. It was mostly a thing of the past, and executions were only performed in extremely rare cases, with people so dangerous they could hardly be considered human at all.

"You can't just...kill him?" he stuttered.

"He *killed* our *commander* – an honorable man of the realm and the Kadoshi. Why, I don't know, and he doesn't have the eyes of a man that would tell the truth of it." Isaiah looked at Tzelem who'd finally managed to get to his knees. His long face was overtaken with pain, and still there was that ever-present sense of stubborn unyieldingness.

"We have important matters to take care of, and I, for one, don't want to waste any more time breathing the same air as this *snake*. A trial will be faster if we only bring you along, and all of us will have fewer *complications* that way. Men who lie about who they are, are the very worst kind."

"You're wrong, he is Tzelem Huxley... I swear he is!" He damned Tzelem for not bringing these stupid papers of his. Surely, he had them, and clearly, it was more dangerous to be no man at all than a gentleman.

"A man can have many names. Many masks and faces..." Isaiah looked at Tzelem's again. He hoped he'd say something to his own defense, but instead he stared at the ground as the wind blew smoke and ashes towards him.

"Do you really trust this face? Would you want to spend the rest of your life sharing a cell with it?" The commander pulled his graying hair back, forcing Tzelem to look straight at Isaiah for once.

"No." The answer escaped him before he could actually consider the question.

"Isaiah, you can't listen to them. They're turning you against me and leading you off course."

"Is it true? Have you been hiding in Hoshonto all these years, while leaving me imprisoned?" It had not occurred to him till just then, that though absurd for the brave adventurer to have stayed cowering in a village so close to the fortress, perhaps it was true – as he was yet to say anything about his absence.

"*No.* I was there for a few months while healing from an injury. The one with my leg that I told you about." Tzelem's voice lost its coolness, as doubt washed off of the boy's young face. What he'd just said was more truthful than many of the other lies he'd fed him with. Even so, it was too incomplete and too overdue to hold any weight.

Isaiah saw it now – that filthy shame in his eyes. Had he even visited his grandfather? No, he doubted it.

"I will give you one more chance, Tzelem. Tell me everything, or I'll let him do it."

"Don't be a fool! I *will* tell you everything, I swear I will answer any question you have – just do not give them the pleasure of winning this game. This is *nonsense!*"

But it wasn't nonsense. It was the first time in a very long time, Isaiah truly felt he had a saying in his own future, and suddenly there was not a single doubt in his mind. No hesitation or consideration. Not only had he left him to rot inside his brother's prison, but he was a liar, a killer, and it was in fact *he* who had tried infecting his mind with corruption – making him just as bad of a man as he himself was.

"Do it." he said, and with those two, short words leaving his mouth, Isaiah had killed his first man – experienced this so-called thrill that made the journey worth living for. Although they'd both predicted it would happen that night, it took them equally by surprise. For Tzelem, it lasted nothing but a brief second, as the Zura knew well how to cut a throat open. As his eyes blinked one final time, the knight didn't see his hard, lengthy life flash before them. All he saw was the crucial incident that had led him there. No more than a week ago, just before Dove had come to have his boots fixed. It could have ended there, if it hadn't been for the man that had entered the shop right after. The bell above the door (that the shop owner had him polish every damn week) had rung in its peculiar way. Deep in his seams, Tzelem hadn't bothered raising his gaze.

"Tell me, shoemaker, have you always made shoes for a living?" The customer had asked in a hoarse, rather casual voice.

"Have you always worn them?" Tzelem had responded. Absentminded, while pushing his needle through Dove's large, left boot.

"It is time for you to finish what you've started." His voice had suddenly deepened, as if coming from the bottom of a hollow well.

"Which shoes have you…"

"Not shoes. You need to go get the boy, Tzelem." Only then, Tzelem had paused his work and looked at the man – a dark skinned fellow with strands of gray hair showing underneath his hat. He had one, deep, olive green eye. The other one was as pitch black as a bird's, and from this sinister gaze, he'd understood playing the fool's game would just lead to a longer, even more unpleasant conversation. Fate, it seemed, had caught up with him after all.

"I was wrong about that. Just…following a silly tale."

"You were only *partly* wrong. The boy *is* the last Aronin." The man said, grinning strangely as if someone had just whispered a joke to him.

"It must have bothered you a lot, having to depend on someone so young and clueless. I can emphasize, but self-pity isn't a good look on you." He spoke and shook his head slowly.

"Who are you?"

"Nobody of importance. Just like you yourself are trying to be nowadays – or failing to be, I should say." The man grinned again.

"I've left that life behind…"

"I can see that and I am curious, Tzelem, why haven't you taken what's left of you and crawled back to your brother's fortress? I've heard the wine there is exquisite." Tzelem flinched.

"Does he know?"

"Your secret is safe for now, and it will likely continue to be so if you answer my question." The messenger said, though Tzelem's gaze alone did well in confirming his suspicions - before him stood a man so proud he would rather appear dead, than to be exposed as a failure. That was a part of it at least, but there was always more to a story than what met his eye.

"That place is *poisonous* and I want nothing to do with it. I'll rather rot out here…" He said, and the customer's eye flickered ever so slightly.

"Though I respect your choice, you're still much too bitter of man, Tzelem. For this, you'll be punished, I'm sure, but all in due time. You shouldn't hide here for much longer, though. The plague is on its way to every corner of the land and believe my words – it will take you first if you're foolish enough to stand still."

"*Who* are you?" Tzelem repeated, taken aback and lacking in other words. The one thing that had made Hoshonto bearable was that people gladly left him alone as long as he got the job done. But this man was not from Hoshonto. No, he doubted he was even an Araktéan.

61

"You may consider me a messenger – as well as a believer in the maintenance of balance. Thus, I did bring some good news as well." He pulled out a coin from his pocket, rubbing its edges with his leather gloved fingers. The instant it was put on top of the desk separating them, Tzelem remembered a dodging line from a hero tale his father had used to read. "When the man was given the sorcerer's coin, he knew there was only one decision left for him to make; what sort of death he would like to die – one of silent acceptance or one of fulfilling glory."

"Why are you bringing me this? You say you bring good news and then curse me with a death sentence!" Tzelem's reaction made the loon chuckle a little. It'd been some time now since he'd given anyone a coin. It still seemed that no matter how far down they'd fallen, there were few Araktéans who dared objecting to prophecies or ignoring what they'd heard from village lore. Even funnier was the fact that the ones who did, tended to encounter worse fates for themselves.

"Because I'm a messenger. Haven't you ever fantasized about it, Tzelem? Your eyes tell me you have – and now the time has come. It's such a wonderful thing for some of you…"

"No, I … I don't want to die!" He didn't want to live either exactly, as life was as big of a curse as any. Still, whatever awaited him in the afterlife, he knew it was worse than any suffering he knew. He felt afraid, remembering that last, daunting expression left on his father's face. A man notoriously known for feeling no fear.

"In these times when many matters are delicate and complicated, your task is not. And you can still have some glory, Tzelem. Perhaps even salvation if you do well."

"I don't care for glory…"

"Aaah, do not pretend you don't. A little crow suggested to me, it's one of the few things you've ever seemed to have wanted. Did you believe the forest wasn't listening to your little talks?"

"I just want peace now." It felt as true to him now as it had when he'd made his first vow to the gods. A promise he would be good if they just had mercy on him and that he wouldn't attempt going back south again. A promise he'd soon chosen to forget. Was that why he was here? Was it *they* who had sent him?

"Peace doesn't come for free for men like yourself, Tzelem, you already seem well aware of that. There's a task for you." The sorcerer said finally before pausing again, awaiting Tzelem to compose himself.

"What do you want me to do?"

"Be the shadow that leads him there." He said, and Tzelem knew that was all – the entire rest of his life told in seven words.

"Shadows don't lead, messenger, they follow." The sorcerer smiled at this, and then said:

"That depends on the direction of the sun."

The memory of the length of the loon's back, his long, black leather coat as he walked out as calmly as he'd walked in, and then the large coin (imaging two men riding on one horse), was the last thing Tzelem saw before the real blackness took him. It was like his father had told him – "Every good curse comes with a choice." If nothing else, he'd died a death of his own choosing. His task unfulfilled, his heart and hands cold, as his mind finally let go of a world that he was done fighting. Soon, another hell would follow, one of new layers of pain, and yet terribly similar lessons.

*

Any Araktéan would agree killing one's master was an awful betrayal, but it felt like justice for the three men left around the campfire that night. It took a great many minutes before Isaiah felt remorse of any sort, and it came accompanied by a realization of having participated in the death of two men, in one night. It was such an unthinkable thought, that he had no idea how to grasp it, and to his relief, Dove came over to him at the very same moment.

"Why would you choose to pair up with a fraud like him?" He asked – not a hint of anger in his voice, despite their previous feud. Isaiah knew it might be a trick – or a mask, as the Zura had called it. At the same time, he thought it to be a good question. In four years, he hadn't told anyone about how he'd ended up in the fortress, but seeing he'd been deceiving enough to try slicing the man's throat in his sleep, he felt he owed it to him. Apart from being in his debt and wanting a distraction, he'd never felt a night more crucial for truth. He started thinking his way back to when he was an innocent child, without a drop of blood on his hands, or doubt in his mind about whom to trust.

"It's a long story." He warned him, and Dove nodded as the Zura sat down across from them.

"Most good stories are."

CHAPTER EIGHT

HOSTS OF THE GARDEN

THE morning of Isaiah's fourteenth birthday he had woken up in unease. It had nothing to do with the fear of getting older, that often came later in life, or frightening dreams, that he just barely remembered tormenting him earlier. Rather, its origin was the book sitting on top of his tiny nightstand – a beautiful gift that he'd been given the year before. Its thin, brown, leather binding, slightly rougher after being brought around their house, their garden and to the surrounding forest that belonged to nobody at all. Despite its journeys, it still didn't have a single drop of ink in it. It was missing two pages that'd been torn out on the first day, and so, if anything, its insides were even more hollow than it'd been before belonging to him.

Isaiah's only comfort was that it could have been worse – and it had almost turned worse on a number of occasions. The book could've just as well have been filled with bad writing and silly stories that'd the world would be better off without. Having discovered how easily such useless words came to him, he'd been waiting patiently for an idea – one good enough to put down on paper. It had seemed like a good strategy, seeing there was no real urgency to the matter. Yet, it had occurred to him some days before, that since he would receive a new gift today, it would be quite a bad thing not to have anything for his grandfather to read. A story, then, needed to come to him, as he couldn't bear seeing him disappointed.

* * *

Isaiah was not completely wrong to worry, for this same morning Theodore was just as excited about making his request to read, as his grandson was dreading to decline it. Lately, the boy had been even more quiet than usual, but he'd felt certain it had to do with him finding his *niche*. Such things took time, as an academic he knew this well. Though more of a reader himself, he'd known and even taught a few skilled storytellers in his days. He'd been careful not to make his grandson one of his students, however, teaching him nothing less and nothing more than what he ought to know. Ever since he was a child he'd been a clever and curious boy - qualities Theodore would've appreciated more, had their circumstances been different. Subject wise their focus had been on simple, relevant things, and though this had manifested a certain ignorance and enclosement within the boy's mind, it seemed a necessary and rather innocent evil within the much larger picture. He was safe.

For some time it'd been inevitable that his grandson was coming of age. Had Theodore been a different man than he was, he would perhaps have seen the increasing silence that followed with this, as a completely natural evolution– another phase that would come and go as it should. But he'd lost a boy to restlessness before, and rather gradually his mind had started imagining the worst. After many sleepless nights, contemplating on how to prevent the many disturbing outcomes in his head, he'd finally found a solution to the matter a year back. It seemed that what his grandson needed was simply something to put his thoughts into, and that writing might be that perfect something. He'd seen how the pen could keep a man's wilderness condensed. How it could protect him (and others perhaps) from himself.

As Isaiah walked down the stairs, one year after receiving his very first book, his grandfather was too blinded by his own excitement to see the worry in his eyes. Having waited so patiently to read his first work, the possibility that he hadn't written anything at all, hadn't crossed his mind.

"How is my storyteller doing?" It should not have been the first sentence coming from his mouth, but since it was, Isaiah's nervousness doubled.

"Good," he responded, resisting the impulse to run up the stairs again. "Though I didn't sleep too well... " He added.

"Oh, what's the matter? So excited about the day ahead perhaps?" He nodded, not wanting to worry him. His grandfather had an ability to fix almost any concern he had, but there was very little anyone could do with his obvious lack of talent.

"Something like that."

"You've been sleepless for the best of reasons then, for your birthday begins right *now*." Theodore opened up the oven and just as he'd smelled from his room, he'd made the world's tastiest apple pie, with too much of everything in it. A good solution for almost any problem, and the only reason he'd finally decided to come downstairs.

"*Only* on your birthday, my boy – and no matter how old you get." Theodore said, smiling from ear to ear, as he cut out one large piece for each of them. What he said was not completely true, for though it used to be an exclusive detail for his birthday, he'd been making it almost every moon span lately. This fact didn't make it any less delicious, and for some minutes Isaiah was able to forget about the book – fully indulging in the sweetness of the mushy apples, with the cinnamon and cardamom. A year ago he'd just barely stomached two pieces, but he now had four before his belly forced him to put his fork down. His grandfather then held up a small gray seed, his earnest smile reaching all the way to his kind, hazel eyes.

"Ready?"

Leaving their plates uncleaned on the table, they walked out to the garden. Compared to their modest house, it was nothing less than enormous, and it would take anyone with a normal set of feet at least five minutes to reach the hedge that marked the ending point of their property. Nobody had ever reached it at that pace, mostly because very few were welcomed to enter, and because whoever did, always stopped in awe – admiring the gorgeous variety of flowers and shades of green along its paths. Standing at the right end of the garden, was the Sterculia alata. Surrounded by herbs and vegetables, it was beyond a doubt the tallest tree there, and carried strange, large fruits at its branches. Isaiah did not have a favorite out of the hundreds of species they hosted, but if he'd had to choose, it might be the one he appreciated the most. It wasn't only its size and fruits that impressed him, but the way it swayed in the wind. The way its bole twisted elegantly from its roots to its top, making it both firm and flexible – at least for a tree that had been standing still for over a hundred years. It seemed this tree had, and would always, be there.

Their garden was his favorite place in the world, and though he'd never been in any other garden, it was unlikely he'd find one that could compare to theirs. Every seed had been precious gifts from all over Araktéa, resulting in a variety almost nobody would even dream of. Despite the blessing, this was a fact Theodore found unfortunate. People didn't dream of beautiful gardens anymore, and the few who did, cherished such dreams only for brief moments, before telling themselves they'd be better suited for brighter days. Days that might never come. He also knew all his blessings came with responsibilities that had to be taken seriously – responsibilities he was committed to fulfil at almost any cost.

As they walked barefoot into the grass, both of them got ready for their annual ritual – one that indeed had kept its sacredness over the years. It was of course impossible to completely avoid looking at last year's plant while it grew, as they spent a great deal of time maintaining the garden. Still, Theodore always insisted it was only on that very day it would reveal its true colors, and though the garden usually calmed both of them, they were always excited as they approached last year's seed.

"Well look at that, Isaiah. Have you ever seen something quite so joyous? Does this mean there will be a great harvest this year and lots of sunshine?" Theodore asked hopefully, as they looked at the tall, bright sunflower, stretching almost six feet over the ground.

"I didn't ask about the harvest." Isaiah responded and his grandfather smiled patiently.

"I know you didn't, dear. Now, are you going to tell me what you did ask about?"

Isaiah usually didn't keep the question a secret from him, for he was a very intelligent man, and could answer most of them almost instantly – without having to drink rain and eat soil for a year.

"It was stupid…"

"No, my boy. Stupid is the one who doesn't share his questions with his wise grandfather." Isaiah sighed. It was a lesson he'd heard many times before, and yet, he still found a great many things too strange to speak about.

"I asked whether I was an adult yet." Theodore looked at him, his eyes unusually widened and disapproving.

"Now, why would you ask that?" Isaiah shrugged, but this response did not seem to satisfy Theodore.

"I don't know. I guess I started feeling different, and it seemed like a logical reason for it..." He'd felt different a year ago but standing there now he felt a different sort of different. Perhaps it was just an adult thing he needed to get used to, for the plant looked tall and bright. Yet, he couldn't say adulthood was something he found enjoyable. As he'd told him some years before, "Adults don't dream, and we worry a lot."

"Nature never lies." Theodore sighed, "I guess you *are* an adult now..." Isaiah was at least relieved he wasn't about to be lectured on the limitations of his questions. Instead, his grandfather had that absent look upon his face now, that hardly ever led to conversation.

"It seems so." Isaiah said at last and forced a smile. It had sounded like a good thing to ask at the time, and he'd been hopeful. Now, he wondered what would need to change accordingly.

"Perhaps I should start calling you Sir, then?" Theodore joked, thinking humor might hide his worry, and stop him from browsing his memory for when this change could have occurred – when and why his grandchild suddenly felt he was not a child any longer. Even if he'd dared to ask, Isaiah wouldn't have told him. As with most, the sensation of change had crept up on him rather gradually. What he remembered very well, was when it had manifested into a question – yet another thing he couldn't speak of. He knew that worrisome look on his face, and that it always seemed to worsen when he attempted to explain something like this. He'd worn the very same one, when a tall, light-haired man had come riding in last year – just a week or so before his thirteenth birthday.

It had been a very long time since they'd had any visitors, and the people that came and went, mostly had not paid any attention to him. His grandfather had explained it was because he was a child, and having none of their own, they were no good conversing with children. Because of this, it'd been a surprise when a young, uniformed man greeted him while fetching water from the well in the front of their house. The encounter had been brief, as Theodore had explained that the two of them needed to talk in private. Isaiah had watched his grandfather's private conversations many times. Not because they were particularly exciting, but the visitors that had once come with more frequency, had often looked different from the Deltans in the nearby villages. Simply observing them had been fascinating. This time Theodore had made it clear, such behaviors would be even less acceptable than usual, and so instead he'd stayed outside with the man's horse – a beautiful, white stallion. Stroking his hand over its soft mane, he thought he'd wish for one for his birthday. Remembering his grandfather was afraid of horses, it had then occurred to him that perhaps if adults spoke to him now, there was a possibility he was becoming one himself. If this was the case, it would mean he could in fact get a horse without anyone's consent. With this in mind, he'd decided this might be the question that could change everything.

One year later, he understood how foolish his thirteen-year-old self had been. How juvenile the idea was, and how up till that moment, he'd imagined life to be an easy thing where he could have whatever he wanted. It wasn't that simple for an adult. Nothing was.

"I guess now that I'm a man, perhaps it means I should have some new privileges?" He suggested, though not so sure if he wanted a horse anymore. His grandfather had convinced him they had no use for one and Isaiah had been unable to answer who would teach him to ride and where in Araktéa he'd want to ride to. Still, he didn't want the question to have been asked in vain. Surely, there had to be some other benefits tied to adulthood.

"Actually, it is usually the other way around. But if you wish *Sir*, I can review your latest writings and share my humble opinion on them. Then *afterwards* we could discuss some privileges." He was ready to give the boy almost anything, just to get a peak of one of those precious pages.

"I really haven't written anything good yet, grandfather."

"Oh, I doubt that, dear. Remember that talents need some time to expand and come alive."

"I would just rather work on it by myself for a little while longer…

if you don't mind." It was just then that Theodore noticed how oddly melancholic he seemed about the matter. "No, he must just be nervous to show it to me." He thought. His grandson had always been such a perfectionist.

"Alright then. I will stay patient." Theodore said, leaving his grandchild ever the slightest calmer. It was a lesson he'd taught him at an early age, and he felt he couldn't force any story out of him that wasn't ready to be read. Perhaps, it was finally time for him to write to one of his old acquaintances in Dabár. In circumstances such as these, the boy finally seemed to need advice beyond what he himself and his seeds could provide.

"So, what will be your first question as an adult?" he asked, bending down to make a pocket in the soil, while his grandson studied the seed of the purple iris. Isaiah had known for almost a whole year what he would ask. Usually it was something he would change his mind about hundreds of times before deciding, but not this time – it had come to him clear as day and stuck to his mind like a hungry leech.

"I just want to know if things will ever be the same again."

"The same as what, boy? Same as when?"

"The same as they used to be." Though he didn't know when or exactly what it was, their world had started feeling different. Already a year ago, he'd been waiting for some time for it to return to normal. Now, he found himself waiting still, and though ready to continue being patient and hopeful, he was less eager to wait for nothing. His grandfather knew this very feeling better than anyone and staring at the boy as he planted the seed, he feared the worst of answers. "He can sense it too." he thought solemnly, and watched him plant the seed, hoping they were wrong.

*

After the seeding, Theodore decided they'd pay a visit to the close-by village. Isaiah found it rather pointless, seeing that all they'd done was to change apples for mushrooms that they might as well could have picked in the forest. Isaiah dreaded crowds. The feeling had amplified further that day, as several villagers had bumped into him, and rather than apologizing, they'd turned around with strange, confused looks upon their faces. Staring out into the air like the clueless sheep he believed they were. "Pay them no attention, Isaiah. They don't know any better." His grandfather had reminded him, and returning home things had turned for the better. They'd played three rounds of cards, before preparing the dinner – finally finding themselves chatting about anything but books and serious questions. Almost having forgotten about both matters entirely, his grandfather's cheerful humming turned silent. Then, listening more closely, he heard the rare sound of galloping hooves.

"Keep on chopping, I just need to go fetch something. *Don't* let anybody in."

Theodore rushed down the steep stairs to his office. Over the years, he'd developed a certain talent for recognizing sounds. It had begun with bird chirps, but now he could almost always tell the breed of a horse, simply from the rhythm and length of its steps. Though he hadn't taken his time to listen closely, he knew it was a rather large horse – meaning it would likely be accompanied by a collector or some noble man. More likely than not, it would be the collector that had been there a year earlier – just as had been promised. He was more prepared this time and had both his papers ready and a copy of the contract he'd signed when he'd left Nagár. It should not be any major trouble to have him leave again – still, his heart was beating as if it was about to get speared, and he couldn't help but think the answer they'd received that morning, had been a very bad omen.

As Theodore ran back upstairs, he heard two heavy knocks on the door. "Damn them for coming right on his birthday," he thought, then he took a deep breath and put on his most solid and authoritarian face. He stood up as tall and wide as a man of his size could, and then opened the door. At his doorstep stood a muscular man with a sharp chin and a dripping, wet forehead. He appeared tall, but was leaning towards his leg, making it hard to tell if he was bowing or just badly injured. Nobody had ever bowed to Theodore before, and so he assumed the latter.

"Good day, Sir." The stranger said.

"Good day."

"I am sorry to bother you, but I've been passing through the woods for days and yours is the first house I've found. I've injured my leg, and it is making riding back home quite... difficult." Theodore measured the stranger while holding the papers hidden behind his back. They were not for just anyone to see, and though he'd felt certain about what sort of individual was coming, life had taught him caution. He stayed on guard, knowing it might be a trick. It would have been a strange method to get into their house, but a clever one, nonetheless. Refusing to help somebody badly wounded was dishonorable, and Theodore even suspected it had become illegal – though he hadn't cared to read the newest laws.

"I am sorry about your misfortunes, but perhaps it'd be better if you went to the nearby village. It is only a seven-minute ride from here, and there will be both doctors and healers that can assist you better than me." The man's clothing revealed he was not just another poor drifter. The odds of him being of the Kadoshi were low, as he didn't carry their uniform – but he could still be *anyone*. Theodore's biggest fear, by far, was that the realm itself had sent him. That his secret was no longer safe and that they were trying to lure their way out of the agreement.

"I understand, thank you." The stranger stuttered, his steely, gray eyes were yet to have tears in them, but the red lines revealed fatigue. With great effort he started stumbling back to his horse. As Theodore had predicted, it was a large breed, but taking a good look at it, he noticed it was not of the common, noble man's horses as he'd first believed. "Peculiar." He mumbled, and then said, "Hold on, Sir. Perhaps I can take a look at the wound for you. I am no healer, but I do have a salve that might help." He damned himself as the words left his lips, but seeing the limping man bending over in pain, and already having been wrong about his horse, made him second guess his judgement. It also made him strangely curious as to who he was, as something about him seemed awfully familiar.

"Thank you for your kindness, Sir. You'll be paid for the trouble."

"Now, none of that." He replied. Noble money was the last thing he wanted in their house.

Theodore did not introduce Isaiah to the stranger, but he did not send him to his room either. Uncertain whether this was one of these new, adult privileges or if he was just being inattentive, he stood silently in the kitchen entrance. It'd been a long time since anyone else had been in the house, and so, he couldn't help but glaring rather unshyly at the man. His dark, blonde hair laid messy behind his ears, looking as sweaty as he smelled. The stranger responded with a short nod of acknowledgement in his direction. Followed by this, there was a subtle, alertness on his grandfather's face before he turned to tend to the stranger. The tall man fell down on their sofa with an awful expression on his face. He bit his lip as he pulled off his right boot, revealing wounds Theodore saw were more serious than he'd prepared for. Many men fell off their horses, down hills or even treetops if they were truly foolish – but these were not wounds of the sort. They were thin and clean, nearly making up a pattern that made it look as if someone had torn the flesh up deliberately. For most, they wouldn't seem particularly threatening. Not very deep, nor showing obvious signs of infection. Having seen similar wounds before, Theodore happened to know that if not treated properly, death was a certainty – and even then, the chances of survival would depend on a thin stray of luck.

"I will get some equipment from my office." He said, rushing back down to the basement with a sudden urge to help. He found his last jar of medical salve, a cloth infused with turmeric and just as he was about to exit, he saw the flask of water once gifted to him. According to his former student, it ought to have miraculous healing qualities and should only be used in emergencies. The past ten years, there'd been none, and though Theodore wasn't sure he believed in miracles anymore, he thought it had to be the only thing that might save the man.

"It seems I came to the right house." The stranger said, looking ever so astonished by the old man's efficiency. The small cuts had turned to a darker shade of red, since he'd last looked at them, and the surrounding skin a grayer shade of pink.

"I will do my best…" Theodore said as calmly as he could, cleansing the wounds thoroughly. Meanwhile, the man stayed silent. His long, pale face revealed no pain until he put the salve on and Isaiah covered his ears as he started cursing viciously. It'd been some time since he'd gotten any injuries, but with the salve's strong smell he recalled the pain from past wounds - this and perhaps the strange words made him feel a little lightheaded for a moment.

"Pardon me. I forgot there were children around." The stranger said, and for a moment, Theodore stopped what he was doing. He looked the man straight in the eyes, before slowly turning his head towards his grandson, still standing silently in the entrance to the kitchen.

"Apparently, there's not..." He uttered.

"What's your name, boy?" The stranger asked, turning his head towards him. Isaiah looked towards his grandfather – oddly empty of instruction. "Speak only when spoken to," he remembered, and then he said "Isaiah, Sir." The stranger nodded with no major interest, while Theodore bandaged his leg as tightly as he could. Raising up from his knees, he noticed he'd left the contract on the table.

"Excuse me for a moment." He said, grabbing it before rushing downstairs, locked it inside the lowest drawer of his desk, and brought back some tea leaves.

Once both their mugs had been half emptied, and the stranger's pain seemed to have settled on a more moderate intensity, Theodore cleansed his throat.

"May I ask where you obtained these injuries, Sir?"

"I couldn't tell you." He responded. While the two of them silently regarded each other through the rising water steam, Theodore felt a growing urge to ask much bolder questions. He knew these kinds of wounds, and if they came from the place he suspected, he couldn't keep himself from believing the stranger had come to their door for a reason. Not out of his own selfish agenda, or even his pain, but reasons he himself might not even be aware of. Reasons worth the trouble of saving him, as well as the risk of being completely mistaken in doing so.

"I heard you cursing in Birdú, and I see your wounds, so, I must ask you...." His lips were narrow, so that his grandson might not hear him from the kitchen.

"Have you gone to... the Parda?"

"What do you know of it?" The stranger asked, almost spilling hot water over himself.

"I... I've heard more than just a few tales, you might say. I didn't believe anyone dared enter these days." He said as casually as he could, while the stranger measured him.

"I didn't get too far this time... As soon as my leg is better, I'll head back."

"Mmm." Theodore responded, and for a flick of a second, the stranger saw admiration along the lines around his eyes. A rare encouragement that made him an inch more relaxed.

"It happened just over a week ago." Theodore nodded slowly to this. Had it been himself, he wouldn't have wanted to know it was his last night alive, and so he smiled kindly and said:

"I don't have much space here, but you are more than welcome to stay in our common room till you feel better."

"You're too kind, Sir."

"Oh no, too kind would be offering you my bed, but unfortunately my back wouldn't bear the sofa these days. Not that it is unpleasant in any way, but I am getting... old." he sighed, and got up from his seat.

"Please have some rest while we finish dinner." The stranger nodded, and for the first time in years, Theodore locked the door to the kitchen before rushing over to his grandson (busy stirring the pot).

"Isaiah, the brave adventurer who is staying in our living room is very ill. He will most likely die during the night, and so, we should go on and celebrate your birthday like usual tomorrow. Tonight, we must try to give him the best time possible, seeing he has very little left. Do not mention to him that he is dying, for it might devastate him and devastated men are difficult to amuse." Isaiah had never heard his grandfather talk in such a way before – nor seen him so eager to share dinner with a complete stranger.

"Are you... alright?"

"Yes, I am quite alright. I am not the one you should worry about – and not the adventurer either, for that matter."

"But he's dying... isn't there anything we can do?"

"I will put something in his food for the pain. He will die with a full belly and in good company – that is the best thing we can do for him."

*

* * *

The tea had made the stranger drift off into a strange sleep, and only an hour or so later he woke up to the smell of Theodore's slow cooked, Deltan mushroom pot. It was considered a luxurious meal for most – particularly for travelers that always found themselves on the move, and he'd personally only ever smelled it from afar.

"Not only do you have impressive healing skills, but you're a great cook as well. Are these the talents unmarried life forces upon a man?" the stranger asked, seeming far less stern than he had before, as the three of them had gathered around the dinner table.

"It seems so – although my late lady was not very talented in either." Theodore cleared his throat and looked down on his plate. He shouldn't talk about Elora that way – if not a talented cook, she'd been an extraordinary woman in her own right. Perhaps even too extraordinary, but he'd be damned if he were to sit there and spit poison upon her name.

"What about yourself, do you have anyone special waiting for you at home? Children, perhaps?"

"I do not, and I intend to keep it that way." The stranger was quick to respond.

"No fairness in keeping a lady caged, even more so if she never sees me. And I don't believe in bringing innocent children into this...*world*." Theodore felt relieved. As most drifters he was a loner, and so, hopefully, nobody relied on him, and few people would need to miss him.

"Wouldn't you rather tell us about one of your journeys then? We would love to hear about them."

"Yes, please, Sir, do tell us a story." Isaiah said, hoping it might inspire an idea for his book. Other than his grandfather's plain tales of life, and a few about the Nagárian revolution, the only ones he'd ever heard had been from a distance – hiding on top of the stairs with his heart in his throat. They'd been tales he'd been too young to understand – ones he couldn't remember anymore.

"Oh, I don't know." Theodore filled his glass a bit higher, and then poured one for himself – breaking yet another house rule, that would make his tongue looser and his laugh louder than usual. He excused himself with the fact that having a good time with a dying man was a hard task.

"You two are a convincing pair." The stranger said with a half-smile and a softening gaze suggesting he was already well affected by both the wine and the food. Shaking his head, he took another long sip of red liquor, oblivious as to how many years it'd been locked behind closed cabinets. Then, he started speaking. He told tales like Isaiah had never heard any of his grandfather's friends do. Of faraway places, large animals, and wild adventures where he'd fought death and won time and time again. Where he had climbed tall hills and swam across the wildest of rivers. Isaiah had asked for a miracle that day, and now, he had a dead man in his living room – telling stories truly worthy of being penned down. All the candles on the table had melted down and the sky was pitch black, before the storyteller started having trouble keeping his eyes open. As his words grew slower and less comprehensive, his hosts finally led him back to the sofa. Theodore then went out to the garden for some air, as the wine had left his head hot, and his thoughts in need of clearance. Isaiah walked towards his room, stopped after one stair step as the dying man pleaded, "Boy, will you come here for a moment?"

"Of course." He said.

"How old are you?"

"I turned fourteen today, Sir."

"You seem… younger." He said, and Isaiah smiled so that his large cheeks seemed even rounder.

"I just wanted to say that—" he took a breath, "you are a very special boy. I think your grandfather might know this, but he's afraid to tell you. Don't blame him– he's a *good* man. One of the best there is…" His voice was hoarse, and he was speaking fast, as if trying to outrun the deep sleep that was trying to grab a hold of him.

"What is it?"

"What is what?"

"What is special?" Isaiah hoped – begged – the adventurer would grant him yet another miracle. That he, as a storyteller, would tell him that he could recognize that he was one too – that he could see it in his eyes or hear it from the few words he'd spoken during dinner. If so, he'd surely write all night and show him the next day. If his grandfather could only be wrong, only this once, and if he could at least live till the next morning. The stranger's steely eyes looked at him considering. By the light of the lantern, they nearly looked golden now.

"I don't know. It's just a… gut feeling, boy." He said, not accustomed to flattery and much too tired to continue any more courtesy than needed. The answer didn't satisfy Isaiah. Even so, he knew he should be happy a man like him, though unknowingly, was spending his last breaths complimenting him, and so he said, "Thank you, Sir," as the stranger closed his eyes, and drops of sweat ran down his temples.

"Don't thank me, you deserve the truth even if it might be an incomplete one." He wasn't sure of what to say, for if these were the last words the man would ever hear, they should be gracious and wise. There and then none came to mind, and so he decided to honor him by writing down whatever he could recall from his stories. Making him a hero to be remembered was the least he could do in his honor.

"You should go to sleep. I will see you in the morning…"

"Good night, Sir. Sleep well." Isaiah said, thinking that "die well" had a very strange cling to it.

*

When Isaiah woke the next morning, he barely dared to move. He couldn't help but imagine the adventurer's dead body in their common room. His striking eyes wide open, his expression angry and perhaps damning both of them for not having told him the truth of his fate. He would have wanted his last words to be something of more importance – he would have wanted to know he was dying, so that his last day might be spent as he pleased, and not in the company of two strangers. And so, Isaiah stayed in his room, writing down the man's stories, and trying to report them as best as he could. He'd begun the night before, till his eyelids had become so heavy, he couldn't see nor write any longer.

"Isaiah." Without him noticing, his grandfather had walked into his room. As he saw his grandson sitting at his desk with the quill in his hand, morning light coming in through the window to his right, he felt his smile widening. He felt his heart singing songs he thought it had forgotten, and took the moment in as if it was his last, before saying; "A miracle has happened. He survived the night."

Both of them did their best to hide their astonishment while observing the adventurer's sudden recovery. Not only was he alive – he almost looked well. The redness in his eyes had moved down to his cheeks, and his breath seemed unforced.

"How are you feeling?" Theodore asked.

"A lot better, thank you. The leg hurts, but my fever seems to be gone. It must have been that bloody, painful salve of yours." Theodore thought it couldn't be possible, as it was composed of nothing but herbs and snail ointment. It led his mind to places it had not been in quite some time – places he'd done his best to avoid.

"I know you told me I could stay for some days, but as you know I'm in a hurry."

"Please, Sir, I recommend you rest for another day just to make sure." Theodore wouldn't admit as much, but he'd grown fond of his company and perhaps more importantly – he wanted to know about the journeys that he hadn't mentioned during last night's tales.

"I am grateful to you, but I must insist." Theodore was about to argue, but could tell he wasn't a man so easily convinced, and nodded instead. It was better for all of them if he left.

After breakfast the visitor asked for a word with him in private, and so the two of them went for a stroll in the garden, while Isaiah returned to his writing.

"You should know, I appreciate everything you've done for me. I believe I knocked on this door for a reason."

"I believe you are right." Theodore was fast to say. Though physically better, the man had lost the cheerfulness from the night before, and again turned serious.

"I have a proposal. One you might not like very much, but I wouldn't feel right to leave without having asked you."

"Oh?"

"I am not quite sure *what*, but I believe your grandson has a bigger purpose than being here. Counting flowers and eating apples day in and day out might be a decent life for a child, but his puppy days are coming to an end."

"I can assure you Isaiah is fine – and he is no *dog*." Theodore frowned.

"I don't doubt he is *fine*. He seems like a… clever enough boy. Still, there's a wilderness in his eyes that I've seen before. I am afraid it will turn ugly if you don't let it loose – if you keep him here for much longer…"

"I believe you are being much too familiar, *Sir.*" The stranger looked unaffected by the sudden outburst and continued.

"If you keep him here for much longer, it will be against the good of both of you." His tone was so sharp and matter-of-factly, Theodore's pulse started rising.

"What exactly *is it* you are proposing? Had I known you came to…"

"I want to bring him with me."

"You must be mad! He is far too young." The man wanted to argue that it wasn't his age that was Isaiah's problem. That rather, it was the boy's obvious immaturity that would keep him from being anything but a burden. There was a chance his many irritating characteristics could be reshaped however, and there was no better place for it than on the road.

"I was younger when I first rode out on my own – Isaiah won't be. If he comes with me, he'll have the guidance he needs. He won't be torn away from you by a collector and tossed into their brutal Kadoshi training."

"He is a hard-working and clever boy, but no adventurer, Sir. I assure you – he wouldn't be of any use in any mission. Besides, *I* have an agreement with the realm." They stopped as they reached the Sterculia alata, where the sunflower stood high and proud – reminding Theodore once again, that Isaiah was no longer merely a boy.

"You seem certain of this."

"He is *my* grandson. I raised him, and he never cared about traveling. He is happy here." Now, Theodore felt he was repeating the same argument with different words, and that such an approach wouldn't make it more convincing. In truth, he didn't need any explanation and could just tell the man to leave and not come back. He would have done so too, but it was not solely the visitor he was trying to convince. No, these were concerns that had been ripening inside his mind for some time, and it pained him to hear how hollow his defenses sounded when spoken out loud.

Tzelem Huxley had never been good at reading people's emotions but could see his healer's eyes turn from angry to saddened, and so, with his very best efforts, he softened his tone as well as he could. Repeating some of the few words he recalled from his time in the south.

"Just like the wind, people change course, expand, quiet down... Perhaps you haven't felt the strange airs we've had in Nahbí yet, but they'll move north soon enough and it won't be safe here for much longer. These agreements you're speaking of, shouldn't necessarily be trusted either."

"Delta is the safest place there is, and don't you speak to me about *my* agreements." Was it possible his eyes had caught any of it when he'd left it on the table? Did the stranger know who they were?

"I'm sorry if I've upset you, but please, consider my proposal. I do not know you well, sir, but you seem like an educated man. My father, the late Lord Huxley, was an academic as well. You remind me of him in some ways." Finally, Theodore recognized what had seemed so familiar about him – it was the chin. The strong, square chin of a man he'd once known. He hadn't seen his father since his name was merely *Sulley* Huxley. Once among the brightest students in the academy, Theodore had always admired him – even envied him for his directness. The ways he'd moved and argued with his arrow proof confidence. Very few had been able to compete with his charms and though his son had perhaps inherited very little of it, he had his resilience and bravery (and unfortunately, some good arguments.)

"If you must take him with you, you need to leave within the hour, for if not, I will surely change my mind about it." Tzelem looked surprised but nodded firmly before turning towards the house again. It'd been a long time since he'd felt anything resembling hope or opportunity, and though thin, it made him grin ever so slightly to himself.

"Please know, he will be in good hands." He said, without turning back to see the old man's solemn nodding, or the crow that made an almost elegant dive through the space separating them. Though an eager bird-watcher, all of Theodore's attention was now on his own two hands that he knew had been shaking for some time now. It seemed there would be dreadful consequences if he didn't let go of whatever grip was left in them.

* * *

"Isaiah." Indulged in last night's stories, the boy looked up from his book as his grandfather walked into his room. This time, the sight of him writing was merely a small comfort.

"I am sorry I didn't give you a birthday gift yesterday."

"That's quite alright. The adventurer is alive, I couldn't have gotten a better gift than that."

"You could, dear…You can." Theodore said, sitting down on the stool next to him, while trying to look excited as he turned both their lives around. Next to the open book, now filled with Isaiah's refined handwriting, he placed the new gift. A necessary but impulsive choice for what was to come.

"I believe I've wronged you by keeping you here for so long." He said, as the boy unwrapped the light brown fabric.

"What is this?"

"This knife was given to me by my father. As I've told you before, we were simple farmers, and he made this so that we could protect ourselves from robbers and such. Luckily, I never needed to use it."

"What would I use it for?" Theodore allowed his hand to stroke the blade. It was a good question.

"I love you more than anything, Isaiah. I love having you here with me… and, for a long time, I've been thinking that if I let you go somewhere else, bad things might happen. However, it has now come to mind that bad things might happen if I *don't*."

"I don't understand. I don't want to go anywhere…"

"As we learned yesterday, you're an adult now – or at least on your way of becoming one. I think it's about time for you to go farther than just the village…" Isaiah turned towards him in nothing less than complete confusion.

"I thought you said the Deltan river was the wildest, most dangerous river in the world, and that I should *never* even think about going anywhere close to it." Theodore had said that, and he thought he had been rather right in doing so too, but it was beyond the point.

"You wouldn't be going that way – you'd be going south."

"To Nagár. Where you studied?" he'd hoped he wouldn't need to study himself, for from his understanding it meant reading books all day long and then being asked difficult questions about them. He preferred the more practical approach of his grandfather, listening as he described the various processes that each plant went through as it sprung. He liked working with his hands, to ask about what he *wanted* to know, instead of reading thousands of uninteresting things about subjects he didn't care for.

"Maybe there. And then – even further south. Araktéa is a large land." Isaiah thought all of this terrifying. Theodore had explained that Nagár was like an enormous village, with enough people to fill their whole garden multiple times. Going beyond this, he didn't even dare to imagine.

"Why?" he asked so thinly and fearfully, Theodore couldn't help but to cover his face with his hands. He'd hoped he wouldn't make it more difficult for him than it already was, but how could he expect him to understand these things, when he'd done everything in his power to make sure he wouldn't?

"You saw how the sunflower you planted grew? How it's now bending away from the shade of the tree, and stretching towards the sun?" Isaiah nodded.

"Only if it grows out of the shadow and into the sunlight, will it survive."

"But you told me it was a sensitive flower, and that it didn't like too much sunlight. Besides, it has grown long and strong already."

"It has, but it won't grow as long as it could have done elsewhere. And I will admit that this time, I was mistaken… I thought it was a different seed. Nature is ever-changing – so are we in our own way."

"You've never been wrong about a seed before…"

"Oh, I have, my dear," Theodore sighed, "I have…" he cleared his throat, composed himself and laid his hand on his shoulder.

"One year ago, I gave you the book so that you could write stories. This year, I want you to start living them, and so, I've arranged for you to go with master Tzelem."

"Is that the name of the adventurer? You want me to *leave* with him?" Isaiah asked in disbelief.

"Yes."

"But I know nothing about horseback riding, or villages or all the large animals that live in the south."

"He will teach you about all of it – he will teach so many things I never can."

"But I want to stay here with you. I would miss you too much..."

"And I will miss you, my dear, but I know you'll return, and then you can stay for as long as you like. If you want to come back, that is. For there are many beautiful places, and many houses that have better pies than mine."

"Of course there aren't." Isaiah threw his arms around his neck, trying his best to hide the tears edging out from the corners of his eyes.

"Alright. I'll go." He said, trying to sound brave, and though he felt certain he didn't want to be an adult at all, it was time to be a man. He would be a good man and make him proud.

"Will I get my own horse?"

"I am sure you will eventually. For now, the two of you will have to share one."

It was in such a way, due to a rare sort of moment where a learned man experienced both clarity and confusion in the same heartbeat, a new agreement was made. Forced upon him by a situation where it seemed, all that might save them was a leap of faith, and a prayer to a god he hadn't spoken to for three long decades. It did not seem the right thing, and yet, with all that he knew, it was indeed the only sane thing to do. He told himself this, again and again, as he waved to his grandson from the back of his master's horse. Then, for the rest of the day, the night and the lonely year thereafter.

CHAPTER NINE

A NEW COMMANDER

AS Isaiah told his capturers about the first encounter with his late master, none of them uttered as much as a word. Other than Dove, shaking his head as he explained how Tzelem's character had drastically changed as they'd ridden to the fortress, they hardly moved at all. It was only when finishing his tale, their questions surfaced. Not of Tzelem, rather, they were eager to hear of his experiences from the fortress. Amongst guardians, it was better known as "Camp Huxley", and though familiar with it, it was not within their domain of authority. Isaiah told them there was not much to say, and that for men like them, it would probably be a very dull place both to be and hear about. Still, they wouldn't leave him or the matter to rest, and so he told them he'd been treated fairly well, which was the truth. He didn't say exactly how well, again remembering, that even if Tzelem might have lied to protect himself, it didn't need to mean the guardians were necessarily well intended.

"Is the Sheppard still in good health?" Dove asked.

"We don't have sheep."

"Ait, but you know the Sheppard?"

"I don't..."

"Lord Huxley – *Sulley* Huxley."

"He's been dead for... many years, it's his son who's Patron now." Dove looked over at the Zura, who's large, dark eyes seemed to jump from surprise to composure before he asked, "Did you happen to meet a man named Khair?"

"Yes." Isaiah said without thinking, and both of them nodded and went silent again. It seemed then, that the triplet had been a guardian once, and considering their somewhat loose morals, it was probably also true that he'd killed a man "in the name of Araktéans safety," as he'd so heroically put it.

Isaiah turned his attention to where Tzelem's body was lying. He had once again, almost forgotten about the incident. Still too numb to feel anything resembling sadness or remorse.

"You chose well, boy. Now this land has one less snake to feed." The Zura said. Isaiah wasn't sure what a snake was, but someone had once described it as a sort of strange, legless lizard. Thus far, he'd never seen one in Delta, and there had been no mention of it in any books he'd ever read.

"Won't there be troubles with the Huxleys?"

"I think nobody will miss him. Animals will probably eat his flesh before anyone stumbles upon him. Not much prey out here these days, so they take whatever they can get – even *poisonous* things." Tzelem had already disappeared once, and Isaiah could not remember anyone leaving the fortress to look for him. Perhaps it was because Araktéa was too large, and as the wanderer he was, he could have been almost anywhere – "dead or alive", as he remembered Lord Huxley putting it. As it turned out, he had only been some forty miles away, sculpting and repairing shoes of villagers – people who, once upon a time, would have kissed the feet of nobles as they came riding in. Luckily, nothing was quite so formal anymore, but the thought of a high-born on his knees polishing shoes – the image of Tzelem as a shoemaker – was still too ridiculous for him to fully grasp or fully believe.

"Should we bury him?"

"You can dig a hole here if you feel like it. I'd rather go back to sleep since *someone* woke me up in the middle of the night." Dove said, and then got up from his seat where he'd already been half asleep for some time. Isaiah looked over at the body. Both in Nahbí and Delta, many claimed leaving a corpse on the ground was disrespectful. He wasn't quite sure why, for if he'd ever had a soul in there, it was surely gone. The body was an empty shell, and regardless if it was put in the soil or not, *something* would surely eat it – perhaps making more use of him than when he'd been alive. "If he'd been a plant, he would have been a bad seed", Isaiah thought. But even if it had been convenient and much more comprehensive, people were not exactly like plants or animals. Tzelem was not one of these snakes. *He* was not a sunflower (less so now than ever, for he had killed or at least commanded a killing to take place.)

"Maybe we should just throw him into the woods..." Dove grunted, getting back up again. Even though he might not *look* like a man that minded sleeping among corpses, perhaps he was – or perhaps, after some consideration, he saw it as a half-honorable compromise. An act that didn't acquire the same effort as digging through the rough ground with his bare hands.

"You should take his boots first. Say what you will of the man, but he was a *damn good* shoemaker." Isaiah hesitated, but as his own were more than well-worn, he decided to pull them off – Tzelem still owed him that much and he certainly wouldn't need them now. Pulling off the left one, he noticed the new wounds he'd been complaining about. They were different from the ones he'd once had – darkened by blood, bumpy, and gross-looking.

"Now look at that, looks like he was doomed already, lad. I hope you haven't been breathing too close to him..."

"No... we kept our distance." Dove measured the boy, and then took a long and unsubtle step away from him.

"Well, yet another reason you ain't sleeping *anywhere* close to me." This, Isaiah felt completely fine with. And as far as the disease went, he was too tired to be truly concerned – they had kept their distance. Before resigning, he pulled off the other boot from the leg that had once been miraculously healed. He'd suspected to see some scarring there, but what met him instead, were fine hatches.

"It's... it's wood?" He stuttered. Turning away from the fire, the Zura glared at it in disgust.

"As I thought. *Rotten* to the core... none of us killed this man." He muttered and then lied down next to the fire, praying silently until the dream spirits took the worst of his anger away.

*

Having thrown one dead man into the woods and hung another

over the horse he'd left behind, the three remaining men were ready to leave early the next morning.

"How far is Hoshonto from here?" Isaiah asked, pulling on his new boots and accepting a water flask the Zura offered him from a safe distance.

"You don't need to come. You can stay here or go home – do whatever you like." It seemed the man they'd mistakenly thought to be the commander, had now quite effortlessly stepped into the role. Browsing the insides of his cape, he pulled out the knife he'd taken from him before, and handed it back to him.

"Your great grandfather's knife."

"You... you are letting me go?"

"You made a mistake. From the circumstances you've told us, they were not of your own making. Besides, we only brought you because you were accompanying *him*. It's a suspicious thing for a man to deny his profession. And there's nothing shameful about being a shoemaker – we all need shoes..." He said casually, and Isaiah wondered if he'd never joined the Zuras when they danced around large fires – their feet buried deep into the mud, making odd roars into the darkness. He'd sensed the guardians had grown more empathetic towards him after the story, but he had not imagined they'd be sluggish enough to let it compromise their duties. Surely, he'd committed a rather serious crime, and even if he'd been unsuccessful, he sensed he deserved being put to trial.

"So, you are letting me go. Even though I almost killed Dove?" He asked, hearing the sudden noise of the large man laughing from behind him.

"You were nowhere close to killing me, boy. If anything, you're only a danger to yourself." Isaiah looked around puzzled, trying to grasp the fact that for the first time in four years, he was truly free. A free man in his prime, with his own horse and four gold coins. No debt to pay, no master to serve and hopefully no disease.

"How can I get to Delta from here?"

"It will be around a five-day ride, go towards Hoshonto, then follow the narrowest road from there heading straight north..." the new commander explained.

"Could I ride with you till then?"

"We're heading back south."

"Oh… I am sorry if I've wasted your time." He had apologized for the murder attempt a great many times already, but it was only then he realized that he'd also taken up time they could have spent keeping the roads safe. The commander made a sound of something in between a sigh and a chuckle.

"That's quite alright. Good luck on your journey." He said, then got himself up in his saddle as easily as most people sat down on a chair.

"Don't ride around with people you don't trust. And by all means, find the ones you do. These days, riding alone and paperless is almost the same as being a ghost." Dove said, and with two friendly nods and one last hand gesture from the commander, the guardians rode off, leaving him free and frightened in front of the dying dim of the fire.

Isaiah knew the four directions of the sky and the stars that marked them, but it was daytime, and they were all in hiding. For a few minutes he sat down, trying to figure out how he'd resume in order to get home in one piece. He'd need to avoid the bears, the Huxley fortress, tribal people, as well as the many other unknown dangers nobody had bothered telling him about. All he had to protect himself was a knife he didn't know how to use, and the rope he'd taken from Tzelem's dead, bound hands. The first, and the only conclusion, he came up with as far as strategy was concerned, was that he needed to ride very fast. Being alone was among the most dangerous things you could do in these woods. If you added inexperience to this, standing still was another, and so, in a hurry he unbound Indra and made her run for both their lives. "First Hoshonto – then straight back home," he repeated to himself, and never had he been so petrified and motivated at once.

CHAPTER TEN

A PERSONAL TRIAL

THE journey back to Delta was as long and gloomy as he'd feared it would be. After one day, his limbs had grown stiff and numb. His throat and hands rasped by the dry, crisp air, and though the road was the very same one he'd come from, he felt a strong distrust towards it. Overlooking the pain, sitting on the mare's back had gradually grown easier on him. This was a good, as well as bad thing. The less he thought about how to ride, the more inevitable it became thinking about how he'd explain what had happened. Gradually, it forced him into an even deeper realization of the many mistakes he'd made over the years. Despite being alert about travelers, animals and cliffs along the way, all he heard were the whispers of rough winds rushing through his ears. During the evenings their accusations grew louder – making it clear that there had been a great many things he should have done very differently. If he'd only thought wiser thoughts sooner, he could have been home long ago. But he hadn't. He'd been standing still, like a broken, spineless tree.

It became increasingly clear to him how far he'd gone from his grandfather's expectations, and so, instead of stopping in Hoshonto for supplies, he made the decision to surpass every town on his way. Prevailing himself from good food and proper shelter might not make him any less of a failure as far as his writing and morals were concerned, but at the very least it would make him slightly more of an adventurer. Even if just for a few days, he told himself, he would need to act bravely. Then, once home, he'd somehow find a way to make it up to him. He couldn't think of a single thing that would, and so the temptation to tell him a so-called half-truth, became quite unshakable. At first, the idea seemed nothing but dishonest and unvirtuous, but as it entered his mind a third time, he realized it would be better than a lie. Besides, he was not only thinking about himself – the complete story would likely make his grandfather remorseful for having sent him into danger. And so, it was possible half the story or less, would be the preferable one for both their sakes.

With this in mind, he rode an entire day and a whole night. During the second day, he allowed himself to sleep for a few hours during the daytime – though he was only half asleep on top of Indra's back – who was intelligent enough to follow the path ahead. On the third day, he felt so tired he could not even think to worry. He simply laid down on the ground and slept so deeply, he'd almost forgotten who and where he was when he awoke. On the fourth day, he finally started to recognize the Deltan forest in its fresh, green, spring coat. It was only there, he finally felt nothing could harm them, and the mild winds confirmed this as they blew through his thick, dark hair, for the first time in four years. They embraced his face with a light tingling he remembered all too well, and though not speaking in words, he felt assured he could finally rest safely.

The morning after they galloped all the way home, and he had never felt so relieved as when seeing their house. It looked just the same as it always had, the bright, peach-colored roses had bloomed around the entrance in a perfectly wild, half-circle. The sun was going down in a similar color behind the low trees in the west, painting a worthy background to the perfect haven. It felt as if his heart would outgrow his chest, overwhelmed and joyous over a sight he'd been dreaming of for years. His excitement was then partly disrupted, as he came to the grim realization that he was yet to decide on a final version of his story. In truth, he had no better idea about what he would say, and which ways he would say it, than four days prior.

Despite the complications this might bring about, he couldn't keep himself from running towards the house after binding Indra to a nearby tree. Knocking on their small, red door, he hoped he wouldn't be asked too many questions just yet. As his knuckles touched it, he felt his heart beating through his chest – almost drumming in his ears as if he'd been in the middle of a dream. For a moment he worried he'd wake up on the side of some faraway road – but he didn't. He was wide awake, staring at the door – their door – thinking it rather strange to be feeling so nervous to see the only person he really knew. When his grandfather finally opened, he did so slowly. First, peeking out between the thin crack of the door, as if expecting him to be an intruder. A few short moments later, his eyes widened, and he almost looked startled by the sight of him. Isaiah smiled, his blue eyes tearing up as Theodore embraced him with all his force. It was not a very strong force, for he was not a large man, but it was all he needed – all he'd been waiting for, for all these years.

"You came back!"

"Of course I did. Oh, how I've missed you!"

"And I *you*. How many years...?" he asked, holding Isaiah's face between his hands.

"Four – four, *long* years!" Now, neither of them could stop the tears from running down their cheeks. Neither of them tried, as it seemed the first time any of them had felt a reason to cry out of joy.

"Only four? Oh, I feel it must have been twenty at least." Isaiah laughed. In a way, it'd almost felt like a lifetime to him. His grandfather seemed smaller, but he realized it was he who'd grown taller.

"Are you well?" He asked.

"Me? Oh yes, do not worry about that. Come, come. I just happened to finish making your favorite dish." Theodore said, immensely revealed to have his boy back. Seemingly unwounded and perhaps finally having outgrown his heated temperaments. As he followed him over the thresholds of their home, Isaiah could smell it – his special apple pie, with too much of everything.

*

Though having worried he might bombard him with questions, his grandfather sat rather silently across from him as they ate. It was not so strange, unlike himself, he hadn't been preparing for his arrival, and with so much time passing between them, knowing where to start was quite naturally a difficult thing.

"Is it good?" he asked him.

"Oh, yes." Isaiah thought it had a slightly more sour taste than usual, but he could certainly not complain, for it was much better than anything he'd eaten since leaving the fortress.

"The apples have not been the best this year. There hasn't been quite enough rain…"

"It's *very* good." He assured him. "Can I go out in the garden?" Other than his grandfather, it had beyond any doubt been what he'd missed the most.

"Well, certainly! You do whatever you want – this is your home."

"Whatever I want" Isaiah thought. It was something he'd need to get used to, and he reflected upon this as he walked out. To his relief, it looked just the same. Except from a few more additions of orchids and petunias, nothing he was unfamiliar with had been seeded. At the right end, the Sterculia alata, standing as high and mighty as ever, greeting him with the subtle waves of its lively leaves. It was not that he'd doubted his grandfather would keep everything together without him, but he'd feared he might get an idea of changing things. Regardless of what people thought, a plant could be moved, and though not always a good idea, it was sometimes necessary. Even in peaceful places like these – plants changed. They died or grew too large and needed to be cut. He saw his sunflower was gone, and he couldn't see his purple iris either. "I'll have to ask him about that," he thought and just then, he felt the first drops of rain falling on the top of his head.

"I've kept it blooming quite nicely while you were gone." Theodore was standing on their back porch, and the sight of him made Isaiah feel at ease again.

"You certainly have. The garden looks beautiful."

"I wanted to ask you…did you by any chance meet Nicholas on your journey? I've been wanting to speak with him for so long, but couldn't dare to cross that *malicious* river and no couriers have paid me any visits."

"Is he someone who's visited here before?" Theodore got a muddled look over his face.

"Well, of course. Your memory must have gotten bad, for you used to ride with him all the time when you were younger." Isaiah looked at him confused, as he'd never ridden with anyone but Tzelem.

"I'm not sure that I know who you're talking about…"

"Well," Theodore sighed, crossing his arms. "Perhaps it is better that you've forgotten – hopefully he has too. I didn't handle things too well with him…I've been wanting to apologize." Isaiah assumed it had to be one of his old friends.

"What does he look like?"

"Honest eyes, a large head, and a grin that would be a king worthy." He chuckled. "Wide shoulders too, but maybe not anymore. It's been… a long time."

"I don't believe I saw him. But anyone would forgive you for anything – you're the kindest man in the world." He smiled, but instead of returning the gesture, his grandfather started laughing loudly, as if he'd made some inappropriate joke.

"Oh, stop mocking me. Don't you know it is rude to tease an old man?" He said, then entered the house, heading towards the stairs to his office at a fast pace. Isaiah followed him inside, and Theodore turned around, looking almost baffled by the sight of him.

"I wanted to ask about the iris and…"

"I have some work to do. Make yourself at home, and perhaps tell me when you're leaving again." "Leaving?" Isaiah thought. He'd just gotten there and had no plan on leaving *ever* again. The disinterest in his homecoming suddenly started to feel more like an insult than a relief, and he suddenly sensed *he* had to be the forgiver of the two. Luckily It was an easy task, for he was ridiculously happy to be back. Surely, he thought, they just needed some time to get used to their old ways again. It would be overwhelming for anyone that had spent four years in solitude, suddenly having his fully-grown grandson back home. "Time," he thought, time was all they needed and despite of the fact there had never been any clock in their home, it now seemed to be as present there as anywhere else.

The next day Isaiah got back into his old routine. He began his morning by harvesting the fruits and berries in season. He then walked around inspecting the plants and making sure they were all in good health. Noticing some species that he'd almost forgotten about, he reread the botany book to refresh his memory. To his relief, his grandfather's strange mood had passed and throughout the day, he wouldn't stop praising him for how helpful he was – how wonderful it was to have him home again. During the afternoon, he once again withdrew to his office. Isaiah suspected he'd found some new study he was indulging himself in, and so he felt himself being drawn to the woods – amazed by the Deltan beauty and silence, that he'd taken ever so slightly for granted before. Now he saw, or rather he felt, just how differently the air filled him there. As he walked the known paths, he collected four kinds of mushrooms, and as they sat down together to have supper, it almost felt as if they'd at last celebrated the promised last bit of his fourteenth birthday. That night he slept like a child in its mother's womb. Safe, warm and worry-free underneath his old, soft sheets.

CHAPTER ELEVEN

INCOMPLETE CLUTTERS

AFTER having finished all the gardening that could possibly be done, Isaiah decided to start organizing the insides of the house for once. After further inspections, he'd noticed there was some clutter that had built up in some of the tiny rooms which they didn't use for much else than storage. He figured he might find some of the things he'd used to like, but other than some useless tools, he only found a few wooden horses his hands had once sculpted. Now that he had Indra (still not introduced nor commented on by his grandfather) they seemed far less interesting.

"I've cleared out every room now – except for your office." He said, as he walked into the kitchen – warm and filled with the sweet steam of pumpkin soup and cumin. He took it all in, the sight of the small, iron stove, the cabinets with the little, blue flowers he'd used to count while waiting for supper.

"Oh, it was not necessary at all. Now please, sit down and rest a little. Supper will be ready shortly." Theodore smiled, winking before returning his attention back to the pot.

"I am more than happy to help. If you'd like, I could clean the office for you too…" he suggested. Usually, he was not allowed down there. Much like the garden had always been to him, it was Theodore's sanctuary – a place he could engage in his studies undisturbed. Having cleaned every other corner of the house, the decluttering still felt somewhat incomplete.

"Well, perhaps tomorrow – if you have the time. It is becoming a bit of a mess but..."

"Don't worry, I'm sure it won't take too long." He assured him. If there was something they had a lot of now, that surely was time.

As the evening turned into night, his grandfather went to bed. Being oddly active himself, and with nothing else to attend to, Isaiah thought it a good idea to start clearing out the office. He'd never actually been there before, so walking down the stairs felt like stepping onto forbidden ground. Halfway down, he suddenly remembered that it was not the first time at all. Once as a child, he'd felt awfully curious about the mysterious office. He'd been quite disappointed discovering there was nothing but papers and books there, and some minutes later, Theodore had fetched him and told him quite firmly that it was not a place for a child and how easily he could have fallen down the stairs and hurt himself. This time, he'd been given permission to do it the next day, but with an invitation to *enter* (as well as generally doing whatever it was that he wanted), he couldn't see how it would be considered an intrusion.

Reaching the end of the stairs, the room felt much smaller than he remembered it, with a large, red-like, wooden desk filling most of the space. The four, short walls had shelves packed with books – some of which he'd read himself while Theodore was still schooling him, but most of them unknown. These were the things he noticed, only after realizing how much of a mess it was. The desk had a thick layer of scattered papers on top of it, and as he moved his candle around, he noticed all the corners of the ceiling were filled with dense spider webs. Almost instantly he regretted having volunteered to clear it out, but then reminded himself *who* he was helping, and that this was the last room he'd have to clear out to finish his house cleaning.

He started by picking up all the papers from the desk. Collecting all of them, he respectfully contained his curiosity knowing that letters could be very private. Still, he thought it was quite uncharacteristic for his grandfather to write letters in the first place, and he'd never seen him sending or receiving any. As he thought about this, he spotted his own name on top of one of them, and the rare sight of it in writing made his heart jump. "If something has your name on it, it would quite obviously be meant for you." He thought, and so he read.

"Dear Isaiah,

I am writing to you this day, to apologize. I am remorseful and very uncertain if it was the right time, and the right way to let you go. I, of course, knew it would be hard having you taken away from me, but the sorrow is far heavier than I had imagined. My mind has been troublesome these past years. Since you've been gone, it has gotten worse, and I am starting to worry I might be losing it all together, as my consciousness increasingly seems to be fading away from me. I don't know where it goes when it is gone, but it is a painless place – so, please, do not be concerned. These moments of clarity might be coming less frequently, and they *are* rather painful if I am to be completely sincere. Something I fear, I should have been more often while you were still here.

If you ever come back home, you should not trust or listen to me like you've done before. By then, you should be a clever and grown man and will know what to do. Know, there are things I've kept from you. Your father and your mother —"

The letter stopped there. The last words sluggishly scribbled, not matching the rest of his otherwise elegant handwriting. Isaiah would have recognized it anywhere, but the words, he did not want to believe were his. Suddenly he was filled with a fear he was yet to know, and as he noticed the date of the letter, it spiraled through him further. Day three-hundred-and-fifty-two, year thirty-one. It'd been written less than a year after his departure. Flicking through the rest of the letters, he saw it was the only one addressed to him. The only other name he recognized was that of "Master Raziel Mongoya". In an attempt to read, he realized all of them were written in a strange, incomprehensible language and after desperately trying to detect something, he finally gave up.

Walking up the stairs, his ears rang like distant bells and he felt increasingly lightheaded. As he reached his room, it was amplified and what had been a wholesome pumpkin casserole nearly made its way back up his throat. With the letter in his hand, he reread it again and again on his bed, hoping there was something he'd missed or misread, but the words remained unchanged. Though he'd noticed his behavior a little unusual, he'd assumed it was just due to age that went beyond common adulthood. Besides, he had always been a little absentminded, but far from mindless. Now, he couldn't help but wonder if the condition had come because he'd felt lonely – isolated for years and abandoned by the only family he had. Even if he had sent him away, he should have had the sense to say no. He should have seen the way Tzelem had manipulated them with his tales, and so, perhaps, all of it could have been prevented. At last, as Isaiah fell into a dreamless sleep, it was the last, incomplete sentence that haunted him "your father and mother…"

*

"Good morning!" Theodore said, quite cheerfully, as he walked into the kitchen the next morning. Yet again, oblivious of his grandchild's concerns, as well as the change of events that were about to occur.

"I found this in your office yesterday." Isaiah held up the letter, unsure if such an uncharacteristic directness was truly a good approach.

"You know you're not allowed down there."

"You told me I could clean it."

"*Clean it*, yes. *Not* snoop around – I raised you better than that." His tone was irritated but casual, and he didn't take note of the dark circles underneath Isaiah's eyes as he walked past him and filled his tea pot with water.

"I saw my name on it and I was worried about you. Apparently with good reason." Isaiah argued. It was the first time he'd ever raised his voice at him and he hoped it might catch him off guard and make him talk – bring out some confession, but he did nothing of the sort. His expression so blank it was hardly an expression at all.

"I have not written any letters for you. You *left* me here and did not tell me where in Araktéa's name you were going."

"Look." Isaiah said, and Theodore gave a brief, squinting glare to where he was pointing to on the paper – to his name.

"I can't keep track of all my letters, but that one is *not* for you."

"*Of course* it is for me…" He walked past him while shaking his head absentmindedly.

"You are always making such a scene – calm down and have some breakfast."

"You have written that you are about to lose your mind."

"Well, of course I am, and there is no wonder about it with a son like you!" He, too, had raised his voice now and Isaiah felt the lump in his throat choking his words.

"There must be something we can do. I can ride to the village and find a doctor." An unconcerned smile, accompanied by a deep breath, filled the old man's face.

"No doctor can fix me, Ares. This is my punishment and I always expected it would come. In a very different manner – certainly – but nevertheless… it's been expected."

"Punishment for what?" Isaiah asked, stunned that he'd just called him by his father's name. He'd never made that mistake for as long as he'd lived. It wasn't worth bringing up, of course, as they needed to focus on the mind matter.

"We need to *try*."

"Sometimes it is better to accept one's fate. This is one of those times." At any other time, and with another fate, Isaiah would have accepted the suggestion. But not now.

"We will ride out this instant." He demanded, fetching his grandfather's thickest coat before Theodore got the chance to respond.

"I said *no*."

"I don't care! According to you, you cannot be trusted as for now. We are *going!*"

"You'll have to hit me in the head with a rock then, for I won't be going anywhere." Isaiah sighed.

"You said… you said there was something you wanted to tell me. About my father and mother…" He tried softening his voice, but his grandfather's eyes were anything but appeased.

"How many times must we go through this? *I am* your father, and your mother was a disturbed woman, whose life you should not obsess over!" Isaiah took a step back, never having seen him even half this angry before.

"I'll leave myself. I will…. fetch someone."

"If you leave again, you are no longer welcome in this house. Do *not* come back." The words didn't hang in the air between them for long, before Isaiah stormed out the door. Still, they hung long enough to grow heavy. The silence had left enough time for them to be taken back or corrected – and yet, they hadn't been. Instead, they'd become the end of their argument, words both of them would be reliving and wishing to change for weeks to come. As Isaiah walked out into the rain, and sat down on Indra's back, he told himself it wasn't actually him. It was a disease and he would find a way to fix it.

"I'll have to introduce you two later. We just need to find help first." He assured her. If he hadn't known how to make up for his errors before, it was as clear as day now. The mind was the most precious thing one had. "Without it, men are nothing but animals – eating, mating, and avoiding danger in a constant flux of survival." He remembered being taught that. Now, Isaiah couldn't avoid danger anymore. He'd need to face it for the sake of both their sanity, and as soon as he'd calmed himself, the idea almost felt uplifting. Almost, but not at all entirely, and only for a few moments in hopeful ignorance about what saving someone's mind might actually require.

CHAPTER TWELVE

OMINOUS FORTUNES

IT took him no more than a few minutes to reach the village, but he spent hours there looking for a doctor. When the fifth villager told him he'd need to go all the way to Duroya – the largest town in Delta – he finally acted on the advice. Riding further east than he'd ever been before, he did not reach it till long after sunset. His hands were red and numb, his clothes completely soaked and falling heavily towards his trembling body. It hadn't stopped raining, but was pouring down less violently than it had, and the settling of the wind bore a promise of a calmer morning. The relief upon his arrival was only temporary, as the residents of the many small, wooden houses either seemed to be asleep or departed. Coming to the acceptance that finding a doctor wouldn't be possible till the next morning, he understood finding shelter would be a big enough challenge in itself.

Riding through the dark, silent main street, he merely spotted one house with light behind its long, mighty windows. Compared to the rest of them, it was a rather large home. This could mean there were good chances they had space for him. It could also mean they were the kind of people that didn't want strangers from out of town interrupting during the late, night hours (or any other hour for that matter). In different circumstances he might have found some roof to sleep under, waiting until spotting a friendly face in the morning – but he was afraid he'd fall ill if he stayed outside for longer. And so, he bound Indra and searched his pack for the gold coins. Though hardly ever used in Delta, the chances were higher with wealthier people, who might value them. Although he suspected one coin was much more than any regular inn would have charged him for a bed, he was very willing to pay – even if it had taken him a year of labor. It was only a small piece of metal after all.

Knocking on the door, he made no efforts to look more pitiful than he felt, and waited for less time than expected, before a young woman in a long, light green dress opened it.

"Hello." She said, in a familiar tone one might use when greeting a neighbor or friend. Her hair was long and wavy, hanging loosely over her shoulder instead of being tied up in the typical noble fashion. In her left hand she had a small lantern, making her dark skin and yellowish eyes almost illuminate in the dark.

"Good evening, I am terribly sorry to be disturbing you at this hour. I have been riding all day and was hoping to find some shelter for the night. I saw your lights were on, and...."

"Stop wasting your breath, dear – please, come inside." Her full lips were curved into a soft smile, but underneath her warmth there was a sharpness – an almost assertive expectation behind her eyes.

"Thank you." He said, panting, as he entered through the doorway and into the warmth. His boots fell heavy towards the unusually dark, wooden floor.

"I'm so sorry..." he said, feeling bad for not having removed them. The woman looked him up and down, seemingly content and unconcerned about the wet dirt circling him.

"I'll find you something dry to change to. Stay here for a minute, would you?"

"Thank you." He said again, just then realizing how cold he really was – how sick he might have gotten if he'd stayed outside for much longer.

"You must be terribly hungry, no?" The woman came back quicker than he managed to collect his thoughts. She handed him some clothing, then turned around, in what seemed to be an attempt to give him privacy.

"I'm alright really, please just let me sleep on the floor and I promise I'll leave first thing in the morning." He felt puzzled, as he'd never been naked in front of a woman before (or behind one for that matter), but too cold and too tired to mind this, as he stripped off into his new ensemble. The cotton felt soft towards his skin – in great contrast from the rough materials used by the sewists in the fortress.

"*Nonsense*, what would you like?" She asked, turning around in an effortlessly elegant movement, before taking his wet rags from the floor

"Perhaps some tea – *if* it wouldn't be too much trouble, my lady." He dared suggest. He would've wanted a warm bath as well but knew it would take too long to boil up that amount of water.

"Wonderful, I'll make you some herbal tea and reheat the dinner. I just happened to make a bit too much today and it would be sinful to throw it out, wouldn't you agree?" From his understanding, making more than what was just needed was uncommon in the villages, and so it needed to be a rather wealthy household. Could the woman perhaps be a servant there? "No", he thought, it was not a very common custom in Delta. She didn't strike him as one in the slightest – despite her outstanding hospitality.

As he followed her down the hallway, he noticed that despite its size, the house was a simple one. Clean, tidy and with walls decorated with only a few paintings and lanterns, it was beyond a doubt beautiful. Compared to the many pompous rooms he'd seen in the fortress, it seemed somewhat empty and even unfinished. Perhaps they'd had to sell their belongings now that times were harder, or maybe they'd just moved there, running away from the plague as many others. He decided it wasn't his place to ask.

After being seated in one of various common rooms, he realized she might actually be the lady of the house. The wife of some rich merchant, or a high-ranking member of the Kadoshi, perhaps. Whoever he was, Isaiah hoped he wasn't home. Regardless of his profession, he felt he wouldn't be thrilled about his wife inviting a stranger in, this time a night – nor requesting one to strip naked in their hallway. Having seen quite a few men and their tempers when it came to their women, it was likely for this anger to be directed towards *him*, along with a fist or a kick that'd lead him back on the cold streets.

"I live alone. So, no need to worry about jealous men startling you."

The lady assured him – startling him with her accuracy. Thoughts of sorcerers and mind control came up and he brushed them away the best he could.

"Oh I... I wasn't." He lied, not wanting to seem like someone assuming she was married. Of course, not all women were, but it was still strange at her age (twenty-something if he were to guess). Even stranger was the fact that she'd own such a large house.

"Please, stay here, I will be back in a minute." He stayed on the sofa as instructed and for a moment he was tempted to lay down. The dark room smelled like lavender and something unfamiliar. It had two stoned walls, as opposed to most Deltan homes that were solely made of timber. In the corner stood a small oven, heating the room, and slowly returning the senses back to his feet and hands. It took only a few minutes before the woman returned with the tea and dinner, and he swallowed the meal rather shamelessly without paying much attention to what it was or how it tasted – it was mostly vegetables and some spices he couldn't recall having tired before. Looking up from his bowl, he noticed her looking at him, and then he saw it again – this odd expectation. He thanked her for the food, not knowing any other way to show his gratitude. At this point, he sensed it would seem a little strange to offer her his gold.

"Don't worry about it." She said, and he nodded and took a sip of the earthy smelling beverage she'd poured him. Surprised by how flaming hot it was, he coughed as it burnt his tongue.

"It's newly brewed, be careful!" She chuckled, and he nodded once again and kept the mug in between his hands to reheat them.

"So, what is your business in Duroya?" She asked. Sat down on the chair facing him and took a good, long sip of her own newly brewed tea – not the slightest sign of discomfort upon her face as she drank it. He didn't know if his mouth was just colder, or if her tea was, but felt his cheeks flushing by the incident. Then cleansed his throat in an attempt to summon a more composed version of himself.

"I am looking for a doctor. My grandfather is... ill." She nodded to this.

"I see. What is wrong – if you don't mind me asking?" He'd thought that he would mind. He'd thought he didn't want to tell anyone about what had happened, but as he started explaining their situation, it occurred to him that sharing the burden with her was just as much of a relief as when he'd stepped into the warmth of her home. It felt like taking wet boots off of his feet after a long day of riding, or finally sensing sunlight on his face in the morning after a long, dark winter. Suddenly able to ignore his physical exhaustion, he talked with increasing eagerness. He left out the bits he didn't think he should ever share with anyone, but told her about his grandfather, what sort of man he was, and what sort of grandson he himself wanted to be. At last stopping himself, he realized she'd barely said a word. Taking in a very long breath and then a sip of a more moderately hot tea, he hoped she wasn't bothered or bored by his breathless rambling.

"*Everything* can be healed, dear. As you've probably already noticed, there are not many doctors left in Delta. Most went to Nagár and other villages in Nahbí when the plague started spreading." His heart sank. Remembering the lonely man they'd encountered in Bharoos, he couldn't see how it would be necessary to send doctors there – there was hardly anyone left to save. Maybe it meant they had died too. What in Araktéa would they do when there were no doctors left?

"Do you know where it spread from?" He asked, remembering the disturbing glare Dove had given him. "I can't have caught it." he assured himself, he would have felt it – seen it.

"Well," She smirked, raising one eyebrow "the realm *claims* it spread from the south... that the Jalas brought it with them from some strange, foreign place *or* that it sprung out from another 'sinister', southern tribe."

"I thought the Jalas were gone now. Some say the last thing the tyrants did when they were chased out of Araktéa, was to take them as their slaves so that they could use their powers."

"They are *now*." She sighed. "Though I don't believe in any of that..."

"Neither do I." Isaiah was quick to say, flushing a little for even mentioning it. Tara smiled patiently.

"Let's leave that subject for another time." Isaiah nodded.

"Where would I find a doctor?"

"You would either need to go to Dabár or back to Nahbí." She said plainly, and it made him want to burn his tongue again, just to distract himself from the thought of having to leave Delta.

"Luckily for you, you don't need one. What you need is *a healer*."

"What's the difference?" He felt silly for asking, as it seemed like something everyone but him knew.

"Come with me." She said, putting her mug firmly down on the tray.

As he followed her through yet another hallway he felt his eyes drawn to her waistline. It stood narrow and perfect under her dark hair and the delicate fabric of her dress, making her round hips look as full and round as ripe peaches. It was something he had never seen in the fortress before, as the women were all dressed in bland, shapeless dresses. As she led him through yet another long hallway, she opened a door at the end of it. Except from her front door it seemed to be the only one in the house, and it led into a small, windowless room. As she moved her lantern around, it illuminated the shelves circling it, beautifully decorated with colorful stones in different shapes and sizes.

"Are those... jewels?" he asked, so fascinated by their shimmers at first, he completely overlooked the long body of a man, laying on top of an even larger, maroon carpet some six feet in front of them.

"Not quite, but some jewels *are* made of crystals like these, so you're not completely off." She said casually, but Isaiah had lost all interest in them. Looking at the man, he felt his heart hammering. He had a blue clothing in front of his eyes and a red one covering his crotch. Other than that, he was naked, with a variety of these pretty stones lying around him and on top of his stomach. Though it didn't look like anything he'd ever seen, it, more than anything, reminded him of the sorcery rituals he'd heard about. It had all sounded like childlike superstition to him. But once again, he was having second thoughts on a lot of his previous skepticism and tried remembering exactly what had been said. He recalled one of Byron's statements, that although there were *some* good sorcerers, most were bad, and so it was always better to keep them at a distance. If you weren't careful, they could lure you into giving them all your gold and marrying them or bind your soul and feed it with their devilish and perverse agendas.

"Don't look so concerned, dear. This is my healing chamber – and that is my client, Geo..."

"What's wrong with him?" Isaiah heard his voice shake and tried to calm himself – the frightened and the weak were the easiest prey for a sorcerer. He reminded himself, it was just a few stones, and not knives cutting through the man's flesh. Stones were not dangerous when laying still, and he couldn't see how they could possibly be hurting him.

"He is struggling with... a sort of *temporal* madness, one might say. Not the same kind as your grandfather's, but in a sense – it's all the same." The lady said thoughtfully.

"You... *you* are a healer, then?" She nodded, and not only did he feel relieved he was not about to have his soul infused with evil, but somewhat lucky, seeing she might be able to help them.

"Would you consider..." He spoke with a low voice, not to disturb the temporally mad man on the floor.

"You can speak normally. He's in trance and can't hear us." Isaiah found the fact that she could remove a man's hearing concerning. Perhaps it was too incredible to be true, that the exact thing he needed conveniently showed up out of seemingly nowhere. Maybe the man was actually her husband, or perhaps some poor fellow she'd tricked into her home. Or maybe it was in fact *his* home, that *she* had taken over.

"How long has he been laying there for?"

"Only an hour or so." Her honey dark face still carried that soft expression. In fact, it even had a purity about it that made it seem impossible for her to be bad in any way. Then again, it could just as well mean he was in a sort of trance himself. It could mean that the sorcerers had the prettiest and most innocent looking disguises, and that this was why they said that once you'd gained their attention, there was very little you could do to protect yourself.

"Is he under a spell?"

"We usually refer to them as incantations. Spells are too associated with the darker magicks. But no, this is just a minor trance..." The lady noticed his face turning paler.

"Let's go sit down." She said, and not knowing what else to do, he followed along. As they walked, Tzelem's voice clung in his head – the one advice he'd thought wise to remember; "trust nobody". It had seemed so very reasonable when he was riding back home, but now, when he couldn't even trust his own grandfather, it only made him feel helpless and alone. This strange woman seemed to be his only chance, and other than his coins, soul and perhaps Indra, he couldn't think of anything she'd might want from him. Noticing himself becoming more tired with each step, trusting her seemed to become an inevitable risk as he realized he was too weak to resist any sort of sorcery.

"Do you think you could heal my grandfather? Could you come with me tomorrow? It's rather urgent."

"I believe I can help." She said calmly.

"But you would need to bring him here. I can't leave tomorrow – I have commitments."

"I am afraid he is...immovable."

"Immovable? Like a mountain?" she asked playfully.

"Of course not..." he frowned.

"I'm no fortune teller, but I sense he might be more movable than you think." He ignored her comment. "Don't you have any medication that might help? Something I could bring?"

"It's not that simple, Isaiah..." A sigh escaped him, and it was as if all the energy he'd had left in him dissipated into the air with it. His knees felt as if they were ready to collapse onto the floor, and he just barely managed to straighten up as the lady turned around.

"I think it'd be better if you went to sleep now. You look *very* tired." He nodded, thinking it didn't take a fortune teller or a sorceress to see where he was heading to. As they walked he felt his steps growing even heavier. Finally, when they reached the stairway, she took his arm, and he felt a strange tingling flowing through her hand. If it was sorcery, it was not painful like some had described it. No, it felt warm and comforting, like a cup of tea that'd had enough time to brew and slightly cool down.

"I will show you to the chambers." Chambers – the word would have normally filled his head with all sorts of torturous pictures, but he allowed her to take him there without resistance. Just barely present as he laid down on the bed, he drifted off to sleep before having time to realize he probably shouldn't have. It had been a long time since he'd had a dream, but this night it grabbed a hold of him almost before he closed his eyes. Like a strong calling from a past he couldn't recall or a future that was yet to be written.

CHAPTER THIRTEEN

THE INSIGHT

ISAIAH woke up to the smell of pastry. The thrushes were chirping, the rain had stopped, and though enjoying the warmth of the sun on his eyelids, it was first and foremost this sweet smell that woke him. For almost a whole minute he felt at ease – warm on the inside from the thought of breakfast, but this all changed as soon as he remembered he wasn't in his own bed. Forcing his eyes open, he looked around the room, bigger than his own and slightly more decorative than the rest of the house. From the sun's position it seemed it'd been up for at least an hour already and through the narrow gap between the curtains (made of light yellow silk), it shed light on his clothes and his pack, laying on top of a plain chair in the corner. They had dried overnight, and so, he put them on and hurried downstairs. Stumbling upon the kitchen, the lady was standing there in another long dress – purple this time, reaching all the way to the ground. Looking as lovely as he'd hoped his iris would have.

"Good morning, did you sleep well?" She asked, without turning her attention from the pot.

"Good morning. Yes, very much, thank you." He was ready to be as efficient with her as possible, and so – if he wasn't able to convince her to come – he would plainly go out to find someone who would.

"And?" She asked, stirring some grains, and a colorful variety of fruits and herbs. It seemed it hadn't been pastry he'd been smelling, after all.

"And I want to talk to you further about last night's subject."

She giggled, for a moment making her sound like a girl.

"For a Deltan boy you have *quite* a fine speech. Have you spent time in Nagár? Some noble house perhaps?"

"No, my lady." He responded, although he knew the fortress wasn't too far from it, and that Lord Huxley was indeed a noble of a sort - a fine sort even, but it was insignificant, and certainly not where he had his good manners from.

"Some people have it in them quite naturally, I guess. Your grandfather is an academic too, isn't he?"

"How did you know?" he asked, sounding more on guard than he wanted. He'd heard sorcerers could read minds, but never that healers could. In truth, he hadn't heard much about healers at all.

"Firstly, because you told me last night. Secondly, because you look a lot like your father." He'd forgotten about his long, rambling talk and damned himself, suddenly not wanting her to know a single thing about him.

"You knew my father?"

"I saw him when I was a little girl." She explained, then she turned towards him, tilting her oval face slightly to the right.

"You're nearly identical to him, but you do not have his smile, however."

"Oh." He said dumbfoundedly, attempting a casual smile of a sort.

"Now, that's most likely the worst smile I've ever seen – you'll have to work on that."

"I'm afraid that is yet another thing that I'll need to postpone, my lady."

"Oh, for the sake of *the gods*, please call me Tara."

"Tara." He repeated, feeling a little disoriented and then he said, "I'm Isaiah."

"I know, we introduced ourselves last night. Don't you remember?" her tone was less so irritated than genuinely curious – and it was strange, for he did not. For the death of him, he couldn't remember saying his name out loud, nor hearing hers.

"I'm sorry… I must have been very tired."

"That's quite enough sorrys, don't you get exhausted worrying so much?" She asked, taking the pot off the stove as Isaiah shrugged.

"Well, did you have any insights while sleeping?"

"Insights?" Tara smiled, as she poured two cups of tea and big bowl of whatever porridge she'd been preparing on the table.

"*Dreams.*"

"Not that I remember." He had to contain himself not to seem rude as she served him a wooden bowl, and a smaller red bowl with thick honey on the side. It looked as delicious as it smelled, and normally he would have eaten with great pleasure. But nothing was normal anymore, and he didn't want to eat or speak of smiles and dreams. He needed to go back home.

"Thank you for preparing all of this, Tara. And for your hospitality, but I am afraid I need to leave straight away – I'm already running late." She pulled out the chair, reasonably expecting him to be polite enough to at the very least try the meal. She then sat down on the other side of the table, stirring her tea with a tiny spoon, her big eyes looking at him expectantly. He sighed, but sat down. He was a gentleman after all, and she'd been kind and most likely saved him from pneumonia.

"Are you sure you don't remember anything from your sleep?" He tried to think.

"Maybe I do…"

"Tell me, then." Intrigued, her eyes turned hungrier and slightly green in the morning sun that had started entering the room.

"I saw my grandfather. And a man I've never seen before." He recalled, little blurbs of visions momentarily reoccurring before dissipating again.

"Did they say or do anything?"

"I don't remember."

"Try." Isaiah sighed.

"They were in a study of a sort… talking. I can't remember about what exactly."

"You'll remember more later. When you do, tell me."

"What does it matter? It was just a dream…" Tara shook her head slowly.

"Some dreams are just that, but *this dream* was very possibly something more – what *we* call insights." She seemed awfully confident on the matter, her mouth slightly twisting to the right and the greenness in her eyes dancing vividly like fresh, summer leaves in the wind. He couldn't help but think how beautiful they were, and rapidly silenced the strange impulse to say it aloud. Though she might be telling the truth about being unmarried, or even about not being dangerous, there was no time for such things. Even if there had been, he wouldn't have the slightest idea about how to court a woman – a skill, possibly even further down his list of priorities.

"How do you know what sort of dream *I* had?"

"Well, normally it's just an inkling you might say… In this case, I'll admit, I might have put something in your tea to *help it…* come up."

"You *poisoned* me?" he'd heard of the gross mixtures sorcerers made, filled with all kinds of strange, perverse ingredients. Animal blood, human blood, mushed intestines.

"Of course not." She assured him. "It was just some calming herbs and plants in your tea. It seems to have done you good – you look a lot better than you did yesterday."

"I can barely remember anything!"

"They don't normally do that to you – maybe I overdid it just the slightest. Forgive me." She seemed to be telling the truth, but it didn't mean he was done being offended – she had lured it into him, and he had slept much longer than he could afford.

"You gave me a whole cup and I barely had three sips. Slightly *doesn't* cover it."

"Some people are more reactive to it than others. I didn't expect you'd be so… sensitive." he frowned and glared down at the mug she'd served.

"Those are just plain herbs, good for energy and digestion." He ignored her comment, once again suspicious.

"Are you going to tell me *why* or do you always drug your visitors?" Tara rolled her eyes.

"I *knew* somebody would come here in need of help last night. First, I thought it was Geo, but when you knocked on my door, I figured there was something more serious occurring."

"Was that this… inkling too?" she nodded.

"And how does poisoning me help, exactly?"

"Stop using that word, please. You'll know the difference if anyone ever *does* poison you – which will probably happen if you don't stop worrying about it." She took a sip of her tea.

"You needed help, so in turn I needed your honesty. You also needed to rest, and even if you were exhausted when you came, you were very alert."

"You could have offered it to me instead of *tricking* me into drinking it."

"You *did* ask me for tea, if not I wouldn't have given it to you." He thought back. It was true, though it hadn't been the sort of tea he'd had in mind.

"Besides, you would have thought I was some sort of a sorceress and ran out the door. Insights don't come unless you allow them in – which an alert mind hardly ever does." She was right, at least in part – it was exactly what he would have done, but not wanting to admit to it, he frowned instead.

"Since you want to help me, you should come back to our house."

"I told you already, I can't leave. Your porridge is getting cold." She remarked.

"I'm not hungry. I will pay you to come. You can have a gold coin – two even, if you want." She shook her head, uninterested.

"I don't care for the gold any more than you do."

"How do you know I don't care for gold?"

"If you did, you'd know that *one* gold coin alone would be enough to buy a house and more than a year's worth of supplies." He didn't know that. And the thought of it made him the slightest bit more concerned about where he would keep them in the future. "I'll need to sew an inside pocket." He thought.

"How is a house – or even three houses – more important than sanity?" Tara made a delighted sigh as she put her mug on the table.

"I hoped you'd say something like that." Their eyes met for a long moment, and spotting a familiar light inside of his, Tara for the first time considered whether what she wanted to say next, was really a good idea and if it was the proper time.

"I can teach you." The four words broke the silence in two. One half where Isaiah still didn't trust her, and another where he felt awfully curious about what she'd just suggested.

"Teach me what?"

"To heal."

"I am not a healer."

"If you were, I wouldn't have had the nerve to offer to teach you, would I?" He looked at her, even more puzzled than before. From his small understanding this was a skill they were born with. A strange phenomenon that went through their bloodline. You couldn't just wake up one day and decide to become one, nor could a healer wake up one day and decide to make one out of you.

"I think you could become skilled at it with some practice. And perhaps a little patience." Patience, what he had once seen as his strongest virtue, had ultimately failed him and only robbed him of precious time. "No," he thought. "I certainly don't have time for patience anymore." Even if it was truly a skill like any other, there was no way he could learn it in time.

"Listen, my grandfather is all alone in that house. I need to go back *today*. Right now, in fact."

"He has been alone there for years, Isaiah. You can spare a few weeks." Weeks? He felt he couldn't even spare another minute. Suddenly it seemed easier to simply drug the man down and take him there by force. Perhaps if he could trick him to drink some of this herbal tea or ask to borrow some of her odd trance stones. "I would only need him to be calm long enough to stay on top of Indra for half a day or so." He thought.

"If someone doesn't want to be healed, they *can't be* healed." Isaiah rubbed his temples – she'd failed to mention this crucial detail.

"Can you please make an exception? As you said yourself, it's very important."

"Not as important as doing things the right way, and that's just not how it works. The laws are here for a reason. Only the willing can be healed."

"How would I convince him then?"

"He doesn't need your convincing, the only one that could convince him is himself."

"But *'himself'* is not present at the moment!" Tara ignored the comment, calm as ever while pouring honey over her food. "Blessed be my bees," she thought, wishing her visitor would at least enjoy some of it. A part of her felt amused by his anger. It at the very least seemed sincere, and it'd been some time since anyone had dared to talk to her in this way.

116

"He needs time. You can't force him."

"What do you suggest I do then?"

"If you had listened and not been so eager to leave, you would've already known. Learn to heal, starting with yourself." He had no idea how to heal, or what he himself might need healing from – if he'd caught the plague, he thought it should have affected him by now. Then it occurred to him. If she *could* truly read his mind, she might have seen corruption spreading through it. As his own was not the priority for the time being, he didn't really want to know if this were the case, but the words left his mouth regardless.

"I am well, am I not?" As Tara reached for his hand, her pupils widened. He allowed this for a few moments, for her hand was as gentle and tingly as it'd been the night before. Then, realizing he did not want an answer, he abruptly rose from the chair.

"I am sorry, I really need to go. Thank you for... everything." He meant it, he truly did, but he couldn't stay.

"You're welcome." She said, hardly seeming offended by the way he'd pulled away from her, or the fact he hadn't even touched the breakfast.

"I might be back." He said, and as he walked out, she opened up the small, wooden box standing on the shelf placed over her kitchen table. She rarely used her deck anymore, finding most matters rather clear without its help, but she sensed her emotions were affecting her inklings. Shuffling the sacred cards her mother had once gifted her, one shortly fell out. Looking at the image of the charioteer (standing tall in his armor of crescent moons and his crown with the laurel and the star), she smiled. "Perhaps he's right." She thought. "Perhaps the time is finally ripe to explore the force of pure will..."

*

Before leaving Duroya, Isaiah went knocking on some more doors. As promised he didn't encounter a single doctor – nor anyone claiming to be, or know, a healer other than Lady Tara, whom many of them referred to as "the lovely" or "precious". They were either all under her spell, or she'd been sincere, and so he decided he'd need to forgive her for the devious tea, as she seemed their only hope for now. He rode home, thinking he would first need to beg his grandfather's forgiveness and then bring him to her. The plan, he knew, was flawed and fragile, but perhaps the idea of perfect plans was as mythical of a tale as any. Perhaps they were made by greater men that knew much more than himself, about their world, its laws and rules.

The ride back home was mostly downhill, and so, by late afternoon, he was close to arriving. He had rehearsed his humble speech over and over again and felt almost certain he'd allow him to enter – despite what he'd told him in mindless anger. It was the conversation they'd need to have afterwards that mostly concerned him. Taking him to Duroya by force seemed an outrageous idea, but he couldn't allow him to stay there and crumble away. Doubt spread to the darker corners of his mind, like a hungry raven feeding on crude uncertainty, as he thought of the letter. It was clear, he could no longer trust his judgment and until he was well again, he would have to trust his own. This repeating insight nearly made him miss him even more than he'd had in the fortress.

He knocked on the door upon arriving. His grandfather did not open, and he nearly felt like an intruder when entering. An uninvited stranger.

"Hello?" He looked around, only to find that he was not in the living room, kitchen, or garden. After browsing the entire house – including his office that was as much of a mess as it'd been – Isaiah realized that unless there were any secret rooms he did not know about, he wasn't home. This wouldn't necessarily have been a reason to panic in another case, but Theodore only left the house when absolutely necessary. Had he gone after him, regretting those cruel, last words he'd said? No – If so, he would have been back home again that same day. Unless, he hadn't found him in the village and thus thought he'd run off and left him behind for good. If he'd swallowed his pride and asked around for him, which Isaiah sincerely hoped he had, they would have told him to go to Duroya,that his grandson had been eager to find him a doctor.

Isaiah damned himself. He hadn't realized just how far away Duroya was - how tired he would feel when arriving. His grandfather was likely not aware of this either. The plan had been impulsive and foolish, worse than that it'd been an outright mess. If Theodore had gone out searching for him, this would need to be a final proof of his decreasing sanity. Walking those roads by foot would take a great many days. For a man his age (who usually didn't stay further than a few miles from home), it seemed an impossible quest altogether. Though Isaiah hadn't seen signs of him on his way back, he knew there were at least two roads leading to Duroya, and so, there was a great possibility he might be tired and miserable along the other route. "I could stay here and wait. Perhaps he'll be back soon." He thought for a moment, but it only took a few seconds before he decided the time for waiting was over for good. With five apples in his pack and no other clues to his whereabouts, he went riding back – feeling as if time itself was chasing him. As if it was a beast, he'd just recently become aware existed. One that would tear him to pieces if he stopped running.

He arrived in Duroya in the late night hours. He'd met a few drifters along the road, claiming to have seen a man walking by, but they didn't remember how he'd looked and hadn't spoken with him. It wasn't likely he'd reach Duroya so fast by foot, but Isaiah prayed he'd overcome his fear of horses and gotten a ride from some good-willed merchant. Though having seen an inn earlier that day, he felt an urge to go back to Tara's house. Perhaps she, or her so-called inkling, had sensed a stranger entering the city. He didn't *want* to trust her, and he felt an increasing number of reasons not to. There was something unsettling about a woman being so unworried about inviting a stranger into her home. Yet, he sensed he was starting to trust her (somewhat against his own will). Though it seemed like outright loonacy to base his next decision on this, there was truly nobody else he could turn to, and so, once again, he found himself knocking on her door.

"Good evening." He tried to smile, but it felt unnatural even if he was relieved to see her. Tara looked content, pretty and unsurprised.

"Back already I see. And still carrying around all that doubt about me." She almost sounded amused by her own accusation, and with a sudden decrease in potency, Isaiah wasn't quite sure what to say – for she was right, and he felt dumb to admit it.

"I..."

"Don't you worry, I am a *very* patient woman. Come in." He nodded awkwardly and as soon as he entered, he noticed another woman standing in her hallway. She looked about as different from Tara as physically possible: her body tall, straight and muscular in a non-masculine way. Her dark hair was braided tightly to her head. She had a narrow forehead and almost black eyes staring at him boldly. For a moment, he thought she needed to be a guardian, as she was dressed quite similarly to the ones he'd encountered – in dark brown leather and a long cape. It only took him a second glare to realize she wasn't. Not because she didn't carry the Kadoshi sigil, but because he remembered seeing her before – once killing a deer from a two-hundred yard. Another time dancing barefoot around a fire, during the most violent storm he'd ever witnessed.

"This is Cyra. My good friend, *and* one of the reasons why I couldn't come with you this morning."

"Son of Ares." The tribal girl said firmly, and Isaiah nodded automatically.

"Pleased to meet you." He said, though in fact, he was a little terrified to meet her, and if it was correct that Zuras could smell fear the same way that sorcerers and some animals could, she would know this already. He hoped it wasn't, feeling more than slightly embarrassed to be this intimidated by two women – neither having acted directly threatening towards him.

"What may I help you with?"

"My grandfather was not home." He turned to look at the woman, or girl, for she seemed to be around his age. He didn't want to share his troubles with more people – less so with a Zura – but she seemed to be in no rush to leave despite of being fully dressed for hunting. Her bow was resting on her back.

"Where is home?" She asked, and he certainly didn't want to tell her where *that* was either.

"Just, a few miles from here." He responded, then turned towards Tara again.

"I think he might have gone out looking for me, and I'm worried. You have not... seen an older man, five-feet-seven, with dark, gray hair walking by here today, have you?" She shook her head.

"Alright then..." he sighed.

"Any clues to where he might have gone? Any friends or family members?"

"No family. And, I don't believe he has had any contact with his friends for some time. Not that I am aware of…" Could he have dared to go up north after all, to visit this friend of his? It was very unlikely, but no more impossible than many other things that'd occurred recently.

"He must be in Nagár. That is where all loners *and* mad men go." Cyra said matter-of-factly, her accent much stronger than the commander that had freed him. "*Many* nowadays. I go tomorrow." She continued.

"Alright…well, have a nice journey then, miss." He tried to sound friendly, but his voice had a slight tremble to it, and he could tell by the looks of her that *she* could tell.

"I cannot help you on this matter, I'm afraid." Tara said.

"Even if I reconsidered your offer and learned to heal?" He didn't really like his own suggestion but hoped she might be willing to compromise. That if he just did as she wanted, she might be more willing to use her inkling more deliberately.

"It is not because you've offended me in any way, Isaiah. I can't find someone who doesn't want to be found, and even if you reconsidered, it isn't simple to heal someone who's not there."

"I would need to find him first…"

"Precisely."

"Come to Nagár. Mad man must be there." Tara couldn't keep herself from chuckling at Cyra's suggestion.

"Seems like an excellent idea." She then agreed, and Isaiah certainly did not.

"I really don't think he would go there – he hates Nagár. But thank you for the offer, miss."

"You told me he's an academic. And so, he would know people there, don't you think?"

"Yes. But I'm sure he wouldn't go that far. He only left to find me and is probably close by. Tomorrow I'll look around the area, he must be …" Isaiah stopped speaking, as bits of the dream he'd had that night reoccurred before his eyes. Not as brief flashes like memories of dreams usually did. Not like vague notions that couldn't be fully grasped. No, it was an almost clear image of his grandfather (his hair dark brown, his face serious, bright and younger than Isaiah himself). Next to him stood a taller, straight-backed man with black shiny hair inaudibly reading from a book in an office of a sort. The letters were not clear or comprehensive, but somehow, Isaiah could sense them – feel the shapes of the words and how they moved across the paper. The message was more so a notion than an instruction. An ungraspable, but strong, pull.

"Teach me, Raziel." He heard Theodore's voice say, and the man looked at him with piercing blue eyes. The next moment the dream dissipated, and yet, Isaiah didn't feel quite as awake as he'd been a few seconds prior. Tara was touching his arm he now realized, and though not directly at his skin he still sensed the subtle tingling of her warm hand. He noticed she wore a ring now. It had a small, black stone that he almost felt was staring back at him.

"What just happened?" he asked, starry, dizziness scattering his eyesight.

"You just remembered your insight. I couldn't interfere, but you said the name Raziel."

"What does that mean?"

"You'll have to ask yourself that. It was *your* insight. Consider me as a sort of... translator." He was pretty sure that wasn't what a translator did, but it wasn't a discussion he would go into.

"Master Raziel Mongoya was his teacher."

"Perhaps then, it simply means you need to go see him."

"He must have died long ago..."

"What makes you assume that?"

"Well, he would have to be very old if he was still alive." He'd always imagined this master to be an ancient ·oldling. The fine-featured man in the dream had looked more like his grandfather's peer than his teacher, however.

"Old and dead are far from being the same thing. Even if he's the latter, he might still be the best lead as to where your grandfather might have gone." Isaiah thought about this. Was it possible he hadn't left to look for him, but for entirely different reasons? Was he perhaps on a quest of healing his own mind and in need of his teacher's guidance? "This mindlessness of his makes everything possible." he thought, but even so, it seemed completely irrational to blindly follow some strange insight. One someone else had claimed to see, in what *they* claimed to be *his* insight. It was so far-fetched, so absurd to go all the way to Nagár, just because he *might* have gone to see this man, that it nearly made him laugh. Just nearly.

"Many teacher people in Nagár." For a moment, he'd almost forgotten about Cyra, who despite of seeming restless to leave, was still standing in the hallway – staring at him with an uncomfortable intensity.

"Perhaps I should go back home instead. He might have returned by now…"

"Son of Ares should come with me. Tara is *never* wrong – you should trust more." The strange tribal girl almost seemed so eager to bring him, he was starting to suspect she was planning on murdering him or what worse was. If nothing else, one thing was for sure – he trusted Tara more than he trusted her.

"His name is Isaiah, Cyra." Tara glared at him, smiling as if there was no doubt the two of them would get along just perfectly. Though strongly doubting this himself, he could see there was at least a certain amount of logic involved. Despite all the unlikeliness of the plan, Cyra was heading *somewhere* and the only place he himself could think of going was back home. Going back a third time would be a coward's choice. Despite the slight possibility he might have returned, or that he eventually would, something told him it wasn't the case. Not because of an insight, but the sad knowing that it couldn't be that simple. Not anymore.

"Alright then." He said, as calmly as he could (petrified to his sheer bones). Though the girl *seemed* friendly enough, she was still a Zura and accompanying her for a week-long ride was nothing less than pure madness. Yet, there he was, accepting her eager offer, either out of a growing bravery or pure desperation.

"Very good." She said, something resembling a smile on top of her strong features. It was the first time he'd seen a Zura smile and felt an odd appreciation for the effort.

"Wonderful. When will you leave?" Tara asked.

"Before sunrise." Cyra replied. He felt an urge to ask for more time, but quickly realized it was better to go before his mind turned on him. If given any more time to think and reconsider, his fears would surely sabotage the journey. Finally, the tribal girl left for a short night's sleep in the outskirts of the city, while he went back to the room he'd slept in the night before.

The next morning, Tara made sure their packs were filled with supplies, and he had accepted her breakfast. His heart nearly ached – leaving Delta just as soon as he'd gotten there. Though a better rider, and a slightly more experienced man, he almost felt more scared than he had the first time. This time, he was not inside an illusion of having some master protecting him. This time, time was not standing still and it needed to be considered every step of the way. It was no longer about making his grandfather proud, but to save his mind and life. Failure meant there would never be another homecoming for either of them.

CHAPTER FOURTEEN

RAW HEARTS

ISAIAH was determined to do everything he could to keep up with Cyra. To his relief, Indra unreluctantly followed her pace, and other than sitting as tightly as he could in the saddle, it required minimal effort. He had to contain himself not to suggest entering any of the villages they passed by. Though he'd gone four whole days without shelter when riding back home, he'd seen this as a very temporary thing that he'd never need to do again. Besides, it was colder now, and he sensed he needed more supplies than what he'd brought (the rope, his knife and book.) He wasn't quite sure *why* he'd brought the book, as it had no other function than reminding him of past failures. Still, it was his grandfather's gift - throwing it away was out of the question.

On the first day, the rain kept pouring down on them in a violent and unpredictable pattern, that'd make anyone in their right mind stop for shelter. He did not ask, knowing it was not the way of the Zuras. Cyra had called her visit to Tara "an exception" from this rule, and so he'd left it at that. A Zura's life was spent outside, constantly moving from place to place, avoiding the villages – and for the most part, the fortresses. From his understanding, it was only during recent years that some of them had started working for the patrons. There was of course, the notorious torturer in the chambers, but more commonly they functioned as hunters, and would occasionally bring large prey (mostly eaten by the patrons themselves). It also seemed some were hired directly by the realm, operating as guardians – like in the new commander's case. He considered the possibility Cyra might be one, but this was perhaps more of a hope than anything else. For the Zuras, it seemed as if no rules applied. Guardians on the other hand, were bound to the law as well as responsible for protecting all Araktéan citizens. At least, that's what he'd believed until they'd killed Tzelem and let him drift off without a trial.

As he speculated more on his theory, he wondered why she wouldn't have mentioned this. As the commander had said, it was strange for a man – as well as a woman – to lie about their profession. Was it possible the incident had reached the authorities in Nagár? Had the Zura commander changed his mind, and sent someone to take him back for his trial? It would certainly explain why she'd been so eager to bring him along. If she wanted to, she could have easily brought him by force of course, but for once, he considered the possibility that his father's reputation might have helped him (making him at least seem slightly more dangerous than he was). With this in mind, he decided to do what he could not to spoil his cover. For now, he was still unbound and could perhaps run off if needed.

They made a few stops along the way, and though the language barrier made it somewhat awkward to communicate, Cyra was in surprisingly good spirits. The rain didn't seem to bother her at all, and riding through the subtle storm seemed to be a completely natural thing. In the afternoon it stopped pouring for some time. But as it darkened, and the woods grew thicker around them, Isaiah once again heard the sound of falling water. At first, he worried it was more rain coming, but as the trees opened the path before them, he could see something else in the distance – massive amounts of water running down a tall hill, violently splashing its way into a pond. He gasped, for some moments unsure if what he saw was real.

"We sleep here." The Zura girl commanded, stopping in front of the vertical river, as if it'd been the most common thing in the world.

"Isn't it a little... noisy?" Isaiah asked. Though fascinated by the scenery, he didn't feel comfortable going much closer to it – little less so, sleeping next to it.

"Yes, but this is only good water for miles. It keep wolves away also. Not bears – they no afraid of *noise*, but it's the season for sleeping, so it shouldn't be problem." After this brief discussion with herself, Cyra jumped off her horse, leaving it unbound, as she walked to sooth her thirst. Isaiah had many questions but realized it would probably make him sound inexperienced. After all, it was just water *falling*, and probably a very ordinary thing for someone like her – as well as for the sort of someone she hopefully thought him to be. He did his best to look unaffected, and with the lump in his throat drumming in discontent, he directed Indra to a close-by tree.

"Why you trap her?"

"So that she doesn't run off." She looked at him, her face ever so disapproving.

"She no run away."

"We're not quite as close as you and your horse just yet..."

"I know her, she is Zura horse. If you good she no run. If she gone from you, you no need search her. Better let her find you – easier."

"Oh." he responded stupidly, remembering the fact she'd been given to the Huxleys by her tribe.

"You no remove stupid clothes you put on her?"

"Yes..." He said hesitantly, realizing how minimal her own horse's gear was – just a thin cover over her horses' back. Before he'd gotten the chance to remove the saddle and the mouthpiece (for the very first time), Cyra had gathered a bunch of sticks and branches. He stumbled around trying to do the same but noticed most of his findings were too soaked to take fire. Within a few minutes, she had managed to light up a small campfire. He threw his small contribution into it, realizing that keeping up with her would be difficult beyond the riding – if possible, at all.

"I guess I should go out hunting before it gets too dark." Isaiah suggested, or rather – he affirmed – with his most confident voice. He'd show her. If no more than a small rabbit, he would somewhat have proven himself – if even just enough to keep her doubting the 'vastness' of his skills. He wasn't sure of how he'd escape. If it'd be necessary or even be worth an attempt. They hadn't passed any village for miles, and though he'd kept up thus far, it didn't mean he'd have a chance of actually outrunning her. Zuras were naturally born hunters.

"Tara give us much food. No need for hunt." He was surprised by her response. She was of course very right in this regard, but he'd always imagined them eating their prey half raw, feasting on its heart and tearing up the liver with their bare hands. Raw flesh was said to be the secret behind their strength and longevity, so he'd doubted she'd even bother touching Tara's light food. Either, the Zura diet was less bloody than the captives claimed it to be – or she was trying to seem civilized.

"Alright, I will go find some larger branches to keep the fire alive." She picked one up from the ground and stuck it into the rising flame.

"Here." She said, allowing the torch a little too close to his face, as she handed it to him.

"In case of danger." He wasn't going to ask her what sort of danger, thinking he would certainly recognize it if it showed up. Instead, he nodded and walked into the woods, hoping that it wouldn't.

After some time allowing his eyes to befriend the dark, he managed to find a few big, dry branches the rain had missed. He had to extinguish the torch in order to carry all of them back, and stumbled around for some time, focusing on not falling over, while following the sound of the falling water. As he walked, he suddenly noticed another sound. Stopping for a moment it became more apparent, and the unfamiliarity of it made his heart skip a beat. Listening even closer, he became almost certain it was some sort of growl, and so he left behind all the branches and started walking as fast as one could without running. As he got closer to their camp, he stopped – realizing the noise was *not* luring somewhere in the darkness surrounding him. No, from in between the trees, he could see its source, standing up tall in front of the vertical river and heading towards Cyra. Hundreds of times bigger than in the paintings he'd seen, and yet, so unmistakably a bear. A very real and very woke one.

Isaiah froze as he took in the size of the beast. At least as terrifying as he'd imagined it to be, *roaring* in fury, and as tall as both of their horses. Cyra was standing a few feet away from it with a torch. He couldn't see her face, but she was bending down (looking as if she was calculating the bear's next move). He tried calming down, reminding himself that the bear had not seen him, and if anyone, a Zura would surely know how to fight it. He decided the wisest thing would be to stay back, and to only interfere if things got worse. It seemed like a reasonable conclusion, but only for some rapid heartbeats, as he noticed her limping. In the dark, he could see her pants had been ripped, and so, it seemed things had gotten quite bad already. Instinctively, he reached for the knife in his belt. He'd left his own in the pack, and only had a slender kitchen knife Tara had given to cut their fruit - insisting that certain knives had certain purposes. Though not its given purpose, he'd thought it would be sharp enough to slay a rabbit, and now wished he knew whether the size of an animal had anything to do with the thickness of its skin.

Feeling the length of the blade under his right hand, he observed the scene for a few long seconds. Again, he felt hesitant, looking for knowledge he realized he did not have. It was still possible that Cyra did – that she could take care of it herself, even with her leg wounded. Before he could finish this comforting thought, he saw her falling to the ground. He hadn't even noticed the bear taking a swing at her, and in a moment of pure panic and something resembling fury, he forgot all about his suspicions. Pulling the fruit knife out from his belt, and without further consideration, he ran towards the beast, and perhaps for the first time in his life, he screamed with the full strength of his lungs. The sound was much louder – much more terrifying, than he'd ever thought himself capable of. It was as if it came from something, or somewhere, else. Running, with the blade aiming straight towards its furry throat, he had successfully gotten its attention, and just as its large body started raising towards him, his own froze. It was a strange sensation. No matter how much he tried he couldn't move in any direction, but the bear could – and the bear did.

As Isaiah thought about his own death, time once again seemed to be in flux – though in a very different way than before. It was as if all surrounding sounds went quiet. As if the world allowed him to hear nothing but his own final heartbeats. The beast raced towards him. It put him to the ground with its large mouth growling inches from his face. Its teeth, sharp enough to dig through his flesh with minor effort, and its breath stinking with rage. As Isaiah completely gave up on his body and life, all his past troubles felt insignificant. His every worry, every fear he'd had the past weeks, suddenly became insignificant and for a moment all he felt was a deep appreciation for the peaceful childhood he'd had. As he accepted his death and got ready to drift away to some eternal dream, he felt the weight lifting from his chest. For a moment he thought he'd died, but the ease seemed far too physical and opening his eyes, he saw the animal standing back up. The release of pressure felt like reaching the surface after being underwater for too long. The humid air filled his lungs. A roar ran through his ears, and with eyes widened, he could see the brief flicker of Cyra's thick braid from behind the animal. He then saw her sword (a large, double edged blade), planted in between its neck and upper back.

"Move!" She commanded, and he just barely managed to roll to his right, as the bear's body fell heavily to the ground. A second later, Cyra was panting on the top of its back, murmuring something before rapidly getting up, reclaiming her blade and wiping it clean. She then turned towards him. He would have never thought it possible for anything, and less so – *anyone* – to look more terrifying than a ravenous bear. Yet, her almost black eyes came disturbingly close, and he felt his shivering intensify.

"Are you *blind?*" She barked. And though he saw her expression more clearly than he'd prefer in the moonlight, he was unable to utter a single word. Noticing his panting, her expression softened ever so slightly, and she offered him her hand. Had it not been for the beast laying right next to him, he would have stayed down for some more minutes to get his breath back, but he took it – allowing her unlikely strength to almost effortlessly lift him back on his feet. She measured him.

"You are without scratch." She said, almost accusingly and with a strict frown between her eyebrows.

"I... I don't know." Blood was rushing through him. It was as if his heart was beating in places it shouldn't – but she was right. Not only had he survived, but somehow, he hadn't gotten any injuries.

"Did you no see this was *brown* bear?"

"I... I just saw...*a* bear." He said stupidly, as he hadn't given much thought to its color. She looked at him, this time more so in disbelief than anger– though not as much as he himself felt about being alive.

"Have you no see bear before, *shelako?*" The last word was said in a tone so spiteful, it made him not want to know what it meant.

"Only in paintings." He stuttered.

"Paintings?" Isaiah nodded.

"Are... are you alright?" he finally got himself asking, hoping to change the subject from his obvious ignorance. Instead of looking at her leg that seemed to be in an even worse condition from up close, she turned towards the bear.

"I'm fine. Bear is no fine. What you did was stupid. I did have him under control." Isaiah frowned. Surely, she should be grateful that he'd come to her rescue – or at least *attempted* to.

"I didn't doubt that you did. It's just... I saw your leg – and then I saw your fall... I wanted to help." In truth, he had doubted her. He'd wanted to save her, and it had taken every bit of courage he had. He wished he could feel at least slightly proud of himself for the act, but he didn't. It was just like his grandfather had said once: "It is the courageous and the foolish who die young, and they often die holding hands – with *themselves* in desperate prayer." He felt like one of those brave fools from the hero tales. The ones who risked their lives to save ungrateful women. Not only didn't this particular one appreciate his efforts in the slightest, but now he'd proven himself to have no skills in combat, and probably blown his cover (if he'd ever had one in the first place, that was).

"*Never* attack a *brown* bear. Stay down. These animals are dangerous but *very* precious. We no slay them unless we must – understand? Black bear, you must stand up and attack. White bear..." she sighed, then she made a hand gesture that made him understand that he wouldn't have been this lucky, had it been a white bear.

"I just wanted to help. I thought Zuras always worked together..."

"You are *no* Zura. You don't know *anything* about Zura." She said, and now that she seemed personally offended as well, he thought it best to keep quiet.

"We sing prayers for it tonight. Prayers to its spirit." She said, more so into the air than to him. Then she walked out in the woods to fetch dry branches he'd failed to bring back.

Normally, Isaiah wouldn't have felt even remotely comfortable taking part in such a death ritual. Compared to almost being ripped apart by it, honoring its death didn't seem like the worst thing in the world. Nor did Cyra's obvious displeasure with him, which he strongly sensed, even if she kept her tongue and distance. After some prayers in her tribal language, she finally cut the enormous animal open. Isaiah, respectfully, forced himself to watch.

"Bear meat no taste good but make you strong. *Zura* don't waste anything." She said the last sentence firmly, making his cheeks burn hot. The truth, he realized, was that he did not know anything about her people for certain. He'd just heard stories. More stories than he could count on both hands, and the flaming glare she gave him suddenly made him remember one of them. One too disturbing to entertain and that he hadn't dared consider for longer than the tiniest blink of a moment. It'd been told one night by one of the oldest captives, a former bandit, who had once witnessed the revolution, as well as the riots that had followed. One who'd seen most corners of Araktéa, and the obscure paths that lead to them. His claim had been that it was not the raw hearts of animals that was the reason a Zura's lifespan far surpassed that of villagers and captives. It was human flesh. The idea had repulsed him so much, he'd chosen to mostly forget about it, and now, as he again remembered the horrid anecdote, he found himself hoping Cyra was a guardian bringing him to trial after all.

"You okay?" She asked. They had spent about an hour in silence. He'd observed her as she'd skinned and prepared parts of the bear (partly petrified and partly relieved something else was for supper that night).

"Yes." He lied.

"Eat some meat." She ripped off a large piece from the spear, chewing it thoroughly. Though more tired than hungry, he didn't want to risk offending her any further, and so he took a piece and started chewing. It had the stubborn texture of a leather boot.

"Well? What you think?" She asked and Isaiah shook his head.

"My master used to tell me what a talented bear slayer he was. How good fresh bear meat tasted..." "Yet, another confirmed lie from the great knight." He thought reluctantly.

"I eat better bear before. This one skinny." The taste itself wasn't terrible, but its toughness made it almost impossible to swallow. Still, Isaiah ate and chewed as if it'd been his last meal. "This could easily have been the other way around." He thought, again recalling that he'd almost been ripped to pieces some hours prior.

"Who was your master?" Cyra interrupted his grim thoughts, and he felt himself hesitating for a moment, before saying "Tzelem Huxley."

"A Huxley... Then I understand why you so eager to kill."

"I only wanted to save you. You were the one who said it was hibernation season." He argued, regretting it as he said it, though her mood seemed to have turned more tranquil.

"It is. I don't know why it awake. Why it is angry... It is male, it can't be because of cubs..." She said thoughtfully, and then concluded: "Nature changing. It is no good."

"We better lower our voices then, there might be more of them around." They had not spoken a lot during the journey, but whenever Cyra said something, she did so with a significantly louder voice than any other woman he'd met.

"You think I speak *too* loud?" He held up his hands defensively.

"That is not what I said."

"But you are thinking!"

"Are you a sorceress?" he asked, wondering if she could read his mind too. Whether she already knew everything about who he really was.

"Don't be stupid." She frowned.

"Are you a guardian?" She looked sincerely surprised by the question, if not amused. He hadn't planned on interrogating her in this way, but the constant apprehension of not knowing her motives was already unbearable. There was no way he'd be able to escape her anyways – less so now that she'd seen how clueless and defenseless he'd acted in nature's company.

"Stop being stupid I say. I am Zura, *only* Zura. No *real* Zura can be guardian. No Zura make sorcery." She made some strange movements with her hands and rolled her eyes excessively as she took another bite of bear.

"Okay." He sighed. Though yet to trust her, he believed she was telling the truth as her emotions seemed to live on the outer surface of her sharp face. When talking with him, it was anger or irritation for the most part – but sometimes curiosity and even excitement. Whatever her agenda was, he didn't think she could lie very well.

"Also, never try save me again, shelako... Understand?"

"I understand." He assured her, having no problem on agreeing, as it might save him some trouble in the future. Besides, he didn't owe her anything, and if he needed to play anyone's hero it would only be his grandfather's. Only for a little while.

As they laid down to sleep on each their side of the fire, he found her a shade less intimidating.

"Where is he now?" Cyra asked, as he looked at the stars lost in thought.

"The bear?"

"Your master."

"Oh… he died."

"You kill him?" Isaiah's heart stopped for a moment.

"No." He said, wishing his tone had been more assertive. Yet another thing he needed to work on – build a firmer, more convincing voice, that might be strong enough to survive out there.

"You are the son of Ares. I had to ask." Cyra explained herself, not seeming suspicious of his answer. He wondered if she would've cared if she knew the truth, if she'd think of him as a murderer despite the fact that Zuras were known as the most violent tribe in Araktéa.

"It's alright."

"Lots of hot blood in your veins …" she said thoughtfully, and their eyes briefly met somewhere in between the campfire. The wind turned, blowing smoke his way. Drying them with hot, gray heat.

"Tomorrow we leave early – you rest." She commanded.

"Yes, your majesty."

"Shelako…" She frowned and turned her back to him.

CHAPTER FIFTEEN

TRUER TALES OF DEATHS

OVER the course of the following days, Isaiah started to feel increasingly more comfortable with his Zura escort. Though quite private about her intentions he'd set aside his suspicions of her being a guardian, a sorceress or simply a Zura wanting to eat him. It was no longer in his interest to pretend to be any more skilled than he was, which decreased his overall tension. That was not to say he was anywhere near comfortable. The days were long, and even if Cyra was more considerate regarding meals and breaks than Tzelem had ever been, he still felt himself longing for a roof over his head, a warm meal that wasn't bear meat, and a morning that didn't start with his back hurting. Most of all, he longed for safety.

The bear was dead. He knew that with certainty, as they'd already eaten half of it. It was a rare animal too, and as Cyra had repeated many times – it wasn't supposed to be awake this time of year. According to her, what had happened to them had been such an oddity, there were next to no chances of it reoccurring. Yet, the forest hosted other threats and the fact that he'd survived seemed more and more like a miracle to him. It seemed he'd been given a new chance, which he guessed was a nice thing, but it also made surviving a second time seem more unlikely. He was still far from indulging in the world of superstitions, gods and protecting spirits that Cyra rambled on about. He didn't believe anything other than a fierce Zura girl (with a sharp sword and quick reflexes) had been the reason he'd gotten away. Yet, he wanted to at least believe in luck, and if he'd ever had any of it, it would seem he'd spent it all at once. Being on the road these days was a dangerous enough thing in itself, and being there, as an unlucky man living on borrowed time, seemed to be nothing less than a death wish. After the relief of his survival had worn off then, it was thoughts of this kind – as well as the ever unfamiliar sounds of the forest – that kept him up at night. It kept him looking at the stars, being the only known things he seemed to encounter while listening to the fire's threatening flickers.

"You say Zura always work together." Cyra said on their third night.

"I also said I was sorry…" He answered, surprised she was still awake. The girl usually slept like a rock from the very moment she laid down – another quality he couldn't help but to envy.

"No," she said, "it is no wrong. I want to know – what else do they say of Zura in your tribe?"

"I…I don't really have a tribe."

"Everyone has tribe, no?" He thought about the captives in the fortress. If anything, it might be the closest representation he had.

"Well, my tribe is very different from yours. I never really trusted their opinions on… most things…"

"You don't trust your tribe? Not even your grandfather?"

"I *do* trust my grandfather – that's different. And he never told me about Zuras."

"What has others of your tribe said of Zura then?"

"Maybe it's best if you didn't know…"

"Why not?" She asked, sitting up abruptly. Isaiah sighed. She was, of course, asking to get offended, but he was afraid she'd get angry again. Though an angry Zura would have seemed terrifying a few days before, it had instead become more of an annoyance – her moods were impossible to keep track of.

"You might not like it." He warned her.

"I *will* know it – and I decide if I *like… it.*" She spit the last words out, and having nudged her fires already, he thought telling her wouldn't make much of a difference.

"I've heard many stories…"

"Tell me the worst." She looked at him with hungry excitement, and he rolled his eyes as he sat up.

"They told me you wear the knuckles of the villagers you kill as symbols of pride." He said, nodding towards the bony looking rings decorating her left hand.

"No. Villager bones are weak and wearing them would be opposite of pride. We wear bones of our dead elders for protection. Their remains – our reminders. Also, we no kill villager unless they come *looking* for death."

"And that thing on your right hand?" her knuckles were covered with some dark, gray metal covering four of her fingers. She raised her eyebrows, and then plainly said.

"For hitting things *hard*. Now, tell me *worst* story." Isaiah scratched his chin. It was perhaps sinister to wear someone's bones, but this was far from the most unpleasant story he'd heard of Zura. "I hope this won't make her hit me hard." He thought, knowing she wouldn't stop asking till she got a satisfying answer.

"Someone once told me Zuras treat children very cruelly, and... and that they eat children from the villages." He was certain she would either make a furious protest or laugh in his face, but she did neither. Instead, she went silent for a moment before saying: "This is true."

"Your... your tribe *eats* children?"

"After revolt against capital, King punish Zura. He force us stay small area, tell us if we hunt outside it, they slaughter everyone. We only tribe left in Nahbí this time, and after revolt very small tribe – only seventeen Zura left in Araktéa, and my mother only Zura child. Not even great hunters could survive. All the land dry and empty – nothing growing there, after short time nothing left to hunt. They almost starve..." Cyra took a breath, as if moved by a past she couldn't possibly have lived through herself. Isaiah had never heard of any Zura revolt before. He nearly asked her about it, but held his tongue, seeing her face with a vulnerability he hadn't thought someone like her capable of.

"Finally, our leader go to villages, *begging* for food. The King had not said anything about punishment for this. It was big disaster – Zura *never* beg. Many say this bring big humiliation and dishonor to us and ancestors. Our leader thought nothing else to do. Some agreed – letting tribe starve to death would be bigger sin. Leaving the bloodline die in pain and weakness, when we are a people of strength. Other say he should have taken the sixteen and attack capital again – burn it to the ground." Her eyes turned almost black from the other side of the fire. She'd made it with two rocks and it had taken her no more than three seconds. three, tiny seconds to light up a fire without a single match.

"All of them would have died…" Isaiah uttered.

"Yes, but Zura would have died in honor – we would have died *fighters*. But – that is not what happened. Story say he was refused by three first villages. The third one not even let him enter. When he come to village four, his starved demon finally take over his body. He look weak, no meal for weeks, but on his way out, he fight five grown men alone. Then, he stole one fat child that the last seventeen feast on that night. It was after this, rumor of wild, evil and hungry Zura spread in Araktéa. Almost nobody tell true story, but we survive better with their false fear than our truth." She stopped talking, looked at him as to see his reaction, while he allowed what she'd just told him to sink in. He was almost tempted to take out his book and write it down, for though it was a similar tale to one he'd heard in Captive's Cave, it told quite a different story.

"What did the villagers do then? They attacked the Zuras?" Cyra shook her head, a sly smile forming on her lips.

"Each of four villages offered their fattest, spoilest child so we would leave them alone forever. This is reason we never enter now. We did make pact, and we keep our word. As I tell you before, me meeting Tara in Duroya – exception."

"But *you* never ate anyone. You wouldn't do that?" Isaiah swallowed hard and she smiled stiffly.

"I did not eat but my mother did. The other sixteen did too and tribe leader was my mother's father. In Zura we are one, connected in strength, pain and victory – past and future. I look like I am alone now, but we are *always* together. So, what you said is right – but what you thought was wrong. Understand?" Isaiah didn't think he quite did. Still, he felt he could understand her – or rather them – better. She was a *them*, much like he and his grandfather were a *we*. She was a part of a whole he couldn't see and they were all around her, around… *him*. The notion gave him chills.

"Just like you want to save your blood, we will always do what we must to save Zura. No matter what, we follow Zura law. It is all we are."

"But your grandfather broke the law, did he not?" She shook her head.

"He did *not* break *the law*. He chose life, so he broke rule nobody agree on. It is only the true laws, we cannot break. Old laws..." She thought for a moment but seemed to conclude this was too complicated for his *shelako* mind to comprehend.

"That is why all of them did eat. Even they who say it shameful begging for food or eat children, they ate and he allowed it. Some still say he is coward. Others say he is great savior of Zura."

"And what do you think?"

"I think I can not say before I starve myself." Isaiah thought he'd never eat human flesh, but again, maybe that just meant he'd never really felt true starvation. Considering just how awful he'd felt after a whole day without a meal, going for several weeks was nearly unthinkable to him. And so, he realized he was perhaps in no position to make his own judgement on the matter either.

"What happened after they'd eaten all of them?"

"After, more animal found in area. Then many new children born. They say, it was same children that had been eaten. That they came to live *better*, and that they choose Zura so tribe could live and so that they could learn our way." The theory sounded absurd, but Isaiah didn't say anything. If she wanted to believe herself to be the wandering soul of some fat, village child, that was her business entirely.

"If it hadn't happened, you wouldn't be here now." He said instead, and she laughed.

"Yes. Here we both are, living life on top of other's deaths." The comment turned his chills into shivers. She said it with an ease that almost seemed joyous, and though it was somewhat true, it seemed too brutal to be said out loud. Too vicious to be said underneath a bright, starry sky like the one above their heads.

"Now you tell me about your tribe. *Fa.. family*, that is what you call it, no?"

"It is." He said hesitantly. "I only have my grandfather. My mother died right after I was born, and it seems you already know who my father is."

"You must be told about them."

"Very little..." he said, remembering the unfinished letter. Wondering if his grandfather would tell him more once he found him. "My grandfather told me my father left home just before he turned fourteen. He wanted to go out on adventures, slay beasts, and find faraway castles that didn't exist." Cyra laughed, and perhaps for the first time, it was not out of mockery. But he was not kidding. As far as he knew, this had always been the truth.

"It's ridiculous, I know. Other people claim he was a great hero – *the one man* that truly dared to challenge the realm after the revolution. I guess, what you just told me contradicts that..."

"Villagers..." Cyra spat "Always praising idea of being 'only one'." There was a pause between them as they both looked towards the night sky.

"Some people claim he went to the Parda, afterwards. And that he then didn't come back to fulfill the promises he'd made to the Nagárians – or anyone else for that matter. If this is true, I don't understand why so many people call him a hero. I don't really know what, if any of it, is true anymore."

"You think you nothing like him?" She shot in, and he felt glad it'd been made apparent.

"If any of it is true, I *know* I'm not." Cyra did not look as disappointed as he'd thought she would by this. Rather, she looked like she understood him more than it would make sense for her to do.

"Many Zura admire Ares. We say he not normal villager. Moving faster and with more fire." She tapped her belly with her fist, before continuing. "In some ways, he share his strength so we could raise up against King again... some also believe gods sent him to free us."

"Free you?" he asked. To him the Zuras, as well as other tribes, had become the very symbol of freedom – moving around and never settling anywhere, like leaves in the wind. Nature as a whole was their home, and nature was a large place. Then again, he'd also thought them to be lawless, when it in fact seemed their laws were just different ones from theirs – strange ones at that.

"After revolution, Zura grow strong again. But new King even worse than old King. His men come to slaughter us. Most escape alive but my grandfather die and my mother new tribe leader."

"That's terrible." Isaiah had never thought the realm could act so violently.

"Yes. And now, there is less good land to share – even if we free to wander again. Even if Nagariáns don't dare to hurt us anymore." He remembered what Archilai had said, about the soil not being what it once had been. It almost sounded as if nature was getting smaller – as if it was gradually killing itself and bringing everyone inside it along. "Is this too due to this corruption?" He wondered, again worrying about his and his grandfather's mind. Taking in a long breath, he looked at the stars. Whatever might happen, they would stay the same at least.

"You should go to Delta. There is a lot of land there – good and fertile land." He said, noticing a bright star that he'd used to see through his window before going to bed. Looking down again, he regretted the suggestion.

"It not so easy. Nothing is so easy." More than anything else she'd said thus far, he agreed with this, and so he didn't make any further suggestions to what might move her tribe closer to his home. Cyra seemed to be somewhat sensible – even civilized. Her tribe as a whole, (with all their bony rings, sharp teeth and terrifying fire dances), was something quite different. Though not murderous perhaps, they were too wild to ever live in harmony with Deltans. As an afterthought, he realized he didn't really know the villagers any more than he knew the Zuras. He knew both believed in gods and blessed their food before eating. In some world that might have been enough – but not in theirs. He'd seen too many captives criticize each other's prayers – even fighting over them and spilling blood over something as innocent as pretty words said out into the air.

"Look!" Cyra pointed upwards, and his eyes followed.

"What is that?"

"A falling star. A sign of fate." Her tone was uncharacteristically clear, and then she laughed delightfully, as if she'd been wishing for the sky to fall down all her life. Isaiah crawled his body back together to sleep – seeing it as a sign he'd been looking upwards for a little too long.

*

As the following days would reveal, Cyra had not exaggerated when she'd said that Zuras didn't waste anything. After they'd chewed their way through the meatier parts of the bear, she'd started preparing its intestines. They had no spices of course, adding no other taste to their meals than its raw, natural flavor. The oddly shaped organs were not disguised inside some stew, like they often did in the fortress, it was put on a stick, and though well-cooked to avoid potential poisoning, there was no tricking yourself while you ate it. "We must eat with open eyes." Cyra had explained, noticing the repulsiveness as Isaiah tried forcing down a piece of tongue. It wasn't pleasing, but he did his best to eat as she did. This animal's life was on him after all, of which she kept on reminding him. Still, she let him sleep on its skin at night – claiming she had hot blood that kept her warm.

Only on their sixth day of riding they'd finally eaten every last edible bit of bear. By then, Isaiah had gotten somewhat used to the strange taste. He'd even learned to enjoy it, though mostly due to the fact it had spared them the time and hassle of hunting. Now, as nothing edible seemed to be growing in the area, they were left with no choice. Fishing would have been an option a few days prior, but according to Cyra, there were no clean lakes or rivers for miles.

"Our best chance here is shooting something that flies."

"You mean a bird?" Isaiah suggested.

"You name it as you wish." She sighed nonchalantly, slipping off her horse's back and pulling a long arrow from her leather quiver. She hadn't hunted yet, but it had been on her back since they left, accompanied by her elegantly shaped bow. Though Isaiah still wasn't sure about her skills in combating bears, he knew what a wonder she was at archery – and despite his personal dislike of it, he felt a certain expectation about seeing her in action. They left their horses close to the path, and as they wandered into the forest, its shades fell cooling upon them. It was now both dryer and warmer in Nahbí than it had been a few weeks earlier, and they had finally been given a rainless day. Had it not been for the fact they were about to assassinate something; Isaiah perhaps would have appreciated the forest's beauty more. It was no Deltan forest. The grass and leaves slightly dry, yet, with the sunlight falling in between the trees, leaving skylights shining over moss clothed rocks, it had a

142

pleasant ambience.

They watched the treetops, and their every movement, carefully – listening for anything that wasn't their own steps or breaths. Only after what seemed like a small eternity of intense focus, Isaiah spotted something at the edge of his left eye. It was not a bird or any other flying thing – but a large, brown rabbit, eating grass peacefully by a thin water stream. He held out his arm, signaling his finding to Cyra – who of course, had already seen it.

"You want to try?" She whispered, then handed him the arrow, before giving him a chance to respond. Isaiah looked at her, disbelief washing over his face.

"Always kill with prayer." She whispered, and he took her bow like he'd seen her people do it from afar. It was heavier than he'd expected. His hands were not shaking like they had been the first time he'd held a knife (or the second or the third time for that matter). They were steady, and he felt a rare sort of presence, seeing the rabbit from behind the arrowhead. As he let go, with a small prayer for it not to suffer, it swooped steadily through the air and penetrated its soft flesh. Cyra made a loud scream that would've made any flying thing fly, if there'd been any, but the forest bore no other movement just then. Just the sound of a satisfied crow closeby - and nobody ate crows as far as he knew.

"You did it, shelako!" She exclaimed, her smile wider than he'd ever seen it.

"I did!"

"You say you never use arrow."

"I haven't. I have watched others do it a few times...." He admitted. He wanted to tell her he'd seen her do it before, but in the danger of seeming like he'd spied on her, he stopped himself.

"Maybe you are more like father than you think. Or maybe I am *great* teacher." She concluded.

"Yes – one that suddenly decided to test my hunting skills, right when we're out of food in the middle of the woods."

"Sometimes no preparing is better. Makes necessities more necessary, and so nature gives whatever you need. Also, *you*..." she said, raising her sharp eyebrows as she pointed her finger to his forehead, "spend too much time *there*."

"You were the one looking upwards for birds, when there were perfectly, fat rabbits down here on the ground." She rolled her eyes and snarfed.

"You got lucky, shelako." He shrugged.

"Maybe next, you could teach me how you made fire without matches?"

"What is matches?" She asked, and he contained a smile.

"Nothing you will ever need, your Majesty."

"Stop calling me *that*." He had started saying it as a joke. He never really made jokes, but he'd thought it rather funny, since Cyra sometimes reminded him of the fierce queens from hero tales.

"But it is true in a way..." he said. Now that he knew she in a way was the upcoming Zura leader, he thought it suited her even better.

"*No*. I warn you, shelako – stop calling me that." Her eyes had gone dark and serious in the scary way – as opposed to the more commonly, annoyed kind.

"Okay." He said, raising his hands apologetically, as he walked over to claim his trophy. He suspected he in reality had the aiming skills of a seven-year-old Zura child, but this would still make him a better huntsman than most people. Regardless of this, Cyra seemed content with his progress, despite his numerous misses as they resumed the hunt. Though both knew she could have done it herself quite effortlessly, he finally felt he was making a sort of contribution to their temporal, little unit.

"Since there are more rabbits than bears, are their lives worth less?" he asked, as they sat down to prepare their mid day meal.

"No."

"But you *never* kill bears? Yet, Zuras eat things like deers and rabbits all the time."

"You saw me kill bear."

"Only because you *had to*."

"I did not *have to*, and were you normal villager, I wouldn't do it." Usually it was her archery or her two daggers that called for her hand, both in hunts and combats. With the bear incident, It'd been the first time she'd pulled her father's sword out of her own initiative. Mostly, the heavy weapon rested on her back like some sort of

144

symbolic reminder.

"Thank you." Isaiah said and she shrugged. They looked at each other for a moment, and though he had questions, he decided to leave them unsaid as she seemed oddly pensive. They ate their lunch in a silence of a pleasant sort, and then Cyra gave him some advice regarding his shooting technique – confirming that he indeed, had the aiming skills of a child, but that it was better than most shelakos. Better than she'd expected.

CHAPTER SIXTEEN

THE GREATEST GATES

THE day after the hunt, Isaiah for the first time caught himself almost forgetting about his mission, enchanted by the landscape that had started to unfold before them. Now, with many miles of road behind them, the path was becoming more and more open, leaving them with hills and beautiful views he'd only ever seen in the Huxleys' paintings. The closer they got to Nagár – the bigger the fields. There had been two large ones inside the fortress, but both were incomparable in size. From the height of the hills they looked like giant pieces of a puzzle – or like square, plain, (and oddly enough) empty gardens. He'd suggested they could collect something to eat. It appeared the harvest season had ended sooner here, but there was always something left if you looked closely enough. Also, whoever owned the fields probably wouldn't mind a few of their potatoes missing. Cyra had objected, making it clear she didn't give a dry twig about how the owner felt, but she will not eat "villager food" under any circumstances, and neither should he.

As the sun went down, leaving the sky a dark shade of rose-pink, they decided to camp under an oak tree next to a lake. Sliding out of their saddles, Isaiah noticed her doing it ever so slightly more carefully than usual. It wasn't a very evident thing, but as he paid closer attention, he saw a subtle limp in her walk.

"Your leg..." He said, and Cyra grabbed her cape as if to hide it.

"It's nothing."

"Let me see it." she made a loud sigh. Rolled her eyes like a child that had just gotten dull instructions from their mother.

"Come now." He said, and finally she exposed a considerably more-than-nothing wound, marking four deep lines in her tanned flesh.

"It's not bad as it look." She said unworried, but her leg was in poor conditions.

"Cyra, it looks infected. Why didn't you tell me? It must have been hurting a lot."

"Zura are trained not feel pain. The less you worry, the less you feel – the less the hurting." Isaiah thought this sounded like an awful excuse to not cope with their children's whining, but he knew better than to criticize if he wanted to convince her.

"Let me at least cleanse it for you." She snarked again, but then made a subtle nod. Unprepared, he had not brought any medical supplies with him, but with his grandfather in mind, he'd at least remembered to grab the last bit of salve from his office.

"Wait here, I'll go look for leaves we can cover it with and maybe something anti-inflammatory. In the meantime, go clean it with the water from the lake."

"Anti..?"

"Something to help take away the... the bad, burning feeling." He tried explaining. It was getting dark, and so he hurried to search the area. Shortly, he spotted a few leaves that he recognized from the botany book and picked them to use as wound dressing. He then walked a little further, but as he looked around, he couldn't see anything else that might be of use. "The salve will be enough." He thought. Tzelem's leg had been in a much worse condition. He then recalled his new, wooden one, wondering whether it truly had. The remembrance made his face twitch, and he then turned to walk back. On his way he found something he thought was basil. He picked a few leaves, and smelling it, he became uncertain.

"Cyra, do you think this is basil?" He asked, walking towards her. She'd of course had time to make a fire, and the sky had turned to a deep purple, with darkly painted clouds left by the sunset.

"What?" She asked, and he held it out for her to smell.

"I *think* these might be anti... uhm, good for your leg." He suggested, thinking it would be the sort of thing a Zura would know about, but Cyra just shrugged her shoulders, fairly uninterested in the leaves. Either the world of plants wasn't considered quite exciting enough, or that their wounds were not important enough to be properly dealt with. He smelled it himself again, knowing some plants could have the opposite effect and make matters worse. He didn't think holding it in between his fingertips wouldn't cause any harm, but he wasn't so sure he trusted it on top of an open wound. It seemed strange to him how it didn't smell of basil. It didn't smell like anything at all.

"It is just leaves. It is fine." Cyra said, and he felt it was finally his turn to lecture her.

"Actually, this could either be a good leaf to put on your wounds, or it could be a very poisonous plant that could kill you."

"Brown bear, black bear." She said, slightly more serious, and Isaiah nodded.

"Maybe even white bear." He added. She had explained to him that there used to be white bears in Nahbí, but now you could only find them far north – if anywhere at all. Cyra had never seen one herself, nor had anyone she'd ever met. She'd explained, this was either because they'd gone extinct, or because the white bear didn't let people live to talk about the encounter. Isaiah took another look at the leaves.

"I am pretty certain it's the good kind. I have a salve that I brought from our house too."

"It seem Tara was right about you being healer."

"Don't be stupid." He mimicked her. "My grandfather is an academic, and he specialized in plants. He taught me a lot when I was younger." He explained, sitting next to her to study the wound more closely.

"I don't remember all that much about the healing remedies... but I am pretty sure it's a good leaf." Seen away from some herbal mixtures for stomach aches, he'd never really had to use any of the knowledge. "More important than healing, is prevention. When you know caution, my boy, you won't need a plant to lick your wounds." He heard his grandfather saying. Cyra didn't know caution, and he didn't think for a moment he'd ever be able to teach it to her.

"You already say this. I trust you." He looked at her in surprise and felt his cheeks flushing, having never thought he'd hear those words coming from a Zura's mouth. It felt strangely good, and so did being of actual assistance. Though worried he might make matters worse, he knew by the look of it, something needed to be done to avoid further infections.

"This will sting a bit." He said, but Cyra seemed completely unaffected as he spread a thick layer of the sharp smelling salve.

"Doesn't it hurt?" he asked.

"Zura only scream in battle, in rage, or in silence."

"Not in birth?"

"Birth is the biggest battle of all." He noticed the slightest bit of tears in her eyes, and it gave him some relief – as if the salve somehow had lost its healing powers if it didn't cause any burning. He then put the basil leaves on and covered it up with the large ones he didn't remember the name of.

"We'll need to leave it like this for at least twelve hours."

"*Not possible*, we need to move in early morning. We leave it tonight – no longer." Isaiah sighed.

"It would really be better to give it some time. Your leg's condition… I won't lie to you; it doesn't look very good."

"Mission is more important than *some* leg. If worse, I will cut off when we get to capital tomorrow." As usual, her ideas sounded too insane for him to even comment on. She didn't want to tell him what her mission was. When he'd asked, her reply had been not to ask her again, and that doing so would only be a waste of his breath.

"As you please, then. Just for the night." He agreed, not wanting to spend their last evening arguing. He'd promised not to save her, and he intended to stand by that promise like a man of his word – like the gentleman he was. Putting some salve and a leaf on her leg, was not truly breaking this rule – seeing they'd both agreed on it. It's something anyone would have done, his duty as an Araktéan almost.

"We will reach Nagár tomorrow, then?" Cyra nodded absentmindedly, looking towards the road that led over many more hilltops ahead.

"Perfect." He said, though his eagerness to arrive had somehow dissipated. Just as the forest's road had started feeling comfortable, he was about to enter a whole new territory and the capital city was truly something else.

* * *

*

Isaiah had seen paintings of Nagár before and the one most clear to his memory by far, was the large canvas in the fortress's ballroom. Being an image rich in color, framed in gold and strategically placed between the two, long windows showing the Lady's garden, it was the first thing to catch anyone's eye upon entering. The Patroness had explained to him "Greatest Nagár" had been painted right before the revolution by an unknown artist, who'd become notoriously known as the Great Osman. Till this day, he was considered the most masterful painter to have ever walked the earth. "He painted with more than oils and colors, you see. He painted with heart and raw emotions that most people would never even be able to feel. That is why even commoners, who care and know little of the arts, become so captivated by his work." He remembered the silhouettes and shades of the painted, multicolored humans, selling fruits and playing instruments he'd never seen. He remembered thinking it was beautiful and wondering how the city might have changed since 40 A.A. (this date was scribbled in its lower right corner). Lady Huxley had explained they'd started a new calendar in Nahbí after Amnos the First had freed them from the ruthless ones who'd ruled before.

Approaching what was often referred to as the center of their land, if not the world, he'd suspected to be met with a very different image. From the fortress he'd heard Nagár was a joyous and exciting place, filled with everything you could possibly imagine regarding supplies, food, inns, bars, and tailors. They even had various forms of entertainment – offering magnificent shows and plays of all sorts (and at all times). Others seemed to be of the same opinion as his grandfather, stating things like "a chaotic, filthy hole of godless people and temptresses". If little else, many villagers seemed to agree with the Zuras, that the capitalers were the worst scum in Araktéa. What nobody had ever cared to mention, and that first struck him as they reached the top of the infamous hill heading towards it, were the large walls surrounding it.

"It looks like a prison..." he stuttered, and then he thought, "It looks like the Fortress. Just twenty times larger". They found themselves at the exact position as the Great Osman had once sat down with a blank canvas. Yet, even with his vivid imagination and superior emotions, Isaiah doubted he, or anyone else would ever be able to paint it that beautifully again.

"Wall was built to keep us out – us and now most others too. Not worry, stay close by and follow me." Cyra said easily. "In Zura we have nine heavens and thirteen hells. Some Zura say 'Capital is gate of two of the hells.'" She added, and Isaiah wondered if she was trying to comfort him, as she certainly didn't seem to be in humorous spirits.

Riding down the hill, the city grew even more hideous – and more importantly, a lot *noisier* than he could've ever anticipated. Not even a large waterfall (which apparently was what these vertical rivers were called) inside of Captive's Cave on a cold winter's night, would've been able to compete. Outside the walls there were shapeless tents and numerous formations of crowds. As they got closer, their shouting formed words in different dialects. One claiming he had the best oranges in the world, and his neighbor denying it because his own were surely both fresher and juicier. Isaiah took a brief look at them as they made their way through. Not the people themselves – but their oranges, and he quickly concluded both salesmen were mistaken. Compared to the ones growing at home, the fruit was almost greenish, and from one simple glare he could tell they had to be both too dry and sour to be enjoyed. They were yet to enter, but though more colorful (not to say more vivid) than the many ghost towns they'd ridden past, he'd sincerely hoped he would find his grandfather as soon as possible, so they could be on their way home and never return.

After avoiding many insane-looking men and women screaming about their bad-looking fruits, garments in strange styles and wines or spirits Isaiah refused to taste, they finally got through the marketplace and to the gates. The arch reminded him of the fortress again, except these gates were open, and only had one guard on each side. Both men were heavily armed, holding large spears and dull expressions, despite the chaos occurring a few yards in front of them. He wanted to ask Cyra about the paper matter once again – knowing the capitaler's obsession with such things. She had already told him Zuras didn't need papers, since they were not ground bound, and that if he just kept quiet, they would simply think he was one too. He'd reminded her that he didn't look anything like a Zura, and she'd lent him her bear skin. Painted some strange tribal-looking symbols on his face, with some clay they'd found by the lake. "They not so clever. You not worry." She'd assured him. It had helped for the time being, but now, seeing the guards, he couldn't help but feel terribly worried. As instructed, he stayed right behind her and was left rather astonished, as she passed through the gates without the guards giving her as much as a glare. When he attempted to do the same, their spears closed in front of him.

"Halt!" Indra stopped at the command, taking a sudden step back and nodding her head in aggregation.

"Papers." The clean-shaved, dark haired man at the left demanded.

"I.. I don't." Isaiah stuttered.

"No papers? You must be registered." The guards looked at each other and Isaiah looked to Cyra, who apparently hadn't thought about *everything*, after all. Their eyes only met for a very brief moment – his silently begging hers to come to his rescue. Her gaze was first confused, then apologetic, and finally it was completely gone, as she dissipated into another large crowd. Once again, he was left on his own.

"Where were you born? What is your business here?" The one at the right asked. Isaiah took a deep breath. He couldn't rely on silence after all, and he'd not come all this way just to be refused at the gates.

"I am Zura. Zura *not* carry papers." He said, with his best attempt to imitate Cyra's accent. It had some effect on them, for they suddenly looked a little less firm.

"*Zuras* don't enter here." The light-haired one to the right said. He seemed to attempt to penetrate him with his eyes, and Isaiah reminded himself he was a Zura right now and wouldn't be afraid of some shelako capitaler.

"I was told to come register as guardian." The guards now looked at each other in a way that told him neither of them had interfered with an *untrained* Zura before.

"We haven't gotten no orders about this... *who* recruited you?" the light-haired one asked and Isaiah took a second to think.

"I recruited by Zura commander, right after death of great redheaded leader." It was a risk. If Dove and the commander were

152

there, he doubted they'd go along with his lie. But since half the story was true, he thought the chances of them believing it was considerably bigger.

"Kyron knows the rules. If he wants to recruit someone, he needs to bring them here to verify them in person first."

"You are wasting *precious* time, *shelako*. I was *only* Zura agreeing to come, and there is many bandit raiding roads now – *killing* commanders. Zura know these woods better than *anyone*. You –" he said with his fiercest tone, pointing towards the clean-shaved one that now looked the most worried out of the two, "*You* need us." He gave them a penetrating stare if he'd ever had one, hoping it would be enhanced by the sinister-looking face paint. He then turned Indra around, hoping the theatrical effect of it would make enough of an impression for them to reconsider. "Come on," he prayed, as he didn't have the faintest idea as to how he'd climb the fifteen-foot wall.

"Wait! You can pass… we will fetch an escort so you can go get verified." Isaiah almost forgot to suppress his smile as he turned to face them. The light-haired man was giving his colleague an annoyed look, but he didn't protest, and so, their crossing spears opened before him.

Riding through the gates he had to contain himself not to show how ecstatic he felt – for once, it was he who had fooled someone. He looked around for Cyra, hoping she perhaps had just hidden until he'd gotten through himself, but she was gone. They hadn't discussed exactly what they'll do once they reached Nagár. Still, he had at least wanted to say goodbye, while she'd seemed more than alright about leaving him outside. He reminded himself he shouldn't be taken so much by surprise by this – he was not a Zura after all. *They* were not a tribe, nor were they family, and in the end, they had no obligation to each other – owed each other nothing at all. "Who am I to ask her to save *me*?" he thought. She'd done so once already, and it'd been more than enough.

"Get off your horse."

"What?" Isaiah said absentmindedly, forgetting about his Zura mask for a flare second. A red-faced man with matching hair and large, crossed arms was standing in front of him. "The escort." He realized.

"*No horses.*" Isaiah looked around. The city was so disturbingly crowded it would almost be impossible for anyone to get around in – little less so on horseback. There were more humans shouting and yelling, than he had even thought existed. Even so, he did not want to leave Indra, as she seemed to be the only one he could trust.

"Are you *deaf?*" The escort groaned in a strong northern accent – obviously less affected by his tribal costume than the guards.

"Where will you take her?"

"To the stables. *With the other horses.*" He pointed to the right, and the intensified redness on his face suggested he was growing more annoyed by the second. Finally, Isaiah got off her back while silently apologizing. "I'll come for you," he assured her.

"Wait here." The red man said firmly, and just as he turned his back to him, Isaiah started running. Leaving the heavy bear skin on the ground, he ran into the enormous crowd as fast as his legs could carry him.

"Hey! Stop!" The man shouted after him, but even if Cyra had been right about them not being clever, anyone knew better than running with the reins of a Zura horse in their hand.

Within three minutes of arriving in the capital, Isaiah had lost his courier, two guards, an escort, and his horse – the last of them, carrying the few belongings he'd brought with him. Indra was the only thing he truly felt bad about, and he promised himself he'd somehow find a way to get her back once he was done there. Though the Nagárians had been as hostile as their reputation suggested, he didn't think them cruel enough to hurt an innocent animal for his little scheme. For now, his priority was to navigate himself through the streets, and he realized he'd given too little thought as to how he'd proceed from there. Oblivious as to how large the city truly was, he'd thought he would simply walk around for some time, hoping to find his grandfather – or somebody who'd seen him. If this turned out unsuccessfully, he'd start asking people if Raziel Mongoya was still alive – then find him and, hopefully, discover his grandfather had been in contact. Now that he was there, he understood how unrealistic this was, and while trying his best to move in between the masses, he concluded that finding *anyone* in Nagár might take an eternity.

* * *

Isaiah tried to think. He knew nothing about the place, and nobody in it seemed to have time to even stop for a breath – less so to help a lost outsider. Even if they had, he wouldn't have known what to ask, and now that the guards might be on the lookout for him, it would be too risky going around knocking on doors. He tried hiding his face underneath his cape, but soon discovered that nobody seemed to give even a slight amount of acknowledgement to his existence. Overwhelmed by the terrible noise and the many bodies pushing their ways forward from several directions, he scouted for an exit point. With the voices of thousands of humans inside his head, thinking became increasingly impossible. Moving anywhere was as much of a struggle as standing still, and soon he could just barely choose the direction of his steps. It was as if he was about to drown in a large river of sweating bodies, and he felt himself growing more and more desperate, looking for something to hold on to. As his breath grew heavier, he instinctively put his hand to his chest. His heart was pondering. Though not exactly the same, it was beating in a similar rhythm it had, just before he'd been put to the ground by the bear. Suddenly, he felt burning hot. He gasped, sensed the noise quieting down and being replaced by an odd whistling in his ears. As if a strange wind had taken over his head. His body felt tingly, his eyesight cloudy, and when he at last fell to the ground, it felt very close to relief.

CHAPTER SEVENTEEN

ARISTOCRATS

WHEN Isaiah woke up, he felt confused. More than he'd done the first morning he'd been back in his own bed. Perhaps even more than when he'd woken up in Tara's house, and this time, he knew for a fact something had gone wrong. Though the sun was up, it wasn't morning. He wasn't in a bed but laying on a sofa, fully clothed. These first observations made him get up more abruptly than he should have, only for his head to remind him of its loss of potency and force him back down. His memory of the hell-like street returned, though he didn't know how long ago it'd been – or where he currently was. Looking around, he concluded he was inside a home. The terrible noise appeared as more of a summing sound in there, luring in through a large, open window some feet away.

"You're awake." The voice came from a man sitting in a moss green chair, just slightly out of his eye-reach.

"Hello... yes, at least I think I am..." Isaiah managed to respond, hoarse and still feeling strangely disoriented.

"Please, drink some water, Sir." The man got up and gave him a big, bronze colored cup that'd been standing on a beautifully crafted, wooden table next to him. It was the first time anybody had called him Sir. He didn't think of himself as one, but as he turned his head to take the cup, he didn't care to correct him.

"Thank you." He drank greedily, feeling he should find something polite to say or ask. Before he got the chance, a round woman with shoulder long, sunny hair and large, sparkly, brown eyes entered.

"You're awake! Hello, dear, I'm Alice." She said in a loud, sweet voice, then squatted down in front of him and felt his forehead. Surprised by the touch, he instinctively pulled away.

"So, so. It's alright, I am only checking your temperature."

"Thank you…" He uttered, but it took even more of him than usual to speak.

"Don't worry about talking dear, just nod for now, alright?" Liking her suggestion, and the warmth in her eyes, he nodded accordingly. At least it *seemed* he'd (quite literally) fallen into good hands and though losing consciousness in the middle of the street was quite an alternative way of getting off of it, he was relieved he'd managed to do so before it had swallowed him alive.

"Your temperature seems fine… have you drunk and eaten well these past days?" he nodded, though not sure if bear meat could be categorized as *well*. Cyra had been very strict about cooking it thoroughly.

"Alright. Well, you look like you've come from a long journey, so it's possible you're just a little dehydrated and exhausted." The explanation didn't completely convince him, and that was when he thought of the plant he'd assumed to be basil. If it hadn't been, and was in fact something else, could it have poisoned him through one of the small scratches on his hand? If so, what would happen to Cyra? She hadn't complained about her leg, and it had looked better when they checked it in the morning. Still, he knew with certainty some poisons could be discrete, and she could just as well not have felt the pain. The terrible images appearing in his head were abrupted by Alice, as she started pulling out strange looking things from a big, red bag.

"There now, I'm a doctor, so you have nothing to worry about." Isaiah nodded again and observed as she browsed through numerous odd-looking instruments (none of them being colorful stones or strange teas). He felt a little relieved she wasn't a healer, but that was only until she pulled out a long, thick needle.

"What is that?"

"This is a cannula. Though, I doubt there is anything seriously wrong, I think it'd be better if we ran your blood through the Analyzer – just in case. Sometimes we can detect diseases with it… and well, my eyes are good but if there is something more *invisible* going on with you, I won't be able to see it."

"Analyzer?"

"Yes, it is a fairly new invention... we haven't found a better name for it yet. My husband, Robert, is a scientist you see." Isaiah thought their Nagárian names peculiar. Robert, now standing over at the window, was a well-dressed man with dark brown, nearly black hair and a finely groomed mustache. He gave a modest nod and a subtle smile in his direction. All Isaiah had ever heard about scientists was that they tried explaining things people found unexplainable. The new academics, some called them.

"I am what you might call a *chemist*." Robert explained. "It is much like an alchemist, only much more *useful* in these modern times." Someone had once mentioned Raziel Mongoya was a talented alchemist, which Isaiah understood to be something in between a scientist and a sorcerer. He didn't exactly know what the difference was, but while a sorcerer created and saw dark things, the alchemist made gold and other precious metals. From his understanding, a scientist could do neither of these things. He would be able to *explain* the metal and its qualities, while a sorcerer probably couldn't make gold themselves and likely wouldn't care to explain it to anyone either. Still, they could make other things – vicious things – and they could make them out of thin air.

Isaiah flinched as Alice stung her needle into his middle finger, and then pressed drops of his blood onto an oval piece of glass. Allowing a stranger to take his blood was not particularly pleasant, but he had little to no strength to resist.

"Can your Analyzer detect poison?" He asked, and Robert, who till now had an overall serious appearance, made a sound of almost childlike excitement.

"I'm not sure. But we'll soon know if it does." Isaiah was nowhere near as excited as his host, but decided that if anything was wrong with him, he'd rather know it sooner than later. He wanted to ask them to check his brain too, but it might give Alice a reason to sting her needle into it – and he was in no such mood. Instead, he used the remainder of his strength to ask if they could close the window, which they did, along with the heavy, blue patterned curtains.

"Rest now, dear." Alice said, a warm, motherly smile forming on her lips, just before he drifted off again' this time, fortunate to already be laying down.

Waking up for the third time that day, there was no longer any sun or noise coming from the street. Turning his head, Robert was sitting in the same chair, reading a new book that was bigger than any other Isaiah had ever seen. It was dark blue, and on the cover, it simply stated "Chemistry".

"Where am I?"

"Oh, you're awake..." Robert said, closing his book. "You are also safe, I assure you. How are you feeling?" Isaiah considered the question for a moment, and other than disoriented he thought he felt quite a lot better. His head less heavy, and his heart beating as usual.

"Okay, I think."

"The Analyzer agrees. I've not reached a conclusion concerning the poison yet, but from what I've seen, it seems perfectly normal. I must apologize if Alice startled you with the needle, she is just always so concerned about people bringing disease from the outside. Not good for their sake – or *our own*."

"So, no poison then?" He asked, hopefully.

"It doesn't seem likely." Robert responded, smiling reassuringly as his reading lantern revealed subtle bags underneath his eyes.

"Did she give me any medicine?"

"No. Alice said it would be better for you to sleep it off first. And it seems you managed to do that without our help." Isaiah was displeased with the way his body had started dismissing him lately, and that Robert was still sitting there, made him feel he was preoccupying people with much more important work.

"I appreciate you taking me in."

"Oh, no trouble at all, Sir." Robert said, walked over to him and gestured for him to give him his hand.

"I'm not the expert on this, but your pulse is still a little low. It's probably just temporary, but you can happily stay here overnight – or till whenever you feel better." He smiled kindly and when the boy failed to respond he added, "Or perhaps you live close by? I would gladly take you in our carriage if you prefer to go home."

"I... I'm not from around here, I'm afraid. But thank you, that is very kind."

"Oh, no trouble at all, Sir." Robert didn't seem surprised and as Isaiah remembered the symbols he still had on his face, he wondered if they thought he was a Zura or some vile tribal man.

"I know what you must be thinking – what feeble people these two must be, having carriages in these days of difficulties. But I assure you – we do not use it often and mostly only for out of town matters."

"I wasn't thinking that, actually. I've just never seen one before, and I thought all horses were banned from inside the walls." Before Robert had the chance to reply, Alice walked in. She'd changed into a green dress that made her rather large bosoms stand up the way he'd heard capital women's garments often did.

"Oh, how wonderful that you're awake! Just in time for dinner."

*

It was the first time Isaiah had sat by a long table that wasn't packed with hungry captives. From what he'd seen thus far, the house was rather big, and the style very different from the fortress. He got the impression everything in it ought to be considered modern. Though there were no pretty rocks or jewels, their walls were generously decorated with paintings, and they had shelves with many odd objects that Alice had told him had little to do with their work and were rather "inherited junk Robert refuses to get rid of". When he finally asked about what had happened a few hours prior, they explained they'd heard people shouting for help. Since they'd been on their way home, and since the infirmaries were either far away, full or best avoided, they'd offered to take him with them. Nobody on the street had objected on his behalf.

"So, young man. Would you perhaps tell us why you're here? Alice and I rarely get visitors and less so travelers like yourself..." Isaiah felt more comfortable being called a young man, than Sir. Calling himself a traveler was a different topic entirely.

"I wouldn't say traveler... I... I am a..."

"My first guess was a guardian – perhaps even a Zura born guardian?" Alice interrupted, looking more excited than frightened by her own suggestion. Once again, he'd forgotten about his face paint and felt himself blushing underneath it.

"I'm doubting it now – Zuras don't talk like you. At least I wouldn't imagine that they do – I've never really met one in person." She confessed.

"Alice, let the boy speak." Robert chuckled, and she rolled her large eyes at him.

"Actually, I just came here to look for my grandfather." Isaiah said, feeling bad for disappointing them with his ordinariness.

"Oh, does he live in Nagár?"

"No, we're Deltans. He... he went missing about ten days back..." Alice's eyes widened at this.

"Oh dear, that is terrible."

"I'm sure Alice could check the infirmary where she works – he's probably fine, but you can never be too sure these days. Must be a rough journey for somebody his age – though I must admit I've never gone to the Heartland before." Isaiah nodded, grateful for the help – not to say that he'd called Delta the Heartland.

"My dear, you have never gone *anywhere* before. Robert was born here, you see, and I'm from Bharoos myself." Bharoos, Isaiah recalled, was the ghost town where he and Tzelem had gone. It seemed so long ago, but it really wasn't. He considered telling her what he'd seen there but contained himself – not wanting to upset the jolly woman.

"Anyways, dear, I will be sure to check tomorrow morning. I hope you'll find him shortly – it is not easy for newcomers nowadays. As you've probably noticed already, the population has increased *tremendously* over the past year." Alice said, shaking her head so her curls danced around her round face. "No, Nagár is not what it once was..." she continued, and then took a sip of wine, which he himself had politely declined.

"My wife helps the plagued refugees from villages and other diseased areas. She sees the worst side of the city every day." He gave her a warmer look than Isaiah had ever seen a man give a woman before, and her already rosy cheeks grew two shades redder.

"I thought the plagued ones weren't allowed inside."

"They're not... not even the refugees who seem to be well are unless they've been granted prior permission. The infirmary I work in is just outside the walls."

"It is a very admirable thing you are doing, my lady." He couldn't begin to imagine how the poor woman spent her days, and he wished he knew where she got the strength to smile. To be genuinely cheerful – even excited – with a stranger practically falling into their home.

"Please, just call me Alice…" she said, suddenly modest and turning towards her husband.

"Robert, tell him about your work."

"Well, I am now observing the new plague that has started spreading. This way we might finally find a cure that can put an end to them – before it spreads further north. Right *now* I am working from home since nobody believes in the possibility of *fighting nature*. Not even here in Nagár – supposably *the center of knowledge*." He frowned.

"I didn't know scientists fought nature, Sir Robert."

"You are not alone in that regard, young man. But it is possible – we've both seen it." He said more softly, looking towards his wife who nodded thoughtfully while circling her finger around the edge of her bronze cup.

"Now we just need to find out more so this city might be saved. No walls are high enough to keep out diseases like these. Though terrible to keep the refugees out, it is among the few things I agree with as far as the realm's recent policies are concerned."

"So that *all of Araktéa* can be saved, Robert." Alice corrected him.

"Of course, but we must start somewhere, my dear. Everything needs to start somewhere… and our fight starts right here in this house." He patted her hand, and they eyed each other as he took a long sip of his wine. Isaiah saw more than just love there, more than passion and desire and whatever else he'd seen in common lovers' eyes. What it was, he couldn't quite put his finger on, but it made an unforced smile spread across his face.

"You look like you have a question." Robert suggested, and Isaiah looked down at his plate, suddenly embarrassed.

"How do you fight something that is invisible?" He asked, yet to understand the way the plague attacked its victims. Some said it came as a shadow during the nighttime. Others claimed it was sorcery and everyone catching it had been rightfully cursed for engaging with the darkness. He'd heard other versions as well, but these seemed to be the most common ones.

"Ah, now that is a fairly good question. First of all, – it is not exactly invisible. That is just village lore. The plague is nothing more than what we in academia call *a bacterium*, and without sounding too smug, I was among the people developing the Analyzer – proofing that it is in fact not invisible or supernatural in any way. Still, you are of course right in that regard that it is hard to see with the naked eye – a very different matter altogether, and yet leaving us with a similar problem." He cleansed his throat and put down his glass, resuming in natural formality. "To successfully fight anything, you have to *know it* first, and so before we can make a cure, we first need to figure out more about its behavior and tendencies..." he stopped himself. "Excuse me, I must be boring you with all of this... I don't get out much these days."

"Not at all, Sir, it is very important work you're doing." Isaiah was quick to say, fascinated that one of the few things even *he* had considered to be a mystical phenomenon, was actually nothing but a bacterium. Not everyone believed in bacteria, but he'd seen it himself. Every now and then, a plant in their garden would get infected, leaving it diseased and weak. If you didn't cut it, his grandfather had explained, it would spread to other plants as well – much like the plague. "Why haven't I thought about this before?" he wondered. Then he realized it was because he hadn't cared. That it hadn't concerned him compared to how many other things did.

"Indeed, and *thank you* - I am trying my very best. Hopefully there will be more results soon, it's been a slow process these past...*months*." he admitted, rolling his eyes ever so slightly, then wavering his hand as to leave the matter to rest.

"Now, enough about terrible things. Maybe if you told us more about your situation, we could be of better help. Deltans are not known to stray this far away from home. Would you have any clues as to your grandfather's intentions with coming here?" Isaiah sighed, he did not want to bother them more than he already had, but knowing Robert was a chemist, the possibility of him knowing the whereabouts of another academic, were bigger than none. It was as he'd just said – he had to start *somewhere*, and even if their dinner table was not the ideal place, it was the only one currently accessible.

"I suspect he might have come here to seek his teacher from his days at the academy…"

"Goodness, your grandfather must have been among the students of the very first academy – among the last living scientists I reckon. How I'd love to meet him and hear about it. I've found very few records on the matter…" Isaiah smiled, not wanting to say anything regarding the current state of his mind. "As to his teacher, it must have been one of the original academics that taught at the Old Academy before it burned. I'm afraid all of them left after the revolution." Isaiah's heart sank and Alice gave him an apologetic look as she placed some more of the buttery purée that he already felt he'd eaten too much of.

"I see…" he sighed, trying to look less defeated than he felt. "His name was Raziel Mongoya. You don't happen to know if he's still alive, if anyone around here knew him, or where I might…?" before he'd gotten through the sentence, Robert burst out laughing, almost spitting out his wine.

"*Oh*, that is the teacher you're looking for?" Isaiah nodded, as the couple's eyes met somewhere in between amusement and amazement.

"He is *still* alive, yes, and the only one of those *ancient* academics that were too stubborn to leave or die. He prefers *Master* Mongoya, but Sir Mongoya would do just fine." Isaiah noticed the hatred in Alice's face, a lot of it in fact, but he still felt relieved – it seemed he hadn't come to Nagár for nothing.

"I just call him Uncle Raz." Robert uttered, chugged down the rest of his wine, and shook his head in amused disbelief.

CHAPTER EIGHTEEN

MASQUERADE

AS the evening had continued it came to Isaiah's knowledge that Sir Mongoya, was a very special sort of Sir. Not only was he an academic and an alchemist. Not only was he a teacher and an uncle, but he had about a dozen other titles. Most of them, Robert said, were either unknown or forgotten, but all were significant to him, as he still saw himself as a highly valued member of the Nagárian aristocracy. Robert simply referred to him as "Uncle Raz", with a certain loathing in his voice that only seemed to occur when there was bad blood within a bloodline. It was the same tone Tzelem had used when speaking of his brother. The same tone his grandfather used whenever mentioning Isaiah's father. With this obvious disliking, Robert had offered to take Isaiah to him, and so the next day he felt oddly excited to see a real carriage for the first time. Mostly due to the fact that he wouldn't need to walk the streets by foot again, which made leaving the house slightly less nerve-wrecking.

"It must feel unusual for you... with all these people, I mean." Robert remarked, clearly noticing his discomfort as he put a small, odd-fashioned hat and long, black cape on.

"A little bit, yes." Isaiah admitted, and Robert smiled as if he understood. Perhaps he did – as he'd told him, he did not leave the house very often either.

"I was raised here – mostly by my mother, and it used to be much more..." he paused. "*Bearable* might be the best word for it."

"You've lived here all your life?"

"I moved to Bharoos a few years back for my studies. I planned on going right back here as soon as I was done, but then I met my dear Alice. We stayed until the plague came just a few months back. Rather ironic, as it was the exact thing, I went to further indulge myself in..." he sighed and cleansed his throat.

"I thought the only Araktéan academy was in Nagár."

"It is, but the kind of research I'm doing is not permitted here. Some of my previous colleagues called it a sensible precaution, but to this I couldn't agree. This is why I am working from home – so please keep what you've seen there to yourself."

"Of course." Isaiah responded, and Robert gestured a nod and that trusting smile that seemed to come so easily to him. Then, he opened the main door, and led him alongside the tracks that lead to their carriage. It was narrow and black and had crisp leaves on the roof that a coachman tried his best to remove.

"Don't worry, they'll fly off on the way, Jerry." Robert assured him, and the slim, serious-looking oldling nodded.

"Certainly, Sir." He said, opening the door. From the inside, the carriage was much smaller than Isaiah had expected it to be, and he realized the ones he'd seen in the painting would've been large and useless in today's Nagár.

"You were lucky you got away in time, and to have such a beautiful home here." He said, attempting to converse casually, as they sat down on red, velvet seats.

"Do not be so easily fooled by the exterior. I was born into a great debt." Robert mumbled and then cleared his throat again.

"This home belonged to my father – and truth be told, I should get rid of it." His expression darkened, then turned serious, and finally saddened as he looked right at Isaiah.

"You are right. Alice and I were lucky to keep our lives. But we... we lost our only child. There was nothing we could do for her." Surprised by his honesty, Isaiah felt his hands tremble and had to fold them together in his lap.

"I am... I'm so sorry – I had no idea." He said, feeling a sudden sorrow come over him. Losing children was a common enough thing these days – a loss he obviously never had to experience himself, and yet, he nearly felt tears coming out of his eyes, and had to turn towards the window to hide it. Robert didn't seem to notice (himself somewhat surprised to be sharing this tragedy).

"Alice had just been nominated to one of the best doctors in Nahbí when it happened. Instead of working in one of the more prestigious care homes when we returned to Nagár, she chose to help the less fortunate. Though the loss of a child is something a mother never completely recovers from, it seems something has given her a new sense of strength. It's admirable to say the least. She's an extraordinary wife. I even believe the tragedy brought us closer to each other." He said thoughtfully, his tone intact and filled with a pride that was every bit justified. Isaiah took a breath, "I won't cry" he assured himself, turning away from the window.

"She seems like a wonderful woman, Sir Robert." He said sincerely.

"She is indeed. Strong, independent. I sometimes sense I need her more than she needs me. If that's not extraordinary, I don't know what is. Do you have a wife, Isaiah?"

"Me? No." He laughed, thinking it absurd, although it seemed to be a somewhat common thing for people his age.

"Good." Robert said. "You're still young. I had no plans on ever being wed, and I didn't change my mind about it until I was five and thirty. Six years it's been. In time, I hope you'll find a woman of great character and not just of great appearance. A real partner." Isaiah nodded and Robert hummed a little before returning to where he'd been heading with his initial point. He rarely spoke this much about private matters, but the boy had a decent silence about him that made it hard for him to stop himself.

"Alice and I now see our blessings for what they are, and we continue doing our best to make sure less people suffer what we did."

"The world is for the living, so we need to look forward." Isaiah felt embarrassed as the words left his mouth. "I didn't mean…"

"No, you are very right. And, despite the masses of people crawling these streets, we need *more* of the living in this land. There is so much potential in rebuilding Araktéa – and unlike some people will tell you, it is not too late." It had been a long time since Isaiah had heard someone speak of such things – if he'd ever heard anyone doing so at all. He came to the realization that if anyone could fight nature, it would need to be someone like Robert Mongoya, and if he could make cures to save them from plagues, there was a possibility he could help his grandfather too. He hadn't told him about the mind sickness, aware he'd already helped him too much. Even so, he would ask his advice if it came to it. He'd thought this corruption disease to be something just as invisible as the mind itself, but perhaps it was no more mystical than plague. It might as well be a bacterium – something that could be seen and removed. But for now, he wouldn't bother him with these speculations. "Find him first, then fix him." He reminded himself, and then, trying to turn the conversation to a more casual subject, he asked, "What did Araktéa look like before, Sir?"

"I don't know." Robert said, dragging his finger over his mustache, "I just know I can envision a better one, that there is in fact enough room for us all to feel... a lot better – much safer than we do now. Most Nagárians argue there are too many of us, but there is so much land that can still be saved. There is *so much* unseen potential." The only thing Isaiah could see through his own vision and window was the wild crowd, and it didn't make him feel safe in the slightest. Robert's vivid eyes did, and so perhaps it was possible they saw something that was truly wonderful.

"You should come to Delta some time, Sir Robert, then you wouldn't need to envision anything, you could just look around and smile." Robert laughed wholeheartedly.

"Perhaps I will. Now, I didn't mean to bore you with our plans. Right now we have much more urgent things to talk about."

"Your uncle..." Robert nodded, the excitement leaving his eyes and replaced with strict hostility.

"I tried sleeping on it – but it sadly seems wine does little to help to clear my head. I still don't know exactly how to prepare you for meeting with him, but if I'm yet to have made it clear, you should know he is a peculiar character. He is crude with *everyone,* so don't allow this to bother you. And stand your ground – but don't be too stubborn, alright?"

"Alright." Isaiah didn't quite know what to make of the warnings, but the nervousness he'd tried brushing off, was luring its way back. This time, it wasn't his father's reputation he would have to live up to, but the perhaps even more intimidating one of his grandfather.

"What should I say to him?"

"If I knew that I would tell you, but frankly I never seem to say the right things myself." Robert chuckled. "You're well-spoken, and probably better off making your own judgement of it."

"My grandfather always told me he was a great man. Has he changed?" Robert hesitated for a moment, moving uncomfortably in his seat.

"For some he *is* and will always be a great man. From my experience, great men often carry with them equally great troubles. The only thing I can say with certainty is that he is unlike any other man you'll ever meet." Isaiah nodded, and decided to be as polite and humble as he possibly could. From the little he'd witnessed of the aristocracy the past four years, great men seemed to prefer the company of agreeable ones. Ones who didn't mind entertaining the idea of their superiority.

*

It took them close to an hour to get out of the city center and reach the lower edge of Sujin Hill (which had Master Mongoya as its only resident). It was high and steep, and placed right in between two even higher hills. One, Robert explained, was the King's palace and the other the Araktéan house of justice (where he would have been taken to trial, Isaiah realized). Both these grand buildings were protected by high walls, making neither visible, even as they reached the top of Sujin Hill. It was at the very edge of the northern side of the walls – high enough to see the entire city but not quite so high you could see the so-called refugee-market in front of the gates. It was silent there. Peaceful even, and so everything else seemed to be in Nahbí, the house was protected by a high fence, allowing them to see nothing more than the point of his rooftop.

"You told me he lived alone."

"I told you he doesn't have a family – apart from myself. He has a few servants. A guard, some cleaners, a personal doctor *and* now I believe he has a few chefs too. A bit excessive if you ask me..."

"Servants, are just like prisoners, aren't they?"

"No, the servants do chores such as gardening, cleaning, serving his food... they keep him and his home alive."

"I didn't think they practiced slavery in Araktéa anymore."

"No, no – they are not slaves either. They stay here voluntarily..." Robert got a thoughtful look upon his face. "Though I have no clue as to *why*, for I could certainly not think of a worse place to be."

"Does he pay them in gold coins?"

"I'm not sure. But I suspect they're mostly paid in a decent bed, food and of course *the honor* of his marvelous presence." Isaiah still didn't feel he understood the actual difference between a volunteer, a servant and a slave, but stopped asking as it didn't seem so important.

As they got closer, he could see the guard Robert had mentioned. He was only one man, but even from a distance he seemed much more intimidating than the two fools he'd met the previous day. Robert gave him a friendly nod as he stepped out, while he started marching towards their carriage, looking less than welcoming.

"Good day, Robert Mongoya – his nephew, if you recall..." The guard made an animal-like grunt, and then stared inside the open door of the carriage.

"Who he is?" He spit at Isaiah. He was surprised to see that despite his size, he was a rather old man. Exactly how old he couldn't say, but his face looked almost like a cracked clay pot – clearly burnt by the sun a few times too many.

"The young man is my guest. The grandson of an old friend of my uncles'."

"Master has no *friends*." He said in a sharp accent. A tribal man, Isaiah figured.

"An old *colleague*, then. A student, his name is Theodore..." Robert looked to Isaiah. He had noticed people had additional names there, but he had never heard his own – nor his grandfather's. He shrugged, and Robert pressed his lips together and turned to the guard again.

"He was his student just before the revolution. My uncle will know him."

"I never heard of this man." The guard crossed his arms.

"Well, could you please go ask my uncle then?"

"Who will guard gates?"

"Oh, for goodness' sake, Julius, he is *not* the bloody King." Isaiah was close to astonishment. The guards at the fortress might not let anyone out of there, but they would've never acted so unyielding towards the Patron's visitors.

"You have my word – Isaiah is no danger to him in the *slightest*." Julius glared at him again. Clearly suspicious, though Isaiah looked ten times more groomed than he had the day before, nicely wrapped into the tight garments Robert had lent him. The little west and the uptight shirt felt suffocating in the city's dry heat, but the Master cared for appearances and would take him more seriously if he was dressed in the Nagarián fashion.

"*Out* of carriage." Isaiah hesitated for a moment, but Robert stepped down and signaled him to follow along. The same moment his boot met the ground, Julius roughly opened up his cape. As he checked his belt and pockets, the roughness of his hands made him feel as timid as he imagined a young virgin might. When he couldn't find anything, he checked him yet another time – inside the west and even the shirt that had taken forever to button up.

"You better not hide anything."

"I am not." Isaiah assured him.

"Then why you look *nervous*?" he grunted, his face so close to his own, Isaiah could feel the heavy, greasy smell on his breath. Exactly what he had eaten that day, was uncertain – but it was certainly not honey tea and sweet fruits. He saw how deep the lines on his face went, his maddening eyes – like those of a provoked hound's, waiting for any excuse to tear something into pieces.

"Could we please get this over with?" Robert asked impatiently, and after glaring at Isaiah for a few, long seconds more, Julius finally barked, "Not stay longer than one hour!" He took a step back, allowing air to flow in between them like an invisible savior from one of the Zura's thirteen heavens. Then, he marched over and pushed the gates open for them.

The first impression of what met him behind this fence, was about as separate from that of Nagár, as it could have been. The house itself (built in beautiful, light gray stones, and with large, multicolored oval windows), was an astonishing sight. Compared to the garden flourishing in front of it, it became nothing but a bleach background. Aside from the bright green grass – perfectly cut and smelling of spring, even if it wasn't – it was decorated with hundreds, if not thousands, of red, pink, and yellow tulips. Though their own garden had an amazing variety, he hadn't seen tulips there since he was around four. They were so rare he'd never even been allowed close to them. Now, they needed to be rarer than ever, and for anyone that knew anything at all about flowers, they showed a level of wealth beyond comparison.

"Sorry about Julius. He's my uncle's last living guard and takes his job a little too seriously." Robert explained, as the carriage halted in front of the building.

"Did all of them... die?" Isaiah asked, and Robert nodded.

"Most of them did from age, and he refuses to hire new ones since he is convinced they would betray him. Not that *one* isn't more than enough already."

"Why?"

"He doesn't trust people he doesn't know... or people that *he does* know for that matter. Among his many troubles, this paranoia might be his largest."

Isaiah could understand why someone might be careful welcoming outsiders, having a beautiful garden as this one. Also, it seemed common enough for old men, not to always appreciate new ones. These observations gave him a certain indication of how their meeting might go, and he worried Uncle Raz would be at least as skeptical of him as Julius had been. On their ride up the hill, Robert had given him a handful of rules – mostly stating what he absolutely *shouldn't* say or mention – but he'd given them with an uncertainty that made him doubt they'd be of actual help.

"I'm sorry if I've concerned you more than I should, really – it will be fine. Just be calm and try to stay composed..." Robert said, as they walked the seven steps that lead to the tall, two-adjacent door.

"I'll put my iron mask on." Robert gave him a questioning look, before knocking.

"I'm not certain what that is, but it sounds useful – so by all means, do it." Isaiah wasn't quite sure what it meant himself, only that he'd seen it on faces before. Both on guards, and seemingly ordinary men and women that appeared strong, but that perhaps were only secretive about what they were truly feeling and thinking. Their composed masks were their strongest armor, and he'd come to think he wanted one for himself, to use in times like these.

"If your grandfather came here, I'm not so sure that he'd let him stay for long. On the other hand, my uncle is full of surprises..." Robert said thoughtfully. "He wouldn't lie about it. At least I don't think he would."

* * *

It took a few minutes before a servant opened the door, and though looking genuinely surprised by the sight of them, the short, gray-haired man (dressed in a similar fashion as the two of them), politely escorted them to the Master. After walking through a long, deeply red hallway with more oil paintings than Isaiah knew existed, they finally arrived at yet another door. After the servant had knocked, the three of them stood in silence. Isaiah looked around, trying to distract himself from the discomfort in his stomach and the lump reawakening in his throat. He noticed some strange inscriptions on the top of the door. First, he wondered if it might be the same as some of his grandfather's unsent letters, but no – it looked strange and was not written in common letters. It was not scripted directly on the wooden door either but carved onto a piece of dark metal. He opened his mouth to ask about it, but closed it just as fast, noticing the polite smile on Robert's face. It was the stiff, polite kind that nobles often carried when mingling at the fortress gatherings – whenever they talked with people they had little interest in talking with. Seeing this, Isaiah forgot about the symbols, and put on his iron face. It was just then that he decided to rename it (though it hardly mattered what it was called, as long as he remembered to wear it).

After they'd been standing there rather awkwardly for a little longer than what seemed natural, the servant knocked again, his hand firmer this time, and then an equally firm voice from the other side, granted permission for them to enter. The little man pushed, and the door moved heavily as they walked into a large room with a high, beautifully painted ceiling, and an endless number of bookshelves.

"Uncle." Robert gestured with something in between a nod and a modest bow towards the left side of the room.

"Well, well. If it isn't my nephew?" Master Mongoya was sitting on top of a high pendulum. He had a wide desk in front of him, with legs of gold and some strange instrument resting next to a book he seemed to be reading.

"And *who* might this manling be?" Isaiah made a slightly deeper bow than Robert, much like he'd been instructed to do when first meeting with the Huxleys'. Out of the many names and titles Robert had mentioned, he knew for a fact that he was not an actual Lord. He wasn't even sure he were to be considered an noble, but reckoned exaggerated humility would serve him better than potential impoliteness. As he moved his spine back up, he did his best to remain it as straight and as long as possible, hoping it might make him seem firm – like someone who was humble but stood their ground. Someone more than just another manling, wanting to go home – thought this was what he was.

"Master Mongoya, my name is Isaiah, son of Ares…"

"—and the grandson of Theodore Aronin." Mongoya interrupted him – and it was in this strange manner that Isaiah finally learned his second name. "Isaiah Aronin," he thought, "so that is my full name."

"Precisely." He said, trying to hide his astonishment.

"Huh." The Master responded, unmoved, but at the very least interested enough to raise his head from the book, and his elbows up to the desk. It was hard to tell (both due to physical distance and time) if this was the man from his insight.

"I haven't talked with Theodore for years." He plainly informed them, and Isaiah felt his heart sink.

"That was actually why I came to see you, Master Mongoya. My grandfather has gone missing, and so I left Delta to look for him."

"And why would you think to come here? Theodore *hates* Nagár." He laughed a short, sharp laugh, not seeming moved by his tale in the slightest. "I've finally come to agree with him in that regard." He then continued, his narrow face moving towards one of the three, long windows facing towards the tulip garden.

"He admired you greatly, Sir Mongoya. So, with no other clues as to where he'd gone, I thought it best to come to you first."

"You rode all the way from Delta to see if *I* knew where he was?" Isaiah couldn't tell if he was impressed or just found him exceptionally *stupid*, as Cyra would have put it. Still, he responded with an assertive yes, not having thought up any alternative story, that might make him sound like the more rational person he'd once thought himself to be.

"Huh." He said again, seeming to consider this for a moment, and even from the long distance between them, Isaiah could see him raising his eyebrows. Interest.

"Very well." He sighed finally, closing the book and bending slightly over his desk again – squinting over oval spectacles, similar to ones he'd seen Lord Huxley wear at times. Then, he stood up slowly and grabbed the black cane that'd been leaning towards his desk.

"Do you need help, Uncle?" Robert asked, taking a hesitant step towards the pendulum, as Master Mongoya cautiously made his way down the stairs – there were ten of them.

"No." he said sharply, and Isaiah wondered why a man his age would even consider such an impractical workplace. Watching him was like watching a child walk for the first time, wanting to intervene, so it wouldn't cry when it fell. When he at last had both his feet safely placed on the floor (clothed by a midnight blue carpet), Master Mongoya stopped for a moment. He took a long inhale. Then, instead of walking towards them, he headed to the other side of the room with surprising ease in his stray. Both Robert and Isaiah eyed him wordlessly, till he stopped in front of one of the many bookshelves. He stared at it, not seeming to be searching for anything, but rather just looking. As if it'd been some canvas he wasn't certain if he liked. Isaiah spared a moment to look around. There had to be hundreds if not thousands of books in there, and he wondered how it would be possible for someone to read them all. He wondered *how he'd* ever thought himself able to write a story, yet to be told.

"Theodore was among my best students. I'm sorry to hear he is gone." Sir Mongoya was still standing with his long, slender back towards them. His breathing was normal now, his voice sharp and loud like a whip. He'd said the words as if reading something in a foreign language he didn't understand – motionless and cold like a frozen lake.

"He is not gone, only missing, *Master* Mongoya." Isaiah cleared his throat, not used to speaking to someone standing more than fourteen feet away. "Though realizing he might not be here, I thought perhaps a man of your intellect would have an idea about his whereabouts. Where he might be heading to…"

"Is that so?" Master Mongoya chuckled. He then turned around, finally walking towards his visitors. As he came closer, Isaiah noticed the way his skin hung over his tall cheekbones. The deep lines on his face, and the descending hairline above what had once been a high, narrow forehead. He was indeed old, and yet, his light blue eyes were almost more electrical and vivid than those of a child. Now that he was on safe ground his back was as straight as his cane – now resting in between his hands, as he walked somewhat elegantly towards them. It was beyond a doubt the man from the dream.

"Do you really believe I keep track of all my students' whereabouts? Do you have the slightest idea of *how many* I've had in my lifetime?"

"I am sure you have had a great many, Master." Isaiah responded, suspecting that any of his guesses were likely to offend him.

"*Vaguely* correct." He stopped some five-feet in front of them and was now resting towards his cane and looking him up and down indiscreetly. Isaiah had never given it much thought, but he realized he did not look very much like his grandfather. If Master Mongoya hadn't met Ares, there was a chance he would doubt his legitimacy.

"What is it exactly Theodore has told you, that made you come to *me?*"

"He said you were the wisest man he ever knew. The greatest teacher in all of Araktéa, and… the most talented alchemist in the world." The last part was something he'd overheard one of the triplets say, but it seemed like something Mongoya would enjoy hearing – and so he said it. Shamelessly lying for the sake of truth.

"Yes, yes. All of this is correct, of course." Mongoya sighed.

"And your young mind would obviously see this as an indication that I would know his whereabouts, is that so?" Isaiah nodded, and they glared at each other. He'd never dared to look a man in the eyes for so many seconds before, but something told him that looking down would mean the end of their visit, leaving him back to the beginning and with not so much as a clue as where to turn next.

"I could certainly tell you where he has gone to, but it wouldn't matter for a number of reasons. So then, I shall instead simply tell you that he is gone, and that you shall better accept this fact and move on with your life." Isaiah felt himself gasping against his will. He wanted to yell that he wouldn't accept anything of the sort, but instead he took a long, silent breath through his nose and tried regaining his iron face.

"With all the respect, Sir, I would much prefer if you told me where this place is so that I can go fetch him. He is rather… ill, you see." Mongoya chuckled again and shook his head smugly.

"If he was ill before, boy, he will be worse now. Even with the courage of your father, you couldn't possibly find him where he is. Or what is potentially left of him there – it is no place for the meek and faint-hearted."

"Uncle, this is no good time for these games of yours....please, tell Isaiah where you think his grandfather has gone to."

"*Silent, Robert,* for we are having a serious conversation that has nothing to do with *you*. In fact, I will rather have you leave. You always put your nose in places it doesn't belong."

"My nose is right where it belongs, Uncle. I'm in fact working on very important research." Mongoya snorted.

"Just because I've retired from my engagements, that doesn't mean I haven't heard about you being expelled from the Academic Federation. I'll strongly advise you from whatever independent research you're engaging in. You're already a disgrace to our family name." The short servant had walked in silently and now slightly bowed at Robert and touched his arm. He sighed and Isaiah hoped he would persuade Mongoya with his effortless, convincing engagement.

"Very well, Uncle." he said, with a slight twitch on his face, and then tapped Isaiah on the shoulder apologetically. The tap felt more like a punch in the stomach, for though he found Master Mongoya to be particularly unpleasant, he was not ready to leave just yet.

"The manling stays." The Master stated, raising his left hand from the cane.

"*What* now?"

"*He stays.* Do not look so worried, I'll give him back later." He rolled his eyes at his nephew, moving his hand in strange circles, and Isaiah saw he had a ring on each finger. Each made of silver, and of course, jeweled. Red, green, a mustard-like yellow and one large black one on his thumb.

"Isaiah, you don't need to..."

"It's quite alright, Sir Robert." Isaiah was fast to reply, sensing that even if his grandfather hadn't come to him, Raziel Mongoya would tell him something useful if he could just play along for a little while longer. Men like him, it seemed, just wanted to be listened to and admired, and he'd come to realize that he knew how to play both these parts fairly convincingly.

"Farewell, *dear* nephew, and please – give my best to your *lovely* missus."

CHAPTER NINETEEN

AN ALCHEMIST'S PRIDE

FOR what seemed like several hours (and according to the large, mahogany clock on the wall had been a mere hour and a half), Mongoya rambled. He had explained everything that was currently wrong about Araktéa, ranging from the delayed policy to keep refugees out to the realm granting one of the patronesses to take over after her late husband (whom he insisted had died under peculiar circumstances). It all came down to one root cause, and according to him, everything had been different before the revolution. For anybody that might be remotely concerned with politics, or that had time to spare, his improvised lecture would've probably been an interesting one. Not only because he was undoubtedly knowledgeable, but because he spoke and moved like a stage performer. Even when Isaiah felt clueless as to the places or people he was referring to, he had a way of keeping his attention from flickering. Staring at him with those mesmerizing eyes. Still, he had little interest in Araktéan politics, and even less time for theater. Finally, when he felt he'd been patient and agreeable for long enough, he realized that if he didn't interrupt, he would keep on talking till the sun went down.

"You're very generous to share your view on these most important subjects, Master Mongoya. Where I'm from we sadly know very little of economy and infrastructure, as we use *the old system* for the most part."

"Of course, Deltans have always been a little behind. I know that *boy*, I am merely *trying* to enlighten you, seeing that you are *here* now.

Many Nagariáns will claim capitalers have entered a more enlightened era. I never thought I would say this, but somehow being slow and immovable in your thinking, has ended up serving your kind rather well in the end." Mongoya confessed. Seen away from the many noblemen (functioning as patrons in the larger villages), Delta had remained rather unchanged after the revolution.

"Surely, and I thank you for sharing your knowledge, Master. I am sure that when I find my grandfather, he will agree with you on all you've spoken of. He always told me everything beyond Delta was on its way to becoming a wild thorn-bush of misery."

"Oh, is this what he has taught you?" Isaiah had learned to be careful when speaking ill of the rest of Araktéa, noticing how easily people tended to get offended. It was only since the Master had been expressing his dislike of Nahbí so intensely, he'd dared to. It was a bold move and for once it had little to do with his love for Delta, and more to do with his cover. After an hour of silence, he needed to make sure that when he finally spoke, he would seem like a man with an opinion – perhaps even one of character.

"Yes." He affirmed simply, biting the insides of his cheeks.

"Ha! *Misery...* misery barely covers it. *First* I was surprised he hadn't sent you to study here, but it seems it is a good thing in fact. The new academy is *nothing* compared to what ours once was. People come with hopes of learning something... and they learn, but nothing of importance, and so *they too* become unimportant – a waste of space – flocking around the city with their *skinny*, pointless books... thinking themselves *knowledgeable. Ha! Fools all of them."* The subtle twitches of resentment that'd momentarily appeared on his face, now seemed to be spreading through his body so intensively, Isaiah almost worried it would shoot out through his cane. The old man seemed almost obsessed about moving the thing around, making it seem closer to an extension of his left arm, than something to lean on. Though the anger wasn't directed at him, Isaiah felt a need to speak more cautiously.

"I've been fortunate enough to have my grandfather as my teacher, Master Mongoya. He said all he had ever learned he'd learned from you." There was a chance he'd overdone the flattery, but thus far it seemed the Master's boundaries, as far as compliments were concerned, went far beyond the average range.

"What you are trying to say then," Master Mongoya said,

drumming his fingers over the cane, "Is that in a way, you are almost one of *my* students..."

"Oh... naturally, I would never think of myself..." The Master started laughing, and Isaiah paused, unsure if it was out of mockery or sudden epiphany.

"How endearing. *Brilliant!* Now, I still believe you might just be a simple, Deltan manling, but there *might* be some hope for you after all – if there is hope left for any of us..." The old man rolled his eyes, and then wandered over to one of the large windows, which even from a long distance had a clear view of the city. Thus far, Isaiah had been standing uncomfortably still, moving his weight from leg to leg, hoping to be offered a seat. Now, he finally felt it might be acceptable for him to move, and so he followed along.

"Hope?" He asked and Mongoya sighed. He hadn't spoken, and even less so felt, this sensation for the past two decades. Likewise, he had fallen into the threshold of hope before, only to discover it'd been the temptress of desperation who'd lured him there.

"Now that you no longer need to take care of your grandfather, you might finally *become* something." He stated matter-of-factly.
"With all the respect, Master. I have not given up hope on bringing him home. And even if you were right, Sir – which you seem to be regarding most subjects – I would need to find him and make sure he is given an honorable death. We bury our dead in Delta, as I'm sure you know." Mongoya turned towards him, and for the first time he found him impossible to read. Isaiah struggled to keep his own iron face in place, as the causal implication of his grandfather having permanently vanished, made him feel like running out of the room sobbing. Forced to stand still, listening to his lengthy rambles had already taken so many layers of iron, he felt sure his head would fall off if he didn't get out of there soon. "He is alive. And Mongoya knows where." He heard himself think and just then his wrinkled face twitched.

"You're not ready to bury anyone, *boy*..." He hissed and turned on his foot. Up till then, Isaiah had felt confident he was at least not boring him. He knew how much Lord Huxley *hated* people who bored him, and thought pure speculation, he suspected this to be one of the characteristics men like them shared, though they were certainly not the same when it came to temper.

"Just like your grandfather – you refuse listening to *sense*." The Master's voice echoed through the room, and he then made his way up the stairs of his pendulum again at a hasty pace.

"I did not mean to offend you, Master…"

"Offend? You could not offend me if you tried, silly *child*." Mongoya spit. "I must say…" he began, his tone still sharp as a blade, as his hands flickered through something inside one of the drawers of his desk. "I am surprised you came here first, not because it was a *directly* unintelligent decision, but having Theodore as your teacher, it should be obvious where he has gone to. This makes me question your *mental* capacity…"

"It seems he has… changed over the years, Master."

"Perhaps a man *can* change, at least slightly… and as I told you before – we have not spoken for decades. If this had been forty years ago, I would have had no doubt about where he'd gone to. But even now, it is still obvious." He came down the stairs again, less patiently this time, and holding a large roll of paper in his right hand along with the cane.

"Consider yourself lucky. Few have witnessed what you are about to see." He announced as his foot reached the second last step. This time, Isaiah was certain he hadn't been lucky. He'd *earned* this information with attentiveness and patience. Every last bit of it.

There was a long, wine red table standing towards the wall on the right end of the room. Here, Master Mongoya finally unrolled his secret, and as Isaiah had half-expected already – it was a map.

"Where is this?" he asked. He'd seen a few maps of Araktéa before, but this one seemed to be covering something else – a smaller area. Sir Mongoya looked at him in annoyed disbelief.

"For the sake of *the gods*, is it still not obvious?" Isaiah wanted to suggest something – anything – but he was clueless. It was beautifully painted, but it had no implications regarding the measures and didn't even include any readable names.

"What is it exactly Theodore has been teaching you? I'm not surprised he's neglected politics, but he must have taught you *something*. History, Literature, *Astrology?*"

"Mostly practical subjects, master. Botany… some Biology, Cooking." The master had suddenly gone silent, and he couldn't tell if it was because he was so taken by his map or because he was thinking. He glared down at the brownish paper, as if seeing it for the first time, mumbling something inaudible in between tight lips, and then he sighed loudly.

"Cooking," he said tonelessly, and Isaiah regretted having mentioned it, "Botany…" he chuckled, rolling his eyes.

"We've been living a simple life…" The master held up a hand to stop him.

"I know Theodore is a man of wide knowledge and various interests. Compared to this…" he said, his long, scorny finger pointing to the middle of the map.

"He cared next to nothing about *any* of it. No… all he ever cared about were these *bloody woods*. You should have seen his eyes during my early lectures. The Parda was his first love – *that* I can assure you of." His icy eyes had intensified, and his lower lip had a slight tremble to it as he spoke.

"The… the Parda?" Isaiah stuttered. "It can't be." He thought and seeing Raziel's strange grin he felt he had to be playing with him. That an educated man would suggest, that he would even consider, that *this* was where his grandfather had headed to, was absurd.

"Surely, Sir Mongoya, he can't have gone to such a place. Now *please*, if you would just tell me where he is for time is already scarce…" He heard his tone growing more impatient and had to use every last bit of poise left in him. He was done with his theatrical nonsense and felt a sudden urge to shake the man like a puppet, till he told him what he knew – if he knew anything. He tightened his fist instead. Focused on the pain of his nails digging into his palms. They stood there for some moments. Glared at each other, much like two hungry dogs ready to get into a fight over a meaty bone.

"*Explain* your ignorance on the matter." Mongoya barked.

"As anyone with sense, I am aware the Parda is real…"

"That it is *real? Real?*" the words echoed through the room, his blue eyes as fiery as blue could get. "*The Parda* is more real than any other place you will *ever* step your feet upon." He rolled the map back together protectively – in a way that made Isaiah understand this was no trick. He wasn't having fun on his behalf, nor was he testing his current base of knowledge. The Great Master Mongoya was convinced his grandfather had enough interest in this forest to seek it. To this, Isaiah did not know what to say, and so he said nothing at all.

Instead, he stared into the air, with an urgency to both laugh and cry at the same time. It just couldn't be true, and surely this man, too, had to have gone mad with age. Both of them stood still in front of the table for a while, as the confused silence grew into an unpleasant one. It was finally broken by an "Oh", and as Mongoya turned towards him, Isaiah was surprised to see a wicked grin spread across his face, before he burst out laughing.

"*Now* I understand!" He held both his arms out, and Isaiah flinched back an inch as he almost hit him with his cane.

"Botany, cooking... *all things* uninteresting and dull. All things safe to hear and seemingly unproblematic to engage in."

"I don't unders—" He hushed him, unfinished with his stream of thoughts, and the loose ends that finally seemed to be untying in his mind.

"No – no, you don't *understand*. You don't understand even in *the slightest*. But I do, I see what has happened here. This is all just marvelous. *Awful* – but marvelous too." Isaiah wanted to ask for an explanation, for though he doubted he could fully trust anything leaving this wise man's mouth, he was still curious as to *what* he thought him not to understand. By now, he knew it happened to be a great many things.

It took a minute or two before Mongoya's almost soundless rambling slowed down, and when he re-composed himself, he hurried the map back up to his desk and returned with a serious expression.

"Whether you believe it or not, your grandfather has gone to the Parda. You can look for as long as you like anywhere else, but you will never find him. Very few have entered and less have come back alive. Sending an untrained individual as yourself would be reckless and foolish."

"I am ready to go there, Master. I am just surprised since... I was under the impression that the tales told about the Parda were... exaggerated." He wanted to say village lore but held his tongue.

"Whatever it is *you* have heard, are likely just that – *cock and bull stories* we call them here. Not necessarily even old ones and mostly just rubbish. All tales come from *somewhere*, though."

"I am ready to take the chances. Whatever might be the truth of it."

"The truth of it?" He asked – or rather – he shouted.

"No, no, you fool. You are by no means *ready* to go there. I don't care how skilled you believe yourself to be with a sword. How confident you feel in whatever other forests you've been to, or how well traveled you are…" Isaiah swallowed against the lump in his throat.

"Have you been there yourself, Master?" he asked, wanting to avoid the topic of his many, nonexistent accomplishments.

"Ha! Of course not, I don't do this sort of *labor*. I am a teacher. An academic that is here to provide guidance for the ones worthy of it."

"Could you teach me then? Like you taught the twelve?"

"As I told you before, even if you had *any* sort of potential – which I doubt you do – it's too late for it."

"So it is true. He did teach the twelve." Isaiah thought, and then he asked, "Is there any way I could prove my… potential to you?"

"Let me be clear. Even the ones who might be considered capable of entering the Parda, need proper preparation to have any chance in there. *You* are nowhere close to any of the ones who've gone before you, nor would you have the time to reach their competence."

"I don't care how dangerous it is. I *need* to go there. Please, Master, if you could just lend me the map, I promise to bring it back."

"*Lend you* the map? How many maps like these do you think exist? *One* - one map in the entire world, and if you think for a second, I would hand it over to you – less than a manling – then your grandfather's supposed madness has surely been inherited." From the mere tone of his voice – not as loud as before, but somehow more threatening – Isaiah knew he had overstepped. He should have known by the way he'd looked at it, but being at least as infuriated, he had to swallow the words he felt like saying. He calmed himself, hoping Mongoya's temper was of the hot, rather than the long-lasting kind.

"I apologize for overstepping, Master. Perhaps if you could just tell me the direction, so I could be on my way and leave you to your important work, Sir." He tried, in a tone so composed, he felt anyone would have thought him a noble man.

"No, no, *no* boy. You have this all wrong. Your ignorance on the matter is simply outrageous." He shook his head, seemingly frustrated, but underneath it, Isaiah sensed something very different – something curiously close to excitement.

"The Parda is not a place someone can just *show* you the way too, you need to know the way *to her* before you enter. What some might consider unexplainable things have happened there, and though one can never be prepared for any of them, one must know certain things not to go in completely blindfolded." He was back to lecturing now, his eyes glittering, and his anger just barely lurking under the surface of what Isaiah now saw as a pasty, soulless face.

"What sorts of things, Master?"

"There is no reason for a young man like yourself to know of such darkness. Better if you went back home while it might still be there." Perhaps for men like him, home was nothing but high walls and a too large, lonesome bed to sleep in. Perhaps he did not understand family since he did not have one, or perhaps he was just saying it to trigger him. Either way, this was not something he would tell him about. He would tell him exactly what he wanted to hear.

"I'll *do* anything if you teach me about the Parda, Master Mongoya."

"What would *you* have to offer *me, boy?*" His response was fast. So fast, Isaiah knew he'd prepared for it.

"To me, it seems you have everything you need, Master. But if anything said of the Parda is true, then I dare suggest that perhaps there's also a treasure inside?"

"You want to fetch me the supposed, ancient gold hidden in there, is that right?" Isaiah nodded eagerly.

"There is no such thing. That is just some childish cock and bull story. Besides – I can make my own gold. You should know that much."

"Of course, Master. As I said, I've been told you are a very skilled alchemist, which is why I didn't offer you the few gold coins I have, in exchange for the map. But perhaps then, there is something else in there of your liking? Rare plants..."

"Stop, stop – enough about *plants* now." He held both his hands up and twisted his head to one side to shake off his annoyance.

"I don't care for them. I am convinced there is something of value beyond gold in there."

"I will get it for you – whatever it might be." The Master looked like he was considering his proposal for a moment. But Isaiah knew he wasn't. He was much too clever. Too clever, not to know desperation when he saw it, and too wicked not to take advantage.

"I would have to spend hours and hours lecturing you... and you will more likely than not fail the mission and disappear..."

"I am the son of Ares. If anyone can find it, it will be *me*." For a flare of a second, something changed along the lines of the Master's face. It left as soon as it'd come, again being replaced by that immovable arrogance. Still, Isaiah had spotted it – and even if it hadn't been actual admiration, there was surely less disrespect there than his words revealed.

"Oh, do not get overly confident. Your father might have been the *last known* man to enter, but he too failed, just like the others, and *now*, too many people *fail* to talk about that fact."

"*Please, Master* – teach me." There was a long silence, before Raziel Mongoya finally said, "Huh." He sat down behind his desk, holding his hands together casually and studying some of his rings.

"Consider yourself privileged, boy, and don't you ever raise your voice at me again, understand?" Isaiah nodded, and though his expression was strict and serious, his eyes could not lie – not even from afar. It was quite obvious he was content, looking at him much like a child would look at a new toy. It seemed as if Raziel Mongoya owned him differently than any other master ever had.

CHAPTER TWENTY

EAVESDROPPERS AND RULE-BREAKERS

THE impossible plan became for Isaiah to learn everything he needed to know within a period of five days, with the initiation day counting as day zero. As the master had initially made a point out of, this was far too short, as well as far too long, if he was both to find his grandfather alive and come out in one piece. It might have seemed like a hopeless, if not an impossible quest altogether, but he had found Mongoya within a day of entering the city. He had convinced him to make him his student – though it hadn't been his initial intention – and so, there seemed to be a certain hope rising within him. Hope there perhaps was something guiding him. Something unseen that he couldn't touch or make sense of. Perhaps for the first time, he had something resembling true confidence and though it seemed to be of the naïve, childlike sort, he was committed to holding on to it as tightly as he could to get through the lessons.

Returning his mind to more realistic considerations, he reminded himself that his grandfather had left Delta no more than a day before himself. Adding to that, he and Cyra had ridden fast, and even if Nagár was a slight detour from the south, it seemed unlikely he had gotten much further than them. There was an actual possibility he was currently on his way to his old teacher. If so, he would be there waiting for him, which would undoubtedly be the most preferable solution to their troubles. On the less desirable spectrum of possibilities, he'd left his fear of horses behind and was already on his way over those vicious mountains. With this in mind, Isaiah had carefully suggested to the master it might be better to find him before he reached the Parda at all. To this, he'd replied that unless Isaiah knew how to go through all six routes leading through the mountains at once, that was the worst idea he'd ever heard, and if he ever mentioned such nonsense again, he would have him expelled. Nahbí was a place of many paths – so many, that finding *anyone* (and even more so someone as specific as a grandfather) could only be done by going directly to their final destination.

Despite his annoyance, Isaiah suspected he was perhaps right and had agreed he wouldn't leave before the final day. Just to be sure he would not get any similar "wild thoughts", Mongoya made him sign a contract. Being nothing but a large piece of paper, stating the terms the two of them had already agreed on, Isaiah had no objection to this and for the first time he signed "Isaiah Aronin" with big, proud letters.

Once everything had been formally settled and signed, the Master announced they were ready to start.

"You told me Theodore had taught you *some* of our modern history, correct?"

"He has, Master."

"Very well. It can't have been more than a fraction. It is about time you knew the truth of the events leading to the *revolution* in forty-four." Though he couldn't quite see what it had to do with the Parda, Isaiah felt ever so curious to hear about it from someone outside of the fortress (it was hardly among the most debated subjects, and often spoken of with a certain caution). The excitement shortly washed off, as Mongoya saw it necessary to first cover all of Araktéa's history. He was kept from asking about its relevance, as one of the Master's primary rules had been not to interrupt him. Slow hours went by before the old man paused. Isaiah got ready to speak but had to stop himself as his teacher placed one strict finger in front of his lips. He looked as if he was listening for something, but other than the wind carefully drumming a branch towards the window (no differently than it had done since he arrived), Isaiah couldn't hear a sound. Finally, Raziel moved his finger and pointed it towards the door. Nobody had knocked, but he kept on staring at it intently, and then turned impatiently towards Isaiah.

"Eavesdropper." He whispered, almost inaudibly from the top of his pendulum, then more exaggeratedly, but still silently, he gestured for him to open it. Isaiah walked, confused as to who would care to listen to a lecture – not to say, how Mongoya would've heard someone listening with his aging ears. He was surprised when he opened the door, for instead of an empty space of paranoia, it was a round pair of brown, frightened eyes that met his.

"Who's there?" the Master's voice echoed through the room, and Isaiah's mouth shaped into a questioning hole of a sort. He was ready to say something, but the young man sat down on his knees – clearly scared witless, silently begging for his silence.

"Nobody." He heard himself saying, then closed the door as he gave the boy a sharp look. He'd made him break the Master's second rule on day one – No lies.

"Is that so?" Isaiah shrugged. He still could have admitted to such a fresh lie perhaps, but he didn't want to be the reason a young boy lost his workstation – and less so an ear. This was of course no longer a legal practice in modern times but seeing Mongoya's preference for anything conservative, he sensed it wouldn't stop him.

"You must have heard the wind. It is quite wild today."

"I *know the wind* and it certainly doesn't sound anything like unwelcomed ears." Mongoya barked. "Since I am up here, and you have already checked, there seems to be no other option than for me to trust you." Isaiah felt relieved, surprised, and though certain lying had been the right thing to do in the situation, he even felt the slightest bit of guilt. Breaking a man's trust was not something to be taken lightly – especially a proud man like Mongoya. Luckily, he was much too eager to resume where he'd left off to notice the cracks in his iron.

"So, as I was saying, after King Amnos the second had been *removed*, the revolutionists decided to put one of their own on the throne. The issue, of course, was that he was just another *somewhat* charismatic individual that had led a dozen protests or so. In the spirit of victory, very dumb ideas can seem like very good ones you see, and thus everyone was convinced he'd be the ideal leader of the country. Can you guess what went wrong?" It was the first time he'd asked him a question regarding the actual lecture.

"Perhaps he wasn't fit to rule…"

"Obviously not – I already told you that. What exactly are the qualities that would make a man fit to rule? What makes him a good king?"

"I... I don't know, Master. Knowledge... Patience? Strength?" The Master glared down at him, impatient and unimpressed with these hopeful adjectives.

"And? Do you think this is all?"

"I apologize, my knowledge of our kings is not very broad, Master."

"The only thing we should ever *care* to learn from our kings, is hidden in their mistakes – so you're not a complete fool for not knowing of them. The idea of a man being strong is an ancient way of thinking, boy. Only primitive tribal men need physical strength to lead. What a *real* king needs to succeed is a mind sharp as a sword, and most importantly he must be *strategic*. The revolutionists all thought themselves to be strategists, and this was reaffirmed when they overturned the realm, but once this was done, they only saw what they wanted to see. They were not able to admit to themselves; they'd merely been *lucky*. They also ignored the fact that they had made a mess out of things. Do you understand the mess they caused, boy?"

"A great many people died, Master." Isaiah tried, not wanting to suggest any number.

"*Thousands*. But I am mostly talking about the destruction. People are born all the time – gross masses of them." He said, clearly disgusted. "Ancient buildings – and books – are *irreplaceable*. And that is what made it not only bad but unforgivable." He thought it to be a very sinister point of view, but kept quiet.

"Don't you have questions?" Isaiah took a breath. He couldn't appear disengaged, and so he asked what he'd felt the most puzzled about.

"Forgive me, Master, but I've been under the impression that you were among the ones *wanting* the revolution to happen." He was underplaying this, of course, for what he'd been told was that Raziel Mongoya had been one of its main advocates. Hearing this, the Master's face turned red, and Isaiah was certain he'd poked another nerve he should've never had gotten close to.

"I will only forgive you for this mindless assumption because it's a common one." He spit.

"I *condemned* it. The old realm was far from perfect, the Amnos rulers usually not as wise as one would wish, and the system insufficient in a great many ways. Still, change is not something one must aim for in itself. One must have a straight vision of where one is going with it. That was my intent with my writings and lectures. It seemed that I overestimated my students' brightness, not to mention *their patience*. In only a few weeks' time, they'd made a mockery out of me and speared my good reputation. Your grandfather too - not to mention *your grandmother*. Elora was among the worst of them – *but* she has paid for her sins and I no longer carry any resentment towards her. Worry not..." Isaiah's grandmother had given birth to Ares the very same day the revolutionists had taken over the city. She'd died in labor and Isaiah had oftentimes wondered how it would have been like to have her around growing up. Though his grandfather spoke little of her, and had always seemed content just being the two of them, he was sure *she* had been the love of his life and not some strange forest.

"Did you know her well, Master?" He was hesitant to ask, but knew it might be the only chance he'd ever get to know something about her, other than the fact she'd had fiery, red hair and a laugh that could make almost any crowd stand up and dance.

"She was my student." Mongoya responded plainly. "One of my better ones, I must admit. A bit of a wild card... tremendous ideas, clever but way too impulsive. Poor Theodore had a hard time keeping up with her. I never quite understood how they came together in the first place – a very *unlikely* couple."

"My grandfather loves playing cards..." Isaiah said, and the Master made something of a frowning chuckle.

"Does he now?"

"I believe they were happy together."

"Happiness... such a misunderstood concept." He sighed.

"Is it?" He felt odd discussing such things with him, but he was interested to know more about his family – even if he would never be able to meet any of them.

"Both of them were ready for change and hungry for truth, but different parts of it. Elora was always more fond of the *pleasures* in life. She loved the parties and the spirit this city once cradled. Not to say spreading the youth's revolutionary ideas. Theodore took his studies more seriously, far more reasonable – most of the time. I told him early on 'that woman will always be reckless, and you will always be *too* patient with her.'" Isaiah felt surprised he knew so much about his grandparents. He could almost picture it, the two of them – young and promising in what they thought would be a new and better Araktéa. He hoped Robert was right. That it wasn't too late.

"Brighten up now, Elora was happy enough while she lived. She walked these streets as if she owned them – back when there was still space for such pretentiousness. She wouldn't have enjoyed this world she participated in making." Mongoya cleared his throat.

"Anyhow – enough about this personal nonsense and let us move on to my favorite subjects: the three-day king, and how the Amnos family came back to power after his tyranny."

*

When his first lesson finally came to an end, the giant clock on the wall appeared to be just past midnight. After abruptly declaring himself done, Mongoya had handed him a book. He'd told him to read it, and then he'd left the room wordlessly. The title said "The Early History of Araktéa", and despite the agony of having to read, and the exhaustion from listening to Mongoya's voice for almost a whole day, Isaiah felt content to at least be spending the night indoors. His host had said nothing about where he would sleep, and in lack of options, he made his way to the sofa. It was made of a dark purple velour. Narrow, stiff and clearly not made for anything other than sitting up very straight. He thought it would still be more comfortable than laying on the ground, but somehow this wasn't the case.

Coming to terms with the furniture's impractical design, he decided to start reading his curriculum – thinking there couldn't be anything better to bring him to sleep. He reread the same three pages thrice with little more comprehension than if it'd been a different language entirely. This cycle was finally interrupted by the door being pushed open. It was pushed as silently as a door of the sort possibly could and left him holding his breath. First, he pretended to be asleep (not wanting a conversation or confrontation if it could be avoided). Only when hearing the sound of something larger than a cane being dragged over the floor, he opened his eyes. He just barely dared to turn his head to peek, but when he did – half expecting to see a ghost of some sort – he felt relieved to see it was a boy, no – *the* boy, standing on top of a ladder leaning towards one of the grand shelves.

"What are you doing?" The boy gasped, then turned around so abruptly he got close to falling. Regaining his balance, he was quick to rush down the fifteen steps of the wooden ladder.

"I'm sorry for startling you!" Isaiah said as he sat up.

"No, no. It's fine. I am just surprised you are... still in here." Isaiah noticed how much taller he was now that he was no longer on his knees. Tall and lean, narrower over the shoulders than himself, yet not skinny. His posture straight, his black west open but his linen shirt nicely tied in a loose hanging bow.

"And I am surprised that you are... *here.*"

"Yes. I'm so terribly sorry, Sir. I thought he would have placed you somewhere...more comfortable. I will leave you to rest now." He said, turning away and then looking at him again, "First, I would like the opportunity to thank you – for earlier, that is." Once again, he felt awkward being addressed as Sir, but took the opportunity to use the heightened position.

"Were you eavesdropping before?" The boy, or rather – the young man only slightly older than himself if he were to guess, was about to say something but then stopped himself.

"I was. I *beg* of you, Sir – it took a great deal of trouble for my family to send me here. Please, don't tell him. I'm just a chef with an inconvenient and distasteful curiosity."

"I won't," Isaiah assured him, "but may I ask why?"

"*Why?*" the boy said, sudden disbelief spreading across his sculpted face. In the dimly lit room, his skin looked darker than it had earlier. Not as dark or as illuminating as Tara's, but as if it'd been touched by cinnamon and honey.

"Master Mongoya is the most brilliant academic who ever lived. Unfortunately, he doesn't teach anymore – at least that's what I thought until today. You've been *most* fortunate, Sir!" Isaiah shrugged his shoulders, feeling fatigue come over him.

"I guess that's one way to see it."

"It is said he hasn't had a single student for a great many years. You've been *extremely* fortunate. As have I, as I might finally get to hear some of his last ones?" He bravely suggested.

"I could ask him if you could join us..." The boy shook his head hard at this, his dark, shoulder long curls falling across his face.

"You must either be joking, or you are quite foolish for someone so clever, Sir." Isaiah looked at him, surprised by the sudden change in his tone. It was almost playful, and yet he was not sure if he'd just insulted or complimented him.

"Clever you say?"

"Not just anyone could convince the Great Master to teach him. I might not be quite so clever myself, but enough to know that he'd never even consider a simple chef worthy of his lectures."

"I am to find him some sort of treasure in return...and I probably just got lucky. He still hasn't even told me what it is..." He remembered. Hopefully, he would reveal more the next day.

"If you believe you were *merely* lucky, then perhaps you're not so clever after all."

"Should I be insulted?" Isaiah asked, mostly jokingly. He knew it was the iron face that had gotten him there, but that would've been a very strange thing to say. It was gone now anyhow. He was tired, and it seemed oddly unnecessary to wear it with this young chef.

"That depends. Do you prefer to be clever or just lucky? A clever man wouldn't allow himself to be offended, but a lucky man might – at least occasionally." He suggested.

"Which do you think would serve me better here?" The boy's eyes lightened up as he took a brief moment to think.

"Obviously as I'm not enough of either, I couldn't possibly tell you." He concluded, though Isaiah wasn't convinced it came from a place of humility.

"If I was in fact *clever*, I would say you were the lucky one of us, seeing I didn't tell you earlier." The boy nodded to this, suddenly more serious.

"That would be true, and seeing that you now have a lucky, as well as very grateful man at your service – it was also very clever on your behalf."

"You owe me nothing..." Isaiah said, his tone putting an end to the foolish ramble.

"But I do, Sir." He insisted, "In fact, I believe I owe you both my ears."

"I don't think I'll need either of your..." Isaiah stopped himself.

"How long have you been here for?" he asked.

"Four years."

"And seen away from cooking, your task is...rearranging the shelves at night?" The boy moved his light feet around while tilting his head from side to side.

"You could say I am doing some... self-study while I'm here. The master hasn't really told me that I can't, but..."

"Your secret remains safe." Isaiah said, not seeing what sort of damage it could possibly do for some servant boy to know things. In fact – quite on the contrary.

"Thank you once again, Sir – Do you mind me calling you Sir?"

"Isaiah would be better."

"Isaiah it is then, Devus Donovan at your service." He smiled broadly, exposing perfectly white teeth and taking his hand to his heart as he made a light bow.

"Devus, I might need your ears after all."

"I thought you might." Devus grinned, and Isaiah thought there might be a chance he could actually get something out of these lectures.

CHAPTER TWENTY-ONE

SON'S OF LEGENDS

AFTER having received an impressively detailed summary of "The early history of Araktéa" (which Devus had read three years earlier), Isaiah ended up sleeping in an unoccupied bed in his chambers. His room, placed on the third floor, was small and humble compared to the rest of the house, but had a good view of the tulip garden and an overall decent standard. As the sun woke him the next morning, he ran to the lecture hall, just to wait for the Master for an hour while trying to rehearse what Devus had taught him. When Mongoya at last arrived, he had no questions for him, and said nothing of the Parda that day either. Nor did he the next day. Adding to this, each time he felt he'd gained some understanding of whatever subject was being taught, Master Mongoya changed it to something else. He went through a wide variety of topics. A great deal of things and events he'd never even heard of before. All far less intriguing than stories from the fortress. His only comfort during these lengthy hours was that Devus was right outside the door listening, so that when the evening came, he would summarize them.

On the third night, each of them flickered through the pages of the two new books he'd been assigned. Devus on the menacing sofa, and Isaiah on the midnight blue floor, as the clock approached the first hour of the following day.

"I just don't understand – what in Araktéa does things like sculpting styles in these 'golden ages' and bird quitters have to do with me going to the Parda?" Isaiah asked.

"I don't know about the birds but in Dabár, we're taught that the Parda is the only man-made forest in the world. Due to this, some consider it a piece of art as much as nature." Mongoya had explained to him how important the arts had once been. How painters, writers and performers had been cherished "back when the aristocracy had taste, tact, and true wealth". He'd come fairly close to showing him his own collection of canvases, but Isaiah had managed to distract him, so he wouldn't catch Devus as he ran down the hallway.

"Who was the man who made it?" Isaiah asked.

"The Parda? Many did – men and women together. The first humans that came here long before us, in ancient times..."

"Were they sorcerers, then? Is that the reason that it's supposedly *enchanted*?" he smirked, wishing he had not asked that question.

"No." Devus said, closing the book firmly.

"The tribal people in the north, the Agátis, tell us they came from another world. That they were like gods there and could fly like birds and breathe underwater like fish. There, they had carriages made of metals and lighting that could bring them around faster than even our best horses. They could communicate with each other even when they were miles apart. All of this power, they left behind to come here, and all the knowledge has vanished..."

"Were they also made out of stars and glowed like jewels?" Devus thought for a moment.

"I don't know, but your tone is suggesting you don't believe in it."

"Sounds like village lore to me." Isaiah shrugged.

"And maybe it is. I'm yet to find literature here that confirms any of it, but sorcery and magick is very real, Isaiah." Devus' eyes seemed to measure him oddly, as if just then discovering he had a third eye on his forehead. He almost felt it himself. A strange pressure that seemed to heathen the space between his eyebrows.

"I'll believe it when I see it." He said. Having more than enough on his mind already, he figured he'd be better off not entertaining the idea of its existence at all.

"The Parda will make just about anyone a believer."

"Would you ever go there yourself?" Isaiah asked, thinking of his father, of Tzelem, and the twelve. They had all entered despite the risk.

Searching for treasures, knowledge – secrets perhaps – while all he wanted to find in there was his family.

"Possibly."

"What do *you* think it's hiding? What's this treasure I am to find?" Devus looked at him with a wordless, unreadable expression. "The only thing the Master has told me to bring back is water, and he wouldn't say anything more of it." He continued.

"Though I might owe you my ears and my knowledge, Isaiah, telling you more about the Parda would be no favor done to you." His tone was uncharacteristically strict, as he turned his gaze up towards the tall ceiling. Tiny and large flowers. Perfect circles of blue, black and silver symmetry.

"So, you *do* know?"

"As I've told you, I haven't gone there myself..."

"All the stories I've heard seem out of this world... None of them are true, are they? They can't be." Devus sighed.

"Do you at least know more than these books of his? Mongoya tells me to read between the lines to prepare, but it's useless..." Devus took a deep breath and looked at him hesitantly. Biting his lip. At last he said, "My father is one of the twelve." Isaiah raised his eyebrows at this, looking for a hint of a joke that often accompanied their sessions. But he was grave serious.

"I grew up listening to the lesson that he and the other survivors brought with them – from both the academy *and* the Parda. It wasn't until I was older, he told me they'd gone there themselves, and that they were training us so that someday, we might do the same."

"Did he... did he not go mad afterwards?" Devus shrugged.

"Madness is relative. He might have changed, I wouldn't know in which way, but my father is a good man."

"The Master..."

"Does not know who I am, and he can't know. Even telling you is... I shouldn't have." He got up from the sofa in a rapid, distressed movement. Then he turned. "You see, people will expect you to be a certain way, and I am not. I am just a cook who likes to read. That's it."

"I can imagine how it feels." Isaiah said. With the vocabulary of a noble and the wits of a merchant, he'd already suspected Devus was more than just the Dabárian villager he'd portrayed himself to be.

"Sorry for keeping the truth from you. I just don't want there to be any talk about it in the city. I will need to ask you to keep this to yourself." He remembered what Archilai had told him of their culture of honesty. Keeping something so essential to himself for three whole days, was proof enough Devus was not your typical Dabárian. Isaiah considered telling him about his own father, as Devus didn't seem to have overheard this part of his first meeting with Mongoya.

"It's alright." He said instead, deciding it was perhaps enough confessions for one night. Devus nodded, eager to resume on the original topic.

"The Parda, among many things, is notoriously known to be a place of ancient treasures, but it is more importantly a place of secrets. It will often tell you a very personal story... It even made the northerners that went there believe, certain things are better kept within their own memories."

"So, your father never told you what happened there?"

"I've been told no more than what he's been told to tell me. For the most part..."

"And what is the wildest story you've ever heard?" Devus hesitated for a moment.

"Nothing of my father's, but there have been rumors stating there is a tree of truth there. It sees all this world's past and current events and has the memory and eyes of every seed ever planted in Araktéa. It catches people and forces them to listen to their own truth. It then keeps them trapped until they... eventually kill themselves – most times." Devus shook his head as to steer away from the thought.

"Can every person's truth possibly be that terrible?" Isaiah asked, and Devus' lips tightened.

"You asked for a story, Isaiah. That's what it is. One that none of my teachers have confirmed."

"None of the ones who came out alive..." Isaiah thought, but then hushed the thought away and resumed with his reading.

"I'm tired." Devus announced, though he did not seem as such. He then walked out on light feet and closed the door. That large, heavy door that seemed to want to keep the entire world out.

The next morning, Devus was back to his usual spirit and over the next few days, they developed a routine of browsing through the numerous books in the lecture hall (trying to find more specific information than Mongoya's curriculum provided). With Devus explaining the essence of both the lectures and the books, Isaiah ended up understanding slightly more than nothing at all. Just enough to feel a shade more enlightened about the world. They slept late and got up early, and when both their heads were too tired to think of large, worldly matters, they spoke of smaller ones. Small things that seemed to find a natural place in that large, empty room under the dim yellow light of its five lanterns. The kind that flows easily when your mind has no strength to reconsider or keep words entangled.

"Where are the other servants? Other than Julius I never see any of them unless they're bringing in food – not even in the halls." Isaiah asked on the fourth night.

"They mostly stay in another part of the house. Mongoya is only *one* man and eats for no more than half a woman. I don't even think he eats my food at all, but the other servants do. At least they enjoy complaining about it."

"What does he eat then?" Devus shrugged, laying on the sofa with a heavy book on his chest. Allowing his mind to select and perfectly recall the pages that might matter someday.

"And how did you even get to work here? His nephew told me he never hired anyone new. The rest of his servants seem... well-established here."

"Oh, you wouldn't believe me..."

"Tell me." Isaiah demanded. Devus sighed.

"I showed up at the gates and brought some cake for the guard."

"And?"

"That's it. You'd be surprised how persuasive the sweet taste of Dabárian cake can be. I had false papers with me of course. Devus *Donovan*, a name I'm yet to have had any use for before meeting you."

"And he brought you in? He gave you a room just like that?"

"Well, no – Julius convinced the Master to take me in." Isaiah looked at Devus, and when he realized he was not joking, he burst out laughing. It was a loud, broad laugh, spreading from a place deep inside his gut, and he couldn't have stopped if he'd tried. Devus laughed too, nearly as uncontrollably, realizing how long it'd been since he'd done so.

"So, here I am. Not even the Master's chef in truth – I just cook for his pet. His precious, guard dog." He managed to utter, and when they'd finally managed to calm themselves down, they were both teary eyed.

"Don't you ever feel alone here?" Isaiah asked after a while.

"No. It's been terrific. In the north, people talk breathlessly. Everything is *loud*. Here, I finally got some time to read undisturbed…"

"Sorry for interrupting." Isaiah said.

"After four years a little interruption is much welcomed. I finally have someone to discuss the work with. Holding on to all these ideas and knowledge feels a little maddening sometimes." He confessed. The truth was he'd been starting to feel an overbearing boredom creeping in on him the past months. A heavy stagnation he'd never thought would reach him with this current abundance of literature. The very sort that could make a man, and perhaps specifically a man like himself, make bold and even reckless decisions.

"Why doesn't he teach anymore? Mongoya is old, but he seems to have no problem lecturing nine to eleven hours a day." Isaiah wondered.

"My father claims it is due to all the students that died during the revolution – that he feared his teachings would bring about another one."

"But you don't." It was more a statement than a question, and taking a breath as to think, Devus looked at him with his large eyes. Humorless now.

"I think my father believes it to be true. But after all these years, I can't say I believe he would stop talking for the sake of the youth's sanity. Master Mongoya is the kind of man that teaches purely out of his own pleasure." After four days, Isaiah was still confused as to Devus's true opinion of him. Usually he praised his genius, and so he hadn't complained about him as much as he'd liked to. Still, he could sense a certain loathing in his tone and Devus was certainly no fool.

"I am leaving the day after tomorrow." Isaiah said, changing the subject to something he realized was much more urgent. "He hasn't told me anything *real* about the Parda yet."

"I wish I could tell you something that would calm your nerves…"

"You could. Your father went, and you told me they've basically groomed you, so you could go there yourself someday." He said, failing to hide the sudden annoyance coming over him. Except for making the topics of the lectures much more comprehensive, he was no more helpful in this regard than the Master himself. He had thought he would come around. That something might be a slip of the tongue, but he'd been as silent as a fortress morning.

"My father has spoken of his journey *going* there, and he has told me about the aftermath. But as I've told you, next to nothing about his time inside. If you must, you can read the book Master Mongoya wrote based on their descriptions – I won't be able to tell you anything more." Devus had mentioned this book already, and though it was considered the most (if not the only) academic book on the Parda, he'd assured him there was really no good reason for him to read it.

"I had... an insight before coming here." Isaiah said with some hesitation and Devus looked at him expectantly. "I saw the Master speaking with my grandfather. He was holding a book..."

"And you think this is the one?"

"It might be." Devus sighed.

"If this insight was more than just imaginative, I doubt this is the book you saw."

"Why is that?" Devus covered his face with his hands, then looked at him – clearly frustrated with all the sudden questions. It was too late for this. Too late for proper discernment and not spilling the many things he needed to keep to himself.

"Because there's another book. One my father told me about just before I left."

"About the Parda?" Devus nodded.

"Then why are we wasting our time reading about all these other things – let's find it!"

"I looked for it for years..."

"It must be on one of the higher shelves! Why haven't you mentioned this before?"

"It isn't. And because I knew it would misdirect your focus. There's so much exclusive information the Master is gifting you. Even if I can't explain exactly why it's relevant..."

"This book, Devus. I *need* the book if I am to stand a chance."

"It's not here." He said firmly, and after Isaiah had suggested numerous other places it might be hidden – ways they might be able to climb the shelves without making a mess of things, Devus gave him a grave look.

"Unless the Master shows it to you, it is not for you to read." On this note, the conversation came to an end and shortly after, they went to bed. But even in his last minutes of awareness, he couldn't keep it from his mind. Somehow, and for some reason, he needed this book.

At last came the final day of lectures, and after a whole night of contemplating on the book and what it might withhold, Isaiah found some courage within his tireless aggravation. As Master Mongoya entered (twenty minutes later than scheduled), he stood up a little taller than what felt natural. Then, after bowing respectfully, as he'd made a habit of doing, he attempted some variation of a poised expression.

"Master, I appreciate everything you have taught me about Araktéa so far. But I feel I know very little as to what to expect inside the Parda, and I fear I won't be able to find this water you wish me to bring you." It was no proper way to start their day, but he had better chances of receiving a reply before giving Mongoya a chance to speak.

"You do know very little." He responded plainly, looking at him with a blank expression as he made his way past him.

"I was under the impression you were going to prepare me to go there. This is our last day of lectures and…"

"The only thing you can expect to see in the Parda is the unexpected. The only way to survive her is through pain. Pain is the toughest of teachers – and the only one that will take you *anywhere*." The last words he said almost as a reassurance (If he had thought *him* strict, he'd better think again). Isaiah swallowed hard, noticing his current teacher looking slightly more tired today. The Master continued, "I must say, you've been more persistent than I believed you would be. But if I haven't sufficiently scared you yet, *she* will. I've seen the most tactful, educated, and fearless of men, come out speechless and with their minds crumbled to strange fairy-dust." "How odd that he keeps calling it a she." Isaiah thought, but then again, the Master said many odd things.

"I do not mind not speaking for a while, Master Mongoya." He replied. At this, the old man chuckled in a slightly different pitch than usual, revealing a new shade of intensity in his eyes Isaiah hadn't seen before. Only a fool would've believed it to be admiration, for there was no possibility Master Mongoya would admire a boy that knew as little as himself. Yet, it looked oddly similar, and so, for a brief second, he allowed himself to believe it was. He measured him for a while with this strange gaze before finally breaking the silence.

"You would do anything for your grandfather, wouldn't you?" He said, so uncharacteristically slow, Isaiah felt the hair on his neck rising.

"Of course I would." He responded, feeling he had no reason trying to convince him of this fact any further. The old man nodded, stretched his neck and looked down on his cane.

"Well then. I believe we are done here. Use today to reflect upon everything I've taught you. You'll depart in the morning." With those words, and without even reaching the stairs of his pendulum, the Master left him. Isaiah worried he would discover Devus behind the door, but fortunately he wasn't there.

It was only in the late evening he walked, grinning and his eyes were carrying their usual excitement, he also looked a little sleep-deprived.

"I went looking for you. Mongoya cancelled today's lecture." Isaiah said, having spent the whole day trying to make sense of the books they'd found the previous evening. One titled "A Traveler's Guide to the South" and another "Ancient Ways to Light a Fire". Neither taking part of his curriculum, and both seemingly of more relevance than the ones that did.

"He passed by the kitchen this morning, so I worried he might be watching me. He never shows his face around there…"

"Well, I might finally have learned how to light a fire in the meanwhile." Isaiah said, closing the book and standing up. He searched through the pocket of Robert's west and pulled out the small, green bag Lord Huxley had gifted him. He'd nearly forgotten all about the gold and had only some days prior realized that Tara had placed it in an inner pocket she'd sewn while his clothes were drying.

"For all your help." He said, feeling he owed Devus much more than just gold. The boy lifted his eyebrows while opening it.

"Your grandfather never taught you about economics either, did he?" Devus' eyes widened as he weighed the four coins in his hand.

"I couldn't... It is too much."

"You can. Gold won't allow me to enter where I'm heading... At least, do me the favor of keeping them safe for me till I'm back?" Devus smiled, shaking his curly head in disbelief.

"Alright, but I do expect you to come back for them."

"I will. I've signed a contract after all and dying would conflict with the Great Master's wishes." Isaiah smiled, a real, effortless smile. It seemed the guard dog's chef had somehow managed to teach him that too, though his own was not as present right then.

"Alright." Devus said, placing the coins back in the bag, and inside his own pocket.

"How long are you staying? Why are you really here, Devus?" With all the time they'd spent together, Isaiah was yet to ask him this. And from the look on his face, it didn't seem like something he wanted to answer. He might have told him part of the truth, but there was something more. There was always something more.

"I'm here to find some missing pieces, that's all. Books are banned from Dabár, you see..." He explained.

"You don't have any books at all?"

"No educational ones. Only hero tales, cock and bull stories..."

"Poetry?" Isaiah asked, and Devus shrugged.

"Yes, but our people mostly prefer to sing." Isaiah remembered Byron's reaction to his poem – Timotheus and his songs, and suddenly that dreadful night made more sense to him. "I'll never be a poet," he thought, and it didn't sting him the way it'd done a few weeks back. It seemed he'd come to terms with the irrelevance of it.

"Where I grew up it was the other way around. No tales. No poetry or songs – just plain, good facts." He explained, and it just then occurred to him, that perhaps that had been his problem all along. Why his imagination had always felt so limited whenever he'd tried writing.

"My father says truth is found in a place in between tales and facts. That's where true wisdom is, and he seemed to think it's hidden here." Devus held his arms out, and they both looked up at the countless books. Reading all of them, with all the sentences and the lines in between them, would take half a lifetime if you were fast.

"Your father is not fond of the new Academy either, then?"

"He's convinced they're corrupted and only teach their students pointless nonsense." Isaiah's heart skipped a beat.

"There's... corruption here in Nagár?" He asked, and with this Devus looked at him gravely as he said (to this peculiar boy whom he still wasn't sure if knew absolutely nothing or had all the answers he needed). "This is where it was born, Isaiah."

CHAPTER TWENTY-TWO

DEPARTURE

IN the morning, his last morning in that soft, borrowed bed, Isaiah felt alert from the moment the sun met his eyelids. Despite a vague remembrance of some coal-black, suffocating nightmare, reality (though brighter) seemed even grimmer. He wasn't ready for the Parda or any of the roads that lead to it. He wasn't even ready to be on his way out of the city, and yet he had to leave. Looking over at Devus, still asleep in that strange, corpse-like position of his, he considered inviting him. It was not the first time the idea had crossed his mind, but once again it seemed a selfish invitation. He didn't want him to feel he'd tried buying him off with the gold, and so, when his study partner (or perhaps his teacher in a sense) woke up, he tried to seem calmer than he felt.

"Have you figured out how you'll get there yet? You should perhaps bring at least one coin to buy a decent horse, some matches and..." Devus said, moments after having opened his eyes.

"No, I'll have to get Indra back." Isaiah was quick to reply. The very idea of riding a new horse made his stomach twist like a wet, ragged cloth.

"Well then, the guards are fools. If you can't manage to trick them, you should stay *far* away from the Parda anyways." Isaiah smirked, pulling his shirt on. Or rather, the one Devus had lent him. Slightly, if not very, more convenient for his journey.

"Oh, and make sure you watch out for the fire rain on your way." Devus added.

"Fire rain?" He turned towards him, and as always Devus' eyes smiled before his lips did.

"You should be more skeptical of what people tell you." Isaiah rolled his eyes – mostly at himself. Naïve. When had he become this naïve?

"Perhaps the Master's paranoia has brushed off on you." Devus said, reading his mind just a little.

"Or maybe your superstitions have," Isaiah suggested. Devus frowned at this, walking over to the small window where the sun arose in bright orange. The golden illumination made the army of tulips even more spectacular than usual. Isaiah was somewhat saddened by the fact he hadn't gotten to spend any time there. He'd been too timid (and possibly too cautious) to ask, and since Mongoya wasn't one to offer such things, it'd been left undone.

"I was just joking." He said, feeling Devus was being awfully quiet.

"Trust your own senses, Isaiah. That is the best advice I can give you." He said, without turning his attention from the window.

"Ever since leaving home, I've been nothing but skeptical of what people tell me... I think it might finally be time to trust someone." He was a little surprised by his own words. Yet, he couldn't help but feel he meant them as more than just some chivalrous, departure flattery. Devus turned at this. Looked down, suddenly almost as shy as he'd been those first, brief seconds of them meeting.

"I wish you the best of luck. I feel certain you'll find what you're looking for."

"Thank you."

"He chose you because you're special. Please try believing me when that's regarded too." Isaiah felt Mongoya had chosen him because he might have seemed his only chance to fetch this strange water. And possibly because he, deep down, underneath his cold exterior, didn't want his long gone student to die. Though far less certain about the importance of the latter, he hoped there was at least some truth to it. That there was more humanness to him than what met the eye and ear.

"I should go down and talk to the Master before I leave." Devus nodded distantly, and Isaiah couldn't help but feeling he was acting strange. A different kind of strange than usual. Then again, departing from someone who might not come back was indeed a time for strangeness, if any. He felt strange too, but he hadn't felt quite like himself since arriving there. Exactly who he had felt like he wasn't too certain of, but it was as if he'd lost himself inside the lectures. Become a student and nothing more. A role to play just to prepare for yet another one.

"I'll come back." He reassured him (though it was a ridiculous promise). When he gave no answer, he left him standing there by the window, where Devus would still be scouting down as Isaiah walked away from the grand building that no longer felt particularly safe.

Isaiah had assumed he'd need to walk all the way to the city center, so to state he was simply surprised when Indra stood waiting for him as he and Master Mongoya walked towards the gates, would've been a serious understatement.

"I have a horse you can use." Mongoya said matter-a-factly, pointing his cane towards her, as if it wasn't obvious where the magnificent animal was standing. She wore the same gear and carried his pack on the right side of her saddle.

"How...?" Isaiah stuttered.

"Some believe keeping a Zura horse against its will is bad luck. The guards sent her to me to decide what to do with her - poor fools do not understand the difference between alchemy and sorcery..." He explained, waving his hand and rolling his eyes. "Apparently, some *primitive*, bear-clothed tribal man came riding into the city the other day... anyways – you can have her - *if* you dare." For a moment Isaiah considered telling him the truth, as he was rather proud of his little scheme. But no – though he'd sworn his honesty to him, certain secrets were better kept, and so he gave a short bow and thanked him instead – just as a humble student ought to.

"Consider it a gift. A symbol or perhaps a reminder of our *agreement*. I've marked her with my sigil, so the guards won't ask any questions when you ride out." Isaiah nodded subtly. Now it seemed he owed him even more. Perhaps he even wanted to scare him into thinking, he might be riding a cursed horse that was under his alchemist-control. He felt relieved and safer as he climbed her – knowing exactly who's back he was on.

"I will do my best to return shortly, Master Mongoya. My grandfather and I will be seeing you soon." There was an odd twitch that crossed the Master's face, and brushing it off with a movement he said, "I made a simple copy of the map for you yesterday. You may consider this *a loan* and an indication as to where you are, rather than an accurate explanation of it. Araktéa has changed over the years." He pointed to an additional pack he'd hung on the other side of the saddle, then looked at him motionlessly. His skin was pale. So pale, it seemed it would crumble or burn if he was to stay outside for much longer. "There's also two water flasks in there – refill them and leave the horse before you enter." These were Raziel Mongoya's final commands, before turning around and walking back to his shell. No wise message for his student to untangle, very little hope inside that void in his chest and yet it seemed something had reawakened deep inside of him. Something that had been lost and numbed for a very long time.

*

On his way to the gates, which surrounding-area luckily was less crowded than the last time he'd passed them, Isaiah went to see Robert and Alice. Though perhaps not directly concerned about him, he felt he at the very least owed telling them about his whereabouts – as well as the fine garments Robert had lent him.

"Well, if it isn't Sir Iron mask himself?" Robert's face lit up seeing the boy at his door. He embraced him (an action rather unpredicted by both of them) and then led him to the living room where they'd first been introduced. Since then, Isaiah had used any minute he could spare looking for past indications of his grandfather's supposed obsession with the Parda. Making no more sense than it had before, he still felt more certain than ever this was where he was. At least enough to risk his life to find out. Trying to explain this to a chemist didn't turn out as he'd hoped. If anything, it sounded even more ridiculous said out loud than it had inside his head. When he couldn't think of anything else to say, Robert uttered some discontent mumbling.

"They say the twelve believed themselves *destined* to find this gold. I didn't think you were that sort of man, Isaiah. I still can't seem to think that you are..."

"I am not doing it for some gold, Sir Robert. I am doing it to find him. Even your uncle doesn't seem to believe there's any gold in there, he just wants me to bring some water..."

"Regardless of what he wants you to find, my uncle always has his own agenda. You might feel *destined* by him taking you in as his student – for all I know you might even be special for convincing him to do so. I'll admit, it was strange how he actually didn't seem to... detest you. It took me by surprise – no offense to your persona..." Robert said, holding up one finger. Isaiah noticed how their hands looked much the same. His were clearly much younger and they only bore one ring (the golden kind used in marriage in Nagár). Even so, it revealed a family resemblance Robert's hatred couldn't erase, unless he'd had them cut off.

"We've made an agreement. I don't know how *just* it was, but at least I know where to look. This has nothing to do with being destined for anything... I just want my grandfather back." Isaiah said, slightly offended by his lack of support. He hadn't expected Robert to be particularly pleased by the idea, but he'd at least wanted some of his encouraging words to bring with him on the journey.

"You do realize, he has *nothing* to lose and everything to gain by sending you in there?"

"I do." Robert shook his head in disapproval.

"I need to do this, Sir Robert. I'm sorry." Isaiah said, with no more time to convince him of a decision that had already been made.

"I told you not to let him get to your head, Isaiah."

"I haven't. Please understand, I *must* go now."

"You do." Robert said thoughtfully, his hand resting over his forehead as he got up from his seat.

"You've signed a contract with him. Whatever you do now, you cannot break it. Your situation is a hopeless one, I do not know what else to tell you... Our door is of course still open for you *if* you come back." This pessimism sounded far more alarming coming from him, than from his uncle's more dramatic lips. They struck through his chest, and he felt he had to physically force himself up from the sofa.

"Thank you for all your help." He said, realizing it might be the last time they'd see each other. Robert just shook his head with a saddened smile.

"I'm not so sure I've helped you, boy..."

* * *
*

As Isaiah rode south through new fields, he thought of Robert's grim warning. He thought of *all* the problematic variables of his mission, and in the cluster, he came to discover a whole other layer adding to the problem. As he imagined the different ways and places where he might encounter his grandfather on the way, it seemed impossible to imagine any sort of sensible conversation occurring between them. Having no more power in changing the old man's will than before, he had little certainty – or even faith – he'd suddenly listen to sense. As Tara had said, with his current mind, he couldn't convince him, and so perhaps there wouldn't be any humane way of bringing him back.

A moon span ago, such realizations would've made him give up on the quest. That, as well as Robert's daunting words, would've made him run back home, hoping he'd returned and found a way to fix himself — hoping he could talk to Mongoya and have him free him from their contract. Somehow, being on the sort of mission that had seemed impossible for some time, with the unlikeliness of both his shallow preparations – and knowledge – these things became less relevant. Simply details he couldn't be bothered with. Instead, he focused on the hope he'd seen in Devus' eyes and that momentary flare of respect he thought he'd spotted in Mongoya's. Even if they were both delusional in their expectations, he came to terms with that being so himself, might just be the only way he could get there. To the end of the world, after the path would split in two after the vicious, unnamed mountains.

CHAPTER TWENTY-THREE

THIEVES AND INTRUDERS

IN the two first days of the journey, Isaiah was pleased not to encounter any major surprises. First there were fields. A great many of them, and so, he took the opportunity to gather some vegetables. After that, he encountered small-sized lakes and plain forests with far fewer trees than when they'd ridden from the north. Mostly, the path ahead was an open, predictable road of nothing much at all. It didn't rain, but there were mild winds that turned chilly during the evenings (making him wish he hadn't thrown the bearskin away so carelessly). Still, he was yet to find himself truly distressed, and pleased not to have met anything but a few refugees and merchants. It was only on the second evening, as he searched his pack for his book to scribble down potentially useful membranes from his lectures, he encountered his first preoccupation. He'd already discovered that the guards had taken his knife. His book, they'd quite unsurprisingly not cared for, and as his hands browsed for it, he noticed that its cover felt strange. It was no longer leathery. It was no longer the same size – in fact, it was not his book at all. Squinting at it in the moonlight he saw it was not among the ones he'd attempted to read either. No, it was *the* book. He looked at it in disbelief, realizing he'd browsed the pack the Master had given him and not the one he'd left with Indra. Had he decided to give it to him after all? Had he hidden it there for him to find on his way? Before he could consider what Mongoya might gain from doing this in secret (other than the thrill he seemed to feel from being ahead of everyone else), he noticed a small piece of paper sticking out from its side.

"Dear, Isaiah

What you now hold in between your hands is of higher value than words could ever tell you. So, first of all, you are welcome – this is the book you wanted to read. Secondly, I must apologize for giving it to you in this manner. I've made a thief of you against your will, and there is no reason you should ever forgive me for this. This book is said to be a source of the truth of all things. After having given up looking for it, I finally found it the day before you left. As to where, is not so important, but let us say I was surprised – such as you might find yourself surprised right now.

How will you use it? — I do not know. It is written in a foreign language I do not know myself, and I don't expect you to know it either. Still, as I know you are cleverer than you think, I am sure you'll find a way to interpret what it says. I felt it needed to be given to you, and if nothing else I've tried teaching you these past days has helped, I pray this will. Take care, and when you come back – please blame me if you must. I now owe you both my hands as well as my ears.

Your friend, Devus"

Isaiah wasn't sure if he should feel angry or grateful for his gesture. He opened what seemed to be very old (if not ancient) scriptures. The alphabet was common Araktéan, but still no less comprehensive. No matter how precious it might be, it seemed useless for him to carry it around – not to say dangerous. He wouldn't lose an ear if the Master found out about this, he would lose his fingers, or Devus would. More likely than not, they'd lose all twenty of them, as Master Mongoya had the tendencies and ruthlessness of a nostalgic traditionalist. There, alone in the dark, with the most precious book in Araktéa – one he'd so desperately had wanted to find – he heard himself laughing.

"Oh Devus, what have you done?" He asked out into the air, regaining his breath. He tried to comprehend how someone he'd thought to be so exceptionally bright, had stolen this treasure and given it to *him*. An incompetent nobody. Raziel Mongoya was perhaps not a noble, but Isaiah had a feeling that stealing from him (stealing this particular thing from him) was much more foolish than it was bold. More foolish even than blindly following some day-dream insight. Even more foolish than stealing a noble man's cape and giving it to a fragile, little boy. "Perhaps I am cursed to be surrounded by stupidity," he thought, but he still didn't feel the fury he thought he ought to. Perhaps because he was still far away – both from Nagár and the Parda. Perhaps because, despite the loonacy and unlikeliness of it all, having found yet another piece of his insight – his long since vision, gave him some confidence he'd find the third one as well. The one he was truly looking for. A beautiful, lost mind searching for rescue. His own flesh and blood.

*

With the path he'd chosen, Isaiah expected to ride through a similar landscape for a few more days before reaching the beginning edge of the mountains. Instead, the ground started changing around mid-day, and shortly, there was nothing but a strange, powdery, ground surrounding them. "This must be the place they call *the Dunes*," he thought. Looking at the map he'd been given, it stated nothing but the word "sand". A place deprived of anything even resembling a path, it indicated it was not a particularly large area, and so, seeing it was wider than it was long, he decided to ride straight through it. After many hours battling through its winds and doing his best to ignore the dead remains of horses and riders, he finally stumbled upon a town. Small and isolated in the middle of the Dunes' nothingness. Riding towards it at full speed, chased by a deep, red sunset that would have been magnificent if his eyes hadn't been fixed southwards, he soon learned it was even more lifeless than any other village in Nahbí. Clearly depopulated, he thought the risk of entering a plagued home was better than entering no home at all – and most certainly, better than joining the dry, fleshless bones.

He left Indra unbound after giving her some water and walked into the first house to the right (a small home of brick and clay), and just before falling asleep on the stone floor from fatigue and dizziness, he saw a shade at the edge of his left eye. The sight got him up abruptly, and he saw it came from a small girl dressed in a white linen dress. Her physique made her look no older than ten, but she had the calm eyes of someone older. Large and clear as ice. Her hair was the same golden colors as parts of the dunes bore, braided down along her narrow back.

"What are you doing in our house?" She asked softly.

"I... I am so sorry, miss, I didn't think anyone was here. I'll leave straight away."

"Go where? It is late and there's a curfew, Sir."

"I... I don't know where." Isaiah stuttered.

"You can stay here I think."

"Okay," he said hesitantly. "Thank you."

"Your accent is strange. Are you from far away?" The girl smiled, her little head tilted to the right.

"Yes, I'm from a place called Delta."

"I don't know this place."

"Of course, she wouldn't know." Isaiah thought. Villagers hardly had much sense of geography beyond the miles surrounding their town – which in this exact place would mean, nothing but this dreadful *sand* area.

"It's far away. Many miles north from here." He explained.

"You must be tired then, Sir."

"I am." He admitted, rubbing his eyes.

"I am tired too, but I can't sleep."

"Are... are your mum and dad sleeping?"

"I have no mum anymore, but my father is sleeping. He sleeps a lot nowadays..."

"And you don't think he would mind me staying the night?" The girl shook her head seriously.

"He doesn't mind anything, really." She assured him, then she took a step closer with a shy smile on her face.

"Do *you* mind reading me a story?"

"I don't really know any... *good* stories, I'm afraid."

"I am sure you do. Travelers and drifters always do – and there is no need to be afraid, Sir."

"Yes, well. I guess I am not a really good traveler." Isaiah admitted, rubbing his fingers towards his temples.

216

"If so, why don't you read one from the book that you brought?"

"My... oh. You saw that." She nodded. He'd brought it inside with him and left it on the little, wooden table, wanting to keep it as close to him as possible.

"It's quite pretty."

"I guess it is." He said, looking at its brown binding. Old, but firm. Not common leather, but some other animalistic material he didn't recognize.

"What is your name?"

"Isaiah Aronin."

"Isaiah..." the girl repeated. She had a delightful smile on her face, and Isaiah never thought he'd heard anyone saying it so sweetly or so softly before.

"That is a beautiful name. Mine is Amelia." He almost felt himself blushing, but the heat in his cheeks felt different than usual. More like a fever. Strange and almost overbearing.

"That is a beautiful name too."

"It isn't – not really. It means hard work."

"Oh." He responded dumbly, his head aching increasingly.

"Please read to me, Isaiah. My father always reads to me before sleeping, but he's asleep himself now, and I'm too tired to be awake and need to hear a story."

"I don't think you'll like this book very much..."

"I'll be the one to judge that." She said, her tone suddenly making her sound ten years older than she looked.

"If you insist, then." He sighed. If he could get away with staying the night, he'd show her the unreadable pages. Amelia nodded contently before sitting down next to him. As unworried as a tame lamb. Smiling as if he'd been her long-lost brother. He understood right there and then that he really liked children. Their innocence. That fierce curiosity he was uncertain of when he himself had lost, and perhaps was on an inevitable course of rediscovering – redefining. On the other hand, there was something very uncomfortable about the expectations of a child. Too close to disappointment and oftentimes impossible to fulfill.

"Try this page." Amelia said, opening the book somewhere close to the end.

"Normally, you should start at the beginning of the story, don't you think?"

"Yes. But sometimes, you should start in the middle or the end instead – you can also make it up yourself as you go. That's what my father says."

"Your father sounds like an interesting man. Very well, let's see what it says." Looking at the page, he was tempted to make it up as he went, but his mind was much too tired for any creative play of words.

"I'm sorry, Amelia. It seems I can't read this language."

"Maybe I can." She suggested.

"Oh?"

"Maybe, but I can't *read* you see."

"What if I read the words out loud as clearly as possible. Could you maybe understand it?"

"We could try that." Amelia shrugged easily.

"Okay. Let's see, Sri fraku persinova estilp broch harisn arom. Lemmu serina faruk persin shanatti heravo bicsi oldovo." He read the first line, and the words felt strange on the tip of his tongue – numbing, like overripe fruit in a dry mouth. Amelia looked at him attentively.

"That translates to – The elements' whisperers will grow louder once he opens the gates. Fear not the pain of the departed as their cycles are completed..." Isaiah turned towards her, no attempt in trying to hide his astonishment. She couldn't possibly have made something like that up.

"I don't think you like this story. It scares you, doesn't it? We can stop." She reassured him. Her voice was like that of a mother speaking to a child.

"How do you know this language, Amelia?"

"It's Birdú. I've always known it. At least I think I always did... but maybe I remember it wrong." She said thoughtfully.

"Amelia, could you... could you maybe translate more of it for me?"

"Yes, but not right now. I'm so tired, aren't you?" Isaiah nodded – he was in fact very tired. Despite the excitement of – at the very least – having translated *something* from the book, he suddenly felt he was barely able to keep his eyes open. Dozing off on the floor's carpet, he could see the girl moving towards what he suspected to be the bedroom, and though he doubted her father would be as calm about a stranger inviting himself in, he couldn't find the strength to worry right then. Closing his eyes, he simply hoped she would speak in his defense if needed be.

Waking up some time later, he gasped for air with a sudden alertness about his surroundings. It was dark out still – almost uncomfortably so, and the wind was vile and hollow in its calls. He'd always thought the south to be mild, but he felt cold. Terribly cold, as if the sun hadn't been up for days.

"Amelia?" He asked, annoyed for having allowed himself to sleep in there – on their floor like some beggar or a bandit. A man who thought it a good idea to begin a story in the end or the middle, most likely wouldn't listen to any excuses before hitting him in the head with a spade.

"I'm here." Amelia's voice came from their kitchen. He found her sitting by a tiny table. Her hands tied around her legs and a gloom alertness on her little face.

"Did you get any sleep?"

"I'm not sure. I kept thinking about the story."

"It was just two sentences. Better not to think too much about it."

"Some stories are short, Isaiah. But I think this one might be very long. So long it seems exhausting to even start it. Maybe that's why everyone is so tired now..." she said, clearly preoccupied with these strange and unchildlike thoughts.

"Your father is still asleep?" She nodded.

"To tell you the truth, I think he might be ill."

"Has there been a doctor to see him? A healer?"

"No. Not for a very long time..." Her big eyes were filled with great concern, and Isaiah felt a sting in his chest.

"I'm sure he'll be fine." He said, or rather, he lied for he wasn't sure – far from it. He'd never wanted to be the sort of adult that lied to children either, but it was perhaps too easy of a thing to be avoided in circumstances like these.

"Would you mind checking on him?"

"I am no doctor, Amelia. And I don't think he would like me to wake him up at this hour." He searched the room for a clock, but there was none.

"Please. As I said, he doesn't mind anything. He only sleeps – *all* the time. I would really like you to see him." He felt chills down his spine as she said it, and he wondered – wondered if he'd been sleeping in a dead man's house.

"That's the bedroom?" He asked, pointing to the door she'd walked through earlier. She nodded.

"Alright. I will go and check on him."

"He keeps a knife in there, but he doesn't want it anymore."

"A knife?" Isaiah asked, suddenly more alert, as it could be an awfully bad idea *if* the father was actually alive.

"Yes. But don't worry, it is only made for protection. It has never cut through anything, and he wouldn't hurt you with it either."

"Just like the one I was once gifted," Isaiah thought. It was probably not unused anymore.

"Are you sure?"

"Yes. And you can have the knife, it will be good for protection on your travels. He normally keeps it underneath the madras." The thought of touching a corpse repulsed him, but he did need a knife if he was to get through the thorn-bush and defend himself from whatever might come after – *if* he reached there and *if* he got through it, that was. The disturbingly clear memory of Tzelem's wounds, told him a sword would've been much preferable for the task. He should have thought about that while in Nagár, gone to a blacksmith while he could instead of being so eager to leave.

"Alright then." He sighed, deciding that a dead man's knife would have to do.

Isaiah opened the door slowly. It quirked as an old door usually would, and he carefully peeked into the room. It was small, just like the rest of the house – rooming no more than two beds, a coat-stand (without coats or any other clothing), and a mull-eaten rug in dull colors. It only had one window with a thin curtain covering it. Though it was closed, it felt even chillier there than it had in their common room. He wasn't sure how he'd expected death to smell like, but thought the room didn't smell like anything at all. He took a step towards the bed where Amelia's father was laying, and his widely opened eyes confirmed his suspicions. They were the same as his daughter's, and though drier and less vivid, the color was still as bright blue as a cloudless sky. His hands were gracefully crossed above his chest (much like Devus slept, he noted), and more speckled than even a lifetime of harvesting could do to a man. Still, the skin of his face was clear – not gray as he'd heard a dead or plagued man ought to be. Rather tanned, from hour-less days of working under the sun. Isaiah wondered how long he'd laid there for. How much he'd suffered from his illness and felt a sudden sadness rushing through him. It came with an unexplainable knowing that he'd not been a fool like he'd ignorantly presumed. That he'd been a good man that'd deserved a much better life than he'd been given – a better death. Though this might have been just as true for so many other Araktéans, seeing the stranger lying there in a body that almost looked warm still, made it very different. It almost made it feel like a personal loss.

As Isaiah came back to at least some of his senses, he remembered there was no time – nor reason – for him to grieve the stranger. Sadly, that was something he'd have to leave for the poor, orphaned girl. He didn't know how, or if, he'd be able to explain death to her. Out of all the stories he'd heard of it and the tales suggesting the odd occurrences that followed, he was yet to hear one that made sense. From his own perception, a man's death meant he was gone, and an empty body had no use for protection – while his own, most certainly did. He noticed himself still compelled to get the knife he'd been promised. "He won't miss it any more than Tzelem misses his boots," he thought. Besides, since his daughter remained, he knew the laws said that whatever had once belonged to him, was now hers to keep or give away. With this in mind, he tried lifting up the madras (the man had left a body of heavy bones). He then tried slipping his hand underneath it carefully – unsuccessfully.

Glaring at the man, considering how he'd proceed in moving him, he noticed something underneath his hands. Looking closer, he saw there would be no need to move him at all, as a thin knife was resting right on top of his chest. Carefully, he lurked it out with the tips of his fingers. Though the silver wasn't rusty, and the pattern in the wood was smooth and nicely cut, something told him it was a knife of a very long memory. It looked nothing like the ones used for slaughter. Nor for cutting leaves, or vegetables, and it was much more delicate than the large one his grandfather had given him. It was unlike any knife he'd ever held or laid eyes on. Slender, almost weightless, even a little beautiful.

"Thank you." He whispered out into the air, and just as surely, he could have sworn he saw the dead man blink. Stumbling backwards, he assured himself his mind was playing tricks again – that it was too dark there for him to trust his eyes. Quickly, he rushed out and slammed the door shut.

"Amelia? Could you come here, please?" He looked around. The house was all silence. He wasn't sure what to tell her, nor what would be the best thing to do with an orphan. Though he'd gladly take her to a neighbor, he worried the town was all out of living ones. Another option was to bring her to the next village, but he was in a hurry and the map hadn't suggested there were any villages at all in the area.

"I am here." Isaiah flinched, discovering the little girl standing next to him.

"You startled me."

"My father is alright now." He took a deep breath and then squatted down to meet her eyes.

"He isn't, Amelia. I am so sorry to tell you this, but... he's not alright. He *will be*, but right now he is sleeping very deeply, and he won't wake up again." He tried compensating for the message with a gentle voice, but it proved to be a hard thing to do while scared senseless.

"No." Amelia shook her head, seemingly unconcerned. "He is alright now." Isaiah realized she'd said it as a statement rather than a question, before. Not a hysterical one that one might expect from a child that had just lost their last parent, but with the certainty of an academic and the confidence of a guardian.

"Do you know about death?" He asked seriously. She nodded without blinking.

"It is that thing that moves you to somewhere new and shows you who you were." He thought about this for a moment.

"That is a nice theory." He said, scratching his chin.

"You could come with me in the morning, but I will have to leave you somewhere safe along the way... I'm on an important mission, you see."

"I could tell that you were – you have light in your eyes." She said and looking into hers he felt his heart beating louder. They were so old, those eyes – so strange and so familiar at the same time.

"I'll come with you for as long as you need me." Isaiah smiled. Her tears would come soon enough. When they did, he would do his best to comfort her.

"We should get some sleep."

Waking up the next morning, the headache and at least parts of his disorientation had passed. He drank some water from his flask, and then walked towards the bedroom. Though he'd insisted she shouldn't sleep in there, he hadn't felt it was his place to refuse her one last night to say goodbye.

"Amelia, we need to leave now." He said, knocking the door. When she didn't answer the third time, he opened it and his chest tightened as he noticed she was not in her bed. Had she run off somewhere? Turning his head towards where the dead man had laid, he just barely managed to suppress a scream. The man he'd seen, so freshly departed the night before, wasn't there either. That was not to say the bed was empty or that his daughter was laying there (either case might have been preferable). Instead, resting under the thick, gray covers, there were bones, and on the pillow the eyeless scalp of a fleshless skeleton. After almost falling backwards out the door, Isaiah grabbed his book and ran. He got on Indra's back, and he left the town as fast as he could without looking back. Guilt came upon him as soon as he thought of the little girl. He wondered if she'd truly been real or if he'd been so tired he'd made her up inside that strange fever. Her words hadn't been those of a child, but he would've never made up such an odd saying himself either (unless he'd unknowingly had grown himself an imagination). He had never prayed before, but for the rest of the day he prayed that was what it'd been. Some vivid dream made by an overly heated head and a tiresome heart that all of a sudden seemed to mind solitude.

CHAPTER TWENTY-FOUR

FIRE AND WIND IN THE NAMELESS VALLEY

FOR two whole days, Isaiah rode through the Dunes and encountered no other villages. There was nothing but this sand, that along with the wind, did what it could to blind and misguide him. Finally, some forty miles or so away from the deserted town, he saw the first tree. Then another one, and gradually a sort of forest formed before him. It bore a dry, metallic smell, and finally, after another day of riding, he glimpsed the two notorious tops of the nameless mountains. The Master had said Araktéa was a place of many paths – that it had changed, and so, these tops had been the only sight he'd felt certain he had. Each of them taller and wider than all the three hills in Nagár combined – but this first sight of them withheld no true astonishment. The unexpected didn't appear before he got closer, and was not so much the presence of something, as the absence of it. It was clear that mountains didn't change from wind or rain like the ground did – that they didn't move, sink, shrink or grow. What struck him was that the purposely malicious river (said to have drowned so many travelers) wasn't dividing them. Instead, there were large rocks and an otherwise clear road leading to the other side. For the first time in days, Isaiah felt a smile forming on top of his shriveled lips. They didn't need to climb, and he would reach the Parda faster than anticipated. Then again, he realized, it also meant his grandfather might already have reached it. "We need to be fast." It was the first words he'd said out loud for days, and he thought his voice sounded like a stranger's now. Hoarse and hollow. Perhaps even mature.

* * *

The hills did well at keeping any battling airs away, but also laid shadows upon them early. Stopping for the night, he thought it would've been a good place for a campfire and with two rocks, he tried the technique he'd read about (the same one he'd seen Cyra do many times). It didn't work and when he realized there were no trees or other flammable materials in near sight, he gave up. It wouldn't be the first time he'd fall asleep cold, and at the very least the moon was full again, making the darkness a little less daunting. "It has been a whole moon span since I left the fortress," he thought. It felt like a year – if not two or five. Looking up while leaning his back towards a rock, he failed to notice the slender silhouette approaching him. It didn't speak a word until Isaiah saw it from the edge of his eye and turned in its direction. The stranger was small and scrawny, and bore a grayish, white robe that reached to their bare ankles.

"May I join you, young one?" they asked, the voice as unrevealing of its man- or womanhood, as its appearance. It didn't matter, as the sight of a living soul oddly made him feel more relieved than threatened.

"You can. But I have no fire tonight, I'm afraid."

"I did not ask you for fire. And there is no reason to be afraid." Their voice was slow and steady, and they had a ghost of a smile on their wrinkled face.

"I have some food if you're hungry."

"I did not ask you for food either, but if you're so eager to share, I would be grateful to you." Isaiah realized he didn't really want to share. He'd been vastly careful with his supplies thus far, and instantly regretted the impulsive offering. Yet, he had already presented it and the sight of the skinny oldling made sharing seem like a duty. Personally, he was much too thirsty to eat, and since bread did few favors for a dry mouth, he gave them what was left of it. If they were as hungry as their exterior implied, they hid it well. Taking patient, small bites, chewing all of it thoroughly. Not until finishing the last piece, did they looked in Isaiah's direction. Smiling in peaceful contentment.

"What is your name?" Isaiah asked, uncertain what else they might find themselves talking about.

"I left my given name long ago. It used to be Phax."

"And what do you call yourself now?"

"I call myself many things. But my people call me Wind, and you can call me this too, if it pleases you."

"So, you prefer to be nameless... like these mountains?" The stranger nodded to this, their eyes blankly staring before themselves.

"Why?" Isaiah asked, suddenly curious. Despite being among the most infamous places in Araktéa, nobody knew the names of the mountains. They were simply referred to as "the nameless mountains" or – more often than not – "the vicious, nameless mountains".

"Words can be dangerous. Especially the ones worn as names. It can empower a thing but also make it harmful or vile. So, I chose to be Wind instead – not bad nor good, but always carrying the air forward. At times vicious but mostly an essential thing for movement." They turned towards him, their eyes were light blue and almost transparent looking.

"What is it you seek here?"

"My grandfather."

"You seem like one that might seek answers – as well as questions."

"Seeking questions?" Isaiah asked, and the oldling nodded.

"Perhaps that too." He admitted.

"Good. For they are seeking you." The oldling smiled out into the air again, as Isaiah moved uncomfortably – unable to tell if his chills were caused by the cool air or the oldling's oddity.

"You prefer the certainty of cold feet, over the possibility of burning ones." Isaiah thought for a moment, realizing they were referring to the absence of fire.

"Maybe I did before..." He admitted, "but tonight, I just failed to make fire. I didn't bring matches." They nodded ever so slightly, then got up on their feet with surprising ease. Isaiah stared as they picked up two rocks the size of fists, then, digging in the sand, they quickly found some dry roots.

"There can be a short and surprising way from failure to success." They said, spending no more than a few moments to make fire out of their humble findings. Isaiah eagerly reached his hands out towards it.

"Thank you." He said earnestly, and the oldling sat back down again, now facing him from the other side of his creation.

"You killed your shadow." It sounded like a suggestion – one they seemed neutral and yet certain about. Isaiah instinctively looked behind himself. With the fire shedding light, he could briefly see it, stretching out long.

"No…" he said hesitantly, feeling gullible for having humored the idea.

"Have you not caused death, then?" Isaiah gave them a puzzled look. Then, he remembered what the Zura guardian had said after the silent commander's death: "When the word reaches the Birdús, they'll be ruthless." Could the oldling be of this tribe? Had they come there to punish him? To kill him in the middle of the mountains, where nobody would hear him scream? Had he come all this way, just to die out there in the cold, with nothing but nature as his witness?

"I swear I didn't kill the guardian. It was my master who did it, he…"

"I speak not of a guardian, but a shadow – as I told you." Their voice was calm and unthreatening, and Isaiah bit his tongue not to let the wrong words escape him. "No," he thought. This small, weak oldling couldn't possibly be there to punish him. He was getting as paranoid as Mongoya, if not even delusional. It seemed this was the real danger long, lonely roads brought upon you – not bandits or beasts. And clearly, this individual was just another strange creature that'd been wandering these roads for far too long.

"If not masters, we are wisest to let our shadows be our teachers. Yours taught you how to cradle resentment and fear, but it is time for wind to carry away the last of it. Then, you might learn the lessons that serve you." Isaiah looked at them, again confused to what seemed more like poetry than conversation. Then it occurred to him that perhaps they were referring to Tzelem as his shadow, the same way they referred to themselves as wind. He had been his teacher after all, and now that he thought about it he'd made him feel all those unpleasant things.

"That man stole me away. He lied to me and broke my trust – twice."

"Did he steal your trust?" Isaiah thought about this for a moment.

"No, but…"

"Did you give it away to him?"

"No. I... I only went with him to get out of there – to go back home."

"Many speak of the act of trusting as if it is a choice we make. But you always knew this shadow was not worthy of your trust. Did you not?"

"He was a bad man. I... I had to let them do it." Isaiah stuttered, and feeling his hands growing cold again, he rubbed them together.

"Perhaps he was. Perhaps he was not, but do not blame him for breaking things that were never in his hands. *They* say this shadow completed a part of his mission..." They looked up from the fire and into Isaiah's eyes. They were so blank – so disturbingly pale and motionless. Perhaps the oldling was a true sorcerer – one that saw through people and their deep kept secrets. One that could speak with fire and have it expose them.

"And what can they say of *my* mission?" Isaiah asked, surprised to find himself more curious than afraid of such dark things. The oldling's face softened a touch.

"What is it you carry with you?"

"Not much..."

"Show your little to me, then. And I will show you some questions." Isaiah opened his mouth and looked over to where Indra was standing.

"You do not like showing things. And you dislike the visibility you've given yourself even more. There is no better company, then, than that of the blind." They said, and Isaiah turned his attention back to them, studying their dry, wrinkled face closely he was again struck by the eyes.

"You are... blind? How do you walk around here without vision – and all alone?" They didn't even have a cane or a stick to support them.

"Only without sight, young one. *Not* without vision." They blinked. "Do you feel the place where your skin ends?"

"In a way." Isaiah concluded, sensing the coolness tingling on his naked hands and neck.

"It is *in* and *on* this way, that I move." What increasingly seemed like a creature – rather than a human – turned towards Indra, signaling for her to come towards them and the mare obeyed just as surely. "If you trust them, then perhaps I should too." Isaiah thought, and so he walked over to her and browsed through his two packs. Seeing the ancient book, he hesitated for a moment. He could leave it there, but though blind, he felt the sorcerer would see right through him if he attempted any sort of lie. Perhaps they could translate something for him.

"This is all I carry." He said, laying his few belongings in front of them.

"Two books – what richness in ink and paper..." They said, excitement spreading on their face.

"Both are not mine, I just...stumbled upon one of them. I was wondering if..."

"You've been taught to ask some questions but not common ways to seek their answers. This can be a good thing. Many seekers now, but with them, even more diluted questions. A great many are out searching, and yet here you are – just *stumbling*..." They said the last word thoughtfully, allowing their crooked fingers to stroke over the bindings of both books.

"I don't know how to read it. It was found by my... friend."

"And will you return it to your friend?"

"I don't think so, he... he stole it without my knowledge."

"Can you steal something that was already stolen?"

"I... I'm not sure." The blind nodded at this.

"Good." They said, allowing their right hand to slide to the handle of the knife. The same moment, their face lit up in almost childlike excitement.

"This is from the mirror world. An ancient time too..." They said, grabbing it as uncarefully as if it'd been a stick.

"It's sharp!"

"A harakiri knife... What a precious treasure. You seek the Parda I've been told..."

"Told by whom?"

"The elements that your blood fears. How appropriate to bring treasures to where people go searching for them. And what an appropriate treasure this is."

"I am only seeking my grandfather and the treasure is for someone else – just water really..."

"Can we seek what we've already found? Is water just water, or is it a friend or perhaps even an enemy to some?"

"I don't understand..." Their blind eyes widened as they turned towards him.

"And I don't *see*, so it seems a good thing we've found each other. And perhaps also a good thing I have given up my given name... I might have been tempted to make you a trading offer, if it hadn't been the case. But now, time is on your side."

"An offer? For the knife, you mean?" Isaiah asked, and they nodded.

"And your eyes. In return, I would have led you to the one you seek." Isaiah's heartbeat speeded up.

"Do you know where my grandfather is? Could you take me to him? You can have the knife. I'll lend you my eyes, guide you home or wherever you need to go..." The oldling took in a long breath then released it in his direction. The fire between them distinguished into thick, white smoke as they whispered, "I am Wind now." Then they walked and seated their light body next to him.

"What did your mother tell you?" They asked, softer and much more human-like.

"I don't have a mother. The only family I have is my grandfather and..." Isaiah flinched by the touch of their hand on his arm.

"One is lost, another has been freed." They said, their fingers cold through the thin fabric of Devus' shirt.

"I don't see how that..." The oldling let go of his arm again and held their skinny knuckles together, their face somewhat illuminated under the light of the moon.

"I seem to have given you an answer, when I only promised questions. Forgive me. I am usually a wind of my whispers." They got up on their bare feet again, light and graceful as a leaf – as wind itself.

"Thank you for showing me your treasures." A slight bend in the neck in his direction – though far from a bow, before walking away in the same direction they'd come.

"Do you know what happened to the river that was here?" Isaiah shouted after them, and the silhouette stopped for a moment.

"It left to make room for a new one. We have been praying for its arrival." Isaiah thought of the heavy rain up north and said, "I think it might have landed in the wrong place." The oldling didn't answer but kept walking until he couldn't see them anymore. Isaiah regretted not having asked them about the Parda, or to translate something from the book, but decided their riddles wouldn't have helped him anyways.

CHAPTER TWENTY-FIVE

THE PARDA'S DANCE

IT took half a day before Isaiah saw the end of the valley. No oldling – no anybody on the way – and he felt nearly ecstatic to discover the almost Delta-green forest on the other side. More importantly, or at least more essentially, there was water. Fresh water that he bathed in and drank greedily from. According to the map he was now but a few miles away from his destination. He'd thought he'd have the chance to think more on his way. Plan more, make more sense of the things he was supposed to have learned about the strange place during his mountain crossing. But there seemed to be no more time to pause or to get ready, and he guessed perhaps nobody was ever ready for the Parda.

A short hour later he reached a place resembling an open village. The hovels were spread around a vast, spacious area. Small, mostly wooden and with openings rather than doors. The area itself was small too, but probably home to as much as a few hundred souls. Some of them were outside. Most were children and along with a few adults, they sang and played on large drums. Though sounding different from indigenous lips, the words resembled those he'd said out loud from the book. It was a wholesome sound, and made young voices seem deeper than those of northern children. He didn't get much time to observe any of this, before a small boy spotted him from afar, and as the child pointed in his direction, some others turned too. With this, the song stopped and a muscular, shirtless man shouted something at him. It sounded like a question, but realizing Isaiah didn't understand, he turned towards another man that resembled him. Red, tan skin and stern faces. He'd imagined at least Birdús to be fair and red-haired like the dead Commander, but they resembled Zuras more than anything.

The two men approached him as the rest stayed behind – visibly more frightened by his intrusion. "They could perhaps translate my book." He first thought but noticing the stern, unwelcoming expressions on their faces as they got closer (not to say, the fact that they had grabbed two spears on the way), got him thinking otherwise. It took no more than two pointy, stone-made spear ends to surround him. Perhaps he could have fled, but his body did no such thing. Humbly, he obliged and got off Indra's back. They dragged him along with them, discussing with each other as they walked. He tried apologizing, just to find his foreign blabbering had no effect. Finally, they led him to one of the hovels. It seemed big by their standards but was made of straw and birch bark like the rest. As they led him through the entrance, Isaiah flinched as he heard one of them say the word "Wind" in common Araktéan, and then once again, when he saw the oldling. The hovel was made up by one spacious room, and they were sitting at the end of it. Cross-legged on top of a heightened plateau with many colorful cushions (red, yellow, green). Instead of the white rags they'd worn on their last encounter, their body now bore deep, red fabrics. Something was burning close to them, filling the room with a thin, white smoke. In a low voice they said something in Birdú to the armed men, and just as surely, they left their grips off Isaiah's arms and left.

"Forgive them, they haven't seen one like you for some time. I explained you're not all as threatening as you might look."

"It is… it is *you*. How did you get here so fast?"

"By going slowly. Do you enjoy the sage?" They asked, nodding towards the burning plant. Isaiah recalled smelling something similar. Remembered it'd been in Tara's home.

"It's nice…" He stuttered. "I thought they would kill me."

"We are peaceful here, but we must sometimes take precautions to maintain our peace. Did you come to ask me something?" They asked, waving him closer.

"I... I want to know about the Parda." He said.

"The only way to know her is to meet her. But this, you've already been told." He'd suspected this kind of useless reply. As he suppressed a sudden annoyance, the spear men returned – though instead of the spears, they'd brought a wide plate of food. They placed it in front of Wind who gave them an affectionate smile.

"Let us eat first. Then, we might speak and think more gracefully." Isaiah nodded at this, noticing he was in fact ravenous, and thought the savory meal might get him into better spirits.

As they ate, he did his best to do as Wind did – surprised by how much focus it required of him to eat at such a slow pace. Even if he was half-starved (his last meal had been in the Dunes) and wanted to hurry, so they could perhaps tell him something, he did his best to chew properly, appreciating every piece of the delicious but unfamiliar flavors.

"Hunger is a scary thing north from here." The oldling remarked, finally having finished the meal.

"For many it is."

"And for yourself?"

"Sometimes, yes." Isaiah admitted. "Though, much less than it used to be." He realized.

"What else is?"

"Not finding my grandfather." He responded and the oldling nodded, their blind eyes seemingly in some distant thought.

"And the rest of them?" They asked and Isaiah thought for a moment. Had he been somewhere else, he would have thought their questions inappropriate, but he was south of the nameless mountains now. In a very strange place, that seemed to require equally strange conversations.

"I have many more weaknesses than I'd care to have... but I can't think of anything particular."

"Maybe a lack of imagination then." The oldling smiled and thought it didn't seem to have been a serious suggestion, Isaiah couldn't help but agree.

"I believe you're right."

"Such a weakness will help you here. Not with writing untrue things in empty books, but to lead you to the one you seek."

"So… you are saying my lack of imagination will help me find my grandfather?" They gestured for him to come closer, bending over the empty plate they'd shared.

"You cannot meet anything in there that you could not imagine." Isaiah sat back again and took a breath.

"And?" He asked, "What else?"

"The less you know of her, the better. The emptier your mind is, the more she'll welcome you. The more she will *show* you."

"*Please* – I need…" Isaiah begged, but he wasn't sure what he needed. Only that it would have to be some unshakable fact that was more than a riddle. Something to make him feel prepared for what was coming. The oldling shook their head.

"She likes to dance." They stated at last.
"What?"

"That's why we always play music." They held their hand up to their long, right ear, listening to the drums from the outside. "Unbelievable." Isaiah thought.

"I sense you're displeased. But you asked to know what I knew, when you should question what it is you yourself need to know."

"Thank you for the food." Isaiah said, ignoring their implication.

"You have walked a long way in your shadows' shoes. You've felt their heaviness and dangers. Now, it is time you take them off and enter as yourself. This way you might finally reach your true destination." Their face had a delightful expression now, like someone seeing light for the first time in years, and Isaiah couldn't help but think they truly were trying to be helpful.

"I will leave the boots then, if you think it matters." The oldling nodded.

"It is time for us to leave each other again. You're in a moving state, and it is time for me to have my silence. Two of my eyes will show you a shortcut."

"Finally something practical," Isaiah thought. He was fetched by the same men – or eyes as they called them. They pointed him in a direction leading southwest and said "Go." And so he did, thankful to be leaving well-fed and un-speared at least.

* * *

As he rode, he wondered about Wind's peculiar presence. It'd been many days now since he'd had a normal conversation (if the ones with Devus could even be considered as such). It made him consider whether Mongoya had been serious when suggesting madness ran in their family. If he was trying to save someone from the same corruption he himself had either caught on the way or inherited. For a few lengthy miles he considered this, and only when he arrived did he come to the odd realization that perhaps it did not matter. Many had lost their senses in there, and so, having lost his in advance would only make the quest less of a risk. He'd wondered how he'd recognize the Parda, but the moment he saw it he knew her – perhaps even a few moments before. It looked just the same as any ordinary forest but differed the way a painting might do from a true view. There was no thornbush he'd need to cut his way through. It had a clear opening to a path; So obvious that any bypasser would see it if he knew what he was looking for. He left Indra outside and took his boots off. At last, it was time.

CHAPTER TWENTY-SIX

THE WHITE NIGHT

AS Isaiah entered the Parda the sun disappeared. Not as it did at dawn, or as the sky was covered by dark clouds. The sky remained a pale shade of blue – far from dark, and yet utterly sunless. The air felt crisper in there and the nearly motionless air made the silence seem hollow. Even in the nearby dead forests he'd gone through before, there had always been sound, if you listened closely. Rustling leaves, bugs crawling up trees, the flickering of wings or some distant stream of water. In here, there was none of it, and though it seemed any sound would have made his heart jump out of his chest, the silence seemed unnatural and unsettling. It scared him very differently than the open, dry dunes had. At least there, the winds had kept him company. At least there, he'd had a certainty (or perhaps a delusion) that nothing could appear out of nowhere. He would hear it first – see it first. Here he sensed anything could appear from everywhere, or at least (if he were to trust the oldling) anything he could imagine.

He walked for some time, barefoot as instructed, wondering if he should be mad enough to start dancing. But he didn't know how to dance, and so, he took a breath instead, trying hard to think. Then, he remembered what the oldling had said about emptying his mind. He made an effort to look around without thoughts, like he'd often done in their garden when he'd been a boy. It took some minutes before the urgency finally slipped off of him. There it was. That beautiful ease. Just like that. "How could it be so simple?" he wondered, and as the thoughts came back, he once again focused on where he was. There – right there, in some forest he (and perhaps nobody else either) really knew. Trees and stones. Nothing in sight to fear and nothing unimaginable in the hiding. Quiet. Very, very quiet.

"You will have to master yourself before entering the threshold of these gates." A broad,masculine voice leaped out of the void, and he turned to where it came from just to find there was nobody there.

"There were no gates..."

"You *saw* no gates, ignorant child."

"I apologize for my blindness. Forgive me, I am only here to find my grandfather." He turned around again – trying to find the origin of the voice – but as he'd feared, there was no visible thing talking to him. He started walking faster. Although he'd suspected he wouldn't find his grandfather in any ordinary way, it didn't seem the voice's source was well intended.

"Run, Isaiah." It was another voice speaking this time. One young, sweet and familiar – Amelia's. He turned around again. Had she followed him there? Had he brought that poor, little girl into danger?

"Run!" It was a woman's voice commanding him now, and he ran. He ran as fast as his bare feet could carry him, until he met with an odd mist that rapidly turned into a thick, cold fog. Suddenly he sensed little pieces of ice landing on his face. Melting on his heated cheeks. Looking behind him, the green forest was no longer there – nor were any of the voices. He allowed the chill, almost steam like air to enter him, and there, in the pale white of it all, he felt the same bravery he remembered having once felt inside a lucid dream. The coldness still *felt* real, so, he kept on walking fast to stay bearably warm. But he did not run, and he did not turn around.

After some minutes of listening to his own breaths, he finally heard the first true, natural sound of the Parda. It was no human sound this time, nor was it one completely unfamiliar to him. His heart started beating faster, as his mind threw it back to the first day he'd ridden with Cyra. To the moment the Zura girl had no longer been what worried him the most, and nature had shown him what true wilderness was. It took some seconds before he saw the materialized origin of the sound, its whiteness blending in and out of the fog as a cloud, before moving towards him. It's coat, beautiful, and clean. Its body was long and slow and its breath loud and pacing. The fog and the little pieces of ice surrounding it, made it look unreal – still it seemed much more alive than the smaller brown bear he'd met that night that seemed so long ago now. Yes, "alive" was the best word, as well as the only word he could find for it.

He froze as the bear kept walking in almost majestic patience towards him. The two of them stared at each other as if they'd been the last two creatures alive. As if they'd reached the end of the world together, and both were wondering who'd be the last to remember the other. Isaiah broke the moment. Once again able to move, he stumbled backwards a step. He felt for the harakiri knife in his belt. Had it truly been a dream – had anything been possible – he could have saved himself by aiming it against the animal's heart, or perhaps that deadly spot on its neck, once it attacked him. He could survive or maybe wake up. But the cold told him this was far from a dream. That this would spill more unnecessary blood on the white ground than what was needed.

With the touch of the handle, he felt a strange, sinister solution occuring to him. The idea that he could at least keep himself from being ripped to pieces if he died by his own hand. It seemed wrong, cowardly, and yet it was as if the blade called for that action. As if its purpose was to free him and this was the only way. Compelled, he pulled the blade out and held it towards his stomach. The bear, no more than twenty feet away now, stopped abruptly. It left him gasping as it stood up on two legs, exposing its true, massive height. With this, the knife slipped out of his hand as he fell down to his knees. In sudden surrender, he saw there was no victory in fighting nature. There was no reason to escape it once it had made its judgement, and so he decided he would not die a coward's death. He had reached his destination, his final trial, and so he prepared as well as one could for the animal to rip him apart.

Three seconds went by, the longest he'd ever lived, but the bear did no such thing. Instead, it lowered itself down to the ground and out of the tense silence that followed, Isaiah swore he could hear the sound of drums. The beats hit him in the chest as sudden beams of lightning –

almost as if it'd come from inside his body. He looked up, just to find the bear staring at him, and it felt oddly the same as a human stare would. Painful, exposing, but not unkind. He stared back, and its black eyes looked almost saddened for a moment, before it turned away – dissipating into the thick kingdom of clouds it'd come from. Once again, he'd been spared. Once again, he'd been abandoned.

Regaining enough strength to get back on his feet, Isaiah walked for hours in the fog before finally being too tired and cold to continue. "Grandfather!" he screamed, like he'd already done hundreds of times. Once again, nothing but his own echo returned to him, and so he sat down and wept. Sobbing like he'd thought a scared fragile little boy would, after having lost everything. Alone there in a world of nothingness. He thought of all the places he'd seen on his way. He'd had enough gold to buy a house, but instead he'd come here like a fool – well knowing it was a place for the doomed and the reckless. He thought of all the people he'd met. Any one of them, even the ones he'd thought rather awful, would have made him laugh out of pure joy if they'd appeared just then. "Anything and anyone at all." He stuttered, with no attempt to scream this time.

He felt himself wishing neither of the bears had spared him. That Wind's eyes had speared him on the spot or that the Zura commander had taken him to trial. It seemed so clear now, that suffering was the price of life. That was what adulthood truly was – the only certain privilege that came with it. Though wanting death needed to be the most selfish idea to have ever occurred to him, he felt too much fury to feel ashamed. Angry with himself for ignoring all the warnings – for ignoring his obvious weaknesses and unreadiness to enter a place like this.

For half a night he cried out loud and shamelessly, feeling so close and yet so far from death. When his throat was finally so sore it couldn't bear making another sound, he laid down, understanding well what laying down in such a place might mean. His feet had gone numb a long time ago and the initial needles had passed. Soon, his entire body seemed increasingly senseless and after some time it even gave up shivering. As he laid there, looking up towards the moon that had found him in the fog (slightly less than full), he prayed it would be the last time he'd fall asleep cold. He prayed it would be the last time he would need to fall asleep at all.

CHAPTER TWENTY-SEVEN

GOOD MEN AND THE DEPARTED

"THE night has passed." Whether the voice came from a fading dream or not, Isaiah was uncertain of, but in either case it was what awoke him. The ground felt less viciously cold. Opening his eyes he saw it was now green and that the air had cleared around him.

"Will you allow me to guide you?" The voice asked, and he thought it sounded like the same one that'd been rather displeased with him when entering.

"I want out of here!" He yelled, trying to get to his feet. His right hip was aching, his chest was tight, and it was just barely that he managed to stand up.

"What is the fastest way out of here?" He tried more softly. Once again, he found himself in a lush, green area, but he did not trust any of its directions to lead to an exit point.

"Death is." The tone was neutral, and he swallowed hard at the earnest response. It seemed this was the Parda's wrath, and surely how the twelve had ended up either dead or severely disturbed (perhaps his father as well for all he knew). Worse was the fact, it seemed a tempting offer, though he felt a shade less fragile than he had some hours prior. Even this voice, unhuman and unemotional, seemed better than that endless silence.

"What did you come here seeking?" It asked.

"I swear on my life. I only came looking for my grandfather...you can keep your treasures." he said and all of a sudden, the clear view started dissolving. First it was replaced by colors. All kinds of colors, brighter ones than he'd ever seen, inside of patterns he thought not even the most talented of sowers could recreate. Then, a total, blind blackness.

"Stop looking." The voice was closer to him now, and he stumbled around trying to keep his balance.

"Give me my vision back!"

"Be calm, Isaiah." Another voice (a woman's) said, and he felt the pressure of a warm hand on his shoulder, gently pushing him forward. He thought he should scream, throw his arms around and try to escape, but resistance seemed futile. Instead, he let go, no longer caring much if he lived or died. No longer feeling fearful or opinionative on the matter. As if there was nothing left to lose or gain for remaining in his flesh. Shortly after, he felt he was no longer walking. With the warm hand still on his shoulder he felt himself floating like he imagined someone would do on a river. Instead of being on a fleet, he somehow *was* a fleet – blind as wood, thoughtlessly allowing the stream to carry him to any place it desired.

When his vision returned, it appeared like stars circling and dematerializing before his eyes. The first thing that met them was a waterfall. It was running down a tall hill and splashing into the beautiful, bleak blue lake that now reached him to his waist. His eyes followed it from the top down, and when he turned towards the shore behind him, he didn't see his shadow or his reflection in the water. What he saw was his grandfather – his family, his flesh and blood. Theodore Aronin was sitting calmly by the shore, in the same garment (now slightly torn) he'd worn the last time he'd seen him, as if it'd been any ordinary day. Suddenly noticing him, he stood up on his bare feet and waved. Isaiah ran towards him and embraced him with an appreciation that only someone that'd just walked through a hell or three could.

"You are here..." Theodore cried hoarsely. His eyes filled with puzzlement.

"Yes! But we need to leave at once. I believe corruption has entered your head and you need help." Theodore shook his head, his mouth half open.

"No. I am staying." He stated.

"Please, it is important that you listen to me. You're not thinking straight. We *need* to get out of here."

"You, listen." Theodore was calm, a peculiar steadiness behind his initial confusion, and though Isaiah sensed this, he felt alert. Suddenly aggravated, as if he'd just woken up and parts of his dream were still circling around him. "I know that I'm not." He said, the faintest of smiles on his face.

"Okay." Isaiah sighed, thinking as he had, that this part wouldn't be easy. With no straightness in either of their minds, it seemed clever convictions or arguments would not lead them anywhere better. He hoped time would, that it was on his side now, as Wind had said.

*

Two days later (if they were to guess) Isaiah and Theodore Aronin still found themselves inside one of the Parda's hidden gems. A place beyond any map ever drawn, where each person was left in their own navigation and narrative. They stayed close by the waterfall, feeling at least remotely safe and sustained. Other than some bushes of elderberries they lived by eating its fish and drinking its water. Theodore had, for the most part, been awfully quiet and Isaiah hadn't minded much that he was. Having found a sense of calm, he felt happy just to see him alive, physically well, and at ease.

"How is your mind?" he asked, feeling (despite previous failure), it perhaps was time to reevaluate the subject.

"A wonder." Theodore answered distantly, as Isaiah sat down next to him. They leaned on a big stone some ten feet away from the waterfall. Both felt the ghost of sunlight warming their faces.

"When we leave this place, we will get you help. I've found a healer, a doctor, *and* a chemist. One of them must be able to..."

"As I've told you, Isaiah, I will not let you trick me out of here."

"I'll stay here till you're ready." It was no new conversation – and in exceptional patience, Isaiah had already accepted the same answer thrice.

"You never go into the water." He commented, finding casual subjects to flow easier between them.

"I'm afraid of water, you know that."

"I'm sorry. I do know that." He admitted, having heard the tale of how both his parents had been taken by the Deltan river when he was a boy. How he'd watched them drown, unable to do anything to save them. Theodore sighed.

"Do not be sorry, nature gives and nature takes. That is its way. People mostly just take..." He took a long breath. "I drink this water. It clears my mind, but it is no longer what it once was." He'd already told Isaiah the water had some sort of miraculous healing qualities, which at least partly explained Mongoya's thirst for it. If not ill, a man his age was undoubtedly vulnerable to become so. They'd also concluded it was this, rather than the herbal salve, that had healed Tzelem's leg. Isaiah was yet to tell him about the leg's (and his master's) final fate.

"Maybe you need to walk into it. It's okay if you're afraid, I'll be here to help you."

"Another day, perhaps." His lips smiled hopefully without fully reaching his eyes.

"Why does me being here make him sad? He should be happy." Isaiah thought, and then he asked, "What kind of thoughts have come to you here?" Knowing it to be a question that required a longer answer. Theodore bent his neck backwards and closed his eyes. "Very few were kind, but many have been honest... answers to things I've wondered about for ages."

"Like what?" Theodore sighed, avoiding his gaze as he looked in the direction of the waterfall.

"I've always thought that if your father had grown up with a mother, things would have turned for the better. I see now that a mother like Elora perhaps only would've made it worse. That she was... disturbed and unfit for motherhood. I should have never made one out of her..."

"You told me you loved her more than anything."

"I told you I loved her more than I loved myself – but it was a brief love... and I have come to realize that perhaps it wasn't as true as what we led ourselves to believe. I convinced myself that I saw her differently than everyone else, which I still believe to be true in part. That's the only reason she'd ever chosen a fool like me – not rich, handsome or even charming." Theodore made a joyless, chuckling sound.

"You can't possibly have been a fool. Mongoya told me you were among his greatest students."

"If you only knew..." he said, his eyes seeming to be half the world away. "If I had only known it would come to this."

"I'm sorry..."

"No." Theodore cried, breathing heavily through his nose.

"For the first time I feel I'm loving all of her, or at least someone closer to who she truly was, even if she's no..." he paused "no longer here. It's just like falling in love with a ghost. Someone who will never return." Isaiah wanted to suggest that perhaps they sometimes did. That at the very least, the voices of the departed were still among them somehow, but he could see that it wouldn't ease his pain. No words could, and it occurred to him that perhaps they shouldn't even attempt to. He saw it wasn't his duty to remove it and that any heartache that came from love was one that needed to be felt. The pain with which the Parda taught her tough lessons.

"What thoughts have come to you, my boy?" Theodore asked once he'd gathered enough air. Isaiah bit his tongue. Over the past days he'd strangely noticed himself going back to the memory of the white bear. It was not a fearful one, rather, it seemed to walk around his mind, with an almost holy mercy about it. At first it'd arrived with an ache – almost like an uncanny longing attached to it – but now it seemed to mostly bring him an odd sense of ease and safety. Resembling the calmness he'd discovered during his first minutes in the forest. It was a beautiful thought, and yet, he felt his grandfather wouldn't understand whilst being within this miserable enchantment with the long since departed.

"I've wondered about why you sent me away the first time." He said instead, making Theodore look even more miserable.

"There were many reasons, Isaiah – none of them good enough, and none made by the man I once thought myself to be."

"I forgive you." Isaiah said, thinking he did and, if not entirely, knowing for certain that he wanted to. "Now, please tell me the worst one." Isaiah said. Theodore looked at him, confusion adding another layer of sentiment to his teary, brown eyes.

"The day Tzelem came, I thought he was a guardian coming for you. I was very relieved to discover that he wasn't, and thought it an opportunity to send you somewhere... safer. I used to know his father. He was a very resourceful man – and so I took a chance, assuming his sons too would be... *good men*. Men who could protect you."

"Did you know of the Huxley fortress? That's where I stayed all those years... as a captive." Isaiah felt relieved as this truth left his chest. A captive. That was what he'd been, and the shame of this fact seemed to have dissipated. It seemed his grandfather didn't care if he wasn't a writer, and by being there now, he knew he needn't say anything about the wild journeys he'd been on.

"I had heard rumors of it – both good and bad, but I never imagined they'd keep you there. He seemed so... fascinated by you." Theodore paused. "Perhaps it was because of your name... some get blinded by names. Desperate men especially." Isaiah wanted to tell him of Tzelem's death – have it lifted off his chest once and for all, but he once again felt afraid he would see him differently. "He already does see you differently." He heard himself thinking. As Theodore looked into the air, he opened his mouth to confess, but his grandfather was faster – faster to tell him the worst of the whole matter in three words so innocent, that nobody would think much of them at all.

"He saw you."

"Saw me?" Theodore shook his head and abruptly got up from the ground.

"You asked on your 14th if things would ever be the same. I knew there and then the answer was *no*, and could have told you *right* then, but I didn't." His tone was suddenly sharp and accusing. "I had to bring you all the way here to tell you that..." He said, mostly to himself, as he strayed off.

"What is it you're *not* telling me?" Isaiah followed him till he finally stopped in front of the pond. They both stared at the waterfall for some time, as if it would manifest some common ground for them to connect again. Understand each other as they once had.

"For some time after your departure..." he sighed, turning to look at him. This boy who he'd spent years looking at, and was now so exceptionally similar to his son. His son who he'd sensed since entering the Parda but was yet to find. "I was convinced you'd never existed at all. And a part of me... still believes you're just an illusion. A trick of my own mind."

"I... I'm *here*, grandfather. How can you say that? I was only away for four years!" Isaiah had thought he was ready to hear just about anything – no matter how strange, confusing or heartbreaking. He thought he'd be able to make sense out of it with this new, more neutral, state of being, and that whatever truth his grandfather had kept from him, might finally bring him some peace and understanding. Seeing the fear and confusion in his grandson's eyes, there was nothing Theodore wanted more than to make it go away. He'd always feared this would happen. That his tongue would slip and reveal this fundamental question, that made every other question he'd ever had, seem utterly irrelevant. That of the boy's (perhaps a man now) very existence.

"I've been wondering for much longer than that."

"I don't...."

"You don't understand... and that is my fault too." He breathed heavily.

"Then explain!"

"When your mother brought you to me, she had one mere wish: that I would keep you safe, for as long as I could. I thought the best way was to make you believe you could have all your questions answered from me and our ritual. That if I kept you from believing in things that seemed strange or unexplainable, things that might make you want to fight for something, you wouldn't stray away the way your father did. There are few things more important than a mother's last wishes..."

"You kept me from believing in what? Gods... places like this, even though you believed in it yourself?"

"I do not know what I believe in anymore. Gods are good for people who need hope. For those who need guidance and salvation. You didn't need that – you were just fine until I... ruined you. I think there is something in our blood. Something that makes us *mad* if we can't find truth. I truly tried to keep you away and I kept myself away from here too. For so long..."

"I didn't come looking for truth, I came looking for *you*." Theodore looked as he was about to walk away again, but he forced himself to stay put.

"I still don't understand. I don't understand what you came looking for or how you can stand there and tell me you don't believe I exist!"

"They did everything they could to keep me away from this place. To distract me. I came to drink the water... it explains all the things I thought I wanted to know."

"Well, how much more of it will you need to drink before you come to your senses?" Theodore looked at him. His eyes were much more distant now, as if he was staring at a ghost.

"Enough to drown it seems...there are many layers to deception." He uttered, and then Isaiah saw it. All the fear, the remorse, the pain and everything dark and unresolved that he'd been unwilling to witness.

"You have to let me take you out of here. We need to go home."

"My father used to say that when it becomes difficult to live simple dreams, it is time to wake up. It's time for me to do so."

"If you would *just* let me help you... "

"*You* need to *leave* me now, Isaiah."

"No. I am done listening to you." He said, then jumped into the pond just to wade around in it rather aimlessly. There was certainly something about the water there. Something that had made him feel at ease for some time, but just as all things, its effect had dissipated. Panic had taken over his body and he laid down on his back with his ears under the surface to silence its noise. Attempting to exist a little less vividly. To be as lucid as his grandfather saw him.

CHAPTER TWENTY-EIGHT

THE VISITOR

ISAIAH wasn't sure how many days more he stayed, yet they seemed to go by fast, though they were spent doing very little. He taught himself how to swim and how to float more easily on his back. He tried making fire with rocks again but failed. Soon enough, he noticed himself feeling next to no hunger, or even tiredness during the misty nights. He stared at the stars, thought of bears and sat still. Each passing day the world outside the Parda, seemed more and more like a distant dream. He cared as little for it as he now cared about being here. Now that he'd reached his destination, everything seemed irrelevant and unimportant. That wasn't to say he felt melancholic or empty inside, just wonderfully uninterested and disconcerted, as his mission finally seemed over with. He'd found his grandfather. Merely a shell of the man he'd once been – a shell afraid of water, and yet, he'd found him. This someone who he'd never truly known in the end.

It was while he was floating on his back one late morning, he heard the whisperers of something from underneath the surface. It was the woman's voice which he'd heard twice already – commanding him to run and then leading him to where he now was. Now soothing, yet direct and assertive.

"It's time to end your visit." This time, he didn't bounce by the sound, as hearing invisible voices had started to seem normal enough.

"I can't just leave him here."

"He came wishing to see everything. Being told a complete story takes time, understanding it could take an eternity."

"I'll wait. Somehow, I'll figure out how to save him."

"He needs no saving from here, Isaiah, he needs rest. And there is much more waiting to be saved by you elsewhere." He stopped floating. Somehow, he knew the voice was telling the truth, and it triggered something in him. As if that dull irrelevance had left his body in a split second. Suddenly, it was as if fire had been lit up under his feet, and with an urgency to move he swam towards the shore and walked over to his grandfather.

"I will come back for you." He said, and he looked up at him – his face unreadable and pale. He hadn't said a word for several days and Isaiah didn't expect he would now either. He'd made his choice. Bending down, he gave him a hug which he, to his relief, returned. Before giving himself any time to change his mind, he filled Mongoya's flasks with water and left.

When Isaiah would later think back of his departure, he would never be able to recall exactly how he'd found his way out of the Parda. It was as if he'd been by the waterfall one moment and on the outside, where Indra was waiting for him, the next. Riding back, he was relieved to see that the Birdú's prayers for a new river were yet to come to fruition. Riding through the Dunes once again, he didn't stumble upon any strangers or villages. The only unusual thing he saw was a large, triangular creation in the far distance. But the focus and dedication to his northern march spoke louder than his curiosity, and so, he resisted the impulse to stray. He met a camp of five merchants close to the northern edge of the Dunes. They were friendly enough to share their food and water, and with an urgent need for a new pair of shoes, he tried trading them his knife. Clearly less impressed by it than Wind had been, he finally offered to trade his book instead. His *own* book– with nothing but a few stories from the fortress, key points from Mongoya's lectures, his only poem and of course the hero tale of a man that would be known in the south as the Visitor. This burden he'd carried around for years, still had hundreds of blank pages. After some consideration, and perhaps pity for the barefoot traveler, the merchants agreed to the bargain and gave him sandals and bandages to cover up his blistered feet.

* * *

After ten days or so, (he soon lost count) Isaiah reached Nagár. This time, getting through the gates was a rather effortless procedure, and he wasn't even chased when he rode past the masses. They'd grown larger than before, and the guards were too few and too disorganized to keep all of them from entering. The chaos stood in great contrast to the silent roads he'd found himself on, and yet, he felt himself remaining calm. Both the flasks were still full, but he'd permitted himself some drops of it each day to keep his head clear and sharp. It seemed to keep his nerves intact too, and though he dreaded the idea of giving it up, for he was committed to complete the agreement.

Reaching the top of Sujin Hill, he was stunned to discover that Julius wasn't there, and that the gates stood wide open. Entering, he saw the tulips were bland, and their withering made him want to drop all other matters and come to their rescue. It was the first thing that had truly triggered him on his way back – these precious, dying flowers that he felt certain you could not find anywhere else anymore. But he could not waste the healing water on them. It wasn't his water and they weren't his tulips.

Entering the house, he didn't meet a soul until he walked into the lecture hall. There, Devus was standing on top of the Master's pendulum, and when he saw Isaiah (standing there tall, tanned, and dusty) he nearly fell down the stairs running.

"Isaiah! Thank the gods you are back!" he said, and Isaiah looked at him incomprehensibly. For a moment he thought he would embrace him, but he took a step back while holding his hands up. "The book..."

"What has happened here? Where is everyone?"

"They... I don't know. But, the book... *I don't* know what I was thinking – it was terribly reckless of me."

"Oh." Isaiah responded plainly, almost having forgotten about having it in his possession.

"That's alright, Devus. We should... probably put it back where you found it? I left it in my pack." Devus looked at him, as if he'd just suggested they should play a round of cards or go watch a play in the city in the middle of the chaos.

"You're not *angry*?" Isaiah shook his head, for though he felt many things due to the more recent event, anger didn't seem to be among them.

"You really are an extraordinary bastard, aren't you?" Devus laughed, bending his head before him, as he grabbed his right shoulder. "How much he must have worried about this." Isaiah thought.

"I don't think Master Mongoya is coming back, he's been gone for days. Even Julius left."

"And why haven't you?"

"I've been waiting for *you*." Isaiah looked at him unconvinced.

"And well, I couldn't stand the idea of leaving all these books behind *unprotected*."

"Devus – protector of books. You didn't seem to have made much of an effort to save the tulips..."

"I am *not* joking. These are some of the most precious writings in the world. Anyone could just walk in here and..."

"And read?"

"Take this seriously, please! They could burn the place down – they did it before, during the revolution. So many secrets lost in the ashes. As I've understood it, part of Mongoya's work has been to duplicate everything. I can't let all his work go to waste. We... the people *deserve* the truth." His big eyes showed sincere concern.

"We do deserve the truth..." Isaiah agreed, "but I don't think it's safe to stay in Nagár. It's a chaos down there."

"You're right. I guess... I guess it is time to go home." Devus put his hands together looking at the books, as if praying for them. Then he turned towards Isaiah. His strange friend who he thought he'd just started to comprehend before he left, but not anymore.

"Come with me."

"Okay." Isaiah said and Devus looked at him somewhat baffled by his ease. It was as if he was in a different world altogether.

"Perfect."

"I'll need to leave the water here. In case Mongoya returns."

"I guess... yes – yes, of course you should do that." Isaiah didn't trust himself with it. That was not to say, he trusted the Master with anything either, but he would not break their agreement. The delivery seemed to mark an end to their relationship, and besides, Aronin men kept their promises.

* * *

After gathering a handful of books Devus thought to be the most important to preserve, the two of them left the city. With one of the gold coins they bought Devus a decent horse from a friendly-looking merchant outside the gates. The man eyed them as if they'd been heavenly-sent angels, and as he thanked them a fifth time, Isaiah gave him another coin.

"That's hell of a price for a half-decent horse, my friend..." Devus warned him, but Isaiah shook his head as they rode off.

"He needs it more than we do."

"That's beside the point. He wouldn't know how to spend it – he'll just get scammed or *robbed*. Look at this place."

"Perhaps he will, perhaps he won't." Isaiah responded and Devus couldn't help but wonder just in how many ways the Parda had changed him. He was like a well-known lyric with a new melody, or an old melody performed with a new rhyme. It fascinated him, and he couldn't help but think he'd for once been very lucky. That he might finally have something – someone – to show for upon his return.

CHAPTER TWENTY-NINE

THE DABÁRIAN COUNCIL

THE road leading north was a familiar one for both of them. Finding shelter in inns along the way wasn't an easy quest, and perhaps more so than ever necessary, as it'd been raining heavily and continuously over the past weeks. They followed the once thin stream that now was wider than any of them recalled, and it wasn't until it met the river, the one Isaiah had been told to stay away from his whole life, they were finally faced with a proper challenge. Normally, it wouldn't have taken more than a few minutes to cross, but the bridge was no longer there, and the river both wider and more wild than Devus had ever seen it. Their horses battled their way across the angry streams, and when they finally arrived at the Dabárian fortress (some miles up the hills), all four of them were soaking wet and exhausted.

Devus' home was framed by walls like so many other places were, but the gates were open, and as soon as they were spotted by the guards, they were escorted into a warm room and given dry, woolen garments and heavy blankets.

"Thank you for bringing me with you." Isaiah said, sensing this fortress (far smaller than the Huxley's, non-decorative and simple) was every bit a proper home.

"Don't thank me yet. You still need to meet with the council." A slow heartbeat later, the door opened, and both of them turned from the soft chairs they'd crawled up in.

"I was just given word of your return." A man (perhaps in his mid-fifties) with a thick beard with touches of silver, walked in. He was fair skinned, had wide shoulders, and the same boyish smile as his son.

"The situation in Nagár was outrageous, father. I had to..." Devus said, standing up to face him.

"I'm not upset with you. And it's no wonder there's chaos. Rumor has it the king has gone missing."

"What?" The man was about to speak again, but then he noticed the other boy. He opened his mouth, looking as if he'd seen a ghost. "He must have known my father," Isaiah thought, and knowing the harrowing sensation of seeing unreal things all too well himself, he arose to introduce himself.

"Isaiah Aronin, my Lord." He said and bowed. Devus had only just explained to him that his father was in charge of the Dabárian fortress. A detail he'd seemed weary about sharing.

"You're Theodore's grandson..."

"Yes." There was a pause of a longer sort – a sort the commander of the Dabárian fortress rarely found himself in.

"I'm Nicholas Teague. I used to know Theodore well. And I knew your father."

"I used to know him well too." Isaiah thought, and he could have sworn he'd heard the man's name before. He repeated it in his head a few times, but nothing came to mind.

"Pleased to meet you, my Lord, and thank you for having me as your guest."

"The pleasure is all ours. And we've actually met once before." Isaiah searched his memory as to where he'd seen him – the square chin and the dark, blue eyes – but his memory seemed to fail him.

"I'm sorry..."

"Oh, I don't expect you to remember me. You were very young. How is Theodore?"

"He... he is getting well." Isaiah uttered and then cleansed his throat.

"In fact, father, I partly came to tell you the most outrageous story. Isaiah just came back from the *Parda*. He went there to find his grandfather before returning to me in Nagár – alive and *without* a scratch on him." Devus' eyes eyed Nicholas' as if trying to transmit some secret code fairly indiscreetly. He'd already asked Isaiah about a million questions on the way, which he'd mostly responded to as honestly as he could remember. "Alive," Isaiah thought, and from the expression on Nicholas' face, it seemed what he'd accomplished (which he personally felt was nothing at all), both Teague men considered rather miraculous. At least it seemed his journey had been an impressive failure.

"Are you *certain* it was the Parda?" Nicholas asked.

"I am, Lord Teague." Isaiah said, and from his eyes – from the way the boy carried himself – he knew it was true.

"You must be tired." He concluded, then he turned towards his son. "We are having a council meeting as soon as Liv is back from town – she's looking for Philomena..."

"I'll be present." Devus was quick to say.

"I'd appreciate it if both of you came. I promise you will get some rest afterwards." Isaiah nodded, as Nicholas scratched his chin. He looked as if he wanted to say something else, but then stopped himself and turned to leave. It was then, when seeing his back Isaiah remembered – honest eyes, a large head and a grin that would be a king worthy. Even his shoulders, still wide for a man his age.

"My grandfather wanted to tell you he was sorry. He didn't say what exactly..." At this, Nicholas stopped and turned his head towards him.

"I'm the one who's sorry." For a moment Isaiah thought he would say something more, but he didn't.

"I'll tell him... when I go back for him." Nicholas made a short nod before leaving them and just as surely, Devus stepped closer to the fire. Grinning.

"I knew he would like you."

"Your father seems like a good man." Isaiah said, the brief acquaintance having been enough for him to understand, that Nicholas Teague was about as different from the other nobles he'd come to know, as soil was from sand.

"That's what they *all* say. Many people here actually call him the King of Dabár."

"Really?" Devus nodded.

"He hates it."

"The king does?"
"My father does."

*

Except for the two young men (still dressed in thick, unflattering garments to regain some body heat) and the Dabárian king himself, there were seven people present in the council room. All of them standing straight and calm along a table – about the size of the dining table in the ballroom, Isaiah thought, though lacking its polished surface and beautifully sculpted legs. He was somewhat surprised to see three of the council members were women and wore thick, ketill pants – similar to those of the men. Everyone stared as they walked in. A tall, dark-haired woman, standing on Nicholas's right side at the table's end, rushed towards them as soon as they entered.
"Welcome home." She said, embracing Devus with what resembled motherly affection.

"Thank you, Aunt Liv, I've missed you." she squeezed his tanned hand in between her pale ones and gave Isaiah a short nod of acknowledgement before moving back to her placement. As she walked past him, Isaiah felt her measure him so discreetly, nobody seemed to notice it at all. It was a doubtful, suspicious stare that might have startled him in the past, but the discord seemed to crumble down as soon as it'd come.

"We are all happy to see you've returned, Young Sir." The man on Nicholas's left said. His long face appeared less than half as serious as the rest, and was framed with gray, shoulder-long curls. Everyone conceded with nods and polite smiles.

"You may all be seated." Nicholas said, and Isaiah found himself sitting next to the only empty seat around the table.

"You've been lucky again, my friend – that's where Philomena was supposed to sit, but it seems my aunt failed to find her." Devus half-whispered.

"Who is..." He didn't get to finish the question, as Nicholas' wholesome voice silenced everyone's murmuring.

"As I'm sure you can see, other than himself, my son has brought home something truly extraordinary. This is Isaiah *Aronin* – Ares's son." Their eyes changed from what had mostly been a tame and courteous curiosity, to astonishment.

"Now," Nicholas resumed. "I will not have anyone thinking, *he is* Ares. Despite the obvious similarity in appearance – for those of you who met him – my short encounter with Isaiah tells me otherwise." Isaiah gave him a thankful smile. "He just returned from the Parda…" Nicholas stated and hearing this they all started turning their heads and seats, muttering across the table indiscreetly.

"*I am still speaking.*" Nicholas scolded, revealing that his voice could silence a room in a split second if he wished. "Adding to this… miracle, I was given notice this morning from one of our insiders – it seems young King Satta has gone missing."

"You didn't tell me this!" The dark-haired woman hissed.

"I am telling *you* and everyone else now, Liv. You've been gone all day."

"How long has he been missing for?" Another of the women asked almost tenderly. She was nearly unnoticeable in her appearance, short and bulky with brown, frizzy hair, barely reaching to her shoulders. Her oval face had round cheeks that seemed permanently flushed and a flat nose that gave her a peculiar profile.

"It's hard to say. According to the letter – a week long if I am to guess – it hasn't been made public in Nagár yet. My take on this is that our time has finally come." The announcement left the room in utter silence. These were words they'd been waiting and preparing to hear for years – decades even. Yet, they all looked as stunned as if lighting had just entered through one of the gray-shaded windows.

"There seems to be one issue, father, the crossing bridge is ruined. We just barely made it over."

"Under normal circumstances, waiting for the weather to pass would be the preferable solution – but it has been weeks… moons of storms now. So, I ask all of you, how will we get there in time before we lose this window of opportunity?" Nicholas' expecting gaze circled the table till meeting with Isaiah's.

"First, I should apologize to our dear guest." He said, reaching out a hand in his direction. "You seem to have stumbled upon us at quite a rare time, Isaiah." Devus had already explained to him that other than training their youth to go to the Parda, the Dabárian council had been planning a revolt in Nagár for a great many years. That the actual execution of it would happen the moment he arrived, hadn't crossed his mind. Then again, perhaps it should have. As the voice had told him, there was much more waiting to be saved by him *elsewhere*. Remembering this, it occurred to him that perhaps that was exactly what they needed to do. *Float.*

"Forgive me, Lord Teague, but in theory you could drift down south. On the stream leading south from the Del... the Dabárian river. By now it is so flooded that it might bring you there faster than horses could." They all turned towards him. He thought they'd find the suggestion ridiculous (it did seem like an idea made by a child), but their raised eyebrows seemed to either imply puzzlement or fear.

"We have no boats or fleets. Besides, our people have no experience operating on water – most don't even know how to swim." a red-haired man, more so large than muscular, grunted.

"I seem to have read something about this..." Devus said. "Not a lot, as the art of fleet-building didn't seem very relevant to me at the time. I know we have good trees for it in the region, and I have a clear image in my memory on how to tie them together. It might actually work!"

"And what about the horses? We'll *need* the horses later on..." The same man argued, clearly unsettled.

"We'll go as long as the river will carry us, and then walk the rest by foot. Or the Zuras might provide us some if you're too lazy for that, Harvey." The cheerful man on Nicholas's left suggested.

"I *will not* ride a damn Zura horse, Emory. Those beasts are vicious unless they've "chosen you", whatever that might mean. Besides, the Zuras might be good couriers, but demanding anything from them is like telling a crow to say "kra" – which might happen and might not, and yet they might hatch your eyes out instead." He spit, and then the whole council broke into loud discussion.

"Silent down." Nicholas commanded at last, having passed a long minute in pensive silence. "It is a very good idea. Very innovative." He nodded in Isaiah's direction, and he felt himself smiling ever so shyly as Liv made a loud sigh.

"If such an outrageous plan was to even be considered, it would take weeks of planning. First of all, we would need to find a way to take over the Huxley fortress and get our people out."

"Liv..."

"I am not making *a request* Nic – we will need their help. Regardless if it is time to go to Nagár or not – it is time to get them out of that place!"

"Entering that fortress would risk everything we've worked for. Don't be so *sentimental*, woman." A tall, stern-faced man, clearly the oldest of them, said.

"Oh, don't *you* talk to me about risks!" Liv barked, "I want my children safe."

As the discussion went on, all Isaiah could think about was the Huxley fortress. That he now might need to go back right where he'd started. He didn't know how many days it'd been since he left, only that it'd been a great many, and he wondered how the patrons would greet him if he returned without Tzelem.

"It seems our best chances would be to build these fleets as fast as can be done. Then, Ideally, we should be ready to leave in four days' time. The Agátis might be willing to assist us with this. Half of the council will go. The rest will stay here and start preparing everyone for the last part of their training."

"Are you mad? We can't leave in *four* days – this needs to be further discussed." Liv scolded.

"Ideally, it should. But this is too unique of an opportunity – we can't waste it this time." His eyes were harder than before, but still patient.

"I stand by my vote – we at least need to wait till the rain has passed and should rather focus on getting our allies home." Liv searched for words of agreement around her, and the last of the women, pretty with long, beautiful honey blonde braids, raised her hand.

"Liv is right. Although you are well-trained for a great many deeds, gentlemen, water is not among them. And we couldn't have you all drown, could we?" Her voice was deep and seemed to have an easing effect on everyone but the woman she'd defended. Liv gave a forced nod of acknowledgment in her direction, her tone restrained as she said, "Thank you, Josephine."

"Though we do not wish to bring concern upon you, we *must* go. It is time." Nicholas said.

"Do not speak to us like you're some *king*, Nicholas. You're not – none of you are." Liv's moss-green eyes penetrated all of them.

"Does anyone else oppose leaving in four days' time?" Nicholas asked calmly. Though the air seemed filled with tension, there were no further objections.

"Very well then. The women and dear Sir Derrick stay here – we all know you are better rulers than us half-muscular fools anyways." He smiled in an attempt to ease the mood, and then turned towards his right hand.

"I will leave you in charge, Liv. If you're lucky – I'm wrong about this, and I just might drown in the river. Then, you'll be in charge permanently."

"Don't joke about such things..." Liv said, and they glared at each other for what seemed a little too long, before realizing they wouldn't leave the room in the harmony they usually aimed for.

"We will discuss the details tomorrow. Get some sleep. You're all dismissed." Nicholas said, and once everyone had made their way out the door, he grabbed Isaiah by the shoulder.

"Welcome to Dabár, Isaiah. We are usually a little more civilized than this – though I admit, not a whole lot. I always aim to let my people speak freely with me, and I wish that you do the same."

"Of course, my Lord."

"Please, just call me Nic – I'm no *Lord* and no Patron. This noble nonsense is just for show." He smiled and Isaiah nodded.

"I understand you've been on a long journey, and that you might like to stay behind and rest. Usually, I would have recommended you to, but the times we are living in are strange ones. I don't know exactly how things will be changing – only that they will – and your assistance might help shift things in *a preferable* direction."

"You should know I am nothing special, Lord Teague. I did go to the Parda but... it didn't show me some ancient secret... it was just... just painful and..." Nicholas nodded.

"You need to say no more. Entering the Parda is different for every person, but it takes time to make sense of. You seemed to have come out of it extraordinarily well."

"Right now I feel clear, but sometimes the memories of what happened there feel strange. They make me question myself... what is real and what is not."

"Is there anything particularly troubling you?"

"No, it's alright. I know it's better if I don't tell you too much." Nic nodded to this. Though, besides himself with curiosity, the boy was right. If he heard too much, it would take a hold of him. Pull him there like a dog who'd broken his leash, and there was still work to do.

"You don't need to tell me anything, Isaiah. Just the fact that you are here with my son tells me enough. Let me know if there is something you need to get off your chest."

"Thank you." Nicholas smiled in what Isaiah thought to be a proud, kingly way.

"As for now, we need to make a rapid and very *real* strategy. I know there are many talented healers in Delta, and we might be needing some assistance. Is there anyone you trust?"

"There is." Isaiah realized. "Though, I'm not sure that she'd be willing to leave..."

"We'll need to ask her." Isaiah nodded to this. He'd thought about Tara on the way north, sensing there might be things she'd have answers to. The strange things his grandfather had told him – the voices he'd stopped hearing since arriving in Nagár the second time.

"She lives in a large house in Duroya, about five minutes from the city entrance, on the left side. It's easy to spot, and her lights are on till late at night."

"I'll send my fastest couriers straight away, so that she might be here in time." Isaiah smiled. He felt relaxed around Nic and realized he hadn't worn his iron face since departing from his last master. A teacher he realized they shared.

"I must warn you about getting involved with women of this sort."

"Oh, we're not... I'm not *involved*." Isaiah stuttered. "She's a... she has helped me before."

"Very well, then." Nicholas said, seeming to have noticed something Isaiah wasn't quite aware of himself.

"Emory will show you to your chambers. Get some rest." Isaiah had hoped to share rooms with Devus, but Devus was not just some guard dog's cook anymore. Here, he was a Patron's son – the King of Dabár's son – even if Nicholas didn't like these titles. "How quick things change," he thought as Emory approached him.

"It is truly an honor to meet you, Isaiah." He shook his hand firmly, his eyes showing no signs of fatigue despite the late hour. Walking down the long hallway, there were no paintings on the walls. Only torches lighting up the way and a dark, purple carpet resting upon the gray-stoned floors.

"I believe this chamber is available." He said as they reached the first door around the second corner. The room was mostly empty but had a large bed with huge, puffy pillows.

"Do tell me if you're in need of anything. Nic's guests are my guests, and nothing is more important than keeping them happy."

"Alright. Thank you, Emory."

"Also," he said, as Isaiah was about to close the door behind him. "Nic says you're not like Ares, but I, for one, don't think you're a lot like your grandfather either. That is not an insult or a compliment – just my humble observation." Isaiah nodded silently to this, before he said goodnight and almost instantly drifted into a deep, dreamless sleep.

CHAPTER THIRTY

SLITHERING HOPES

AFTER four days of construction, the two large fleets were nearly finished. As the three councilmen, and their cavalry of around fifty, secured them one last time, Isaiah saw two horses approaching from afar. When he saw her, he momentarily managed to set aside the thought of how outrageous this plan – his idea – really was. Her head was covered by a deep cherry-colored cape. She was wet to the bone, but when seeing him she waved – smiling joyously as if it'd been a sunny, worry-free day and not one where it seemed likely they'd either drown from the rain or the river stream.

"How does someone go out looking for their grandfather and end up partaking in a Dabárian revolt?" Despite the seriousness that lurked behind the playful tone of her question, Isaiah felt himself involuntarily grinning. He saw her noticing and blushed as her brown horse stopped in front of him.

"I've been wanting to ask you the same, Lady Tara." He reached for her white, gloved hand and helped her down from the saddle. The gesture seemed to please her, though she showed no signs of needing any assistance. Her escort had already turned his horse south. With little less in common with Dabárians, Zuras were not much fond of water either.

"I'm sure there are other things you've been wanting to ask as well?" She suggested and though not bothered by the rain, he led her towards the fortress' wall for shelter.

"How have you been?" The casualness felt odd to him, and still, somewhat mandatory.

"Wonderfully safe. It's been a little slow in Duroya lately, so I appreciate you finally bringing me into some proper danger."

"I'm sorry… I shouldn't have brought you here – nor allowed myself to be brought I believe." After the Parda it was as if some part of him had understood something. Some very profound answer he wasn't certain he'd even had the proper question for. It'd been accompanied by a strange courage that had made everything seem in order. A wordless knowing that had dissipated over the past days and left him wondering what in Araktéa's name he was doing – what he'd done. Tara shook her head, and a drop of rain ran down the left side of her plump cheek.

"That's alright, dear. We both brought ourselves here, and you did right by sending for me. I'm here to help, and you *will* need it. As I'm sure you're well aware of – you're *all* way in over your heads." She smiled like she often did – like someone who knew everything – and Isaiah hoped she was not being completely serious in her remark.

"Why are you looking at me like that?" She asked.

"You're wearing pants." He said stupidly. "Like the northern women." He added.

"You don't think it suits me?"

"Oh, yes. I'm… just surprised."

"Riding here in a dress wouldn't be practical, would it? Besides, I might have a bit of northern blood in me." She winked at him, and Isaiah was about to say something when Harvey approached them.

"You're the Lady… the healer woman?" He asked, his tone remarkably less crude than during the council meeting, which was the last time he'd bothered speaking with Isaiah.

"Yes, I'm Tara." she said, and instead of returning her smile, he looked down nodding uncomfortably while twisting around in his heavy, wet uniform.

"Liv is asking to see you."

"Very well, then – I'll come and be seen." She said, taking an elegant step away from the wall.

"To be continued." She nodded at Isaiah, and then walked along with her courier, as the people close by glared in her direction.

* * *

A few hours later the fleets were all set to drift them down the river. That was not to say anyone but the commander himself looked ready. It was him and Devus – who'd left his role as book protector in turn for fleet-building commander – everyone seemed to look towards in need of hope and encouragement. Isaiah sensed Devus was different in Dabár. Older and heavier in his movement, with his dark, leathered tunic and furred coat. His face, too, was more serious, but he seemed content with the heavy task at hand, and much more confident about the plan than Isaiah now felt.

"I've doomed us all. We'll drown because of me. Because they think I know things – because you told them that I entered those bloody woods." He said, as he approached him. He'd quite suddenly started to feel very certain about this fact, but Devus just shook his head grinning, losing five years in an instant.

"I'm being quite serious, Devus."

"Oh, come now, you never said anything about you going to the Parda was a secret. It's something you should be proud of – anyone else here would be and are. *Trust me...*" Isaiah shook his head, and Devus sighed.

"And it will be fine. These are skilled men, and my father seems certain about what he's doing." He assured him.

"Your aunt Liv seems to highly disagree."

"Yes, well. That is her task in a way... to be disagreeable. I'd say she does it fairly well."

"Job as what? His sister? I have a feeling she doesn't like me. And she'll hate me once this fails."

"Oh, I'll assure you she doesn't like you – but it isn't personal, she's just skeptical by nature one might say. And she's *not* my father's sister, she is just... my aunt. We're like a large Dabárian family here – bound by disagreement and intrigues rather than blood."

"Well, I apologize in advance for killing your whole family." Isaiah muttered.

"You need to calm yourself, Isaiah." Devus said, irritated that his steadiness seemed to have strayed away. "Why don't you focus on something else? Like the fact that the lovely Lady of Duroya is coming with us. I swear, whenever I think I know you, and that you're done surprising me, you prove me wrong." Isaiah looked at him, suddenly confused.

"Are you talking about Tara?"

"Yes – Lady Tara of Duroya herself. You never mentioned you *knew* her."

"Are you saying she's *the* Lady of Duroya?" Devus' brown eyes widened at this implied oblivion.

"Well, of course she is. The Patron of Duroya died around a year back – then she became the first woman to continue the patronage of an Araktéan city *alone*. The council was quite delighted you had a connection to her, and they had no idea she was a healer as well. This just keeps getting more and more marvelous." Devus stopped talking as he saw the horrifying look on Isaiah's face, thinking he at least had given him something else to think about.

"You really didn't know any of this?"

"I didn't..." Not only had her husband died, but he'd been the Patron of Duroya – and *she* was a true Patroness.

"Come on lads, we're ready to sail!" Emory waved at them, as he and some Agátis (the large, pale faced tribal people of the north) prepared the horses to drag the fleets to the river. "There is no sail." Isaiah thought, wishing he'd chosen to stay behind.

As they reached their starting point, it didn't help that the rest of the cavalry started looking increasingly less confident, as they secured the fleets one final time. There were about thirty other people who'd followed them there, and as they pushed the fleets out from the mud, allowing them to rush down the river, every single passenger screamed. They had to move to the shore to lift fallen trees and rocks out of the way five times within the first two hours. After this, there were fewer obstacles and three of the men fell overboard. There was no saving them, as the river's force left them with no choice but to hold on tight while it carried them south. Fortunately, as the sky gradually turned into a darker shade of gray, a tree had fallen just at the edge of the Deltan border to Nahbí.

"We need to stop here for the night. I know a place we can stay where there's room for all of us." Tara said, or commanded perhaps, as all forty-four of them stumbled off the fleets. They looked towards Nicholas, visibly discouraged and fatigued.

"You heard the Lady. Pull them up to the land. We'll continue tomorrow morning." Some of them still river-sick, and others plainly exhausted, used their last forces to drag them up to the shore. Then they made their way through the dark mud, falling over each other like heavy drunks, until reaching Tara's shelter. It was a cave. A long, large cave, hidden behind some fallen pines. Fortunately, the Dabárians were resourceful even in utter exhaustion, and soon they had fire by the opening. Everyone took turns to reheat themselves, while agreeing that being cold from hours of wetness was a very different kind of cold, than that of the Dabárian winter air. The only one who seemed unaffected by the journey's hardship was Tara. She stood inside the cave, looking unimpressed by, though not directly judging, the northerner's vomiting and shivers.

"Are you certain they'll manage this sort of mission?" Isaiah overheard her asking Nicholas as the two of them walked deeper inside.

"Most of them have been training for this their whole life. I'm as sure as you could be about a matter such as this one. They've been ready for years..."

"I hope you're right. The stars are aligned now, so it is at least time for something to occur."

"We're the right people, m'lady. And our prophecies suggest the same as your stars do."

"Have you told him about it?" The conversation lulled or got so whispery Isaiah couldn't hear it anymore. He felt certain they were talking about him.

As the fleet riders had gotten some warmth back in their bodies, they huddled together upon their animal hives to sleep. Isaiah was surprised to see Tara laying down only a few feet in front of him. Other than Nicholas himself, it seemed he was the only person who dared being close to her. Devus had told him before, most Dabárians were particularly superstitious and frightened by anything even resembling sorcery.

"What are you thinking about?" She asked in a quiet voice.

"Nothing." He lied, resisting to turn from his back to his side.
"You haven't quite advanced to that degree yet." She teased him, and for the first time he understood what she was talking about. That ease. The ease he'd sensed he lost.

"Perhaps you could read my mind, then." He suggested.

"You should be aware that by saying that, you're giving me actual permission."

"In that case, I take it back. You never told me you were the Patroness of Duroya..."

"A person can have many roles, and this one wasn't relevant when we met. Besides, you didn't ask me who I was."

"I guess you're right." He realized, at last, turning towards her.

"Did you and Nic talk about me earlier?" For the first time since he'd come to know her, her eyes revealed the slightest of surprise. Healers did perhaps not know everything, but Tara knew something important – something he sensed he needed to know.

"We did." She confessed.

"I have a feeling you're keeping something from me."

"An inkling is what you have – and you are right." She said, biting her lower lip. "First, I want you to tell me if you know anything about where Cyra might be."

"I don't. She... left me at the gates as soon as we reached Nagár." Tara raised her eyebrows at this. Then she sighed as she stroke a strand of black hair behind her ear.

"I've known the girl since she was born, she's always allowed me into her dreams – but I haven't been able to see anything for days..."

"She didn't mention you'd known each other for that long."

"Did she mention something else of *importance*?"

"Like what?" Tara seemed to search his eyes for a hint of an answer.

"She didn't tell me about her business in Nagár if that's what you mean." She took a breath and got a little closer to him, so that she could whisper even more quietly.

"The reason she went was to kill the king." He looked at her, and he thought he should have felt more surprised, but somehow, he didn't. It seemed nothing could truly surprise him anymore, and he'd already felt certain she was on some sort of outrageous quest.

"Does Nic know this?"

"He suspects it's what has happened. Nothing has been confirmed yet."

"I didn't think the Dabárians were looking for a violent revolt. Devus told me this would be more of a war of words."

"They don't, but Zuras want revenge. And Zuras do as Zuras wish

270

– I'm sure you've learned that by now."

"No wonder she left me behind..."

"Don't assume too much, Isaiah." He gave her a puzzled look, and her eyes, nearly black in color that night, softened again.

"I didn't think it appropriate for *me* to tell you this... it seemed better that she would tell you herself..."

"If you had told me she was going to kill the king, I would have never gone with her. I would have never gone to the Parda at all..."

"That is not what I'm referring to." Tara interfered.

"What then?"

"Cyra is... she is your sister." As Tara finally said it, she was met with a blank expression that was followed by one of astonishment. She knew a great lot more would need to be said on the matter, but with the current lack of details, this truth was a clear one. An unshakable fact nobody could argue with – one she herself had witnessed.

"She can't be." Isaiah mumbled at last. But she could – of course she could. To believe *his* mother was the only one his vile father had impregnated on his journeys. Suddenly, he couldn't believe he'd never wondered about it before. Wondered if he was his only son. Whether there was someone else.

"Did she know this all along?"

"Why do you think she was so eager to bring you with her? She wanted to get to know you..."

"And still, she left me at the gates."

"She had her reasons, and there is much more to it than you think, but I suggest we'll talk about it in a more private setting."

"Yes. Once we arrive at the fortress, I'll... I will find somewhere private." He stuttered and Tara nodded. Her hand – though slightly colder than normal – felt warm on his cheek. He opened his mouth to say something, but it became a gasp instead, as he noticed something moving in between them.

"What in the nine hells is that?" People hushed at him, tired and oblivious to the presence of what looked like a long, legless worm in lizard's clothing.

"It's just a snake. Don't worry, it won't hurt you as long as you leave it be." Tara said, her hand leaving his cheek. "In fact, it's a good omen..." she whispered, stroking the snake's green, shelled skin as if it'd been a newborn lamb. "I haven't seen a serpent since I was a little girl."

CHAPTER THIRTY-ONE

TRUE ROOTS

THE next day, all of them were pleased to see it was raining a little less than the last, and that subtle cracks of faded sunshine beamed its way through the clouds along the way. There was not a lot of light. Much too little to produce even the faintest rainbow, yet it brought enough hope for them to sing songs as they continued rushing down the stream at a horrendous pace. When the stream finally came to an end, much further south than it usually did, they all clung to the ground and swore they'd never go near a fleet again.

"We're in Zura territory, Nic..." Harvey said, looking more concerned than relieved to be close to their so-called allies. "Though my guts would like to tell you otherwise, we should split up and move towards the villages as fast as possible."

"I promised Liv I'd do all I could to get her boys out of there, and my memory tells me we're at walking distance from the Huxley fortress."

"Nic, I'll only tell you this once – that's a damn foolish idea. Liv is sharper than any of us, but when it comes to these things..." Harvey rolled his eyes and shook his head, water drops sprouting of his now dark, red hair. "That new *lordling* is an uncourteous dog – if he gives word to Nagár that we're here..."

"I see your point, Harvey. Still, we all need to rest and there aren't any villages for miles. We'll storm the gates and find him before he realizes we've even arrived. The Huxleys are not exactly known for their arrow-proof guard system." Harvey sighed loudly as he looked up towards the sky.

"As thy wish then, m'lord." He said, bowing before him (only half sarcastically) before whistling for all the half-fallen men to continue the march on their own two legs.

As the cavalry arrived at the fortress, after battling winds and a soaking, hungry ground, they were relieved to see there were no guards to keep them out. The gates were closed, but simple enough for forty men to break open. Two dogs came running at them when they did, but Isaiah soon recognized them as Dusk and Violet. It seemed they recognized him as well, as their barks and flickering teeth turned to a rather hysteric recognition. It was a more effortless takeover than any of them could have imagined, or endured, right then, but it added to their confusion. Nicholas split them into four groups, each searching one of the buildings before finding themselves back on the empty courtyard.

"Where to in Araktéa has everyone gone?" Emory asked, and Devus looked discreetly towards Isaiah.

"Do you know of any secret chambers we might have missed?"

"Yes, but I doubt that's where they are."

"That's where I'll end up if the Huxleys get their hands on me," he thought solemnly. Looking around, he felt it seemed so much smaller than before. A tiny, pointless and hollow place – an actual prison.

"Maybe they lost their senses and ran away and hid in some cave...." Harvey suggested.

"Should we search the area around here, Nic?" Emory asked.

"That won't be necessary... Harvey is right. I think I know where they are." Isaiah said. They all looked at him expectantly, and then Nicholas nodded and commanded twelve of the men to join him as he marched over to Captive's Cave. When he entered, it felt like going back in time. Most of the regulars were there, and the Cave was as warm and humid as ever. Some guards were there too – drunk and unconcerned by the sight of the intruders. One of them got up and offered drinks, which some Dabárians gratefully accepted – they'd had a long few days after all.

"Where are the others?" Isaiah asked.

"Some were taken away, mostly the women and children... the rest, I think, are either in the chambers... or in the basement, trying to manage the damn flood." Isaiah didn't even know they had a basement, but according to the drunk man (whom he'd forgotten the name of), there was indeed one underneath the main building. Rushing his way over there by himself, he met Nicholas.

"We've found Lord Huxley. I need you to come with me and talk with him." Isaiah felt the nausea he'd had on the fleet returning. He didn't have the slightest idea what to tell him about his brother. Though no longer his slave, being back there made him feel he was about to be badly punished.

"Alright." He stuttered, somehow feeling as loyal towards Nicholas Teague as if he'd known him his whole life.

"We should tell someone to go to the basement in the meanwhile, there are probably some captives down there."

Nic led him to the ballroom, where he explained they'd found the Lord drinking and playing card games with himself. They'd bound him to a chair (thought it'd hardly been necessary) and seeing him almost made Isaiah feel embarrassed on his behalf.

"Well, isn't it my *best* worker? I knew you'd come back!" Lord Huxley's ruddy face lid up as Isaiah entered. He looked like he wanted to stand up and drag the chair along with him, but one of the two Dabárians behind him laid a heavy hand on his shoulder.

"Sit down."

"I am not so sure if I like your new friends very much, *however*. What is it you think you're doing – bringing all these obnoxious northerners here?"

"So much for being in the Lord's good graces," Isaiah thought.

"We need you to tell us where Lady Huxley is, my Lord – and the missing captives."

"I already told them. Celeste went with our guests after the event. She was meant to take care of some... diplomatic matters I believe. What, I cannot recall. Oh, and they brought some captives with them too, those greedy, high-born capitalers..." He rolled his eyes, frowned and looked over to a half full glass of wine standing on the table to his left. Walking closer, Isaiah saw the wood had dark, oval marks from where he'd left it before. Though his moderate drunkenness wasn't uncommon, it was hardly ever so excessive he would neglect his furniture.

"What happened at the event, Lord Huxley?" He asked.

"Oh, it was the most *marvelous* evening – you should have seen it. Amazing dancing, great drinks – really, Nahbí wine at its best... you may try some if you like." He nodded in the direction of some green bottles spread around the table. "If you'd pour me a glass too, that'd be lovely."

"No, thank you."

"I forget – never much of a drinker, this one." He said to Nic, who gave him a hard, spiteful look.

"We need to find your wife, Lord Huxley. You must know something more specific about her whereabouts." He said.

"I wish I did. In fact, if you could go and get Celeste back for me, that'd be stupendous – I'll give you gold for it, and I'll forget how rude you were for just marching in here like... savages." He smiled stiffly, and then he closed his eyes, starting to hum the tune of a song.

"I swear to you, if you are *playing* a fool with me, you will regret it. You'll be better off telling us everything you know, so we won't need to hand you over to our much less merciful allies." Nic said this slowly enough for it to reach through Lord Huxley's veil of drunkenness, his eyes, two, green merciless holes.

"Whatever is it you're talking about? Know about what?" Lord Huxley asked and Isaiah sighed.

"He's not lying." Nic turned towards him.

"Are you sure?" Isaiah nodded. Lord Huxley wasn't playing a fool anymore than Nicholas was playing a commander. It was not only his excessive drunkenness, and the dazed look on his face that told him this. He'd sensed it from the day he'd arrived there and chosen to ignore it, like he'd ignored so many things in the past.

"Yes. He doesn't know anything."

"I do know *some* things," Lord Huxley argued.

"He knows of poetry... all imaginable sorts of wine and jewels – but he doesn't know anything useful for now." Isaiah thought out loud, and just as surely, Devus entered with a quick, loud announcement.

"We found around twenty people down in the basement, Tim and Byron were among them. They've recruited quite a few people."

"You know Timotheus and Byron?" Isaiah asked.

"They're my aunt Liv's sons." The triplets – or at least two of them -

were among the insiders there. He was about to ask whether Archilai was too, but Lord Huxley was faster to ask his own pressing question.

"You haven't come here to take any *more* of my captives from me, have you?" he whined and perhaps for the first time Isaiah felt true sympathy for Tzelem, as his brother clearly didn't have any concerns for him at all. He probably barely remembered the fact he'd ridden out. The dead knight would lay and rot in and nobody would miss him – just like the guardian had predicted.

As they walked outside to meet with the remaining two of the triplets in the basement, Isaiah spotted Rim – looking lost as miserable, right by the clay oven, in the middle of the courtyard, where she'd used to prepare their meals.

"Rim, what are you doing out here? You're going to get ill." The elderly woman looked at him wide-eyed as he appeared before her.

"Isaiah." She said, grabbing hold of his arm and pointing her crooked finger westwards.

"Archilai is out in the fields." In their peculiar raid, they hadn't even bothered checking the fields, as it was unthinkable that anyone would be harvesting during the storm. He'd expected they'd find him in the basement with the others, but then again, the fact that the strange man was somewhere else completely didn't sound all that unlikely.
"There is somebody else out there. I will meet you in the basement in a bit." He told Devus, who nodded and brought the old woman with him.

Out in the fields it was pouring even more violently. Mostly he had to look down at his feet, trying his very best not to soak down into the mud. Finally, scouting outwards, there was nothing but water, soil and drowned roots. "She must have just been confused." he thought, and he was just about to let the wind carry him back, when he heard someone calling his name. It was Archilai's voice, coming from inside the small forest next to the fields. Prowling his way towards it, he sensed an unsettling turning in his gut. Something wasn't quite right about it – why would he be out in the forest in this weather? He then remembered one of the things he'd told him that day – "You don't need to know why I do the things that I do just yet." Back then, he hadn't really cared about the things that Archilai did – he'd mostly only cared about being left alone, but now he found himself much more curious. If he was one of the insiders, it made sense why he'd been so eager to make him escape. Perhaps he'd known all along that captives would be taken away during the event. Perhaps he also knew where.

"Archilai…" he finally spotted the back of his head, or rather – the peculiar hat, that couldn't possibly provide shelter, as it was raining from several directions at once. "Archilai, what are you…?" he stopped himself from finishing the sentence, as his attention was taken by a large, moving tree standing in the middle of the common looking oaks. He hadn't seen it from the fields, but it was at least fourteen feet high – its bole thick as a house.
"Don't be afraid, lad." Archilai assured him, and he took a step back.

"What in the nine hells is that?" he asked, for it wasn't swaying the way any tree would do in a storm. No – by the very first sight of it, he could tell it was moving its branches by its own will – as if it was dancing. As if it was truly alive.

"That's the seed you planted."

"No…" he stuttered. "No, that's impossible!"

"I'm afraid it isn't… you can't trust strange things given to you by just any gardener, lad."

"I…" Isaiah stuttered, and he walked closer in pure amazement. He wasn't quite sure how long it'd been since he'd thrown the seed away in anger – but it had to be no more than sixty days. Trees didn't grow in sixty days and perhaps even more importantly – trees didn't move like this one did. Not even in the Parda had they swayed like that.

"Listen lad, what I am about to suggest to you is going to scare you. But trust me, this monstrous thing will tell you things – they'll be hard to hear, but I assure you none of it will be lies."

"Tell me things? Whatever do you mean by that? Let's get away from here!" He had to scream for his voice not to be drowned out by the sound of thunder.

"You need to let it catch you." Isaiah looked at him, his large, blue eyes looking even larger and bluer than usual. He had shaved his beard, which made his cheekbones stand out like two, dull knife blades.

"There is no way… you're mad!" Isaiah turned to look at the tree again. Of the many things nobody had ever taught him, one of them was that you should never turn your back to a mad man, and as many other things, it was a lesson he was about to learn the hard way.

Archilai, who had long since learned that some people needed a bigger push than others, gave him the strongest one he had left in his skinny limbs. Isaiah fell forward in the mud, and before getting a chance to even grasp what had happened, wild branches grabbed a hold of him. He screamed. He twisted and battled against the hardwood binding his legs and arms – but there was no battling nature of this sort. The tree had none of the white bear's mercy and soon enough, he found himself all consumed by it.

"I've been waiting for you, seeder." He heard a voice say, as he felt his body falling against a hard, cold surface.

"What is happening? Who are you? Let me out!" There was a wicked laugh filling the dark space he found himself in.

"Do not worry, seeder – I'm the Tree of Truth, and I'm here to enlighten your tiny mind on big things." Isaiah stumbled around, just to discover there was no space to truly stumble. He could barely move. He'd left the Parda without any prophecies – with no ancient secrets, or knowledge beyond his grandfather's confused words. Now it seemed it had caught up to him. Exactly what *it* was, he wasn't sure of. All he knew was that it seemed to have been planted by his own hands, and as much as he struggled, there seemed no way of escaping it. At last, he found himself in a dark chamber of his own creation, and so it seemed there might be answers for him this year after all.

Thank you for making it to
the end of this book!
Your feedback on GOODREADS.COM
would be highly appreciated.
— Victoria ♡